ATLAS

of

UNKNOWNS

ATLAS

of

UNKNOWNS

TANIA JAMES

Alfred A. Knopf
New York
2009

This Is a Borzoi Book Published by Alfred A. Knopf

Copyright © 2009 by Tania James

All rights reserved. Published in the United States by Alfred A. Knopf,
a division of Random House, Inc., New York, and in Canada by
Random House of Canada Limited, Toronto.
www.aaknopf.com

Knopf, Borzoi Books, and the colophon are registered trademarks of Random House, Inc.

Grateful acknowledgment is made to Universal Music Corp. for permission to reprint an
excerpt from "I Don't Know How To Love Him" by Andrew Lloyd Webber and Tim Rice,
copyright © 1971 by Universal Music Corp. (ASCAP). Copyright renewed. All rights reserved.
Reprinted by permission of Universal Music Corp.

Library of Congress Cataloging-in-Publication Data
James, Tania.
Atlas of unknowns / Tania James.—1st ed.
p. cm.
ISBN 978-0-307-26890-7
1. Sisters—India—Fiction. 2. East Indian students—New York (State)—New York—
Fiction. 3. East Indians—New York (State)—New York—Fiction. 4. Host families of
foreign students—Fiction. 5. Kerala (India)—Fiction. I. Title.
PS3610.A458A92 2009
813'.6—dc22   2008051860

Manufactured in the United States of America
First Edition

To

Koduvathara L. James, my father
Mariamma K. James, my mother

and

Christine, Neena, & Raj

By me, the hemispheres rounded and tied,
the unknown to the known.
—WALT WHITMAN, "Prayer of Columbus"

Silence is the keeper of the keys to secrets.
—AGHA SHAHID ALI, "Things"

Contents

I.

ORIGIN

Kumarakom, Kerala, India

1995

2.

The DAY BEGINS WRONG. Melvin feels it upon waking, as though he has slipped his right foot into his left shoe and must shuffle along with a wrong-footed feeling all day. That today is Christmas Eve brings no comfort at all.

It is not the first morning to begin this way. Throughout his forty-five years, Melvin Vallara has periodically awakened to a nuisance in his stomach, an inner itch of ill portent that could bode anything from a bee sting to a gruesome bull-on-bus accident. Both events occurred on his seventh birthday, and he still has not forgotten that bull, how it bounced on its back before landing on its side.

This is what the Bible says: *I tell you the truth . . . no prophet is accepted in his hometown.* Nor, Melvin would add, in his own family. His mother believes that the inner itch has more to do with gas than foresight, and like her mother before her, Ammachi calls upon an arsenal of unwritten remedies. She prepares a murky white goo from the boiled grounds of a medicinal root, while her granddaughter Linno watches from the doorway of the kitchen.

"Which root?" Linno asks.

"The name, I don't remember. A *multipurpose* root," Ammachi decides, borrowing an English phrase she heard in a Stain-Off! commercial, one in which a cartoon soap sud possessed eyes and a smile.

Linno delivers the bowl of multipurpose root goo to her father, who is draped across his bed, an arm over his eyes. When he sees the bowl, he responds by turning away, onto his side. He is a man of few words, but clearly he and the goo have met before.

Linno believes. She is thirteen and dutiful, convinced that part of her duty is to champion her father's prophecies, even though he lacks the frothy beard and brooding of biblical prophets and his name falls short of the weight and might of an Elijah or a Mohammed. In fact, he more closely resembles the icon of a gloomy-eyed saint: slight, balding, his forehead growing longer by the year. Linno tries to make up for the little attention he gets by bestowing as much as she can, so she supports his decision to stay home from morning Mass. She also hopes that Ammachi might let her support him from home.

It is not to be. In the end, Linno leaves along with the rest of the family and returns from church to find Melvin still asleep, his hands in fists by his face, as if to pummel ill fortune away.

BUT THEN, there is the Entertainment to consider.

Melvin forgot to purchase the Entertainment from the Fancy Shoppe the day before, and now here they are—Linno and her younger sister, Anju—home from morning Mass with less than sixteen hours until midnight Mass, and no Entertainment? Unacceptable. Unfair. The Entertainment is tradition, a promise upon waking, a beautiful, blinding answer to the holy punishments of morning. Without the Entertainment, there is only the looming threat of carolers who travel from house to house, proud as roosters in their red mufflers, belting melodies and collecting church donations all through the night.

Late afternoon breezes swell the sun-gilded trees that lift and sigh, sifting the light between their branches. There is still time left in the day to visit the Fancy Shoppe, if Melvin can be persuaded. Ammachi refuses to go back out once she has unpinned the Christmas brooch from her shoulder, a brass dove that she nests in its velvet-lined case, where it will remain until next Christmas Eve. She removes the embroidered shawl draped over her shoulder and goes about the house in the white chatta and mundu that all Syrian Christian women used to wear, so few now still starching their blouses and pleating their wraps despite the patterned profusion of saris surrounding them.

Her brow still furrowed from the severity of her worship, she sits in a plastic chair, her eyes closed, her swollen, lotioned ankles perched on the daybed across from her as Linno reads aloud from the newspaper.

Ammachi takes pleasure in knowing the happenings of district politics, lambasting corrupt politicians as if they are standing before her, a row of sulking children. But lately, large-scale developments have been attracting her rebuke, particularly new plans for the construction of a national highway, a network of roads and bridges, three to six lanes thick, that will send vehicles speeding from Kashmir to Bangalore, and west to east in a third of the usual time. "With double the waste," Ammachi warns. Examining the map, the dark passages splayed across the country, she rejects its unpronounceable given name—the Golden Quadrilateral—and coins it instead "the Golden Colon."

During Ammachi's indictments, Linno sketches her grandmother along the margins of the newspaper, paying special attention to her bun, a silver-gray swirl that maintains its integrity without help from a single hairpin. These sketches interest Melvin more than the news itself, so much so that he neatly tears out and saves his favorites. Gracie, his wife, used to tease that he would turn anything, even a bottle cap, into a souvenir. He is sure that had Gracie lived to see these sketches, she would have saved them as well. They seem to belong to the hand of someone much older, who understands not only the anatomy of the face but the way muscles hold emotion, the way eyes possess life. He keeps the drawings in a faded cigarillo box that bears the face of a mustached white man on the lid.

WHILE LINNO DRAWS Ammachi, Anju follows her father through the bedroom, the sitting room, and even hovers around the outhouse, reciting in English from the Book of Isaiah as he does his business. At nine years old, Anju is a valiant Bible Bowler, her brain an unbeatable vault of Scripture that she draws upon to give herself authority, even when faced with a sighing audience. Unlike Linno, Anju will not accept defeat; at least five times a day, she pulls on the tip of her nose, believing that her efforts will somehow win her a straighter one. With similar persistence, she follows her father into the sitting room, translating and interpreting the text as verses of fortitude and godly reliance, closing her case with the reminder that he never got her a birthday gift.

When logic fails, Anju's argument devolves. She whimpers, tugging at the hem of her T-shirt ("*Eddi,* stop stretching it!" Ammachi warns), and threatens to run away, which is a predictable threat, as she is always running away and Linno is always sent to fetch her. The only mystery lies in which neighbor's house Anju might choose as her sanctuary. Usually Linno finds her sitting on someone's front step, bleakly toeing patterns in the dirt until she spots Linno in the yard. Anju always comes away quietly, gradually softening beneath the weight of her sister's hand on her shoulder. Sometimes, after a silence, Anju will ask, "What took you so long?"

Melvin retires to the daybed with his arm over his eyes while Ammachi lectures, while Linno draws, while Anju continues to flit around him with her runaway threats, until at last he says, "Enough." Melvin sits up and rubs his eyes with his fists, muttering that it is better to disappoint God than to disappoint daughters. "At least God forgives."

LINNO ACCOMPANIES HER FATHER to the Fancy Shoppe, riding sidesaddle on the back of his bicycle, her heels held away from the spokes. They cut through mingled smells of dung, earth, freshwater, pesticides. They bump along between paddy fields that, in stillness, reflect the sky's blue with such clarity that grass seems to spring from liquid sky. At the water's edge, a medley of palms bends low, each falling in love with its likeness, while webs of light spangle the dark undersides of the leaves. Whenever a bus appears on the horizon, Melvin pulls over to the side and waits for it to groan past, spewing dust and diesel in its wake, before he plunges his foot down onto the pedal. Her view of the road is blocked by his shoulders, dark and tense all the way down to the unsettling clutch of his fingers around the handlebars.

Linno wonders what kind of gut feeling struck Melvin on the day her mother died. Perhaps he had seen her funeral face in dreams, with skin so spackled over with paint that she seemed a porcelain replica of the person she had been. Here was her lineless forehead, every wrinkle erased like a past swept clean. Here was her tiny smile, as though amused by a secret.

After the funeral, the albums were all packed away in trunks, but a single photo of Gracie remains within reach: the newlywed photograph, a black-and-white double portrait that every couple took in those days, tucked in a back pocket of Ammachi's Bible. Gracie appears vaguely pretty but in a sharp, plain way, considerably shorter than Melvin, and cheerless. Husband and wife stand next to each other, shoulders touching, gazing sternly up into the camera as if being summoned into battle.

·   ·   ·

THE ENTERTAINMENT COMES in a paper bag, folded down and stapled shut. Linno and Anju spend the evening dutifully guarding the bag from interference, though no one wants to interfere more than they do. Fixated on the bag, they shove wads of chapati into their mouths. They argue over who should hold the bag and how. Anju tries to educate Linno about a rarely read passage in the Bible, which suggests that younger sisters should always get their way. Anju is a strange little sieve of general knowledge, continually dribbling answers to questions that no one has asked. This one Linno knows not to believe, just as she didn't believe it that last time with her Cadbury Fruit & Nut.

After dinner, the girls have no choice but to wait on the front step, swatting at mosquitoes, the Entertainment placed equidistant between them. Theirs is a small brick and stucco house with a thatched ola roof, humbly crouched among the slanting coconut trees that are charming by day yet spindly, looming and long-armed by night. Two lanky tree trunks span the brook in front, making a shaky footpath that the girls race across, testing their balance and bravery, light as birds on a branch.

AS THE NIGHT SOFTENS WITH FOG, the family collects on the front steps. Dragging a plastic chair behind her, Ammachi mutters that this is a show she has seen before, and what it has to do with Yesu's birth she does not know. For the first time in history, Melvin allows Linno to assist him, while Anju is told to sit on the steps. In mute protest, Anju takes a pose beyond her nine years, legs crossed, head tilted, fingers laced around her knee, like a woman in a magazine.

From the paper bag, Melvin lifts a parcel whose label displays two words in red block letters: RAINBOW THUNDER. Out of the parcel, plastic crackling, Melvin pulls a bundle of sparklers.

These Linno lights as reverently as if she were lighting candles at church. All else around her dissolves into shadow and there is only the single captive star, its spitfire warmth belonging, however briefly, to her alone. Even Ammachi accepts a sparkler and, equally transfixed, begins circling hers in figure eights, watching the wild spray of orange light, frowning a little when it dies to a glowing ember.

And then, what fire! One aerial miracle follows the next. There is the Volcano—a small cone that splutters before erupting into a great geiser of liquid flame, rising, rising, borne on a splendid gushing noise. The Mouse, which Melvin lights from the throat of an empty toddy bottle, a faint sizzle before the white-pink bullet shoots into the trees and spirals over the branches. And finally, the Necklace, a length of tiny dynamite that Melvin ties to a low branch of the jackfruit tree. When he lights the fuse, everyone plugs their ears against the sound, a violent rifle crack, mercilessly loud as it *pop-pop-pops* all the way up to the branch.

A silky smoke roams over the ground as Ammachi murmurs, grudgingly, that firecrackers are not so bad. "But if it were me, I would buy a nice set of mugs over these light tricks any day." In a rare embrace of Western custom, she cites the examples of other countries where the father gives Christmas gifts to the entire family. Even his mother.

Melvin points out that his sister, Jilu, is American. "When was the last time she gave us anything?"

"Hah, Jilu *was* American! Now she is in Canada. And what do you mean anything?" Ammachi rattles off a list of items: "Soap, socks, a fitted sheet, Tang . . ."

"Those socks were used. And that fitted sheet fit only half a bed."

While Ammachi and Melvin argue over Jilu's largesse, Linno begins untying what is left of the Necklace from its branch. Several links remain on the blown fuse.

Anju calls out, "Eh, Linno, we already lit that one."

Linno is studying the remnants of the Necklace when she looks up at Anju, then at her father. She is pinned, suddenly, by the look of fear in a grown man's face.

"Drop that—" Melvin says, or begins to say, she cannot tell.

Because from this point, everything happens with a slow grace, in the space of seconds. Linno feels nothing and sees everything, in all its strange clarity. The links exploding in her palm, fire flowering and blazing above the watch that she wears facing in so she can check the time discreetly when she is at school. The face of the watch, splashed with light, now a flickering gold coin and above it, her hand held captive by a star, the shifting folds of flame and heat giving way to that time when her mother slit her finger while scaling a fish, how astonishing it was, the scarlet simplicity of what dripped from her, wet petals on the edge of the sink.

And then Linno realizes that what she thought was the screaming of wind is a sound that only a girl can make, a girl on fire.

2.

ℒINNO'S RIGHT HAND suffers third-degree burns, the rest of her unscathed. Bedridden in the hospital, she winces if so much as a breath rakes the back of her hand, the pain racing up her arm. As a nurse reaches over her, Linno studies the burns, the cooked skin, the pink tissues, wet and peeling. Her stomach lunges. Vomit down the ruffles of her Christmas dress.

For days afterward, her hand is cocooned in gauze, the skin within laboring to forget its wounds. With pills, the pain lessens slightly but never leaves, a slow and steady throb that seems to possess its own resonance, a volume that drowns everything else in the hospital.

Ammachi brings her Bible, from which she murmurs Psalms, squinting and dragging her finger across the pages. While Ammachi is caught up in these verses, rocking back and forth as she reads, Linno recalls another: *If thy right hand offend thee, cut it off.*

Every time the doctor pulls away the gauze, he looks offended. The flesh has begun to rot. Infection is chewing at her hand and will climb its way farther through the body if left untreated. So two weeks after the accident, the doctor cuts off her hand, just above the wrist.

Gradually, the scars heal, but she will let no one, not even Anju, see the aftermath. Linno rejects all short-sleeved clothing in favor of long sleeves; the right cuff she cuts and ties into a knot. This she does in private, before school, an animalistic maneuvering of left hand and front teeth. She has Ammachi plait her two braids each morning, though the result is clumsier than she would like. The only hair Ammachi can do properly is her own.

These days, Linno rarely looks in mirrors if she can help it, for she knows what others see, not only a deformity of the hand but a deformity of fortune. Accidents belong to the unlucky, and ill fortune can travel along bloodlines, a gene that surfaces and sinks across generations but never disappears.

LINNO WAS SEVEN YEARS OLD when her mother died; Anju was three. Until then they had lived in Bombay as a family, in a flat where the suburbs were hardly less hectic than the city's center. Their mother hung an orange sheet in the doorway between the kitchen and the bedroom, where they all slept together on bedrolls and a charpoy that the last tenant had left behind. The first thing Linno saw upon waking was a luminous red cloth tacked over the window, through which she could hear the magnified echo of the muezzin's call to prayer. Once, she woke in the middle of the night and saw her mother's profile, traced in dim light by the window. Her mother was perfectly still, a cord in her throat taut enough to touch; she seemed to strain for a view that the window could not afford her. Linno assumed it had something to do with the glossy postcard that had arrived that day, the one with the Statue of Liberty on it. "What is that?" Linno had asked, but her mother slipped it into her purse without an answer. Later, when Linno studied the postcard in secret, she was not especially impressed by the massive, mannish, sea green woman planted on the ocean. What held Linno's interest was the writing on the back of the postcard, in Malayalam:

See? Their most famous statue wears a sari. You will have no problem here.

Bird

Where was her mother going and when? Who was this Bird? Every question led to another, none that Linno could bring herself to ask aloud. She was wounded by the woman her mother might be, and choosing not to know further, she convinced herself of the necessity for silence; such is the way that questions in the family remain unasked and unanswered for years. In time, Linno learned how to tuck all her questions away, like the fancy saris that her mother never wore, tightly folded between leaves of muslin in the bottom of a drawer.

AFTER LINNO'S OPERATION, Melvin calls several hospitals which give him the numbers of businesses that deal in prosthetic limbs; the nearest is a hundred miles away, in Thiruvananthapuram. The approximate price of the cheapest prosthetic, quoted to him over the phone, makes him want to laugh and cry at once. Not to mention that affixing such a prosthetic to his daughter's wrist would be as inviting to ridicule as renaming her Hook. Still, he writes down the figure in small, careful numbers and folds the paper into his pocket. Later that day, he loses himself in toddy and cigarettes until he grows sick, then hurries half a mile from home, tight-lipped and retching, to throw up in a place where his children will not see.

For the sake of Linno's rehabilitation, Melvin fashions himself into a general of optimism. Everything, he announces, is mental. If Anju, tugging at her sweat-stained blouse, complains about the weather, Melvin replies, "All in your head. Think positive. Think cool." He once catches Ammachi weeping while praying in her room, asking God about fate and suffering and other not-positive topics. The next day, when Ammachi opens her prayer book, she finds a magazine clipping inserted between the Psalms. "Today Is the First Day of the Rest of Your Life!" She uses it to line the floor of the chicken coop.

For Linno, Melvin buys a new writing tablet whose cover displays a cartoon elephant in a tiny pink skirt. The pages are thin and gray, with faint blue lines. Using a ruler, he draws dashed lines across the page, like fences, and sample letters at the beginning of each fence.

While her classmates are reducing fractions, Linno is struggling with the alphabet. Until lunch, she sits with her right wrist fixed to the top of the page, the book drastically slanted, her left hand gripping the pencil so hard that the lead breaks. Trying to muscle a steady grace into her left hand—this is not unlike an elephant squirming itself into a skirt.

For months, Melvin makes her begin each day with penciling while he watches and offers bouquets of positive wisdoms loosely translated from the English: "Every cloud has silver in it." Or: "If someone gives you lemons, make a glass half full of juice." The quotations were imported straight from America, via a faded self-help booklet written by Dr. Roy Fontainelle that Melvin found in a book stall. The booklet inspires nothing in Linno but irritation. She hates Dr. Roy Fontainelle, with his fishbowl glasses and salesman smile, for using her father as a puppet of positive talk. Hers is a misguided hatred, she will later understand, but it is hate that steers her around the wallow of self-pity. It is resentment that pushes her pencil up and down her father's fences while he sharpens her pencils with a kitchen knife. It takes months for her hand to fully relax around the pencil, but gradually her letters grow less wobbly. Full sentences begin to walk smoothly across the page with a measured calm, hardly a stutter.

Apologies and gratitude would embarrass Melvin, who, likewise, is not given to dispensing praise. There comes a day when he simply stops glancing over her shoulder and speaking on behalf of Dr. Roy Fontainelle. This is also the day he opens her elephant notebook and tears her new signature from the corner of a page. That scrap seems to him like a picture of her, more truthful than any on film.

. . .

LINNO NEVER NOTICED how quickly the days were rushing by so long as she was swept up in them. But having spent the last two months of school homebound, she returns to find the classroom an altered ecosystem. Her peers have not only surpassed her in studies, but new inside jokes are leaving her on the outside. Girls are wearing jasmine bracelets around their left wrists. There are stories and memories to which she can only listen, popular film songs to which she does not know the words. Her classmates have grown at accelerated speeds, in ways imperceptible to the common adult eye. Linno, in the meantime, has changed only for the worse.

She trudges between classes, her wrist tucked into the pocket of her gray school skirt. She catches other children staring, if only to glimpse what is within her knotted sleeve. Linno is the only student allowed to wear long sleeves among the dozens of bare brown arms and ashy elbows.

One morning, during the earthworm dissection in science class, Linno excuses herself to the bathroom. Opening the door, she is welcomed by the dull stench of bat droppings collected along the sinks; her eyes go to the eaves, where the culprits are roosting. Asleep, the bats are a ceiling of fuzzy heads tucked within leathery wings, but startled by her noise, they ripple into a cloud and escape out the window.

Dank as it is, she takes shelter in the sludgy drains and slimy walls that she remembers, the white nub of soap whose cleansing properties are questionable. She tries to forget how her teacher has just impaled a long pink worm to the tray of tar, between two pins, its shiny ends still writhing. Soon she will have to return; every comfort has its limit. But she continues to rinse her hand beneath the faucet's drizzle for longer than necessary.

Two girls enter the bathroom and, upon seeing Linno, lower their voices. Linno turns off the water. She has seen these girls and knows them to be older from their single braids.

Linno is about to move past them when the tall one addresses her: "*Eddi.* Don't you have to wash your other hand?"

Linno's feet feel stuck to the floor. She has no idea what to answer, except that she does not have an other hand.

"What does it look like?" the second girl asks, flicking her chin at Linno's knotted sleeve. Her smile is almost kind, almost. "You can't show us?"

"She can," the other one says.

As Linno moves past them, her eyes on their blue chappals, she notices that the tall one has two wiry hairs on her big toe. In science class, they learned that having hair on the toes is the result of a dominant gene, and some girls curled their toes under, ashamed.

The tall girl grabs Linno's right arm, a gesture that could seem playful, but Linno pushes her away with undue force, sending her staggering back a few steps.

Dominant, recessive. Tiny struggles turned large. Linno steels herself.

And then the girls are upon her. The back of Linno's head hits the wall. She squirms, but there are two of them, laughing at the ease of it all, one with a hand over Linno's mouth, the other clawing at the knot. The tall one squeals at the other to look at it, look at it!

It is here that Linno stops struggling and wilts under their weight. She looks at her wrist, a bump smooth as stone, the bone jutting sharply beneath, and a dark, shiny welt seaming the skin back together. For the first time, Linno sees it as they do, freakish in its simplicity.

The girls release her wrist and step back. They exaggerate their disgust with wrinkled noses and frowns. "Tie it back up," the tall one orders, as if Linno forced them to see it. But Linno remains pinned to the wall, hardly noticing the sound of their soles peeling from the ground, the door swinging shut behind them.

By the time Linno goes to the sink, she does not know how many minutes have passed. Using her teeth and her left hand, she reties her knot. She smooths her hair. With her fingertips, she drops water into her eyes, to flush the red from the white, and returns to class.

ON THE RARE OCCASION that an assignment requires drawing, Linno excels. Her maps of India and the state of Kerala are scaled and detailed and gaudy as treasure maps, with color pencil legends of sprawling palms and scalloped water waves, tiny symbols of tea leaves and rice sacks to represent the regions where those industries are thriving. While she draws, the classroom falls away. She keeps her chin tucked, her shoulders hunched, as if she might dive into the page.

But words leave her when she is called upon to read or answer a question. "Speak up, SPEAK UP," her teachers demand. With every order, she shrinks.

Another year goes by like this, with Linno forced to repeat the same grade and Anju surging ahead. Family friends ply Ammachi for hints to Anju's academic success: What does the girl eat? How much does she sleep? When and to which saint does she pray? Ammachi refers to a stockpile of "brain foods," the tried-and-true diet of intellectual warriors, which includes raw almonds and spinach and Tang over ice. Yet no snack or prayer can account for the fact that Anju can rattle off multiplication tables and African capitals as one might recite her own birthday. No rival can jostle the edifice of her accomplishments, top rank in all her exams and champion of the statewide Kerala Bible Bowl three years in a row, from age nine to eleven. After retiring from the Bowl, Anju skips a grade and Linno again falls back, resulting in their side-by-side seating in Math.

At twelve and sixteen, the Vallara sisters are known as the bookends of the class, both in age and intelligence. On the first day of school, Anju pretends not to notice the general classroom murmur and busies herself by selecting pencils from her *National Geographic* pencil tin, unaware that her new peers refrain from childish pencil tins. Linno, meanwhile, can feel herself petrifying, growing solid as the bench on which she sits, trapped by the table in front of her. She stares out the window, at a tree thick with birds. Without warning, the birds leap from the tree in one gray conflagration.

Sister Savio takes roll call. When she arrives at Linno's name, she looks up from the spectacles that she wears on a chain around her neck. There is Linno, a head taller than Anju.

"And Linno Vallara," Sister Savio says. "Next time sit in the middle of the bench. You've gotten so big you might tip the whole thing over."

Anju goes still, but Linno can sense a quivering within her sister, from rage or maybe sadness, almost imperceptible, a silent tremor as laughter travels around the room. Linno smiles at the surface of the desk, one long crack forking into two like the lines that frame Sister Savio's lips. One must smile at the ridicule, or be consumed.

LINNO NEVER RETURNS to school. To Melvin, she argues that Ammachi is growing older and slower, and help is needed around the house. "Why pay for a servant . . . ," she begins to say, before realizing the logical end to this sentence: *when I could be the servant?*

Her father hardly fights her on the topic, as he has just lost his chauffeur job with a wealthy couple, the Uthups, who are moving to California. It is a common sight these days, so many beautiful white houses, all empty, undwelled, like moneyed monuments to the pursuit of wealth made elsewhere. Jobs are scarce so men and now women, bearing degrees and suitcases, are pouring into other countries or going north.

Melvin was once one of those men, peering hopefully through the barred window of a train bound for Bombay, a journey he would later count among his greatest mistakes. Those were optimistic times, but now, for Melvin, optimism does not seem to apply.

"Money leaving my pocket faster than it's coming in," he sighs.

FOR LINNO, a day spent at school yawns endlessly. A day spent at home is a constant race with the sun.

Linno cooks, sweeps, scrubs, pickles, washes, whisks, dries, irons, and answers the door and the phone. Within the walls she knows, she quickly learns her way. The failure of chewy papadam is brief, excusable, and the very next day, she seals the papadam into an old biscuit tin so that they retain their crisp. Ammachi is happily relieved from most of her duties, so when the traveling handicrafts salesman asks for the woman of the house, Linno answers to that title. He hesitates only a moment before calling her *Auntie,* which seems to Linno, at sixteen, something of a compliment.

Melvin finds a job with a tea estate, driving a lorry that ships crates of tea to purchasing agents in Kochi. The cab of the lorry is a carnival of blues and pinks and greens, flourishes and florals painted along its sides and below the name: *Erumathana Tea Estate,* though he would have preferred a girl's name to join the ranks of *Priya Mol* and *Annakutty* and all the other lovingly named lorries on the roads. Each evening, Melvin shines his lorry's yolk yellow hood and complains if so much as a small pothole imperils the tires. "If only the Golden Colon came to our house," he says. The National Highway was all but abandoned in Kerala, after newspapers reported rumors of corruption amid resignations. To Ammachi's relief, the provincial curves and gullies have remained, but the growing number of cars still bothers her. Wealthy families have two, and the round-eyed Ambassadors of old are slowly being retired for Korean and Japanese models.

"In town you can hardly breathe the air anymore," Ammachi complains. "Someday we won't see the stars."

"World is changing," Melvin says to Ammachi. "Two options: eat or be eaten."

This is his attitude on the days when it seems that Melvin is the eater. Then there are other days when he is told to stay home, as there are too many drivers and lorries, not enough crates. During those times, Melvin wonders if he should sell off the land that came with Gracie's dowry, a small stretch of teak trees that he was planning to divide between his daughters for their own dowries. But he cannot bring himself to carve up their inheritance. He simply watches as his paychecks thin, vanish, and he waits, heart suspended, for his wages to return the following week.

3.

*B*Y THE TIME LINNO REACHES NINETEEN, Melvin has collected too many of her drawings to fit into the cigarillo box, which seems a shabby place to put them anyway. So with an absolute faith in the capabilities of his hands intrinsic to many a man his age, he decides to make her a sketchbook.

This is during a lull in his lorry job, after he has already completed other manlier tasks in order to distract from the most vital of these—bringing home a paycheck. He has patched up the hole in the outhouse wall. He has pulled a whole new batch of ola fronds onto the roof. And now, after running out of tasks: the sketchbook.

THRESIA PAINT HOUSE is owned by Kochu Thresia, a compact bundle of a woman who has a habit of cracking her knuckles whenever Melvin speaks, smiling all the while, as if his very presence is a question she yearns to answer. Though she has always seemed sweet on Melvin, he hardly thinks of women anymore, having assumed that the libido-centered lobe of his brain has iced over, gone dead, except for those moments when a certain lady reporter's sweltering alto comes over the BBC radio. He is soothed by the thought that there may yet be some life beneath the ice, but Kochu Thresia would not be able to restore it. She has so many moles on her face that he has a hard time looking at her without trying to mentally connect them.

As smitten as she is, Kochu Thresia readily agrees to teach him how to make a book. He buys twine, reams of drawing paper, and two thick pieces of cardboard. She shows him how to line up the holes along the spine, how to fold the pages into valleys. She gives him a leftover can of paint, a regal red, with which to paint the covers. Happily bemoaning the ineffectuality of men, she takes over the task and stitches the pages together herself.

After dinner the next day, Melvin presents the book to Linno. He has never made anything for anyone, as far as he can remember, at least not since he was drawing pictures for his mother at age six. The whole ceremony of it all suddenly seems childish. A simple bracelet or necklace would have been more appropriate, black beads on a gold chain.

Linno lifts the book into her lap and stares at the cover. She thanks him quietly, her fingers gliding over the blank pages as if she can see sketches yet to come. Ammachi asks how he crafted such a sturdy, handsome thing, and Melvin admits a tiny bit of guidance, though he prefers not to specify from whom.

"Look what he made," Linno says, offering Anju the book. *"Kando?"*

Anju reaches out and strokes the cover, then rubs her fingers against each other. With a vague smile, she says it is nice.

AROUND THIS TIME, Melvin receives a used television from Mr. Uthup, who has returned to sell his property. "For your faithful service," Mr. Uthup declares, waving to the small, surprisingly heavy television behind him. Melvin hefts it onto a borrowed wheelbarrow which he pulls all the way home, picking up a pain in his shoulder along the way. The family gathers in the sitting room, patting the thing, dusting it off, fiddling with its antennae, ogling its backside, waiting for something besides snow to show up on the screen. Melvin's cousin Joby, who works for the cable company, gives him a discount on the monthly package, whose installation introduces the family to a selection of semiclear, colorful channels. Immediately Ammachi befriends the television, enjoying its company to a greater degree than she did the radio's. Mostly she watches the news.

But Melvin grows to dislike the very gift he brought home. He does not enjoy the fact that the news is now ever present in his sitting room, a guest that brings unfamiliar faces to dinner (one of whom, the BBC lady reporter, has turned out to be a high-pitched man). Melvin tries to watch as little as possible until an evening in September, when he cannot bring himself to turn the television off.

Family and neighbors gather in the sitting room to watch a plane stabbing an American building through its middle. Another clip shows the building fall while its sister building remains standing, and then another clip in which the sister, too, gives out in a swarm of dust. Over and over, the buildings are folding. Melvin remembers watching the Windsor Castle Hotel rising up in Kottayam over the course of a year, but to watch an even taller building fall in a matter of seconds is like watching rain in reverse, flying back up into the clouds.

Violence seems a global contagion. Later that year, Melvin finds himself sleepless in front of the television again, as India and Pakistan toe the Kashmiri Line of Control. Political pundits foresee nuclear fates. India points a finger at Pakistan. America warns against pointing fingers; the following year, it points its own at Iraq. The television shrinks the world and drops it in Melvin's lap, a Pandora's box of terrors that seems to show how these days every country is stepping up to some line or another, lines that have grown filament thin and are easily crossed, lines that lead nowhere but form a web that make it impossibly unclear who is on whose side anymore.

4.

AT TWENTY-ONE, Linno goes in search of a job at the Princess Tailor Shoppe, something small to pad the family income. She has been coming to this tailor for years, a stout, laughless woman who grows incensed if a customer's opinion conflicts with her own. "You want to be a seamstress?" the tailor asks Linno, eyebrows raised behind her spectacles, implying what the other seamstresses think. They are Linno's age, perhaps younger, one waifish and one chubby, both with oiled braids and chalky hands. The waif darts looks from behind her Usha sewing machine, a blue sari blouse passing beneath the needle. The chubby seamstress is sitting down to her lunch, a steel tiffin of rice with a pocket of vegetable curry. The whole shop is a room no larger than the sitting room back home, with a back doorway that opens onto a dusty patch of yard beneath the bare blue sky.

"I came to bring you more business," Linno says. "I came to paint you a window."

The tailor glances at Linno's knotted wrist. "Paint what?"

Prepared for this reaction, Linno pulls her sketchbook from her satchel and opens to what she has designed in pencil. A woman stands smiling demurely in a sari, its fabric like liquid silk over her hips, the pallu billowing behind her and tapering into the needle of a sewing machine. Behind the machine is a plumpish woman in spectacles, smiling with motherly satisfaction at the sari-clad woman, her muse.

The chubby seamstress hovers at the tailor's elbow, cooing over the picture with pickled breath. "This looks just like you, Chachy!"

The tailor makes a noise of grudging agreement and points at the sketch of the woman in a sari. "But my hips should be a bit wider than this." The chubby seamstress begins to protest but, reconsidering, keeps quiet.

By this time, the waif has come to peer over the tailor's shoulder as well. "Make the sari red," she suggests.

The tailor waves the suggestion away. "Better to be subtle. Maybe rose . . . or *peach color*," she decides. "You know what peach color is?"

So she is hired! Elated, Linno asks for a measuring tape with which to measure the window, unless—

"Wait, wait," the tailor says. "Just because a woman can stitch doesn't mean she knows how to work a sewing machine."

The tailor bends behind a counter, on top of which are binders full of possible dress designs and collar cuts, and surfaces with a large roll of white parcel paper. She unravels a lengthy piece which she slices with a swipe of her scissors.

"Make it in color." The tailor pats the paper. "On this. Then we will see."

MEANWHILE, Melvin's job search has become something of a passive hunt, as he spends more and more time in the company of a bottle of Kalyani beer and Berchmans, the bartender and owner of the Rajadhani Bar. Berchmans, named after the seventeenth-century saint, thinks himself a fairly god-fearing and compassionate man, which would have made him an excellent psychologist, if his father had allowed him to take his master's degree in psychology. Instead, his father demanded that Berchmans take over the family tavern.

In all parts of his life, Berchmans exercises temperance: he does not smoke, barely drinks, exercises, and eats well. So he remains younger than his years, with a drum-tight belly and pectoral muscles that he can activate separately—left, right, left—beneath his shirt. At the risk of losing business, he tries to advise his patrons with priestly patience to forgo the next drink or add roughage to their diets or see the argument from the wife's perspective. As well, he watches out for patrons like Melvin, on whom he could rack up quite a bill over time, if he wanted to.

"I found you another driver job," Berchmans says.

Melvin straightens up.

"For Mercy Chandy's family. She's been looking for someone since their last man left."

Melvin scowls at his beer. "Abraham Chandy's wife?"

"Yes? So?"

"Don't you know about . . ." Melvin gestures at the stool next to him, as if the stool will elucidate everything. "My wife. Gracie and him."

"*Edda,* they broke it off! So what? That was twenty years ago! You think a rich man like Abraham Chandy, a man with a wife and two sons, you think he even thinks about that old business?"

"He might. Sometimes."

"Did you know that he has put seven girls through nursing school on his own donations? *Seven.* Not even relations, simply poor girls whose parents went up to him at church. This is not the kind of man who holds on to petty feuds." Berchmans pushes his sour-smelling towel across the counter. "It is you who can't put the past in the past."

IN THE EARLY EVENING, Melvin irons his second-best shirt and leaves for the Chandy house. His best shirt has a pearlescent sheen that Ammachi deemed too "disco." Melvin has no idea which TV show gave her the word "disco," but he agrees that this might be the impression he would make under intense lighting. He has a feeling that Abraham is the type to install so many bulbs and fixtures that one might mistake night for day.

Melvin walks slowly, taking the time to inhale the damp exhalations of the earth. After rain, the air always has a gentle, smoky taste, and it was this that he missed most while in Bombay, where the air was ripe with competing odors. At a street corner, he pauses by a cold drinks vendor slouched on a stool in front of his stall. Melvin asks for a cold bottle of Coke, to which the vendor spits over his shoulder, a sickle of crimson paan on the dirt. "No Coke," he says.

"Pepsi?"

"No Pepsi."

"Thumbs Up?"

"No Thumbs Up."

The vendor explains that he, like all shopkeepers in the area, is partaking in the boycott of Pepsi and Coke products. "Anti-var protest," the man says in clipped English, between chews. He points to a poster on the side of his stall that reads: *Boycott superpower business like Pepsi and Coca-Cola! Protest military action in Iraq! Brought to you by the Anti-War Samithy's General Council.*

"For how long?" Melvin asks.

The vendor shrugs. "I'd sell it to you, but the Anti-Var Squad will come and bother me if I do. Not worth the trouble." He scratches his chest and squints at the sky. "But all these things can't go on forever."

THE HOUSE IS a two-tiered stucco structure with a tiled roof the color of cinnamon and an upper-level veranda where a hammock swings languidly in the breeze. Standing before the house in his second-best shirt, Melvin pictures Gracie in that hammock, her slender arm hanging over the side, a glass of lime water in her hand.

The servant leads Melvin into the sitting room, where Abraham rises from a plush armchair, his hand extended. He is tall with hairy wrists and a chest like a slab of wood. His handshake has all the brevity and precision of a military salute.

"She is in the kitchen," Abraham says. "My wife."

"Ah."

"Hm."

They stand for a moment, lost without a woman to direct them.

"Sit!" Abraham almost cries out, both shocked at his own ill manners and glad to say something useful.

They sit. On the television is the ever-present Mammootty, the mustached megastar whose classic swagger Melvin had long ago tried and failed to emulate. Here, Mammootty is turning away from a man who possesses two traits quintessential to villains: a sleazy voice and a boulderlike paunch. The villain calls out: "Hey big shot, wait." He scratches his cheek with a smile. "You can't leave just yet—"

Mammootty turns and smacks the man across the face with a loud *dshoom!*

In shock, the man clutches his cheek. Mammootty says: "How about I leave now?"

Meanwhile, Abraham is talking about the satellite that he recently installed on the roof so he could capture channels from around the world. "We also get American channels, but all we want is our Mammootty. Isn't it?"

Melvin nods, though he is more of a Mohanlal man, the huskier, equally mustached counterpart to Mammootty.

At that moment, thankfully, Mercy Chandy emerges from the kitchen with a plate of cutlets and a dollop of ketchup in a crystal bowl. Melvin rises. "Sit, sit," she says, and glances at the TV. "This one again?" Sheepish, Abraham mutes the TV, leaving Mammootty to swagger, slow-motion, in silence.

Mrs. Chandy is one of those women who moves easily through any social circle, whose greetings are like an invisible hand on one's shoulder. Melvin admires the nobility of her chin, something Greek and classical about her profile. As one with a rather prominent nose, Melvin envies those whose prominent noses somehow work in their favor.

The interview is conducted by Mrs. Chandy, though mostly she asks about his family's health. No one mentions anything about the driving job, and Melvin is suddenly stricken by the thought that this is not an interview at all in the Chandys' minds, but simply a house visit.

"About the job," Melvin says carefully, "I used to drive for the Uthup family. If you need a reference letter . . ."

"Reference letter?" Mrs. Chandy tilts her head. "What for? This is not an interview."

Melvin hesitates. "No?"

"Of course not. This meeting is to discuss a schedule. You had the job as soon as Berchmans suggested you to us." Mrs. Chandy looks to her husband for reassurance.

"No, no, we don't need an interview. We know you. And Gracie, of course." Absently, Abraham gazes into his glass in which a lime rind is floating like a dead fish. He looks up with a sudden smile. "What more is there to know?"

Melvin clears his throat and thanks them. He feels as though he is courting two people who are both out of his league, a feeling with which he is not inexperienced.

CURRENT CUT.

It is announced from house to house as if the snap-sudden darkness and slowing of ceiling fans were not explanation enough. Small children are ordered to stay still. Fathers tell sons, "Find the torch, the torch," and sons go blazing the flashlight around the house, attempting to rescue whomever is stuck in the bathroom, mid-bath, without a light to distinguish floor from toilet hole. Out of the darkness, mothers appear around the corner, bearing candle flames behind cupped palms. Candles and flashlights are kept within easy reach in every house because this evening, as with many evenings, the electricity workers are on strike, unsettled by their wages, powerful in their unions.

Linno lowers the candle to the floor, where Anju sits behind a small barrier of books. The past year has thinned some of the baby fat from her cheeks and she has gotten reading glasses that now cast slanted shadows up her forehead, a set of evil eyebrows above her own. She bites her lip, scanning the page as Linno sets another lamp before her, a cylindrical white light that sizzles stray mosquitoes.

Linno crouches on the floor before the large square of parcel paper and a set of oil pastels that Jilu Auntie sent her last Christmas. She has never used them but has repeatedly run her fingers over the sticks of color lined up in the box, hues richer than the words that are found on the sides of crayons. The oil pastels transcend naming. They are made for professionals. They are paralyzingly perfect.

The woman's figure will come smoothly, all the gatherings and ripplings of fabric around the body. To make the fabric recede deep into the page, to create depth through distraction, this poses more of a challenge. But when the page is blank, she harbors no doubt, which makes drawing unlike anything else in her life. It is strange, this pent part of herself, this smallest kernel of confidence, pure as gold, that whatever her mind summons to the page will eventually appear.

From behind her book, Anju watches as Linno maps the ghosts of figures to come. Anju returns to her books, then looks up again. "Is that for the tailor's window?"

Linno nods, drawing an oval shape. A face. She loosens the lines across the figure, the bosom, the hip. Huge, outlandish hips. She slims them.

When Linno looks up, Anju is still watching her.

"I'm bored." Anju yawns, collapsing on her side. Casually, she adds: "Sister Savio told us about a scholarship today."

Linno pauses to listen, her pencil hovering over the face.

It will be awarded to the best student in all of Kerala, Anju explains. A panel of judges. Two weeks of indecision. And then, finally, one student sent to a school in New York called the Sitwell School, for a full year. A year—an expanse of time so long, it rolls out like a scarlet carpet. And who knows where it will lead once her visa is renewed? An image comes to Linno, perhaps from a movie, of Anju at the bow of a departing ship. A fluttering handkerchief. Broad-brimmed hats and blown kisses. Linno realizes that she has never even been to an airport.

"Are you going?" Linno asks.

"I'll apply. If I get it, I will go."

For a moment, there is only the soft scrape of lead and the humming light. Distracted, Linno angles the chin too sharply, throwing the face off-balance, a heart-shaped cartoon. She always knew that this time would come, that Anju would leave, but so soon and so far?

Anju stretches extravagantly. "Did you know that in America, husbands and wives sleep in different beds?"

"No they don't."

"Not all the time but most of the time. There's so much space in America that everyone has her own bed, her own room, her own bathroom, her own closet."

"Where do you get all this?"

"That American show, the one with the wife who dropped chocolates down her blouse."

Linno tries to lighten her voice. "Next you'll tell me there is no color in America, only black and white."

Anju flips onto her stomach and studies what Linno has drawn so far. Smoky features, a face with plumed lashes and a darkened lower lip. Linno feels suddenly embarrassed by her box of oil pastels, their smallness, how they command such importance in her life. And they do look like crayons.

"Is that supposed to be you?" Anju asks.

"No," Linno says sharply.

Anju returns to her books. "I was only asking."

Linno spirals her pastel over the woman's face until a vortex of scribble swallows the features completely. She flips the paper over. The mere suggestion that Linno would be blessing herself with a pictorial, imagined beauty seems pathetic, and more or less true.

ALONG WITH every other eligible student in Kerala, Anju applies for the scholarship. She brings the forms home so that Linno can fill them out, as Linno's penmanship possesses an elegance that Melvin believes might win extra approval. With care, sometimes by candlelight, Linno copies Anju's test scores while Melvin hovers over Linno's shoulder, hands clasped behind his back, as in the Fontainelle days.

During the mornings, Linno is also painting the tailor's window. On the first day, she plots her drawing in chalk, bringing the smaller painting up to scale. The tailor emerges from her store every so often, fists on hips, to offer warnings and criticisms: "Don't make me too dark, understand? I am not a fig." At the tailor's behest, Linno adds a gold bangle and a dainty, pert nose in place of the one that, in actuality, looks slightly squashed.

With an advance from the tailor, Linno buys paint from Thresia Paint House, where a woman who claims to be Melvin's friend gives her a good discount. Over the chalked lines, Linno strokes the first layer of colors, flat carnation pink and peach, then hollows for the eyes, black frills for the lashes, and lighter accents to pinch folds within the fabric. Over the course of two more days, passersby linger while children on their way home from school stop to watch, unblinking, silently reverent in the presence of one who is allowed to vandalize private property. Uncomfortable with their worship, she takes to painting earlier in the morning, in the few dawning hours before the tailor arrives.

When finally Linno is finished, three days later, she stands back and finds the whole thing a hideous, bosomy, burlesque mess. Is that a colander hiding beneath the rump of the woman's sari? Her eyes are of two different latitudes beneath heavy eyebrows, and the pallu, dear God, is a juvenile rendering, a wrinkly peach mess.

"*Aiyyo*, look what you did to my cheek," the tailor says from behind her.

Closing a paint can, Linno begins to stammer that everything is removable with ammonia and water, but the tailor is not listening.

"My cheek," she repeats, her gaze fixed on the window. "It glows."

Taking a few steps back to where the tailor stands, Linno looks at the window. Sunrise has filled the colors with rose and in this light, Linno glimpses her dim reflection, all baggy eyes and fuzzy braid, a lick of paint across her forehead. She sees what the tailor sees in the painted lady, an inner phosphorescence at the summit of her cheek.

Over time, Linno gains a small fame as people congratulate her on what they call "Linno's window." She is hired to paint another window for Frames & Optics, which consists of a giant diapered baby with a pillowy chest, wearing oversized, black-rimmed eyeglasses. Upon the owner's request, she makes the eyes shine like pool blue marbles, though she has never seen a brown baby with pool blue eyes. The tailor's window remains her favorite, and she elaborates upon the parcel paper painting that she initially designed for the tailor. In each corner, she adds a thicket of roses, and in the lower right corner, she draws her name in a tiny, undulating vine unlike the others, thorny and leafless, the green gone brown. Ammachi hangs the picture on the side wall of the sitting room.

Whenever she passes by her windows, Linno slows her step and tries not to linger for too long, but she derives a pleasant vanity from staring, the kind that she assumes a beautiful woman must feel upon looking in a mirror. Sometimes the truth creeps up on her in a quiet, inner explosion—she made these things. On more than one occasion, the tailor has been known to say, "Linno can do more with her one wrong hand than anyone else can do with two!" And for the first time, when she hears mention of her wrong hand, Linno is proud.

IN APRIL, Anju is notified that the panelists have selected her to be one of ten finalists, and that the primary judge, Miss Valerie Schimpf, will interview her personally. Miss Schimpf is an art teacher and counselor at the Sitwell School, and has spent the spring semester on sabbatical, teaching children at a fine arts school in Kochi.

In a letter that is read and recited and handled like a relic, Anju is told that the interview will take place at "the Vallara residence." Five days of cleaning ensue, but no matter how thoroughly Linno and Anju tidy the residence, the door appears ramshackle, the walls a funereal gray as soon as Miss Schimpf crosses the threshold. Linno notices things to which she rarely gives attention, like the creased poster of three pink-skinned babies in diapers, all sharing frustrated faces of constipation, next to the phrase CUTE AS BUTTONS! She wants to ask her father why he hung such a thing over the doorway, but he is conveniently out driving Abraham Chandy.

Fortunately Miss Schimpf does not seem bothered by the poster. She is a confident pixie, dressed in an out-of-fashion salwar, too short for the times, with a shawl bound about her neck like a noose. Her green glass bangles clink when she presses her hands together in Namaste. "What a lovely home," she says to Ammachi, bowing low like a geisha girl. After a moment's hesitation, Ammachi tries to bow even lower.

Only then does Linno recognize the awe in Miss Schimpf's gaze, unnaturally bright and bursting with empathy. It calls to mind a celebrity she once saw on the news, an American socialite crouched in the dim hut of a Rwandan family of eight. The socialite was on a two-day mission, her publicist said, "to draw attention to a growing crisis." Miss Schimpf's eyes move slowly over Ammachi's cracked toes, the starved mattress across the daybed, the stuffed animals trapped in curio cabinets, and Linno's knotted wrist, before returning to Ammachi's elastic smile. Perhaps Miss Schimpf sees something authentic in the shabbiness, the possibility of what could be, a future for which she can pave the way. Unmet need is standing directly in front of her, in the form of a girl, her handicapped sister, and a virtually toothless old woman who pelts Miss Schimpf with her limited English: *Havar you? . . . Es, es, Iyam fine.*

Miss Schimpf is ready to give.

While Ammachi takes Miss Schimpf on a tour of the curio cabinets, Anju dumps spoon after spoon of Tang into a pot of water, clouds of orange swelling and settling to the bottom. "Stop it!" Linno whispers. "You want her to pee orange?"

"Which cups, which cups?"

Under normal circumstances, they would provide their guest with the fancy Pepsi glasses from Jilu Auntie, which read on the side: YOU GOT THE RIGHT ONE, BABY, UH HUH. But this time, Linno insists on using their humbler cups, primitive-looking and made of steel.

Linno unscrews the Nescafé jar which has stored sugar for far longer than it has stored coffee, just as the apricot jam jar now preserves pickle, every vessel possessed of an afterlife. Through the jar's glass, she can see a few ants tunneling paths; she spoons around them. A drowned ant floating on the surface of one's tea is exactly the type of thing that might push a woman like Miss Schimpf from pity to revulsion.

Anju whisks the tray of Tang into the living room. From the kitchen, Linno can hear Ammachi saying, "Velcome my house," as she exits the room.

As soon as Ammachi enters the kitchen, she lets loose a battery of whispered curses, lamenting her idiotic granddaughters for using the inferior drinking vessels, thereby compromising Anju's chance at America. All because of a glass. The idiots.

LINNO CAN HARDLY BELIEVE IT. Anju's interview is going terribly wrong.

From behind the curtain that separates sitting room from kitchen, Linno spies as Anju fumbles over her English, continually asking for questions to be repeated. Over and over, Miss Schimpf reassures her that everything is okay, that they are just having a chat. Is this the same girl who kept Linno awake at night, contentedly purring over her future American adventures? "Why are you so quiet?" Anju whispered. "You know I'll come back for you."

"So what makes you different from all the other candidates out there?" Miss Schimpf asks. "What makes you stand out?"

Anju crosses and uncrosses her ankles. An errant piece of string is caught in the hair at her temple, resembling a patch of premature gray among the black. Her voice issues forth in robotic monotone: "I have made excellent marks in all exams and have made top rank in all subjects such as in maths, English, all these things, and I also was winning many Bible Bowels throughout Kerala—"

"Bowels?" Miss Schimpf repeats.

"Bowels," Anju insists.

They go back and forth like this, until Miss Schimpf brightens and says, "Oh, you mean *bowls*."

"Yes, this, and also I am leader of my school's band."

"It's amazing how accomplished all of you are, the candidates I mean. We've got one boy in Malappuram who started his own Koran Competition." Despite her smile, Miss Schimpf's tentative tone expresses that the question has yet to be answered properly. "I guess what I mean is, what makes you unique? You know that word—'unique'?"

"You-neek?"

"Yes! Exactly. What is it about your personality, not just your awards and your grades, that makes you unique, different, special?"

A short but tortuous silence as Anju waits, leaning forward, straining her neck as if to peer into Miss Schimpf's mouth, where the definition of "you-neek" lies. She sits back and takes a sip of her Tang, and then, the final blow.

Just as she blurts the first words of her answer ("I think"), out comes a spray of spittled Tang onto the back of Miss Schimpf's hand.

"Oh!" Miss Schimpf gives a small, tense laugh. Anju mumbles "Sorry" over and over, attempting to wipe the Tang-laden hand with her own. "It's all right, it's all right. Let's just take a deep breath . . ."

Linno takes a deep breath. Last Sunday, she woke from a dream wherein Anju failed her interview, a dream whose aftertaste, in the morning, was strangely sweet. She both wanted Anju to go and wanted her to fail. Not only to fail, but to know the lasting heaviness of failure. Guilt-ridden, Linno spent an hour with Ammachi's prayer book, summoning up long, sorrowful prayers, and for the rest of the day she went on with her chores, taking special care when ironing her sister's school blouse.

And now, her prayers have been answered with this.

"Get away from there!" Ammachi whispers, then begs: "What is happening? What?"

"They are almost finished," Linno says.

LINNO SITS on the back step just as Rappai's rooster struts into the yard, eyeing her as if she poses some sort of challenge. She hates Rappai's rooster. It boasts all the lesser qualities of its owner: knotty legs, a bulky middle, pecking after ladies in a way that sends them skittering off. Its feet are surprising—large, taloned, and violent—recalling the mightier pterodactyl from which it has descended, disappointingly, into Rappai's yard.

Rappai lives in the house behind theirs; she can see him gawking from his doorway, craning his neck. He wears his usual off-yellow mundu tied far too high above his knees, exposing thighs barely wider than his calves, and a towel over his shoulder. He works in construction, laying down brick and mortar for the new consumer store that is rising up in Baker Junction, and he walks as if he were still supporting an invisible basket of brick on his head.

"*Eddi*, Linno!" he yells from the doorway. "Did she get it?"

In an effort to quiet him, Linno shakes her head furiously, waves her hand *No*.

"No?" She can see the dark shadow of Rappai's mother inside the house, lying down on her mat, lifting onto an elbow to hear.

With her finger to her lips, Linno makes a hissing noise. Finding this attractive, Rappai's rooster swells its chest and shrieks while flapping its wings. She claps it away.

Through the space between Rappai's house and an adjacent banana tree, she can see another ola roof and another farther back, all of these and more homes making up Kumarakom, a village at the delta of the Meenachil River, a dot not even mapped on a globe, unlike New York, which seems almost a nation unto itself. The whole family was assuming that Anju would win the award and go traipsing off to that glittering place like Raj Kapoor, whistling with her stick and bundle as she sang her way into the Technicolor hills. Linno even allowed herself to fantasize that she might follow, one or two years from now. But true life, hers in particular, will require far less color, very little imagination.

She wonders sometimes, not often, what it would be like to be married to a man like Rappai, someone whose matinal nose blowing can be heard from the next house over. Maybe after a while, the wife's subtle disgust settles to the bottom of her being, like a sediment, allowing her to wash his underwear, hang his *sheddi* on the line, and spread Tiger Balm across the shallow basin of his chest without dread, without any feeling at all. It seems quite probable that were Linno ever to marry, her husband would have to be someone poor or ugly or both. Even then, she would have to supply a substantial dowry, though less than what would be required for someone not so poor and not so ugly.

Who has the stomach for this kind of math, when the result— a vaguely repulsive housemate—amounts to so little?

Three days before, Rappai's mother hobbled over to Ammachi, who was hanging damp bedsheets on a laundry line. From the kitchen, Linno listened as Rappai's mother said that she had suggested Linno to a woman whose brother was looking for a wife.

"Is the brother old?" Ammachi asked, already used to and suspicious of these rare inquiries.

"No," said Rappai's mother. "He is from a good family, very upright. A church man. Only thing—he is blind. *Pagathi*, not fully. He can see colors and shapes but someone has to help him with stairs."

"Hm," Ammachi said, her lips tight.

All this time, Rappai has been lingering in his doorway, arms crossed beneath his chest, gravely waiting for news. At last, he goes back inside, and his rooster, eyeing her for a moment, also loses interest and struts away.

That Ammachi has not mentioned the blind man indicates that she has not dismissed the possibility.

As it did that day, panic flaps in Linno's chest.

LINNO RETURNS to the kitchen to find that Ammachi has taken up the forbidden post by the doorway. Ammachi's eyes are closed, head bowed as she listens through the curtain, gleaning what she can.

"What's happening?" Linno asks.

Ammachi whirls around, caught but triumphant. "You were wrong. Something good has happened."

"How do you know?"

"I can tell. Lots of *ooooh* and *aaaah*."

And though Ammachi flutters her hands to shoo Linno away, Linno spies through the space between the curtain and the door frame.

The two cups of Tang have been abandoned on the table, still sweaty with condensation. Miss Schimpf is now standing in the middle of the room with her back to the kitchen. She is looking down at something cradled in her arms, speaking in a low murmur while Anju nods like a desperate, loyal child. Before Linno can make out their words, Ammachi pulls her from the curtain and forces her to sit at the kitchen table, beyond hearing, lest Miss Schimpf suspect them of being unmannered.

WHEN THEY GATHER on the front steps to bid Miss Schimpf good-bye, Linno finds it strange that Anju is sweating so much. Dark splotches have appeared under the armpits of her white blouse, which will turn yellow if Linno does not wash it tonight. She nudges a handkerchief into Anju's palm.

Wiping her brow, Anju looks ahead without seeming to see the leaves, the moat, the bridge, or Miss Schimpf. Nothing at all. It is Linno who rushes over to help Miss Schimpf across the twin trunks of the bridge, her eyes on the water not two feet below her, trembling as though she were several stories higher. On the pretense of hospitality, Rappai and his mother come to watch as Linno leads her safely to the other bank, where a driver is leaning out of his auto-rickshaw.

Before Miss Schimpf climbs into her seat, she embraces Linno and says, "Your sister truly has a *gift*."

TWO WEEKS LATER, the *Malayala Manorama* publishes a photograph of Anju receiving a plaque the size of a small window, with her name yet to be engraved. The article explains how she will be given the opportunity to study in New York City for the fall and spring semesters, at the Sitwell School, all expenses paid.

In the picture, Miss Schimpf and Anju are underexposed, their faces smudgy with gray smiles, joined by the plaque between them. The paper quotes Miss Schimpf: "Anju is a true Renaissance woman: an excellent student, a leader, and a brilliant artist. I am especially thrilled about displaying her artwork during the Student Art Exhibition."

OVER THE NEXT TWO MONTHS, friends and acquaintances ask Linno about every detail of Anju's itinerary, and jot down phone numbers of their second cousins' neighbor's niece who lives in New York and would be happy to help her. No trouble at all, they say, patting Linno on the back, quick to claim their New York connection. Anju is not the only one, *ha ha*.

"We hear your sister is an artist now!" they say, smiling.

"Of course," Linno says, attempting an equal measure of joy, as though she were the one awarded. "You never know with her. She can do anything she wants to do."

Except draw.

But there is hardly time to speak to Anju about such things. She is never at home, rushing around to obtain a student visa, a letter from this school to that embassy, transcripts of school records. Just yesterday, she and Melvin arrived home from an overnight trip to the U.S. Consulate in Chennai, another city that Linno has never visited. And even when Anju is home, she isn't. She casts her eyes around the walls and ceilings, grazing over every possible object before fleetingly meeting Linno's gaze.

And Anju is not the only one. Even Melvin takes care not to mention the scholarship in Linno's presence, except for one evening, when he returns home late from a celebratory night with his friends at the toddy shop. He sits in the good chair, eyes closed, as Linno puts a bowl of banana chips on the coffee table, something to soak up the liquor pooling in his empty stomach. The first drink always goes slowly, harmlessly, but Melvin downs every one after that until he begins to squint, as if caught in his own mental fog, which means that he has long lost count. He squints at the chips, dreamily surprised by their existence, then slowly his gaze swims up to her.

"Abraham Saar says congratulations."

"Why?" she says sharply. "I didn't do anything."

"To all of us." He stares at the table, then abruptly straightens up. "There is good and there is bad, Linno. And then there is bad for good's sake."

Linno encourages her father to eat some chips.

Melvin selects a single chip and examines it before placing it between his molars. He crunches with concentration. "Your mother, she always wanted to go to New York. It was the one thing I couldn't give her. That and a happy marriage."

"Did you have dinner?" Linno asks.

Melvin looks at her. "She is doing this for you too."

"Who is doing what?"

"She. Anju. *This* . . ." He shakes his head forcefully, deeply irritated. "This is for the best."

The word "this" he pronounces with eyes closed, whether from reverence or need of sleep, she cannot tell. Linno knows, has always known, the definition of "this." She wants an admission from Ammachi or Melvin, both of whom have gone about the house maintaining the careful pretense that Anju's newfound artistry is perfectly natural.

With a hand pressed to the table, Melvin rises out of his incoherence and shuffles to the back of the house.

Linno wades her fingers into the bowl of banana chips. Is this the moment when she should knock the bowl to the floor, drag Anju out of bed, call her thief? But her rage will not come. Instead, she feels a slow-growing sadness in the pit of her stomach which she has tried, time and again, to uproot or ignore. She collects the few crumbs from the table and takes the bowl to the kitchen.

SITTING ON THE BACK STEP, Melvin thinks of what he wanted to explain to Linno, about an old friend known as Eastern Bobby. No richer or poorer than anyone else, Eastern Bobby had aspirations that began with a keen sense of destiny, a conviction that he had a starring role to play in the world. So he was disheartened at having to marry a woman double his heft; more than once his friends had asked him if his Dollie ever got tired of toting him around on her hip. But those same friends had no wives with visas, and it was Dollie's visa that landed him in what he believed might be a dream destination: Normal, Illinois.

On his first trip back from Normal, Eastern Bobby brought a film camera, a heavy, monstrous machine that he set up outside his parents' home. He then ironed one of his grandfather's mundas with a care he had never invested in his own clothes and nailed the munda to the side of the house. At night, he invited all his friends and neighbors to watch the projection. Melvin sat back, his elbows digging into the hard dirt, listening to the symphony of crickets and camera noise beneath a crackling stretch of black. A huge, blurry eye burst onto the munda, watery and blinking, apocalyptic, but out of focus. More black. And then—Eastern Bobby's top half appeared, his slight frame huge on the makeshift screen.

"*Namaskaram!*" on-screen Eastern Bobby bellowed at the audience. "Thank you for coming!"

On-screen Eastern Bobby waved the camera into the kitchen, while real-life Eastern Bobby watched with the cool appraisal of a film critic, frowning, his chin in his hand.

The cameraman followed Eastern Bobby to the refrigerator. Eastern Bobby opened the door to reveal a giant jug of milk, a blue carton of twelve perfect eggs, a brick of yellow cheese, and a box with several sticks of butter. In the freezer: a slab of steak and a whole chicken, beheaded and plucked, sitting upright like the guest of honor.

"He just bought all that food for show," someone whispered.

Another audience member disagreed. "Have you seen his wife?"

The screening went on for an hour, beginning with bathroom and closet tours, and ending with greetings from various men and women whom Eastern Bobby had visited in Chicago, sending their best wishes to their relatives. Naming the relatives took up considerable time, and all the camera jostling made Melvin slightly nauseated, but still he watched the nouveau celebrities. Thrilled and sick, he imagined himself on-screen as well, with a fridge of his own full of milk and meat.

This was during a simpler time, when he had only himself to place at the center of his fantasy home in Illinois, with all its wide-open space and stalks of nodding wheat, the Normal supermarkets big as amusement parks. And while on-screen Eastern Bobby pointed out the items in the fridge, Melvin noticed through the window behind him a few children playing. Black children, but still, when Melvin squinted, he could imagine that they were his own.

THE DAY BEFORE Anju's departure to New York falls on a Sunday, and despite the many minor tasks that have yet to be completed, the family attends Mass. It is only proper, Ammachi says, though even she harbors doubts about Anthony Achen's proficiency as a priest. Anthony Achen has cultivated a roundish beard; its pure whiteness disagrees with his black eyebrows, fanning the general belief that he bleaches his beard in order to attain the semblance of divine wisdom. His sermons are lacking in that regard.

"And so," Anthony Achen concludes, "when the angel Gabriel asked the Virgin Mary to bear the fruit of the world, the Immaculate Conception, did she doubt? No. Did she say, 'Can I have a minute to think?' No. Did she say, 'I am the handmaiden of the Lord. Do with me what you will'? Absolutely yes. Because when God calls, we do not think. We trust. We go. We *do*."

In the audience, the Kapyar nods along as if he and Anthony Achen are engaged in a private conversation. As right-hand man to Anthony Achen, the Kapyar keeps his robes as white as his superior's beard, bleached with bottles of Ujala. Sometimes, when Linno is bored, she makes a habit of watching the Kapyar's movements, to see what rowdy boys he is glaring down over his shoulder, which ears he is planning to pinch, a small brutality that has earned him the unofficial title of "the Crab." He looks over the congregation, his gaze laced with disapproval. Just before he catches her eye, Linno returns to the conclusion of Anthony Achen's homily: "And then there are others who have nothing better to do than to steal ladies' shoes from the doors of our very own church. Whoever has Pearlie Varkey's shoes, please return them."

The congregation wears grave expressions, not only at Pearlie Varkey's loss, but also the loss of trust among fellow Syrian Catholics. But maybe next time Pearlie Varkey will think twice about wearing her milk-white high heels to church, or any shoes whose insoles declare LIZ CLAIBORNE, and placing them at an obvious distance from the rabble of dusty sandals that belong to everyone else. Pearlie Varkey has family in Toronto and flies back and forth often, always with her tender feet buckled and belted into new styles. Not that theft is ever acceptable. But ask for attention and ye shall receive.

Someday soon, Linno thinks, Anju will return buckled into a shoe like that.

Ever since Anju's plane ticket arrived in the mail, it has occupied a hallowed place behind the curio glass, nestled against her plaque along with her passport. And then came her suitcase, open-mouthed in the living room, collecting the clothes she would wear, the foods she would bring, including jackfruit that Ammachi specially fried and dried for her and hard balls of sugared sesame seed.

These thoughts weave in and out of Linno's prayer, reducing its meaning to a stream of vowels and fricatives. She stands in the back, rows of heads packed thickly all the way to the nave. On the left stand the men, on the right are the women, crowns covered with sari pallus and shawls, and between them the long, wide aisle that leads straight to Anthony Achen. Above him hangs a massive tapestry of Saint George slaying the dragon. With his placid blue eyes, Saint George appears almost benevolent, aloft on his bucking white horse, lovingly plunging his spear into the writhing side of the dragon whose eyes look almost as human, but brown.

On the coir mats, the congregation rises and sits, rises and sits, the soles of their feet stamped with waffled patterns, so they can walk into the world weak-kneed but blessed. The hymns drone through the church like tides of music, a new verse beginning in the front row with the overeager Kapyar before the previous verse has finished in the back.

> *O Saint Yohannan Nepumocianos!*
> *Your heavenly blessings, priceless blessings*
> *Bestow on us, your humble servants.*
> *We pray you.*
> *We beseech you.*

From here, Linno spots Anju standing closer to the front, her hands folded, her shawl draped over her head.

AFTER TWO SOMBER HOURS of church, Ammachi enjoys a bit of socializing. Aglow, she flits through the scrum of people that have gathered around the entrance, asking after children, parents, and ailments. But that day, every question pertains to Anju—when is her flight, which airline, who is to meet her? Restless, Anju excuses herself, claiming that she has several errands to run, while Linno stays behind to wait for Ammachi and, to her dismay, to act as Anju's spokeswoman. The more Linno laughs and thanks everyone for their well wishes, the more it sounds to her ears as if she is laughing at an ugly, exuberant joke in which she has been made the fool.

While Ammachi gossips, Linno makes her way to the nearby cemetery, which is rounded by a short wall, brightly gilded with moss. Teak and tamarind trees fringe the border, shedding dead leaves over the village of crosses and tombs left to bake in the shadeless heat. Linno passes an ivory vault trimmed in pink, a bird-splattered cross planted on top. This is one of the many family tombs that preside aboveground, holding eight to twenty bodies in separate numbered drawers. Those who cannot afford the family tombs are assigned an earthen burial, a mound temporarily marked by a wooden cross.

Once, several years after her mother's death, Linno visited the cemetery with Ammachi only to find strangers at the same gravesite, mourning their dead son. Ammachi told her that Gracie's remains had been dug up and deposited in the Asthi Kuzhi, the Bone Pit on the other side of the church, more than twenty feet deep, gathering to its heart the generations of broken bones that would soften, gradually, to ash and dust. In time, the dead son would be moved to the Asthi Kuzhi as well, leaving the nameless mound to be filled with another body in need, and grieving strangers would continue to converge at the same spot to mourn their different losses. Sorrow was not a space to be bounded.

LINNO FINDS ANJU crouched before the wooden cross that once marked their mother's place. Anju lays a few weak wildflowers atop the mound, her head bowed, her eyes closed as she prays. Her shawl does not match her salwar, two discordant shades of blue. An obvious mistake, but just like Anju to be so careless, and not only with her clothes. A hundred prayers would not change her.

As Anju rises, Linno asks if all is packed.

Anju whirls around. A smile follows, relieved and artificial. Almost done, she says, though she still has to convert her rupees to dollars. Ammachi knows a man who can give them a good exchange rate, under the table of course, since the banks will rob you blind—

"And my painting," Linno says. "Have you packed that too?"

During the long pause that ensues, Anju's hands fall slowly to her sides. "I promise I will be careful with it."

"That's only one of my worries."

"Miss Schimpf wants to put it in some sort of student exhibition."

"As if it's yours."

"Yes."

The softness of her answer, delicate, almost inquisitive, only enrages Linno the more.

"She saw the tailor's painting," Anju says. "And she asked me if I had more."

"You showed her my sketchbook?" The thought surprises Linno even as she says it, as the image returns to her of Miss Schimpf looking down at something in her arms, Anju beside her, hungry for approval. "You went through my things and brought her my sketchbook?"

Anju draws herself up and attempts an innocent expression, without remorse, if not for the way she is wiping her hands against each other, over and over, long after they are clean. "But I'll bring all of it back."

"With your name on it."

"Not written on it."

"So?"

"I'm trying to help us get somewhere, Linno. I'm trying to change our lives."

"Your life first! By stepping all over mine! And then what will happen when you leave? You will go on and I will be here, only a chapter in your life."

Anju stares at the ground, pained, but not pained enough. Linno knows the way her sister will continue, the way her temporary regrets, with time, will become trivialities, things she will assign to desperation and youth. If only it were as simple as that.

"Put that shawl back on its hanger," Linno says without emotion. "You always forget."

Anju looks up, cautiously hopeful, but Linno is already walking away. Linno tramples over the mimosas that she and Anju used to tickle as children, watching the edgy fernlike leaves fold at the slightest brush. Praying Plants, Anju called them as they shimmered in the wind. After a while, Linno slows her pace, as there are people ahead who will notice her haste and ask her questions, who will hear the tears lodged in her throat. She walks, each step more leaden than the last, toward the distant thrum of voices taking their leave.

II.

ORIENTATION

2.

*F*OR YEARS, Anju has made a habit of mentally penning lines to her autobiography. It is almost always the same line, a variation on the epiphanic flashes found in biographies she has read, most recently those of Franklin Roosevelt, Indira Gandhi, and an unauthorized tome on Oprah Winfrey. In each, the line always ends with: . . . *I found myself at a crossroads.*

And now, sitting in window seat 29A, selected for its proximity to one of four emergency exits, she thinks: *In the airplane, I found myself at a crossroads.* At the moment, there is no crossroads, only a gray runway leading in a singular direction that her tiny window will not allow her to see. But recalling the line gives Anju a modicum of control, a sense of promise. A crossroads does not end in a crash.

The sari-clad stewardesses are slim, pretty, irritable. The pleats of their saris are neatly stacked, like Oriental fans, giving the impression that these are women who never sit or slump or sweat. They poke Anju awake when she tries to sleep through a meal. Wrapped in blankets, she fingers the plastic knife and picks at the papadam, while reading the safety manual for the seventh time. She stares at the screen built into the space above her tray table, where she can track her journey as a jagged blue vein slogging along from Kochi to Mumbai, and eventually Mumbai to London, then London to New York.

After dinner, the child in front of her, demanding leg room, reclines to a nearly horizontal position, so that Anju is forced to watch the screen within inches of her face. A Bollywood actor is talking about his favorite restaurant, Lotus, near Juhu Beach. "I highly recommend the strawberry salad," he says in dainty Anglicized English, pointing a forkful of salad at his fans, who toss and turn in their economy seats. "It's succulent, truly succulent."

THE JOURNEY BEGAN with a white jeep that arrived outside her home in Kumarakom, having miraculously navigated the scarred, narrow roads. While the driver roped her belongings across the top of the jeep, family and neighbors gathered in the sitting room. They bowed their heads and, facing east, murmured a prayer for safekeeping, each at his own pace, so that the disparate words—"servants" . . . "bestow" . . . "blessings"—floated around Anju's ears like the slow pulsing of fireflies past her window, the ones she watched for hours the night before, unable to sleep.

Anju mumbled along, focused on the painting of P. C. Mappilla that hung on the wall opposite. When Linno was eleven, Ammachi had commissioned her to paint the portrait of their ancestor, a minor celebrity of his time, according to Ammachi. Having no other model, Linno painted a rosier version of Melvin, with the same hollows in the cheeks, the same bumpy nose, but a fuller head of hair.

According to family history, Mappilla descended from the first Indian Christians, themselves converted by St. Thomas in A.D. 56 ("The *Christian* Christians," Ammachi said. "Not like the latecomers over in Goa, all those Hernandos and Fernandos.") In 1653, along came the Portuguese priests with their swinging censers of incense, their ribbons of Latin chant, intending to spread their brand of Christianity to the Indians, making Hernandos and Fernandos of whomever they could. So Mappilla, along with the rest of his congregation, tied a rope around an iron cross in the courtyard of their church. In protest, they held fast to the rope and swore on the Bible of the Church of Our Lady of Life at Mattanchery that they would never be subject to the Portuguese bishops.

"The *Coonan* Cross," Ammachi called it. "To this day, you can see it in Mattanchery. *Bent* from the force of their pulling."

"Why were they pulling?" Anju, then a little girl, had asked.

"The lesson is twofold. One: force of mind brings force of body. And two: the West is not the best."

And now, years later, Anju stood poised and packed for the less-than-best West.

Ammachi mashed a kiss into Anju's cheek, crying, clutching her grand-daughter's face as though she planned to pluck it off as a memento. Several times, Melvin reassured Anju that he felt no trace of inner itching, so the flight would be fine. When the jeep honked, he flinched.

"It's only ten months," Anju said, though uttering the time frame seemed only to lengthen it.

Everyone agreed: such a short time amounted to no time at all. But what was good-bye between those who had never spoken it? Awkwardly, Melvin folded his daughter's face into his chest and kissed the top of her head, his red eyes all the while on the vehicle that would take her away.

LINNO WAS THE ONLY tearless one. She stood against the wall with arms crossed, a pose that told she was in no mood to be touched. Anju glimpsed the old woman Linno might become, thin and embittered, arms wrapped so tight she seemed to embrace herself.

"Linno," Anju said gently, by way of good-bye. Linno did not move.

"Don't look so jealous, *chedduthi*!" one of the neighbors called out. "Anju will come back and take you too!"

They all laughed, all except Linno and Anju.

The jeep rattled away. Over her shoulder, Anju waved and her well-wishers waved back. They prolonged the wave, palms wagging, faces growing blank until the gesture lost the luster of farewell. Anju wiped her eyes, weeping not for the people who were waving, but for the one person who wouldn't. Not once had Linno broken her silence since leaving their mother's grave. Her face remained as stony as it had been that day.

SEVENTEEN YEARS OLD and here is Anju, stepping on American tile with its slick, game-show sheen for the first time in her life.

The JFK customs officer asks Anju a series of questions. Many friends and acquaintances have prepped her for this interview, have coached her to insist that she has absolutely no designs whatsoever to stay in the States. Even if she has designs (everyone has designs), she is to be firmly bland in her lack of imagination and ambition.

The gatekeeper, a woman with a crispy-looking perm, opens an envelope that had been sent to Anju by the Chennai consulate, with the warning that should she open it herself, she would not be allowed entry. Glancing at its contents, the gatekeeper asks why she wishes to enter the United States, and then, how long she plans to stay. "Ten months *only,*" Anju says. She is about to explain how she was recruited by Americans, but to her slight dismay, the official stamps her papers and welcomes her.

After waiting an hour to retrieve her luggage from its carousel, Anju surrenders her bags to the poking and prodding of another official. He unearths a set of dolls that fit one inside the next, each of them a pear-shaped American president. Anju explains that these are gifts for her host family, while the officer unscrews Nixon and sniffs inside. Anju does not explain how she spent an hour in three trinket shops, hunting for the perfect present. Her father begged her to take frond-woven handicrafts, on the assumption that six dolls did not make an appropriate gift, but this series of presidents birthing smaller presidents epitomizes something unclear yet profound about America, about its leaders fattening with optimism, about growing toward the future while carrying the past in deepening chambers. Surely her host family will display them with warmth.

With all her bags and belongings intact, Anju pushes her cart toward the EXIT sign, where the glass doors part automatically. Once outside, a placard with her new name catches her eye: MISS ANJU MELVIN.

Her real name is Anju Vallara, but at her father's insistence, she lopped off her last name and took his first as her last. "You need a name that people can pronounce correctly," he said.   .

"Why can't I correct people myself?" she asked.

Melvin cited the names of acquaintances who had gone abroad— look at Gopal Ananthakrishnan who anointed himself Gopal Ananth, or Johny Kochuvarkey who became John Koch. Everyone tossed and scrambled their names into something more globally palatable, so likewise Anju found her passport and visa bearing her new title under a picture that rendered her a bit lemurlike, with eyes surprised and far apart, the rest of her face receding to a timid chin.

"Miss Melvin?" asks the uniformed man holding the sign.

A regrettable change, she thinks.

She nods hello as he takes control of her cart. He is a young black-American. Or is it black-African? African-black? Blafrican? She experiments with several more hyphenates, all in her head, though none seems correct and her driver seems exactly the wrong person to ask. They walk out into a world of concrete and glowing brake lights, people clasping one another, a pink balloon floating into the rich blue sky, forgotten, and a couple that meet in a violent kiss, the man's hands locking the woman's head into place as if it, too, might drift away.

The driver opens the car door (For whom? For her!), and she enters to find them divided by a wall of dark glass. In the reflection, she examines her ensemble, the flowery blouse and skirt that swished with a chic nonchalance back home. The outfit has suffered from the journey, looking now like a flowery tent that collapsed into wrinkles all around her.

She shivers, assaulted by mighty gusts of air-conditioning on either side, and pokes her fingers into the empty cup holders. She reviews what she knows of her host family: the Solankis, a Gujarati family of three, with a mother and father whom she will call Uncle and Auntie out of respect, if not relation. Being Hindu, they will likely impose a beefless diet within the house, but she hopes that they will be more forgiving of fish. They have a son, several years older than Anju, currently attending a celebrated college named Princeton. The father is a doctor. The mother is somewhat famous as the host of an American daytime television show called *Four Corners*. Her name is Sonia Solanki.

Though Anju has seen it only once, she is well aware of *Four Corners*, named for four female hosts who debate various news topics and trends, from foreign policy to flattering swimsuit cover-ups. On the one episode that Anju watched, Mrs. Solanki was introducing the practice of Ayurveda to the studio audience. "Ayurveda," she said, "abides by the principle that anything that enters our bodies can have three possible effects—as food, as medicine, or as poison—which is why I refuse to eat anything with high-fructose corn syrup." Her usual antagonist, the spunky and highlighted Young Creationist, facetiously argued on behalf of Little Debbie snack cakes (of which she could "literally inhale a dozen"), earning applause from some members of the audience. As was her wont, Mrs. Solanki laughed and lauded the Young Creationist's tiny waist: "If only we could all have your genes."

"Levi's Low Rise!" the Creationist replied.

Mrs. Solanki gave another desiccated laugh.

On the way to the Solankis, Anju notices a blond, wind-whipped head leaning out the passenger window of a car, possibly a tourist like her, a thought that inspires a comforting sense of fellowship. Squinting, she realizes that the head belongs to a dog. It calmly surveys the puckered water, the elegant cluster of skyscrapers on the horizon. Anju has read of these buildings. During the three months she spent waiting for her visa, she scoured a library book called *America Today* to bring herself up to speed on the nation's recent history and politics, in case her schoolmates might want to talk history and politics. (She read somewhere that New Yorkers routinely quote Nietzsche and Kierkegaard.) According to the book, "The world's first skyscrapers were built by Bethlehem Steel, a company also responsible for laying the nation's first railroad track and supplying steel for the Golden Gate Bridge." The book went on to mention the bankruptcy of Bethlehem Steel in 2001, but failed to name the new transnational titans, the Tatas and Mittals who had run them out of their own country. (This was a fact that Anju's former history teacher, a spirited nationalist, had proclaimed to the class with a victorious double pump of his fist.) And despite Anju's own sense of patriotism, both of these things—the death of Bethlehem Steel and the skyline whose incompleteness she will never fully know—fill her with a sudden gray nostalgia for a country not her own.

Lost in the undulations of power lines, she stops paying attention to the large green signs that indicate unfamiliar cities. The besuited man is driving fast but no faster than the cars around her, each one carrying a person lulled into a similar spell, the boundless speed somehow slowing time. A jet has drawn a chalky scrawl across the sky but seems to move no further. Dozy yet anxious, she focuses on the wisdoms plastered on the bumpers of passing cars, particularly one that leaves her with the militant order to LIVE LARGER, DRIVE SMALLER! NOT EVERYONE NEEDS AN SUV!

THE SOLANKIS LIVE in a vanilla cake. Anju has seen nothing of such spotless grandeur, a colossus with carved accents and curls along its corners, surrounded by a shiny iron gate with the stern, bearded bust of a Roman general impaled at every post. Morning light blushes the windows, whose sills are spiked so as to ward away incontinent pigeons. The driveway circles the front like a smile.

Gold block letters spell THE MONARCH over the revolving glass doors, which usher her onto a red velvet carpet leading past an oasis of plants and fountains, beneath a series of chandeliers like bright, brass octopi, to the front desk. Upon hearing Anju's name, a man in a black suit asks her how she is doing in a way that seems earnestly invested in her answer. "Very good," she says. He tells her to go on up; her bags will arrive shortly.

Alone in the elevator, she finds a bench with a deep green leather cushion. She sits down. The ground rises up. Sitting has never seemed so luxurious.

The elevator deposits her before an open door made of rich, dark wood. Shoes off or on? Her first impression seems to hinge on this decision. Out of respect for tradition: off.

"Hello?" she calls. Hesitating, she steps inside. Her feet are greeted by cold marble, white with wisps of gray.

The living room is full of beautiful clutter, organized to keep the gaze traveling from one piece to the next. A stained-glass window on the far wall first captures her attention, a geometric design built in brilliant wedges and disks of red, yellow, and green. Niches are carved into the walls to house sculptures and vases, like the leaping salmon of glass or the bust of a brass ram with two black, curling horns. And though the Solankis might refrain from cow, they seem to take pleasure in other piecemeal animals. An elephant foot with tough, scalloped toenails supports the round glass top of a side table. Beneath the piano, the skins of two zebra lie next to each other, arms benignly overlapping. Anju catches her foot in the smiling maw of a bear.

"Happens to people all the time," a man says, stepping on the bear's back. In anguish, she notes his cashew-colored shoe next to the nudity of her foot.

Once she is freed, the man shakes her hand and introduces himself as Varun. Around his mouth is a neat, black wreath of facial hair.

And then, the clean *click-click* of heels as a woman calls out from some upper, unseen level, "Is that Anju?" Mrs. Solanki appears in the hollow of a Spanish-looking arch. Overall, she gives the impression of shininess, from the satin tunic she wears over her pants to the laminated look of her bobbed hairstyle.

"Hello, Auntie." Anju makes a small, awkward bow with folded hands. "Uncle."

"No need for that." Mrs. Solanki descends the stairs with minimal trembling of her bob. "You can call me Sonia."

Sonia and Varun. Using these names makes Anju feel as if she is trying to hug her host parents prematurely. Mr. and Mrs. will do.

"How many times have I said to get rid of that thing, Varun?" Mrs. Solanki shakes her head at the bear rug. "My mother is scared to open the door because of it."

"Maybe we should get one for all the doors," Mr. Solanki says.

Dismissing him with an elegant wave, Mrs. Solanki enfolds Anju into a well of spicy perfume.

ANJU SITS ON the slippery edge of a sofa that, like all the chairs in the living room, is heaped with filigreed, loaflike cushions. Mrs. Solanki places a dish of tiny beef samosas on the coffee table, as well as another one of raw carrots and broccoli which she calls "organic." Anju partakes from the samosa plate, only after watching Mr. Solanki plunge two into his mouth.

"My family is from Bombay," Mr. Solanki says. "You've been there?"

"I was born there," Anju says. "We moved back to Kerala when I was small. To a village called Kumarakom."

"Such different places." Mr. Solanki smiles. Like Mrs. Solanki's, his skin is smooth and taut, as though it has been surgically stretched, like canvas, at the corners of his eyes. "Have you heard of my family home, Solanki Villa? On Solanki Way? Pappa wanted to call it *The* Solanki Villa, but Mumma said, 'How many Solanki Villas are there?' "

She marvels at his accent, slightly Indian with a British prissiness to it, like the Bollywood actor boasting of his succulent salad.

"You and your family," Mrs. Solanki says, "you are Keralans?"

"Yes, we are Keralites."

"Ah yes. Kera-*lights.*"

They are strangers, and for the next ten months, they will be living together. This fact becomes suddenly, bluntly apparent, dragging the conversation to a stop. Mr. Solanki stuffs another samosa in his mouth, and for a moment there is only the sound of diligent chewing.

"You have a son, I think," Anju says.

Enlivened, Mrs. Solanki reaches for the picture frame on the elephant-ankle tabletop. The photo features a bored-looking boy in cap and gown, holding his diploma as he would a lunch tray. Mr. Solanki's hand rests on his shoulder, and Mrs. Solanki is smiling so hard that her expression seems almost bestial in its baring of teeth.

"That was Rohit's high school graduation," Mr. Solanki says. "He was attending Princeton—"

"He is still attending Princeton," Mrs. Solanki corrects. "He is simply taking a year off."

"To study at another place?" Anju asks.

"No, it is the fashion with children here, taking time off. As they say, to 'find' themselves." Using her fingers, Mrs. Solanki makes peace signs around the word "find."

With nothing else to break the silence, Anju replies, "Okay, yes." And with her left hand, adds a peace sign of her own.

LATER, Anju attempts to use a telephone that seems to belong on its own pedestal, all pearly enamel and brass buttons. She carefully dials the numbers on her phone card, more fearful of harming the phone than fumbling the digits, but Mrs. Solanki waves the card away and tells her to dial regularly. "We have an excellent global plan."

No crackling phone lines, no curt operators. After three beeps, Anju hears the faint trail of Melvin's voice: "Hallome?"

"Chachen?"

She can hear and see him perfectly, his hands, thick-knuckled, trying to squeeze her voice from the brown plastic receiver.

"IS IT ANJU? HALLO, ANJU? ANJU MOL!"

"It's me! I hear you! You don't have to shout!" It is a suprising relief, speaking in Malayalam rather than navigating the consonants and quicksand vowels of English.

"What's this?" Melvin says. "So clear! Like you're across the street."

"They have a good connection."

"You reached there safely, Anju? Are you eating well? How is your stomach feeling?"

"I ate, I ate. How are Ammachi and Linno?"

She hears Melvin pause, his speech muffled, probably trying to persuade Linno to pick up the phone. "Linno is taking a bath. Did you give them those dolls?"

Anju looks at the sculpture within the niche next to her, a crystal bird magically infused with swirls of indigo and fuschia ink within its outstretched wings.

"Anju? The dolls?"

"Yes, Chachen, they loved them."

LIKE A WELCOMING COMMITTEE, Anju's two suitcases are awaiting her in the guest room, an awkward pair of plastic visitors in the pulled-silk surroundings. The measurements of the bed are a mystery to her, expansive enough for three adults but no higher than her shin, a height that seems customized for a child. The dresser, bookshelf, and desk are all a glossy dark brown, and marigold curtains collect in pools on the carpet.

Mrs. Solanki drapes a thick white towel over the back of a chair and a smaller towel on top of this, both stitched with the letter *S*. "Over there is your private bathroom," Mrs. Solanki says, "and you'll love the showerhead. It has the best water pressure in the whole house."

In the shower, Anju finds herself endlessly shocked by needles of water so fierce and hot that she is forced to shield her breasts with her arms and turn her back against the onslaught. At home she bathed with bucket and cup, savoring the slow fall of fresh water as it seeped across her scalp and over her shoulders. Here, the showerhead treats her as though she is a grease-grimed pan; the scouring leaves her skin a surprised pink. But the soap is beautiful, a translucent ovoid of green, striped with blades of deeper green within. She inhales and inhales its kiwi sweetness. On impulse, she licks the soap, then vigorously wipes the chemical taint from her tongue. For all her achievements, she sometimes feels like a person of unparalleled stupidity.

Entrenched between tasseled bed cushions, she lies wide awake. Is it lunchtime back home? She pictures a pair of hands washing beneath the wobbly pump at the side of the house, rinsing the street from one's chappals and feet before stepping inside. Back home. But they are not back, her family, they are moving forward, on another orbit, divided from her not only by miles but by time.

Anju rises from bed and sits by her open suitcase as she unpacks her belongings. From a cloth bag embossed with the words PRINCESS TAILOR SHOP, she withdraws a red sketchbook, its spine coming loose within beige cloth tape, its corners worn.

Along the inside of the cover is signed *L. Vallara.*

The writing is precise and sharp, and instantly Anju remembers her sister at thirteen years old, her right arm under the table, her tongue between her teeth, her left hand laboring to bring the alphabet to paper. Lines she had mastered for years, unraveling in a hand that would not obey.

Anju fingers the pages that crackle upon turning; she has memorized the sketches on each side. Beginning at the end, she finds a few studies of diapered babies squatting, crawling, sitting, all wearing oversized bifocals. At the bottom of the page, in thick, swirly letters: *Frames & Optics.* On another page, a peacock with its carnivalesque tail spread around the words *Sari Palace.* And above the peacock: *You Are What You Wear!*

Earlier in the book, the drawings lose their words and become messier, lines more frayed, figures in movement. There is a sketch of a coconut cutter, ankles crossed around a palm trunk, a knife between his teeth as he wrestles a coconut above him. Next to this, a magnified rendering of the torso, the tense chest muscles, the strain of a single cord in the throat, a body shorn of excess. All this from the scratches of her sister's pencil. A live current of talent runs through Linno's body, and yet Anju never held her in awe, as it felt strange to hold her sister at a distance. Now, with so many miles between them, this book in her hands, she can and she does.

On the first page of the book is a sketch of Anju studying, the weft of her braid tightly drawn, scattered with highlights from the gleam of a nearby lamp. Every shadow obeys the logic of light. Her arms encircle an open book on a table, her nose near the gutter, something selfish about the pose.

Alone in my new room, she thinks, *I came to a crossroads.*

Turning to Linno's signature, Anju takes a pencil from her bag and, pressing gently, erases the *L* from *L. Vallara.*

Which she replaces with an *A.*

2.

HE *MALAYALA MANORAMA*. At the Kottayam offices, the newspaper is printed and posted to homes as far away as Toronto and Singapore, Berlin and Mumbai, stuffed into mailboxes, smacked onto counters, soggied with potato peels, saved in cupboards even when the new *Manorama* arrives.

Subscribers in Dubai run their fingers along the captions that tell of yet another family suicide, this one in Kollam, below a picture so under-exposed the bodies look charred. Readers in Indianapolis drag pens down the marriage ads, seeking spousal security in four sentences that involve birthplace, complexion, creed, and degree. And everyone, especially those overseas, lingers in the obituary section if only to recognize the name of an old classmate, a former friend, a distant neighbor who has been pressed like an ageless leaf between the pages of a memory.

At the time of Anju's scholarship announcement, the newspaper reaches about nine million people worldwide. One of them is a woman by the name of Bird. She lives in a two-bedroom apartment in Jackson Heights, Queens, with a rotating cast of subletters who unknowingly pay the majority of the rent. Bird used to feel guilty about bamboozling her roommates, who are usually in their twenties, pale and unfettered, wishing to dive into the fresh waters of independence. But now, at fifty, Bird reasons that she is simply transplanting an Eastern custom for the betterment of Western society. These youths should be taking care of their elders, and Bird is reaping her due.

The current subletter, a long-haired blonde named Gwen, is an avid cook. Often she leaves a quiche Lorraine or a stockpot of chili in the fridge, the smells dangling in the air like unattainable bait. And though Gwen never shares her food, she makes Bird promise to share some of her recipes, for lack of anything else to discuss when they scoot around each other in the kitchen. "I bet you have tons of great currying secrets," Gwen says.

In truth, Bird weeps too easily at onions and every curry needs an onion. She loses all patience with dicing. The moat of blood leaking from a hunk of meat makes her retch. Cooking has never been her forte, and she relies heavily on Tandoori Express takeout, two blocks away. Yes, she has secrets, but none to do with currying.

Bird has recently acquired a job not far from her apartment, as a full-time assistant at the law offices of Rajiv Tandon, an immigration attorney. She photocopies papers, answers phones, and tells people to wait until Mr. Tandon is ready to see them. Usually, the visitors are new immigrants from all parts of the South Asian subcontinent, all of them anxious, hopeful, lurching at the sound of Mr. Tandon's voice as it comes rumbling through his office walls. They are used to a bureaucracy that has proven as inconstant as a cloud. They blame and love Mr. Tandon in the same way that metereologists are held responsible for interpreting the weather.

She won the position six months ago, when she took down the number from a poster that read: NEED A JOB? SPEAK ENGLISH + HINDI?

At the interview, she found Mr. Tandon as well groomed as he was well educated. He did not speak Hindi, he said, because his parents had wanted him to fully acclimate to his private boarding school life at St. Albans, which was, by the by, home to the sons of senators and statesmen. "But that's a whole other era, isn't it?" Mr. Tandon smiled. Not so long ago, it seemed to Bird. The luster of his hair suggested that he was no more than forty. Bird used to work at an Indian beauty salon, so she knew the color of true black, not the stark, bluish shade found in a box or a bottle.

She had spent far too long at the salon, a job she took only because she knew the owner well, from the days when they traveled in the same drama troupe. Abdul Ghafoor is his name, a man whose shellacked hairstyle has not changed since he adopted it from the cinema star Amitabh Bachchan, tall on top with sturdy sideburns. Even as Amitabh's star fell in the nineties, Ghafoor maintained the indomitable coif and was only too pleased to see Amitabh resurface as game-show host of *Kaun*

Banega Crorepati, that enthusiastic Indian answer to *Who Wants to Be a Millionaire.*

Equal to his love for Amitabh is Ghafoor's love for his now defunct drama troupe, Apsara Arts Club, which also lent its name, years later, to his Apsara Salon. Bird has been a key member of both. She prefers not to dwell on her acting days, but Ghafoor prefers to think about them daily, launching into the old roles at random, particularly the lines from *Kalli Pavayuda Veede,* an adaptation of Henrik Ibsen's *A Doll's House,* which Ghafoor brought to the Kerala stage. Ibsen had long been championed by Malayali academics, but by the early eighties, Ghafoor was eager to free Ibsen from that stiff and distant realm. "Social realism" was a phrase of which he never tired. "What is more important than to explore the minds of ordinary people?" he asked, uninterested in answers. Taken with the central character of Nora, the repressed and rebellious wife of Torvald, Ghafoor pored over the English text for months. He turned Nora and Torvald into Neera and Tobin, finding the Malayalam words for the desperation and disillusionment that would lead Neera to leave her husband. As director, Ghafoor never had lines of his own, but he memorized some of Bird's lines, which he still recites today while gliding a broom down the aisle, as easily as humming the tune to an old song:

Always I was your myna bird, Tobichayan, your doll made of glass. Only now do I see the truth: that I have been living with a strange man for eight years, that I have given him three children. Now I can stand it no longer!

The customers ignore Ghafoor's lines as most of their concerns lie with their facial hair and how best to get rid of it.

Despite so much shared history, Bird left the salon over a matter of interior design. One day, she arrived at work to find an old show card framed on the wall. She remembered the poster well, the silhouette of a myna bird perched on a branch in the lower right-hand corner, while more birds were depicted in flight, aswirl around the words:

Apsara Arts Club Presents . . .

Kalli Pavayuda Veede

starring the exquisite BIRDIE KAMALABHAI

Bird stared at the show card, unblinking. In a strangely hollowed voice, she demanded that Ghafoor remove it. She would not say why. She would not mention the name on the cast list that plunged her into a pain so acute she had to look away and gather herself.

They fought over whether the show card should stay or go, which became an argument about Ghafoor's poor managerial skills and Bird's unwillingness to learn how to wax or thread. Ghafoor called Bird a prima donna. Bird accused Ghafoor of stealing Western ideas because he had none of his own. Enraged, he countered with Varghese Mappilai's 1893 adaptation of *Taming of the Shrew,* the earliest in a long tradition of lending and borrowing, but Bird stopped him with an outstretched hand. "Just give me what you owe and I will leave."

After he counted out the bills, she pocketed the money and collected her belongings from her station. There was not much to collect as she had never brought photos and frames to work, like the other ladies did, no small, portable windows into her personal life. The show card was personal enough. With so little to tidy up before leaving, it was as though she had never arrived.

THE OFFICE POSITION was a sitting job, clearly a step up. To prove herself, Bird was willing to take a typing test, but Mr. Tandon only questioned her about her commitment to the job and her ability to make chai.

"I am very loyal," Bird said, wondering if she were making herself sound like a dog. "I speak Malayalam, Tamil, some Bengali, Hindi, and English. And I make my own chai masala, not like the gunpowder that comes in the plastic packages."

"Impressive. How do you know all these languages?"

"I was born in Kerala, but I have been traveling since I was young. I was an actress." She regrets this statement, as the response is usually one of amused doubt.

"I believe that." He studied her. She felt semiprecious under his gaze until he added: "You have a certain grandmotherly quality. I think anyone would believe you."

She wondered why Mr. Tandon had not tested her secretarial skills, but since then, she has learned the breadth of her job. Not simply a secretary, she is a presence. When clients give her their names, she can pinpoint their mother tongues with near perfect accuracy. She reaches out with their language, or the closest ones she knows, and the comprehending client relaxes into a chair and accepts a Styrofoam cup of chai. Over the past month, Bird has learned to tell when language and chai are the closest a client has come to home.

BECAUSE EVERY FRIDAY is a half day, Bird's schedule leaves her free to enjoy the *Manorama* at leisure. As is her custom, she spends her Friday lunch at Tandoori Express, a narrow restaurant crammed with tables, the low ceiling strewn with so many disco lights and crepe paper mobiles that the space resembles some sort of electrified cave, thick with neon stalactites. During the day, thankfully, the lights remain off. The waiters know her enough to predict the small packet of honey that she prefers with her tea, and Arpit serves her regular order of dahi batata puri, four crispy disks as opposed to the usual three. Tea, honey, puri, and paper. At her age, consistency is all she hopes for.

She spreads the *Malayala Manorama* on the table for the first skim through. The front page tells of an ongoing fight between a Coca-Cola plant and tribals in Palakkad who blamed the plant for draining the drought-prone land of water and leaving behind toxic wastes. Pictures show the tribals gathered in a sit-in strike, the women's pallus drawn over their heads, while another sit-in takes place nearby, among the families of laid-off workers who look not unlike their opposition. A few policemen in khaki uniforms hover around them, hands held behind their backs, looking off to the right or left but not at those seated below them. Bird knows these lands; her mother was from Palakkad, but it feels insincere to consider their struggle hers. She has not been back in twenty-two years. Who among them would consider her their own?

She looks for lighter stories. On the second page, she comes across a picture of a girl holding on to one side of a plaque, a white woman holding on to the other side. The headline reads KUMARAKOM GIRL WINS NEW YORK SCHOLARSHIP.

This is the type of article that Bird usually ignores. Triumphant parents constitute a high fraction of the *Manorama*'s subscribers, thriving in their dual roles as publicists, phoning in their childrens' successes in spelling bees, national exams, synchronized swimming competitions. Someone's child is always winning.

But this article confronts her with names she buried long ago.

> . . . Miss Vallara is the daughter of Melvin and Gracie Vallara, and the granddaughter of Elsamma Vallara . . .

Three times in one sentence, "Vallara" bobs up like sea-swept flotsam that will not sink.

Bird looks at the waiter beside her, who reaches down to rescue the spoon by her ankle. His face is heavy with concern. What is his name? She knows it but cannot remember. When did she drop her spoon? She did not hear the sound. And even now, it requires some effort to hear his words, as though muscling upward from deep waters, breaking the surface for air.

"Are you all right?" the waiter asks, his forehead creased.

She could say that she knows the girl in the photo, but she does not know the girl at all. It is foolish to think so, from just the two paragraphs that the article offers. But she does know the name of the school, the Sitwell School, and the address will be easy to acquire. For now, the girl is little more than a picture to Bird, just as she herself must be to these waiters, a lonely woman in the corner booth, whose small, hard features bespeak an age older than her own.

3.

TO EDUCATE HERSELF on the social strata of the American high school, Anju watches several American movies on Mrs. Solanki's home theater, a screen that nearly engulfs an entire wall, much like the tapestry of St. George at church. Many of the movies involve a nymph whose beauty goes unseen behind glasses, a bun, and baggy clothing, though during the course of the movie, the nymph removes her glasses, releases her bun, and tightens her belt, thereby wooing her classmates as well as her leading man. The lesson to be learned: assimilation is an equation that can be reduced to two variables—a short, swishy haircut and a few smooth lines.

At the Sitwell School, Anju finds it difficult to cast students into their proper roles, especially when she can hardly tell one from another. Most students come in shades of pink and white, plus the occasional orange of a girl who appears to have slept in a kiln. Most boys bear monosyllabic names—Matts and Mikes and Daves and Dans—while some scions stand alone, like Leland or Grayson or Jackson. Everyone wears the standard white collared shirts, the boys' slacks slung low, the girls' skirts hemmed high. A few, however, stand apart for unique reasons. Like Dena Geisler, who presses her hair with a flatiron that gives her a singed smell all day. And Shane Hootnick, a lumbering man-child who begins every Monday morning in homeroom with a report of the weekend's beery excess.

At first, she expects the other students to ask her any number of questions about Sonia Solanki—what it might be like to eat breakfast with a celebrity, what Sonia looks like in the morning, before makeup. But Anju quickly learns that Mrs. Solanki is only a semicelebrity compared with some of the other stars who have traveled these halls and attended these Open Houses. Someone's godmother is Barbara Walters. Someone else's uncle is a movie director, the one who made the blockbuster about the androids sent to reverse the events of Pearl Harbor. To most of these students, Mrs. Solanki's face is like the flag of a small European nation, vaguely familiar, obviously important in some way, but difficult to classify.

As for the other students, they are distantly welcoming, but often Anju feels that people are greeting her, chatting with her, smiling at her out of courtesy. She is constantly receiving thanks, for no apparent reason. If she answers a question about the time, they thank her. If she gives them a pencil to borrow, they give thanks. She wonders if this is part of a larger national psychology, a combination of good intentions and guilt. Or maybe thanks is simply thanks. She also wonders if her lack of thank-yous leaves the impression of thanklessness, when in truth the gratitude she feels for her classmates, her teachers, this country, all of this weighs so heavily sometimes she can but lift her eyes from the blond wood floors.

In gym, when someone passes her the basketball, Anju says, "Thank you," and immediately another girl steals the ball from her hands.

THE ONLY ONE TO PAY prolonged attention to Anju is Sheldon Fischer, known to his classmates as Fish. His skin possesses a pale vitality set off by a shrub of dark curls, a style that seems to belong on a tortured doll. From time to time, he plucks the shrub with a black comb. Its handle is shaped like a fist.

Fish received the comb from one of his friends, Paz L. Mundo, who performs spoken word poetry at various Brooklyn venues of exclusive repute. "Everyone there is black," Fish says proudly. "Usually I'm the only white guy." Fish has never taken the microphone, but he plans to, as soon as he comes up with a good stage name. (Aided by her the-saurus, Anju comes up with suggestions—Waxy Alabaster, the Achro-mic Bomb, and so on—none of which appeals to Fish.)

His main concern is getting into Yale, which was attended by his mother, his father, and both sets of grandparents, their family tree well-watered by blue-blood educations. "Harvard and Princeton," he says, "are for the socially deformed." "Harvard" and "Yale"—she knows these words as she knows the word "Everest." All are equally gauzy and mythic, names that hang in the air like mist.

She has no doubt that Fish will summit every goal. He is perhaps the smartest member of his class, a role he both relishes and rejects. During democratic circle discussions, he seems weary of the ping-pong of stu-dent opinion, and Anju feels similarly. When all the desks are in a circle, every answer is right. All are equal. Even the teacher sits among them like a big, conciliatory child. Through all this, Fish keeps his arms crossed and his expression unimpressed, as if mutely guarding a multi-tude of truths. From his posture, Anju learns that a certain kind of silence appears weightier and wiser than speech.

During Anju's first week, Fish tells her not to worry. "I'm not going to ask if you're betrothed or if you have a dowry or whatever else these fools have been asking." The truth is that no fool has asked her any of these things at all. "So are you seeing anybody?"

She is not sure what exactly he means, but shakes her head.

"Cool," he says.

How suprising that Fish is so relaxed around her—his new rival—and even seeks out the company of his greatest academic threat. Back home, her #1 threat was Manilal Iyer, a small scholar who clutched his books to his chest with a protective, hungry love. On the rare occasion that he looked at her, he did so with such intensity that he seemed to be lining her up between crosshairs.

But at Sitwell, there is space. One student's success does not imply another student's defeat.

Not only space, but choice, as revealed in the breadth of cafeteria options, a dietary freedom far evolved from what she experienced at her previous school, that virtually changeless trio of dal, papadum, and rice.

But here: a multitude of salads that taste nothing alike! Tuna salad, egg salad, chicken salad, potato salad, seafood salad, not to mention chef's, Caesar, and Cobb. She samples some of each exotic entrée—a pot pie, a casserole, a complicated lasagna. No matter that the lasagna leaks a diluted juice that sloshes around the contours of its squarish bowl, or that certain cups of chocolate pudding come veiled with skin. The opportunity to turn something down, to glance at the achromic cauliflower and move on, to pick at a few foods, guzzle others, and then casually, guiltlessly, slide them all off the tray and into the trash if one wishes—this, Anju believes, this is the essence of Americana.

IN ADDITION TO three fresh school uniforms, Anju receives a student handbook and a schedule that depicts her week as a rectangle, each day divided into blocks of varied colors, a well-manicured garden of time. How she wishes her after-school time were equally plotted. But as she has no friends, no after-school activities, she often finds herself at home, alone, with Mrs. Solanki.

Mrs. Solanki's voice has the dispersive quality of a gas, reaching into every room of the house even when she whispers. At first, Anju is reluctant to close the door to her own room, worried that this might seem offensive or suspicious, but she soon realizes that with her door closed or open, Mrs. Solanki's phone conversations filter up through the vent in the carpet. "She's from Kerala . . . Oh please, Jeff, it's nothing . . . I'm just trying to give back."

Through these overheard conversations, Anju comes to understand that Jeff, like the son taking time off from Princeton, is both a source of frustration and desperation for Mrs. Solanki. Jeff Priddy is one of the *Four Corners* producers, and Mrs. Solanki harbors a deep and unsubtle desire to be taken more seriously by Jeff and his cohorts. More than once, Anju has heard Mrs. Solanki complaining to her husband of the fluff pieces she must often introduce to the other ladies—usually about perfumes, cooking, or on one occasion hatha yoga. Regularly, she brings up Jeff's failure to "push the envelope," as with the Ayurveda episode, in which she wanted to focus on the economic debate between Britain and India over who should control the Ayurvedic market, and in her words, "the Western attempt to steal a global market worth two hundred seventy billion dollars! We are talking about five thousand years of Indian intellectual property here—how is that not riveting?" Jeff's position: Let's be pleasantly educational, not controversial. But during the taping, Mrs. Solanki insisted on mentioning in her otherwise pleasant segment: "And now, popularized by Madonna and Cher, Ayurveda is even gaining the interest of British Parliament, which, two years ago, ranked Ayurveda as hocus-pocus, about as useful as hypnotherapy. Now, it seems, everyone wants a piece of the pie."

Despite these occasional tiffs, Mrs. Solanki is all sweetness and suggestions when on the phone with Jeff. "Oh, I'm happy to be a host parent if it means promoting higher education among young Indian women. Really, I consider myself a global citizen, Jeff, so I think of women's rights on a worldwide scale. I'm sure that even in Kerala, the girls have fewer opportunities. Studies show that in a tiny Tamil village—I don't remember the name—one hundred ninety-six girl babies were slaughtered by infanticide in one year alone. . . . Yes, China's much much worse. But that would be a topic, wouldn't it? Infanticide?"

At times like this, Anju wants to holler through the vent that female infanticide is about as popular in Kerala as *Four Corners*. But here among the lace and pulled-silk pillows, yelling would be unseemly, especially at the one who has provided the pillows.

IN HAPPY TIMES, Mrs. Solanki is girlish and warm, painting the bucolia of her life's history in golden tones. "Varun and I had a love marriage," she says to Anju on one occasion, her palms hugging a mug of Belgian hot chocolate. "A very big upset to his family. They thought I trapped him, you know, because they knew what I came from. A shack no bigger than an outhouse."

Mrs. Solanki glances at the glass shelf fastened to the wall next to Anju. On this, propped among several other frames, is a small photo of a young Mrs. Solanki with eyes like large blots of ink lined with kohl. Her posture in the portrait tells that even in her youth, despite her circumstances, she seemed aware of her potential to rise in the world. Not a single picture of Anju possesses the magnetism of this one. Mrs. Solanki's sisters must have stood by in jealous awe.

"Do you miss them?" Anju asks. "Your sisters?"

"Missing . . . ," Mrs. Solanki says softly. She taps her wedding band against the mug, like the double tap of a conductor rousing silence from an orchestra. " 'Missing' is not the word for it. What is that feeling?" She looks at Anju with sincere concentration, and Anju, in return, finds herself hanging upon every word, as if her own future lies in the answer. "I miss what we were. I miss something that no longer exists. My sisters and I, our simple life among the jasmine and mulberry bushes."

If Mrs. Solanki is just off the phone with one of her sisters, all of whom have remained among the jasmine and mulberry bushes, her tone changes considerably.

"All they want is a visa. 'Bring me! Bring me!' they say. 'Don't you care about your own kind?' My own kind. My own kind are masters of manipulation. I sent my sister a pair of Nike sneakers last month, but her son is complaining that they aren't Air Force Ones. I said, 'You can't get these for fifty dollars!' And she said, 'Fifty dollars? You spend more money to get your manicure!' "

"More?" Anju asks, not meaning to.

"Manicure *and* pedicure."

The thought of her own kind plagues Mrs. Solanki in every way, the thought of them coming just as much as the thought of them never coming at all.

"I am a *someone* here," she says, riffling through the mail. A newsletter from the Indo-American Arts Council invites her to a gallery opening of a Persian miniaturist at the Metropolitan Museum of Art. She often attends such events and writes checks to the Indo-American Arts Council, which she tears from her checkbook with careless panache. "If I brought my sister and her family, where would they stay? With me. Whose kitchen would they swarm? Mine. You don't understand these people. It's part of our culture. If you bring someone, they are *your* responsibility."

But there are other times, such as the nights when Uncle is once again working late, when Mrs. Solanki seems to have no one to phone. She leaves a few messages on the machines of various friends or apologizes profusely for interrupting someone's dinner, and then surrenders to a lone glass of port at the kitchen counter. On occasion, she asks Anju if she wants to watch a DVD in the home theater. Their first film is *My Fair Lady*, Mrs. Solanki's favorite. By the time Audrey Hepburn is pulled from the gutter and pruned into the hourglass fashion of a lady, her fair face blooming from the petaled collar of her pale pink dress, tears are trailing silently down Mrs. Solanki's cheeks.

Hepburn says, "You see, Mrs. Higgins, apart from the things one can pick up, the difference between a lady and a flower girl is not how she behaves, but how she is treated." And with this, overcome, Mrs. Solanki lets escape a small, animal whimper.

WITHOUT MRS. SOLANKI to guide her, Anju dives into the city.

None of it seems true. None of it possible. That a castle so sprawling, so full of books, guarded by stone lions, can be entered—*for free*. That men and women stand on sidewalks and beseech passersby to take wedges of fancy soap, cups of raspberry sorbet, movie tickets, soft drinks, and iced coffee—*for free.* That in the subway, an old man draws a bow across the strings of a violin almost as ancient-looking as he, creating a sound of piercing melancholy, a sorrow almost seductive while he sits, a boulder against the ebb and flow of commuters who sometimes toss a few coins into the balding velvet of his open instrument case, but otherwise listen—*for nothing.*

Land of the free indeed.

It is Saturday afternoon, and feeling adventurous, Anju treks down to the Financial District, toting Linno's sketchbook in her satchel. On the way, she is nearly killed a total of six times, usually when she scampers across the street just as a car is beeping and barreling toward her. In Kumarakom, cars chat in short, giddy honks, as careless and common as the bleating of sheep. It is only from the long bellowing honk of a cab driver, along with his battery of roaring curses, that Anju learns to obey the orders of the traffic light.

But she refuses to turn back, as she still has one last school assignment to complete.

Thus far, art class has inspired in Anju a vague but light distress, the kind of disaster that remains distant enough for time to resolve all things. On her second day of school, she found the class listed on her schedule, and when she tried to remove it, Miss Schimpf objected.

"My father would like for me to focus on studies," Anju told her.

"Art *is* a kind of study," Miss Schimpf said, looking hurt. "Besides, it's an elective. You need an elective."

Poor Miss Schimpf. Here among the smog-spewing cars, her skin has lost its tan translucence, her knuckles gone chalky and dry. Her lofty position as "visiting artist" has deflated to her previous title, that of "art teacher." In Kerala, she cut through crowds like a celebrity, salwar-clad and fairy-tale blond, but here, walking the halls, she has returned to her usual state of anonymity. Sometimes she offsets her cardigans and khakis with wild rhinestoned bangles or a belled choker of black metal, the proud, noisy spoils of her travels. And yet Miss Schimpf is to Anju the same saint she always was, one who performed a miracle and exacted no debt in return.

"At least take your sketchbook around with you this weekend," Miss Schimpf urged. "Draw anything that strikes you. I'm sure you can find something." Anju agreed, not wanting to disappoint her.

Though Anju has never tried to draw before, she has considered using notebook paper to trace a picture of a tree, which she might then be able to transfer to the sketchbook. Or there must be how-to books that show how a circle becomes a nose becomes a lion in a jungle. Wasn't Rousseau, untrained and self-taught, accused of a certain childishness of style? According to the school's art history textbook: yes. In fact, she might try to assume his style as her own. To be brilliant, one must explode into the world with an unparalleled vision. To be gifted, one must simply borrow from someone else who is more gifted.

She continues on her journey down the island, such a tiny thing, changing its colors and contours from one mile to the next. Farther south, the buildings stand closely together, giant hives of industry. Outside the revolving doors, besuited men and women smoke and speak on cell phones, some of them Indian or maybe Pakistani. She is compelled to look at them as if they might recognize her, though it seems that they make a conscious effort to do the opposite.

When Anju can put off her task no longer, she sits on a bench and opens to a blank page in the sketchbook. The white of the pages nearly blinds her. Pressing her hand to the paper, she takes in the rough weave where Linno's hand might have rested before she inked a dark dot—iris, eyelid, lashes, eye.

She remembers when the book, wrapped in brown parcel paper, passed across her lap from her father's hand to Linno's. She remembers the soft tear of paper, the strip of red that appeared, the twine knotted along the spine with what could only be love. When Anju saw the book, her own envy startled her, how it flamed up from a place she never knew existed. A feeling that tugs at her still, makes her doubt the very steps that brought her to this place, alone. Were her intentions ever clean? Her eyes grow full, reminded that there are untapped doors of the mind through which a person can fall and fall.

She shuts the book.

No one seems to notice her, engrossed as they are in the changing of traffic lights. Maybe each of them stepped on someone else to reach their cubicle of success, and maybe each is carrying his guilt, like a leaky pen, in a pocket of his heart. She watches the men with their ties like tongues over their shoulders, the women with their swollen handbags, their serious, sexy shoes. Anju could watch them for hours, imagining herself in similar footwear, expertly avoiding the treacherous grates through which a heel could fall. These are people who do not open doors; the doors automatically part for them. And if the doors do not part, these people fling them wide.

4.

*B*IRD PREFERS NOT TO think of herself as a stalker, not with all these policemen prowling the subways. Two of them, a male and female, stand behind a card table next to a sign that declares their right to search any bag at will. The male fixes his gaze on Bird, and she can picture the abacus of his brain behind the broad forehead, making its weary calculations. Perhaps it is the size of her bag that attracts his attention or the black kerchief tied over her hair. Men used to eye her for different reasons. She wears the kerchief because it is windy, and she has recently come to notice a thinning of hair at her crown, like ice melting away from a thawing plain. Were she a Muslim, she would be no more committed to keeping her crown covered in public, a devotion born of being beautiful in her youth. A cursed gift, that kind of beauty, which takes itself back over time.

The policemen do not make Bird nervous, so much as the duty at hand. To calm herself, she buys a bag of Raisinets from a nearby magazine vendor, a pasty, sullen man with covers of naked ladies lining the top of his booth like prayer flags. In each, the girl looks somehow both chesty and emaciated, in contrast to the row catering to black clientele, in which the rear plays a more prominent role. Bird lingers before the women, snacking, and the policeman looks away.

If he were to ask, Bird would unload the contents of her bag without complaint: a wallet, keys, an envelope. At home, in her bedroom, she stood for a full minute looking at the envelope, a pen in her right hand, wondering what to title its contents. One word gave way to another: *A letter from your mother. To me. About you.*

She left it blank.

A STALKER DOES NOT climb the subway stairs wincing, with one hand on her troublesome knee. A stalker moves along the current of people, does not slog through the masses like an oxcart taking up so much space. But on the prettied streets of the Upper West Side, Bird is fit to stalk, as she is at an age where trees win more attention. Some women, from a distance, seem to know how to live beyond the reach of age, an effect that is sometimes haunting. There are those with long, fawn brown hair or pert ponytails, who turn their withered faces and smile with shiny, graying teeth, ghosts of the girls they were.

Consulting her map, Bird finds her way to the Sitwell School and enters a shop across the street, whose storefront window will give her a clear view of Anju exiting her school. So intent is Bird on her object of focus that she hardly notices the interior of the store itself, until she is confronted with a lacy yellow bra draped on a hanger, each cup the size and depth of a salad bowl. Headless plaster torsos of the chesty/bony build are positioned throughout the boutique, each wearing a complicated lingerie set, one of which looks vaguely like a torture device with all its straps and buckles. Nearby, a young woman in a lab coat is showing a customer a brassiere, using words like "state of the art" and "invention" to explain its functions.

It seems that Bird has picked the wrong store in which to disappear. She explores a rack of white bras embroidered with cherries and squints at the tiny satin labels that warn against machine washing. When the bra doctor approaches and asks for whom Bird is shopping, Bird blurts out: "Myself."

Dr. Bra seems warmed by the thought that a woman like Bird might be having sex. She offers to measure Bird's bustline using the measuring tape around her neck. "You know, eight out of every ten women are wearing bras that don't fit them properly." Dr. Bra relays this statistic with dismay.

Bird knows better. The muscles slacken. The flesh descends. The wrinkles frown around the knees. Why fight? Why should acceptance mean defeat?

"No thank you," Bird says. "Not today."

Ever upbeat, Dr. Bra swallows rejection with a smile and says that she will be nearby, if needed.

Turning back to the window, Bird's heart falls. Students are pouring through the school doors like so many limes rolling out of a sack. Their noise carries across the street, the calling of names and good-byes, messages faintly penetrating the window's glass. Her eyes are too slow to search them all. Has Anju already gone? Would she stay late? The stupidity of Bird's quest suddenly seems obvious.

After the first clot of students pushes through the door, a few strays saunter out. Among them, a slight black-haired girl. Bird's first thought is *Gracie,* whose face seems to ripple just beneath the surface of the girl's, the cheekbones, the small, sharp chin. But there is also a blankness around the girl's eyes that renders her nothing like Gracie, as though she has quarantined her emotions from the world.

Her school clothes fit awkwardly. She needs a mother to stitch the hem and cinch the skirt by adding a button to the waist. These are Bird's thoughts, at a safe remove from the actuality of Anju crossing the street, walking down the sidewalk nearest to the lingerie store.

Bird huddles behind the lacy shrubbery of the bra rack. In passing, Anju looks up at the lingerie displays, two tall, naked mannequins, hands on hips, impatiently waiting to be dressed by the clerks. Bird can see clean into the girl's thoughts because those thoughts were once her own: *Nipples? On a doll?* Though Anju does not notice her, Bird grows short of air. She grips the envelope in her satchel, once again struck by the lunacy of her project, to approach a young girl with a sweaty envelope in hand, and happily, madly insist: *I know you. Here is proof.*

As Anju passes, Bird reclaims her breathing. Her shoulders relax. If, this time, her courage has failed, her patience will not.

She emerges from the lingerie store and follows Anju from a distance. Even while people block her path, waving fliers and pushing strollers, even when stoplights stretch a chasm between pursuer and pursued, Bird always finds her way, her chest pulling in a singular direction. Past Fiftieth Street, Forty-ninth, and Forty-eighth, they turn a corner, one after the other, as if tethered.

At last, Bird pauses before the New York Public Library. Anju is climbing the stone steps. If she follows, what then? She notices Anju's calves, boyish and strong, above narrow ankles. Legs that belong to Gracie. Bird's heart, deceived, goes skipping after those legs.

Was it ever clearer than now? Time is but a circle, and a person might run from the past only to find herself faced with it in the end.

5.

*I*N ORDER TO DROP OUT of art class, Anju has devised a tripartite plan, based on a term that she found in her pocket dictionary. *Circumvention: Avoidance (of defeat, failure, unpleasantness, etc.) by artfulness or deception.* She feels vindicated by the word "artfulness," its favorable and unfavorable connotations coiled in an elegant word. Maybe she is not an artist, but she is certainly artful.

On Friday, after school, Anju begins with the first step of the Circumvention—the New York Public Library. She is unprepared for the library's inner sanctum of marble and lowered voices, and grows ashamed of the amplified clops of her shoes perforating the cathedral quiet. Their echo carries all the way up the swerving stairways whose marble banisters are as wide as a footbridge. Giant candelabras stand at every archway, and not a hall goes without the engraved wisdoms and sculpted busts of notables. As in a museum, she is not sure what can be touched, but she strolls the corridors, light on her heels, with an expression of scholarly belonging.

In one of the smaller rooms, she pauses before a poster encased in glass, advertising a new exhibit called PATTERNS OF MIGRATION:

New societies, new peoples, and new communities usually originate in acts of migration. Someone or ones decide to move from one place to another. They choose a new destination and sever their ties with their traditional community as they set out in search of new opportunities, new challenges, new lives, and new life worlds.

What is a life world? And who is severing? Anju has always pictured her Pattern of Migration as an elliptical track, jogging from Kumarakom to the U.S. and back round again, gaining wealth and funneling money home with each revolution. She will continue orbiting until certain goals are met: an extra room built onto the side of the house for Ammachi, who has always cherished the idea of a second sitting room filled with viny houseplants. A tin or tile roof instead of ola. Enough income for her father to retire. An adjoining bathroom with a sitting toilet, more for show than usage, as the squatting toilet is more user-friendly. She finds it strenuous, looming over the sitting toilets, knees half bent, quivering against the possibility of contact. Sometimes she layers a wreath of toilet paper around the rim but still cannot bring herself to sit.

Mostly she engineers plans for Linno. Perhaps a visa, or a dowry, or tuition to attend some sort of vocational school. All or none or only part of the above, whatever she prefers. Then finally Linno will see that this elliptical odyssey was fueled by love all along, and she will be grateful and sorry for playing mute on the phone every single time that Anju has called and asked for her. And one day Anju will return forever, like a mythic ship gliding into port, and she will unlace her shoes and slip her big toes into her chappals and lie down on a bed all her own—

"May I help you?" asks a woman librarian, standing beside her.

The librarian's eyes are as bright as the cadence of her question. She is fair-skinned, with a black kerchief over her head. She wears brown saddle shoes with rubbery soles that must have muffled her approach.

Anju turns away from the poster. The future will come, but first, the present, one muffled step at a time.

She says, "I am looking for medical texts, please?"

AS IT TURNS OUT, the librarian is a volunteer. Her name, at first, is confusing.

"Beard?" Anju asks.

"Bird."

"Burt?"

"Bird."

Back and forth they peck at the name until Anju finally understands.

On the way to the medical texts, Bird takes her on a tour, gesturing around as they walk. Consuming the height of one great wall is a mural of a white-haired man cradling stone tablets in muscular arms, his hair billowing about him as he glares down on two cowering figures below. "And here we see a painting of God," says Bird, "writing His punishments for Adam and Eve."

Anju reads a nearby sign: THE ADJACENT PANEL DEPICTS MOSES DESCENDING FROM MOUNT SINAI WITH THE TEN COMMANDMENTS.

For a tour guide, Bird spends more time looking at Anju than at the mural-laden halls through which they pass. Bird is not only looking, but scrutinizing in a way that makes Anju suggest that they part ways. "I think I know where I am going now," she says.

This is the best that Anju can do. Crazy or not, Bird is an elder, and to say more would be disrespectful.

"Nonsense," Bird says, as if abandoning a youth would be equally disrespectful.

SOMEONE AT THE INFORMATION DESK directs them to a room with two long wooden tables and shelves of texts so fat that pulling one from its spot makes the shelf look as though it is missing a tooth. Sitting down at a table, Anju consults the index of a medical encyclopedia. Bird takes the adjacent seat, her chin in her hand, watching Anju as if there were volumes to learn in her face alone.

"Malayali anno?" Bird asks.

Anju looks up. The words are a stunning music that fuse the gap of unfamiliarity, which would otherwise take months to fuse between usual strangers. "How did you know?" she asks in Malayalam.

"Big woolly hair." Bird holds her hands away from her head to demonstrate. "You ever thought about ironing it straight?"

Anju says no, though she has, countless times.

"I used to work in a beauty salon, but now I'm a secretary in a law office. Much more professional." From her wallet, Bird pulls out a business card and places it on the corner of the open book. *Rajiv Tandon*, the card reads. *Immigration Attorney*. In the corner is an address. "You come there, and he'll show you how to apply for a green card."

"How did you know I need a green card?"

Bird fidgets with the buttonhole of her sweater. "Your accent," she says. "Sounds like you came off the plane just yesterday. So you want the card or not?"

"Yes, thank you." Anju slides the card into her pocket and writes her own number on a scrap of paper for Bird. "And where are your people from?"

"Me? Oh, from all over." Bird glances at her wristwatch, too quickly to even read it. She switches to English. "Hah, time is flying! Enough happy hour, back to work." Moving away, she bumps into a lectern. "Don't forget to stop by the office. I will look for you. Okay?"

She waits until Anju replies, "Okay," before leaving.

When Bird reaches the doorway, she looks right, then left, weighing each direction. She turns right and disappears. Anju waits. After a few seconds, Bird hurries back the opposite way.

STEP TWO OF THE CIRCUMVENTION: Duane Reade drugstore.

The cashiers wear plastic cards on their chests, one of which reads DANITA. Her nails are squarish and spangled in mesmerizing purple and red illustrations. She clatters them against the countertop while speaking heatedly with her coworker CHEYENNE. How strange, Anju thinks, to be on a first-name basis with a stranger before uttering a word.

"I know he's old!" Danita is telling Cheyenne. "But he got a nice house, no kids. I'm looking for a man with one foot in the grave and the other foot on a banana peel. Nothing wrong with planning ahead." Cheyenne gives a laugh that shakes her shoulders.

Anju remembers a similar sentiment once uttered by her grandmother. "Is it so bad if Linno marries someone older?" Ammachi privately asked Anju. "At least she would be looked after. And probably she wouldn't have to look after him for that long."

When the conversation seems to have reached a standstill, Danita looks over at Anju, and in a blink Danita's face goes from impassioned to passionless, like a light switched off. Despite the name tag, Danita's expression implies that she and Anju are on a no-name basis.

"Ace bandage?" Anju asks.

"Aisle seven, I think," Danita says. "Seven or nine."

THE THIRD PART of the Circumvention takes place on Monday and requires that Anju arrive at school twenty minutes early.

Since her maiden voyage on the subway, Anju has learned certain matters of etiquette. On a gentle Sunday afternoon, Mrs. Solanki showed her how to buy a MetroCard from the touch-screen machine, how to slide the MetroCard to go through the turnstile, how to prepare for the violent rush of sound and steel as the train whines to a stop.

At the time, Anju committed a grave error, rushing into the car against the thin trickle of exiting passengers. She muscled her way through, earning herself a seat within a virtually empty car, and several irritated stares from those she had nearly body-checked. An old man in a sweater vest stared grimly into the middle distance, having seen many like her push and shove their way into his city. Mrs. Solanki took the seat next to her and, with undisguised irritation, said: "It's not like over there. You have to wait your turn."

But weekday mornings bring the third-world battle instinct, cloaked in first-world courtesy. Anju has learned all the moves—the grazing push, the "Not my fault!" group nudge. And now, with the subway moaning from afar, Anju prepares to utilize both tactics. Today is not a day for tardiness. After the doors sigh open, one passenger burrows out of the packed car just as Anju slides her way into the herd, the doors chomping at her backpack. People writhe and apologize. A woman groans into the folded newspaper held an inch from her nose. Fingers cling gingerly to clammy poles.

Anju stands so close to the short woman next to her that with a stretch of her neck, she could kiss the woman on the forehead, a surface so thickly plastered with powder, Anju would prefer to kiss the pole. She focuses on a sign near the ceiling that shows twelve pairs of eyes—sleepy eyes, saggy eyes, kohl-rimmed eyes, Asian eyes—and below this: BE AWARE OF SUSPICIOUS PACKAGES.

Eventually, Anju notices that the woman is glaring up at her with the same lethal intent as the old family dog back home, dead Jimmi, who used to stare up from the base of a tree and growl at the shuddering branches. This woman harbors that streak of animal fury, crackling just beneath her powdered exterior, her great swoops of blue eye shadow. She is either mad or a failed actress. Perhaps both. One stop later, it seems that the mad actress is pushing Anju, steadily applying a mounting force as if to eject her from the moving car.

"Madam," Anju says quietly, "I cannot support you."

The mad actress looks at her. They stand nose to nose.

"You're an idiot," the mad actress says.

"You are heavy," Anju says.

The mad actress cuts her eyes at Anju, gathering herself as much as she can within her confines. "If I weren't a lady, I'd smack the stank right out of your mouth."

Smank the stack? Too confused to take offense, Anju means to ask what is meant by "stank," though what comes out is: "Skank?"

The woman's eyes grow wide. "At least this skank knows how to use deodorant! Ever heard of it?"

Startled, Anju almost declares that she uses talcum powder because, according to Ammachi, a body is meant to sweat. Instead she says nothing.

Pleased, the mad actress turns only her head, since there is not room to turn away completely. Everyone jostles along in silence, wearing blank expressions, as if discussions of stank are quite natural.

I D I O T! C L O W N! Suspicious package of lunacy! As Anju climbs out of the subway, she applies these words first to the woman, then to herself. Stupid to speak so openly, to wear her rage like a vulgar dress for all to see. There is no victory in declaring your true thoughts, but this is how people speak to one another here, candid madness in the air.

While walking, she tries to sniff herself discreetly. No odor that she can distinguish, but who can make out her own odor? Perhaps it would be wise to visit the perfume counters at the department store and hoard the scented paper samples.

She nearly collides with a blue mailbox before she realizes her school is looming in the distance, a boxy, joyless structure of cement taking up half the block, THE SITWELL SCHOOL declared in white letters on its side. Its roof is staked with an American flag too colossal to clean, its white stripes gone gray.

Before she came here, this school was part of a grand fantasy, one she used to carefully embellish in daydreams, never assuming that some-day the actual sight of her school—the hard angles, the dark, secretive windows—would tense her stomach as it does now. She is free from outward torment and bullying, unlike Silas Bloom, a woeful boy whose pants pronounce his rear, whose face, last week, was driven into a toilet by boys whose names he refused to recall. But Anju's torments are her own—her ridiculous rolling accent, her oblivious stank, her misuse of facilities, such as the time she tried to rinse her mouth at the water foun-tain after lunch and as she spat, Mr. Obata, the math teacher, said "*No, no, no . . .*" from across the hall, as one might order dead Jimmi to stop urinating in his cage. The prospect of committing an error looms over every morning, with each step, each word destined for mistake. For this reason, she sometimes lies sleepless in bed, dreading the moment of waking even before falling asleep.

But today demands composure. She unzips her backpack, tears the Ace bandage from its cover. Taking a few deep breaths, she reviews her lines.

WELL BEFORE THE FIRST BELL, Anju steps into Miss Schimpf's office, which emits the scent of aging newspapers and jasmine perfume. Miss Schimpf is reading a book titled *Media, Sex & the Adolescent,* while her fingers stroke a faint rash at her collarbone, presumably from the black metal choker she wore the day before. Behind her, the bolted metal shelves support more books, including *Reviving Ophelia* and *Rais-ing Cain.*

Upon Anju's arrival, Miss Schimpf looks up. "Oh hello!" Her smile dissolves. "What happened?"

Anju touches her bandaged right hand, which she wrapped according to the instructions on the Ace package. It looks a bit bulgier than neces-sary, but therefore more dramatic. "May I please close the door?"

After doing so, Anju sinks into the plastic chair across from Miss Schimpf, one without armrests, shaped like a bowl rather than a chair that gracelessly sucks her in rear first. She thinks of the last lie she told to Miss Schimpf, standing next to Linno's painting, the gathering warmth in the room. Anju truly believed, at the time, that she would never take such a risk again, and now it is frightening to consider how she can lie and lie and lie once more. She is reminded of a game she used to play with other children, jumping off a staircase onto the ground, first two stairs, then three, or the low ledge of a wall. She always won, not because she was brave, but because she never let herself look down.

Keeping her hands in her lap, Anju confesses that she does not want to tell her fellow classmates what she is about to tell Miss Schimpf. The pity would be too much. Solemn, quiet with courage, she says, "I suffer from juvenile rheumatoid arthritis."

As Miss Schimpf listens with furrowed brow, fondling her throat, Anju explains the statistics that she culled from several library books, including *Juvenile Rheumatoid Arthritis* and *Living with Rheumatoid Arthritis:*

> Arthritis affects approximately one in every thousand children. It is an autoimmune disease that can last for months or years, though patients may experience long periods without symptoms.

When she has finished with her statistics, Anju sighs. A risk, she knows, to embark on such a circuitous journey into falsehood, but she already tried and failed, tried and failed to create anything of worth in the sketchbook. Her pencil never listened to what she meant to draw—an eye became a fish, a tree resembled a hand. Anju resolved, then, that it was time to strategize. A sustained lie is a fragile tower of sorts and requires a continual scaffolding here and there, for fear of the uglier truths toppling down tomorrow. What other choice does she have? Continue drawing pigeons and insisting that they are not seals?

"I wear my brace at night only," Anju says. "I don't want any attentions at school. But today it is bothering me very much so." She grazes a hand over her bulging wrist, which lies, she hopes, forlornly.

Miss Schimpf ponders Anju as one might ponder a perplexing geometry proof. Anju waits, her heart in her throat, for interrogation.

"Does it hurt you to write?" Miss Schimpf asks.

"Sometimes yes. But to draw is most painful."

"When did you do all those drawings back home?"

"The arthritis, it comes and goes. I only can draw when my hand is not paining me so much."

Miss Schimpf presses her palms together, as if to say Namaste. Her gold bracelet, a snake-headed contortion with fake diamond eyes, slides down her freckled wrist. Anju senses that this silence is the sort that precedes the final judgment, as pronounced in a court of law.

"Anju," Miss Schimpf says. "Let me tell you a story."

"When I was a girl, I was stricken with scoliosis. It's when your spine starts growing crooked. So in order to correct my spine, I had to wear this terrible plastic brace under my shirts, and as you can imagine, my classmates were jerks about it, especially the boys. They knocked on my brace. Called me the Cagemaster. Keep in mind that the women in my family come from a long line of Delaware beauty queens, so the scoliosis was an even bigger deal because, naturally, I had certain aspirations.

"But I wore the brace all through middle school and finally, after two operations, my spine was fixed. That's a small price to pay for being the 1989 runner-up to the runner-up of Miss Delaware Diamond, don't you think?"

Anju nods, allowing the drone of the air conditioner to fill the room as she envisions a row of lustrous beauty queens in bikinis and heels, one of them trapped in a plastic brace. Nothing is right about these shared intimacies, this photo album of Miss Schimpf's past, presented with a pure and lucid honesty that Anju will never be able to return.

"I hadn't thought of that in a long time." Miss Schimpf studies her bracelet for a moment, her smile fading. "My point is, I know what you're going through, sort of. But maybe the student art exhibition will be your Delaware Diamond?"

Anju shifts in her seat, wondering how best to arrange her facial expression.

"The paintings you showed me in Kerala," Miss Schimpf says. "You brought them, right?"

"Yes, Miss."

Miss Schimpf explains the details of the student art exhibition, how it is scheduled for December 2, how the winning piece will be shown in the Brigard gallery, downtown. "George de Brigard is an alumnus of Sitwell, and he'll be conferring the award money on whomever he chooses to showcase."

"Award money?"

"A thousand dollars. A drop in the bucket to George. He made his money in pharmaceuticals a decade ago, and then ran off and opened his gallery. Never looked back."

To Anju, a thousand dollars is a green cascade, a deluge so mighty that it will wash away all sins required to obtain it, so great that it justifies one last, delicate lie.

"Sound good?" Miss Schimpf asks.

"Sound good," Anju says.

"And how are things otherwise? Is everyone treating you well?" Eager to leave, Anju answers a quick yes, but Miss Schimpf tilts her head like a parrot piqued by a particular sound. "Really?"

"There was a rude beggar on the train," Anju ventures.

Miss Schimpf gives her a wincing smile. "Here, we say 'disadvantaged.' "

"There was a disadvantaged beggar on the train."

"What about here at school? Do you feel at ease with people? Making friends?"

"Fish and I are friends."

"Ah yes, Mr. Fischer." She says his name with a flicker of wicked delight. "He's a character."

"Yes. A character." In the face of Miss Schimpf's luminous smile, Anju wishes she could come up with something more chummy than this, to be the frothy, affectionate person that Miss Schimpf wants her to be. "Miss Schimpf?"

"Yes?"

"May I join the chorus class for an elective? It is compatible with my schedule."

"Oh, of course." Miss Schimpf flips through a binder and makes the necessary check marks by which Anju can be freed from art. Anju sits back in her chair, but before she can relax, Miss Schimpf reminds her to bring in the paintings. "I want everyone to see a side of Anju Melvin that they've never seen before."

WHAT MISS SCHIMPF does not know is that Anju has more facets than a fake diamond. She glitters with all her many, many sides.

There is the side she displays to Fish, who tells her stories with hardly a breath between them, as though he has been saving all his anecdotes over the years of her absence. Once, unexpectedly, he tells her about his First Time at age fourteen, and only halfway into the story does she understand that he is not talking about driving a car. "She was Mormon," he says. "And older. Like sixteen or something."

"Hm," she says. They are sitting on a cement bench outside school, staring with false interest at a fire hydrant. Her wrist feels choked by the Ace bandage, which she wrapped too tightly in the morning. Fish has been kind enough to offer her a copy of all his class notes, sparse and careless though they are.

"She told me to come to her house after school. I thought it was for

Bible study, but I went anyway. I guess she was rebelling against cultural constraints and whatnot."

"If I rebeled in this way, my grandmother would send me to a convent."

"I guess fourteen is kind of young," Fish admits. "But actually I was really grateful to that Mormon girl. I'd never want to be someone's First Time."

"Me too."

Some lies should be properly checked and fueled before launch, but Anju let this one tear out of her mouth prematurely. He glances at her, waiting for her to continue.

With outward calm, she focuses on the fire hydrant while synapses go firing along the corridors of her brain, trying to gather bits of information from music videos and movies, though the raciest she has seen is the kind that cuts from the first turbulent kiss to the morning after, when people are sucking on cigarettes, sheets tucked under armpits, looking languidly out of windows.

"How old were you?" Fish asks.

"Sixteen."

"Oh, so pretty recent. Who was the guy?"

To manufacture a whole new person and past is a staggering task, so she calls upon a name she knows from years ago. "Sri Ram. A Hindu. He was writing me love notes. . . ." (*Abort*, her brain blares. *Dead end. Abort.*) "But he died. Killed in a paper mill. Chopped him to death."

"Wow." Fish looks at her, then back to the sidewalk. "Sorry."

A bloated pigeon goes waddling after a hunk of bagel on the sidewalk, a wealth of food until several others join in, culling what they can. Fish and Anju watch the staccato rhythms of their pecking for an appropriate period, to honor Anju's fallen First Time.

"You're really nothing like I thought you were," Fish says, his voice lightly glazed with awe.

AND THEN THERE IS the side she preserves for Ammachi and Melvin. Every phone conversation has the same cadence and content, so that the questions and answers, leading one to the next, take on the cadence of a broken alarm clock.

"How are you?"

"Fine."

"Are you eating?"

"Yes."

"Are you studying?"

"Always."

At times, Ammachi drops in a bit of gossip or a reference to a sermon, until her fear of raising the Solankis' phone bill overcomes her and she announces that it is time to hang up. During his phone time, Melvin focuses on the process of acquiring a green card. He seems to entertain the naïve, infuriating notion that permanent residency can be procured in a matter of weeks, based on vague testimonies from a friend of a friend of a friend. Anju hates these blurry suspects, the way they raise reckless hopes.

"Not everyone gets it," Anju insists. "And it must take time to apply."

"Then why haven't you started?" Melvin asks.

How can she tell him that, for the first time, she is beginning to doubt the merits of staying here at all?

There is something at school called the Pit, Fish has told her, a backstage section of the school auditorium where girls gather to do unspeakable and legendary things with recorders and ice cubes, pawing at each other behind the scrim of a painted shtetl used for last year's production of *Fiddler on the Roof*. One girl, naked, wrapped herself in the American flag used for Student Council meetings and sang "Happy Birthday, Mr. President," which was videotaped and posted somewhere on the Internet. Sometimes girls can be seen casually leaving the auditorium, tightening their ponytails, twisting their skirts back into place. They roll their eyes at the term "lesbian." "I'm just so over it," the Birthday girl said, during the Women's Rights unit in Social Studies. "I feel like we should be postgender already."

These are the times when Anju feels paralyzed, caught in the eye of a stormy confusion to which she does not want to know the answers. Such things are not discussed during phone conversations with Ammachi and Melvin. Even knowing of the Pit seems a kind of sin.

But Anju wishes her family could know something of her hardships, which are mostly hardships of the heart and therefore impossible to utter. She wants them to know her loneliness without having to say the word "lonely," which does not fall easily from her mouth. She wants them to pity her and praise her all the same, but more, to know her nightmares, such as the one in which she lies supine on the floor of the 1 subway train as sneakers and heels trample her face and chest, leave her drained of voice and breath, while overhead a voice announces that the 1 train is not the 1 train but a new train called the Wrong Train, making no stops until Mexico.

All this until she snorts herself awake against a goose-down pillow, swaddled in Egyptian cotton sheets.

AS PROMISED, Anju brings the paintings to school, scrolled within a tube Miss Schimpf gave her. She arrives at her locker to find a note taped over the grating: *See me to set up!!! Miss S.* Beneath the three exclamation points, a smile.

The art show is being hung in the Fine Arts Wing, a carpeted haven of crisp, conditioned air, cushy armchairs, and orange pots of polished ficus plants. Few people visit the Fine Arts Wing, usually potential donors or visiting parents, leaving its bathrooms the most civilized of the building.

Miss Schimpf has never looked more buoyant, more alive within her small province of influence, plotting the positions of various fruit still lifes and pointillist portraits of horses. Her bangles are perpetually clattering as she directs the students, gesturing to a wall, using two fingers to draw a square in the air.

Students are pinning up their pieces, asking one another for opinions on what looks askew. Everything looks askew. In one series, the fragments of a face are rendered in terrifying close-up, the hair sprouting in thick, snaky locks, the gaze cloudy and detached, like that of a slain animal.

Below these pictures, on a small white card:

ARTIST'S STATEMENT
by Greg Pfeiffer

I am interested in the protean nature of identity, as expressed through a multiplicity of facial distortions rendered by Xeroxing my face . . .

A pair of hands clamps down on Anju's shoulders, startling her.

"Anju, I need you to do an artist's statement," Miss Schimpf says. "Just the usual *I am interested in this or that idea, this inspires me, I am compelled by* . . . Maybe you could mention commercial art in India and its overlap with calendar art or Hindu religious iconography as depicted by Raja Ravi Varma." Noting Anju's stricken expression, she adds, "Or just write your name."

Miss Schimpf leads her to a vacant section and shows her how to mount and hang the three paintings. She then hurries away, calling out the name of a student who has hung his mobile too low.

Before unscrolling the paintings, Anju takes a blank card and writes her name in tiny letters. She pins the card to the wall, below the space where the paintings will go, and takes a step back.

The card is a small scrap in a corkboard sea; most would not even notice it. Her card—claiming nothing, compelled by nothing—is the closest she has come to honesty in a long while. The bell chimes twice, signaling students to first period, but she cannot pull her eyes from her signature, the fine tremble in the line, as if she forged it. The *n* in "Melvin" trails off in a way that she meant as a flourish, but instead looks like a short bit of string that, if tugged, would quickly unspool her name.

6.

AS A LITTLE GIRL, Linno daily passed a statue of the Blessed Virgin on the walk to and from school. She took these opportunities to channel prayers of intervention, that she be made invisible during the day's oral exams, or that Sister Savio fall magically mute for a week. Only now, pausing before the statue, does Linno notice how years of sun have stolen the blue from the Virgin's cloak and the blush from her cheeks. Wind and rain have whisked flecks of paint from her hands. Her arms are outstretched, but someone has made off with her thumb. Through all this, her mouth remains a ripple of patience.

Linno touches the hot stone toes and prays for divine clarity.

The blind suitor, so casually introduced by Rappai's mother, has since taken center stage in Linno's life. It began with a phone call from the man's older sister, a woman named Alice whose voice burst so loudly through the receiver that Melvin had to hold the phone away from his face. They spoke for ten minutes, during which time Melvin mostly said "huh" and "uh-huh." Before Melvin hung up, Linno distinctly heard Alice say "union," a word that sounded like an alliance between tense nations.

Melvin told Linno that the blind suitor's family had been speaking with Rappai's mother. They wanted to arrange an introductory meeting.

Meeting. Alliance. Union. The near future rose before her like a steep flight of stairs.

A WEEK BEFORE THE MEETING, Linno and Ammachi visit Rappai's mother, who hurries back and forth across her sitting room with glasses of tea in her hands, energized by the fact that she has been sought after as some kind of authority on the blind man. She smiles with what teeth she has left, both of them stained brown like a guava slice left out in the sun.

They sit at the table where mother and son take their meals. Though only two live in the house, the table bears six blue plastic placemats, bought by Rappai's father decades ago. Occasionally, when no one is looking, Rappai's mother will peel up the corner of a placemat and graze her fingers over the golden rectangle left behind, proof of the table's better days. Those were better days for her as well, when it had seemed that six people would eventually fill the table, but her first two babies died in the womb. And then there came Rappai, a sickly child from whom no one expected great things, but whom she adored simply because he survived.

After teas are handed out, Rappai's mother sits at the head of the table and gets down to business. There are some details that she failed to mention upon first proposing the match, namely that the blind man's family has been derailed by a few tragedies.

"Curses?" Ammachi asks.

Rappai's mother ponders this, and then decides on the word "accidents." But first, Rappai's mother reviews the factors working in the blind man's favor:

1. He hails from a good family, long established in the rubber plantation business. They own estates near Kasaragod, great tracts of shady land with thousands of loyal rubber trees, dribbling raw materials for which the increasingly synthetic world will always have demand. Because of this wealth,

2. the dowry won't have to be much, if anything at all. The blind man considers himself a modern man, and he finds this dowry business to be a corrupted tradition.

3. The blind man is fair-skinned. Not fair in the way that parents advertise in the newspaper ads, when their children are actually the color of scrubbed potatoes. But truly fair, Rappai's mother guarantees. "Like the color of tea. Very weak milky tea. No. *Yogurt*."

4. The blind man is not completely blind but rather blind to a favor-

able degree. Delicately, Rappai's mother adds that this is a trait that works in Linno's favor.

"The curses, the curses," Ammachi urges.

"It happened like this. The mother wanted to go to Agra for her fifty-fifth birthday. To see the Taj Mahal, I suppose, or maybe to shop, I don't know, not my business. So she and her husband took off in a plane, but they never made it to Agra. Collided." She pauses for emphasis. "With a mountain."

Ammachi puts a hand to her mouth.

"And then the sister," Rappai's mother whispers. "The one you spoke to on the phone? Her husband hanged himself."

"Aiyyo, kashtam." Ammachi shakes her head. "Someone put the Evil Eye on them."

Rappai's mother clicks her tongue dismissively. "People die when God calls."

"God called them into a mountain?"

They begin arguing over the nature of curses and accidents, and at one point, Ammachi fake-spits to stave off any curses that the conversation may have attracted. Though Linno remains silent, she enjoys these discussions, how simple topics seem to take on such electricity between two old women in a dim kitchen. Until recently, she imagined that she and Anju would end their lives this way, echoing the arguments of the women who raised them. But now the world is much larger than the one she knew as a little girl.

SAFE TO SAY that the blind suitor must have researched Linno's history as well. Linno wonders what he has been told and by whom. Yes, she has had her traumas, one in particular that could have crushed the spirit of a lesser child. She could have grown glazed and mute, living forever in her nightmares, feeding off her grief.

Linno has never recounted the story aloud, though she could, she is sure, if pressed. On the day Gracie died, Abraham Chandy had offered to take her and Linno and Anju on a day trip to Kovalam Beach, along with his own family. There, Linno and her mother took a walk farther down the beach, heedless of the oncoming storm that was tossing the tides. While Linno was playing by herself, her mother wandered into the waves in what was later deemed a suicide. A fisherman found Gracie's body by morning. He told police that the beds of her fingernails were blue.

Being the last to see her mother alive, Linno was handled gently, as though at any second she might descend into a glassy-eyed delirium. She could feel the questions swirling around her: *What kind of mother would leave this child?* If anyone had asked Linno directly, she would have said that Gracie was the kind of mother who made the perfect shape for sleeping next to, like a spoon in a spoon. The kind of mother who hit only with the flat of her hand, to know exactly what pain she inflicted. The kind of mother who did not hide her sadness but let it seep into a whole day, unyielding and infectious.

Linno soon learned that the best coping tactic was one sold to her by a self-help cassette tape given to Melvin by Berchmans, urging him to "Live for the Now!" At first, she was unsure how to Live for the Now if Now had been ruined by someone who had Died in the Before. Her interpretation was to bury her mother in a well-tended corner of her mind. There, she visited her mother almost as often as she breathed, but only in brief moments, scraps of memory. Like the mole at the corner of her mother's eye. Or the dryness of her elbows and the velvet of her earlobes. But Linno did not dwell. If she dwelled, she would have to apologize to her mother, and she did not know if she could survive those kinds of words. ("It is common," said the self-help tape, as read aloud by a woman with a thick, oozy voice, "for children of the deceased to suffer a terrible sense of guilt.")

Technically, Ammachi said, one should not take communion without first cleansing the conscience, but what was the point of confessing everything to Anthony Achen? Whenever he listened to Linno's stuttered string of sins, he never even deigned to ask her name. While Linno confessed to coveting a classmate's skirt, Anthony Achen kept his eyes somewhere on the window above her, his hands curled over his armrests as if he were sitting aloft a throne. By the end, he crossed the air in front of her with his hand and sentenced her to a lengthy recitation of rosary beads to be completed on her own time. Confession was nothing special. It all seemed rather anticlimactic.

If she were to write a self-help book dedicated to children like herself, children whose memories made each night a burden, Linno would advise that control is the key. She once read of Jain yogis who believe that the span of a man's life is a predestined number of breaths; hence, the yogic practice of lengthening and deepening the breath cycle. Control breaths and you control life. So in a way, she decides, control is closer to divinity than confession.

.   .   .

NOT LONG AFTER the conference with Rappai's mother, an envelope arrives in the mail, addressed to Melvin. He stands while opening the envelope and drinking a cup of chai, his hips sore from sitting behind Abraham's steering wheel all day.

Inside is a photograph wrapped in a sheet of paper. He knows without looking that this is the blind suitor. Initially, Melvin was elated by the blind suitor's interest, but now that his photo has arrived in the mail, Melvin suffers a quiet terror about presenting it to Linno. Marriage, all of a sudden, has acquired the shape of a man.

Before he views the picture, Melvin thinks of the woman he almost married, how she arrived in his hands twenty years ago, in the same flat fashion. At his parents' suggestion, he had returned from Bombay to marry the wife they had chosen for him. But when he grabbed the girl's photograph from Ammachi, giddy, almost breathless, and looked at their selection for the first time, his future seemed to fold.

Eight months before, Melvin had gone to Bombay with his friend Govind, a Malayali Hindu who said that the city abounded with "civil service jobs." What the term meant, Melvin did not know, though it seemed to mean working for the government, behind a desk, hopefully beneath a fan. But when Melvin arrived in Bombay, he learned that whole fleets of small-town boys flocked to the city in pursuit of the same dreamily vague civil service jobs, only to find that to obtain such a job, one had to be either smart or willing to pay. And, as well, the network of civil servants seemed a twisted family tree of cousins granting favors to cousins; Melvin had no relatives perched in those enviable branches.

By luck, Govind found Melvin a job as a clerk at the Oasis Hotel. Govind knew the owner, but refused to take the job himself, arguing that a Brahmin, however unemployed and needy, should never have to work for someone of the mid-level castes, as the owner was. Telling Melvin of his plight, Govind leaned against a poster-covered wall, the sole of his chappal propped against the face of a pretty woman holding up a tube of Colgate fennel toothpaste. "Brahmins are doomed in this world," Govind sighed. Melvin could think of a few Brahmins he knew working as cooks and cabbies, but kept silent on the assumption that Govind was simply homesick. "Where can I go but back to university?"

"*Another* degree?" From Melvin's last count, Govind already had two, neither of which he was putting to use. "You would rather be unemployed than working in a hotel?"

"Or I could work for my father again." Govind shrugged. "You are lucky, though, you Christians. Serve thy neighbor. Your own Jesus washes other people's dirty feet, *allay?*"

Govind left a week later, while Melvin took a tiny airshaft of a flat and worked at the Oasis Hotel. Strategically positioned near the international airport, the hotel fielded a healthy amount of transcontinental clientele, many European businessmen and Indians able to travel abroad. The Oasis Hotel embodied its namesake, an island of modern, Western calm in the midst of Bombay's shabby ruckus, where the breakfast buffet offered doughnuts and cereal alongside idli and sambar. The glass elevator was the triumph of the lobby. Gliding from height to height, it shuttled its passengers to a synthesized rendition of "Over the Rainbow."

Melvin didn't mind the job, mostly hoisting people's luggage onto carts, which he then transported to their rooms. He hated the pillbox hat he was made to wear, complete with a strap that dug a welt beneath his chin. He also hated his tendency to nod and nod like a child whenever addressed by a resident, a tendency that would follow him into old age, even when addressed by his mother.

As he stuffed more hours into his schedule, he began to dislike Bombay, though he had seen little more of the city than his flat and the Oasis Hotel. His intention had been to climb the professional ladder through diligence and a good attitude, but the past few months had shown him that the ladder was not so much vertical as horizontal and the higher planes would be impossible to reach. Above the clerks was a supervisor who earned a higher salary, and above him, a manager who was godlike in both his power and his absence.

And then there was the bit of Bombay that he observed: the scant villages of people that sprang up beneath bridges; the hijras who paraded in saris while Melvin watched, transfixed by their Adam's apples; the university students protesting a raise in tuition; the scrawny children weaving through traffic and selling plates of sliced coconut like wide, white smiles. In his later years, when he pictured Bombay, it was not a place that he saw but people, tide upon teeming tide, out of which he knew no one.

Upon returning home, he complained to his friends of the smoke, the congestion, the too-sweet tea, the food heavy with ghee, the beggars with sunken, bullet-hole eyes. But as he grew older, none of these reasons approached the real belief to which he clung like a zealot, that his presence in Bombay had kept him from his wife, thus severing the sweet, green years of his marriage. Every zealot has his target, and to Melvin's mind, Bombay was to blame.

OVER CHRISTMAS, he came home to Kumarakom with the express purpose of finding a wife. Marriage was a stage of life to which he was resigned, an eventuality for which he had no way to prepare. He simply told himself that on his marriage night, either carnal knowledge would descend on him like a holy revelation or he would disappoint his wife. If the latter were true, at least they would already be married, and therefore compelled to work on it for the rest of their lives.

But once in Kumarakom, Melvin began to hope, and the thought of his future wife brought a delicious thrill. She would be there when he woke and when he returned home. Her words would break the tedium of days. She would prepare for him a tiffin of lunch to take to work, and when he opened it, his face would be lovingly caressed by steam. On his rare days off, maybe they would point to a place on a map and whimsically decide to take the train there.

Such innocent fantasies ended as soon as he saw a picture of Gladwyn, the girl his father had deemed a good catch because of her dowry and parentage. The only aesthetic quality that concerned Appachen was the girl's fairness; he was otherwise blind to her buckteeth. Melvin felt too embarrassed to object, but he proposed that they let the girl's family wait for a week, lest better offers should come along. "What better?" Appachen asked, genuinely puzzled. "Fine. A week."

The week brought no new offers, and by Saturday, Melvin resigned himself to a future with Gladwyn and children with dental problems. That evening, he attended an outdoor play that was showing in town, wanting the escape of some pretty, fluffy fairy tale. He hoped that this drama troupe would be less depressing than the K.P.A.C. troupe, which performed Communist plays about the injustices of capitalism, or Geetha Theatres, which championed the opposing Congress Party plays. This was a new drama troupe called Apsara Arts Club; he had seen their show card posted on the wall of a tea shop. For tonight's performance, they were presenting *Kalli Pavayuda Veede*, based on a European play called *A Doll's House*, starring "the exquisite BIRDIE KAMALABHAI." Melvin sat in one of the many plastic chairs arranged over the great green lawn of the Thirunakkara Maidan, beneath lofted strings of white lights strewn around the heads of leaning palms.

From the moment Birdie Kamalabhai appeared onstage, the story seemed to close in around Melvin; he felt enveloped by her plight. Neera was her character's name. Her costars were also talented, even the teenage boy playing the servant, his youth apparent in the high pitch of his voice. His costume stripped him of seriousness, a cross between a genie and the Air India mascot, with a bulbous, ruby-colored turban atop his head.

But no matter which actor was next to Birdie Kamalabhai, it was she who possessed the stage. She was beautiful in her desperation, fumbling as she made the Christmas Star, quivering as she spoke: "It is all nonsense. This Christmas will be perfect. I will do everything I can think of to please you, my husband! I will sing for you, dance for you. . . ." And when she danced for her husband, fear swirled and cycloned through her body, gathering to her all the sympathy in the audience, who quietly condoned her leaving of insensitive Tobin. This from a rigorously pious audience who shrank from the very thought of divorce like mosquitoes from marigolds. Contrary to their social codes, they forgave Neera, and it was all due to Birdie Kamalabhai. Never, until now, had Melvin witnessed such miracles of the theater, far more wondrous than those of cinematic special effects.

As Melvin watched the play, another one unfolded in his mind, starring Birdie and himself. He imagined her wearing the kind of flowery muumuus that his mother wore at bedtime, but uneasy with the idea, he mentally redressed his Birdie in a pale cotton sari. The fluidity of her movement translated into the fluidity of her daily chores, singing as she swept the meager floor, straightening the rug with her outstretched toe, his tiny flat thrumming with her graceful energy.

It was at that moment, mid-daydream, that Servant came bustling along Melvin's row. With his performance over, he was joining the audience, all the while staring at Birdie Kamalabhai as if a single blink might destroy the mirage. Lost within his trance, Servant failed to remove his oversized hat when taking the seat directly in front of Melvin.

At first, Melvin tried edging from side to side, but the view of Birdie Kamalabhai was eclipsed by the hat. He tried to make a few hissing noises, but Servant did not turn. Melvin waited until intermission to tap him on the shoulder and whisper, "Eh! Your *thotti* is blocking me!"

Servant turned, putting a protective hand to his hat. They stared at each other, and gradually Melvin was filled with a thick, viscous terror, a slow-growing regret. An English phrase came automatically to his lips, one that he used often at the Oasis Hotel: "Excuse me, miss."

Servant removed her hat. Underneath, hiding all along, was a large, black bun.

A bit wounded, the lady asked if Melvin really thought her hat looked like a bucket. He quickly said no. A fruit maybe, from a distance, but not a bucket. He was unsure of his words, focused instead on the mole at the outer corner of her eye. She said that she was replacing a man who had previously played the servant role, but to mask her gender, she had spent two nights crafting the hat from plaster and paper. She had even visited a fabric store in Ernakulam for the red glitter, which, to her frustration, continues to turn up in the strangest of places, a red fleck in her eyebrow, another between her toes. Very nice glitter, he assured her. A manly glitter.

At this, she smiled. The white of her teeth broke the dark.

As people around them shifted and stretched, Melvin and the lady remained chatting. Her name was Gracie. Later, he would find it difficult to remember the specifics of their conversation, though he did recall asking her if she enjoyed acting.

"I do, only I wish I had more time to improve." She looped her arm over the back of her chair and rested her chin on her knuckles. "You should've seen me when I started. So nervous, so distracted. You would be too if you had to rehearse with Birdie Kamalabhai."

He asked her why she had continued, if she found it difficult.

"Because my mother disapproved." She gave him a rueful smile. "But then I began to like being up there."

Here she paused, her brow furrowed as she scraped a speck of glitter from her hand. Her silence made him fear that he had said something wrong, but she was only thinking of her answer. "To be up there is to be natural. Free."

"Free from what?"

She turned to him. "You can see it in Birdie's performance. As Neera. Isn't she beautiful to watch?"

Melvin nodded but said nothing, worried that his clumsy questions might destroy her reflections. He felt privileged by the degree of her honesty and amazed that she hadn't gotten up and left by now. In the past, interactions with women generally caused him to suffer a barrage of symptoms—rapid heartbeat, loss of humor, profuse perspiration. He treated women the same way that he treated the manicured section of a public garden, appreciating the whole, respectfully sidling around the borders.

He lay in bed that night thinking of the moment when Gracie smiled at him, and how his gut had tightened. She had a slight overbite (not bucktoothed) that nudged against her top lip in such a way that made him ponder tasting it. Until now, he had entertained thoughts like this only about actresses far beyond his reach, as it seemed safer, somehow, to confine his fantasies to the impossible.

He kept the program, and from the cast of characters, he learned her full name. *Gracie Kuruvilla.* He brought up the name to his father.

"You've been making a relationship with her?" Appachen asked, incredulous, scandalized.

This was the most intimate question that ever hung in the air between them. Melvin shook his head.

They were in the sitting room, Appachen in his haggard armchair, Melvin standing over him. Even from that vantage, Appachen held dominion over the room, but Melvin did not want that kind of authority, the kind that put distance between father and family. Ever since he was small, Melvin often acted as liason between his father and his aunts, even if they were all in the same room. The women sent Melvin to ask Appachen questions, usually *Are you hungry yet?* or *Do you want a glass of lime water?,* to which Appachen answered with impatience, as if the workings of his appetite were common knowledge. On the few occasions that Appachen entered the kitchen, he immediately became the eye of a hurricane, the women halting their conversation to flurry around him and make him tea or snacks. Sometimes it seemed that he simply wanted company, but the attention made him uncomfortable, so he went back to his armchair and waited for the snacks.

And when, as now, Appachen deemed himself above certain affairs, he said, "Talk to your mother," and then closed his eyes. A year later, they would find him that way, dead in his armchair. They would also learn that he had been dead for three hours, but having assumed that he was thinking about something important, no one had wanted to bother him. For now, Melvin could tell that the old man was mentally transported to a happier place, where sons remained boys, where young women were never discussed, where his cup ran over with arrack.

A WEEK LATER, Gracie's father agreed to the match. The family was thrilled, he said, to accept the proposal.

Melvin's family had expected a bit of hedging, followed by a rejection. Ammachi's extensive research, which uncovered the girl's denomination, church name, house name, street name, age, approximate height, and enough features for a police sketch, indicated that Gracie was from a fairly well-to-do family. Her father was the head of Kuruvilla Coir, presiding over a factory that wove the fibers from coconut shells into rugs and house mats. She was once betrothed to Abraham Chandy, the son of another upstanding family, who had reneged on the deal after Abraham's father found a better prospect in Mercy. But at least Gracie's family could find her an engineer or a professor. What would they want with a Bombay bellhop? Melvin wondered. He became convinced that he had unwittingly left an impression on Gracie from their only encounter, an indelible mark, as she had upon him. Maybe hers was a liberal-minded family who allowed her the husband of her choosing. Rich people could afford everything, so why not liberalism?

During Appachen and Melvin's first visit, Gracie's father poured a round of cognac for the men, which Appachen happily accepted despite the possibility that Melvin would shame him by taking wee sips. Melvin swallowed in a fierce gulp that tortured his stomach for the rest of the night. Equally unsettling was Gracie's grave expression, not exactly the thrill that he had imagined. She sat on the sofa, flanked by her parents, silent as her father rambled on about the growing demand for geo-textiles and her mother affirmed his speeches with smiles and nods. The mother reminded Melvin of a porcelain miniature, with her changeless smile and her tiny doll hands folded over her knee. Or perhaps it was her husband's size and volubility that so diminished her, but she seemed to be shrinking with age, best kept behind glass.

Gracie was dressed in her mother's likeness. She was wearing far too much makeup, caking her complexion in a deathly hue, with rashes of blush across her cheeks. Later, she disappeared into the kitchen and returned with a tray of teas. When she bent over to serve Melvin a glass, he noticed a strange discoloring at the corner of her cheekbone, a small swelling spackled over with paint. Catching his eye, she hesitated, then smiled. The skin wrinkled around the swelling.

For the rest of the evening, Melvin could not look at Gracie's father, and instead focused on his two rings, thick gold bands of perfect proportion to bruise an eye.

Gracie's father raised his ringed fingers. "Melvin, you like these?"

As soon as Melvin nodded, Gracie's father began pulling and pulling on the smaller of the two rings.

"No," Melvin said. "Thank you."

"Don't worry," Gracie's father said, still pulling. "This is just the beginning. More on the way."

Gracie was leaning away from him with unveiled revulsion as he ordered his wife to bring the soap. Over Appachen's protests, Gracie's father finally soaped his finger and pulled off the smaller of the two rings, one with a small embedded sapphire. This he placed in the center of the coffee table.

And there it remained.

"I don't want that," Melvin said, barely aware that his palms were sweaty. The room went silent. In one glance, Melvin noticed how Gracie was looking at him curiously, with those pupils tiny as seeds, full of pent life.

Appachen broke the silence with a strained laugh. "He's allergic to gold. Some luck, isn't it? Breaks out in a rash every time."

THE MEETING put Melvin in mind of Ammachi's younger sister, Chinamma, whose husband sometimes beat her. Her bruises were a blend of colors, cloudy gray and plum blue, or yellow dappled with purple. He glimpsed them only in memory. Otherwise, the bruises were to be ignored.

Sometimes, Chinamma came to stay with Ammachi for a few days, which meant that things were going badly with Thambi, her husband. She always went back a few days later, but during their time together, Ammachi and Chinamma slept in the same bed, holding each other like little girls, whispering into the night. Melvin had assumed that his mother was healing his aunt, or maybe cursing Thambi and inciting rebellion. But once, while eavesdropping from the doorway, Melvin heard his mother's words: *No, you can't leave him. You are married now. Be patient, it will get better.*

It terrified him to learn that the people he loved most in the world could be such distant specters of the people he had presumed them to be.

But there was Gracie, the woman he could finally rescue, the wife into whose ear he would whisper sweet, healing things. They were not even married yet, but already her smile lines were inscribed in his mind's eye, and thinking of her returned the inner itch to his stomach, a feeling that he thought to be the first stirrings of love. How an open palm could meet her cheek with anything but wonder, he would never understand.

7.

*I*N THE EVENING, Melvin sits next to Linno and pretends to take an interest in the serial she is watching on television. *Sympathy,* it is called. On the screen, a young woman is confessing to her father that she has decided to marry the neighbor's son, even though the families have been feuding for the past six episodes. One modest tear sits on the apple of the girl's cheek, though her immodest sobs resemble the squeaky scrape of a wiper across a windshield. *Never will I disobey my heart!* she shrieks. *I may die of grief but at least I shall meet God with a pure and honest soul!*

Melvin and Linno watch the screen, neither of them particularly moved. Melvin's presence renders Linno acutely aware of the fake tear, the flowery pleas, the heaving, padded bosom. It is a world created for an audience of one. Two makes the experience rather embarrassing.

During the commercial break, Melvin casually places the photo on the coffee table and then examines the state of his fingernails. "That's him."

Linno snatches up the photo and hunts for signs of blindness. But there are no milky cataracts like the ones that have haunted her recent imaginings, no harnessed hound to lead him across streets. He stands with arms crossed, a magnificent red-roofed house with tapioca walls looming in the background. Every time she tries to focus on his face, her gaze slides to the circular driveway patterned in bricks of red and gray, hugging a fountain where a stone cherub fingers a lute. Mangosteen trees line the drive, thick with purple fruit, and ivy gourd vines wander up an elegant trellis. A sudden, wanton desire rises up within her, having little to do with the man. Though he is not so bad-looking. A full head of hair, his skin as dairy-fair as promised. She flips the picture over and reads the name several times before pronouncing it aloud.

"Kuku George?"

Ammachi approaches and looks over their shoulders, squinting through her glasses.

"What kind of name is that?" Linno asks.

"Maybe an accident," Ammachi says. "I never really liked the name Melvin. I thought my great-grandfather's name was Melvin, but he was not Melvin, he was Elwin. By the time I found out, the name was already on the birth certificate."

"Thank God," Melvin says.

They do not talk of the future. They do not talk of the house like a monument to all that is possible, nor the cherub like a baby Gabriel mid-prance in the center of the fountain, come to inform Linno of her destiny. Instead, Ammachi cheerily notes that Kuku does not look blind at all.

Linno wishes her father were more like the father in the serial, a man with so stoic a face that it belongs on a statue, demanding that she marry the blind man immediately. Melvin, at the moment, is scratching his armpit and looking to the window as a possible means of escape. If Linno were more bound and bullied by her family, it would be much easier to flail, to plead, to put up a fight in the face of familial pressures. But freedom of choice makes defiance far less attractive.

Over the course of the week, she begins entertaining other thoughts. What it would be like to eat in restaurants at whim. What it would be like to tuck a roll of bills between Ammachi's fingers each month. Freedom from financial worry holds considerable virtue. She boils her debate down to its elemental parts: marriage means money, *her* money, and this is a freedom too tempting to ignore.

LATER IN THE WEEK, Melvin drives Abraham to his grandmother's house in Changanacherry, and on the way back, Abraham requests that they stop at a house on Good Shepherd Road. While Melvin weaves around the bicyclists and auto-rickshaws, Abraham says, "I just want to visit with the son of one of my oldest friends. Bought him this nice bottle of brandy." Abraham pats the paper bag in his lap. "Very expensive. From France."

"Is it Yeksho?" Melvin asks. "I heard Yeksho is very good."

"Yeksho? Is that the name of a brandy?"

Melvin nods, his conviction wilting. "From France?"

Abraham brightens. "Oh! You mean this!" He pulls the bottle from the bag and points at the gold label that reads xo.

Heat rises to Melvin's cheeks, spreading around his collar.

"Honest mistake," says Abraham.

Disgusted with himself, Melvin almost fails to hear Abraham explain that the bottle is for a man with a fine taste in foreign liquors. "Poor Kuku. He hardly gets out of the house. Blind, you know."

Melvin focuses on the auto-rickshaw in front of him, which is presently attempting to forge its own lane in the gutter of space between two lorries. "Kuku? Kuku George?"

"Do you know him?"

Melvin glances at Abraham, who looks surprised. "I do . . . ," Melvin says, wanting to adhere to the general policy of secrecy where matters of marriage are concerned. He did not even tell Berchmans the day before, after the third beer had loosened his tongue. "I don't know him personally. . . ."

As Abraham directs, Melvin pulls up to the wrought-iron gate of the house, flung open so that he can ascend the steep driveway. Instead, he stalls at the gate.

"What is it?" Abraham asks. "Why aren't we moving?"

"If you don't mind too much," Melvin says carefully, "could you walk up the driveway and I wait down here?"

Abraham laughs. "But if I wanted to walk, I wouldn't have hired you."

Melvin wraps his fingers around the steering wheel; doing so steadies his voice. "I would prefer that Kuku George and his family not see me like this. As a driver. He has shown interest in my daughter—in Linno—and the families have not yet met. We are to meet next week. I am sure he already knows that I'm a driver, but this would be . . . a bad first impression."

"Kuku?" Abraham sits forward. "Kuku showed interest in your family?"

"In Linno, my eldest." Now Melvin's throat feels warm with shame. He knows very well how improbable the match must seem, as odd as a bottle of XO in a driver's hands. He neglected to consider such things when he married Gracie, whose family was also wealthier than his own. And he would come to regret it.

Abraham sits back, gazing out the window with a loose smile around his lips. "Well, that is wonderful news. You couldn't ask for a better family than Kuku's."

"I'm hoping it will work out. . . ."

"Why wouldn't it? Melvin, this is a chance you should not pass up. Their family is very God-fearing, very well off. I'm sure you know that." Melvin looks at the distant door frame of the house, which is all that is visible from this vantage. Passersby can see little of the property, hemmed in as it is by the gate and the pale stone wall.

Melvin relaxes a bit. He had assumed that confiding such a thing in Abraham would have led to laughter or disdain. "I know that the Georges are of a certain class, but if Linno likes him and he likes Linno . . . She can be stubborn, though."

"Oh, stubborn nothing. Every woman can be convinced by a big house." Abraham gets out of the car. "I'll be back in ten minutes. And I'll say I came by taxi."

KUKU AND ALICE receive Melvin and Linno on a sinister evening, a low flotilla of clouds beneath the full moon. Linno peers from under the roof of the auto-rickshaw as they go rattling up the driveway. The house stands noble and old, its cream stone faintly stained with moss. Its height surpasses the surrounding trees, a size that seems less than a blessing from this close, all those unlit rooms a reminder of the absent children and grandchildren, the generations who are not there to fill them.

Kuku and Alice are waiting on the front step. Linno notices Alice first, the way she stands like a man in her bland brown sari, feet apart, hands clasped behind her back. Her smile has a relaxing effect on Linno, who is then returned to a state of vague anxiety upon noting Kuku's hairstyle, a small and sturdy pompadour. His hair does not reflect well on either him or Alice, as she might have been the one to style it.

On the porch, names are passed around:

"Melvin? Kuku."

"Alice? Linno."

"Linno. Kuku."

With his eyes fixed somewhere on Linno's forehead, Kuku extends his hand for a handshake, a gesture that Linno rarely receives. She takes Kuku's right hand with her left and their hands go up and down twice, gently and awkwardly. If he is nervous, she cannot tell. At home, in a last-minute spasm of anxiety, she spent most of the morning trying to decide upon the flirtier of two salwars (the scalloped neckline versus the high, lacy collar) before remembering that her suitor would probably not be swayed by either.

LEAVING THEIR SHOES at the door, they sit around a slick table of blood red wood, a color that somehow amplifies the gravity of their meeting. A small forest of such trees must have been plundered to supply the matching sofas and armchairs, coffee table and side tables, where fake snapdragons are gathered into crystal vases. In keeping with tradition, the perennial framed portrait of Jesus hangs over the front doorway, flanked by pictures of Alice and Kuku's parents, immortalized in black and white before their hair had begun to gray.

Alice serves chai in fine china cups ribboned in gold, along with a tray of buttery biscuits arranged like lines of fallen dominos. Linno smooths the napkin on her knee, a fine, firm linen. She imagines that this is her table, and suddenly realizes that she has never owned anything that she could not lift herself.

At first, everyone takes turns tentatively sipping chai, never more than two sippers at once. She is drawn to the meticulous nature of Kuku's movements, how his hand passes over the cup before grasping the handle, perhaps to feel the heat in his palm. His ways speak to a quiet sensitivity, an inner Zen.

A Zen that does not last. Galvanized by the tea, Kuku turns into an avid conversationalist, though the only topic that seems to interest him is the U.S. visa process. He has heard of Anju from the *Malayala Manorama*, he says, and he possesses a wealth of knowledge about the route to U.S. citizenship.

"What kind of visa does she have now?" Kuku asks. When Melvin says a student visa, Kuku nods. "F-1 or J-1? There is a difference. You know that, don't you?"

His questions remind Linno of a typewriter's noise, clattering on and on until the end of the question, punctuated by a last inquisitive *ching*.

Alice, meanwhile, appears slightly uncomfortable, her smile taut as she continually urges everyone to eat more biscuits or take more tea. If this is an intersibling signal for Kuku to tone down his investigation, he seems not to notice.

"You must declare no intent to reside permanently," Kuku continues, "but the trick is to keep renewing. It is all very fascinating, this process, *allay?*"

Beneath the table, Linno slides a pen from her purse and, as quietly as possible, clicks the tip. It all makes sense now, the reason behind Kuku's interest to move the alliance along: Linno could be his one-way ticket to the States. A union of nations after all. Of course, Linno's intentions to marry Kuku were no less material. She begins doodling on the napkin, politely looking up from time to time.

"Anju told us she is going to contact a lawyer," Melvin says. "An immigration attorney."

"There are lawyers," Kuku says definitively, "who will not take their fees without winning the case."

Alice turns to Linno. "So are you studying still? Or are you working?"

In a fit of self-sabotage, Linno is about to explain her stunted academic career when Melvin steps in. "She is a painter."

Alice raises her eyebrows, genuinely interested. "A painter?"

"For advertisements," Linno says.

"You know the Princess Tailor Shoppe?" Melvin asks. "That painted window?"

"Hah yes! That? You did that?"

"Yes," Linno says. Alice nods slowly, with new appreciation. Linno wishes that Alice would look away so that she could go back to her napkin, where she has been inking the fins of an ornate fish.

"These days you can quickly get a relative visa, once you have your own," Kuku explains to no one in particular. He snaps his fingers to demonstrate the quickness of it all. For the first time, he turns his vague gaze on Linno. "That's good, isn't it?"

"For some people," Linno says.

Doubt flickers over Kuku's smile. "Which people? You wouldn't want to go?"

Melvin looks at her with slight amusement and fear for what she might say. The clink of Linno's cup against the saucer seems to echo.

"But why not?" Kuku asks, almost offended.

Linno hesitates. The only reason she ever really wanted to leave was so as not to be left alone. Instead of this, she says, "I heard that in the cities, you can no longer see the stars."

With a short laugh, Kuku says he hasn't seen the stars in years.

"Ha ha," Melvin says, as if reading his laugh aloud from a cue card.

Beneath the table, Linno twirls and twirls her pen until it falls to the floor and rolls toward Alice's chair. Alice retrieves the pen and hands it to Linno, but not without squinting at the scribbles on Linno's napkin, which Linno quickly covers with her hand.

THE AUTO-RICKSHAW LURCHES over the rutted roads, with Melvin and Linno jostling in the backseat, not a word between them. Across the sky, a sifting of grayish purple begins to darken, and the auto-rickshaw's single headlight gives the impression of tunneling through a black cave. It seems that Linno's own life is equally murky. There is nothing she can promise herself, fifty years from now, the way other girls do—*I want a house and two children, boy and girl*. For herself, she cannot see the husband or feel the rapturous weight of a baby in her arms. What does she want, then? Smooth, weighted paper. A new set of soft pencils. A room in which to draw. A window of time. She is no genius, but sometimes she entertains the thought of someone finding her sketchbook, paging through it to learn that she is more than what the limited light has thus far revealed.

Linno searches the inside of her purse. Only a comb and a folded handkerchief. The napkin. She left behind the napkin.

Melvin asks what is the matter. "Nothing," Linno says.

"Well, I am not going to force you into anything, if that is your worry."

Linno imagines Alice finding the napkin, showing it to Kuku. *We had her to our house, and this is how she thanked us? By doodling?*

"But if I were a woman," Melvin continues, "I would think he looks pretty good. Had a good head of hair on him, didn't he?"

"I suppose so."

"And he doesn't seem that blind either. I kept watching to see if he would pick up someone else's cup by accident, but he didn't. Not once. He always knew his cup. Berchmans told me that blind people have a very advanced sense of smell. Did you know that?"

"I don't think he could smell his own cup."

Taking her curtness as the early percolations of love, Melvin pats her on the back. "Give him time, *molay*. Give him a chance."

8.

*A*T SCHOOL, Anju imagines herself chugging along as if on a conveyor belt, from one destination to the next. In this way, time does not seem to pass. She forgets about Bird and the business card tucked into her assignment book, focused instead on making sense of the English class bulletin board, which displays a large cutout of a cannon on wheels, and in front of this, a dozen black cannonballs inscribed with names like MILTON and JOYCE and JAMES and CONRAD. Where homework is concerned, Anju attends to what must be done for the next day and the next, and much prefers vocab exercises to green card forms.

For some time now, her faith in the elliptical odyssey has been lessening. This country is a puzzle in which she will never quite fit, and if she stays here too long, her own country will become a puzzle as well. Yesterday, Ammachi informed her that St. John's Bakery would be gutted by the time she returned, to be replaced by a shoe shop. And though Anju always hated that bakery—they undercooked the fruitcake and always ran out of payasam—she grew depressed at the idea of changes taking place without her there to witness them. Of course, she knows that such erasures take place in every growing town, and newcomers arrive and settle without knowledge of the city's antique imperfections. But a town truly belongs to those who can see the stretch marks. A town belongs to those who are there to watch it change.

DURING THE NARROW POCKETS of time between classes, Fish leans against the locker adjacent to Anju's and talks about his literary heroes, none of whose names have appeared on the cannonballs. They perform at Brooklyn bars and cafés, dark, classy dens to which Fish gains entry by way of a false ID and a twenty-dollar bill if the bouncer gives him a look. "You could come, too, you know."

"I am not twenty-one," she says.

He looks at her wrist. "Where's your bandage?"

"My wrist is not paining me for now." In truth, the skin of her wrist had been growing paler than her hand, and she hadn't liked the contrast. Also, it was becoming increasingly annoying to have to borrow notes and balance her lunch tray on her left arm.

"Oh. Well anyway, about the ID, I'd get you a fake. I know tons of girls who could pass for you." He scratches the back of his neck. "Not that there's anyone like you exactly. Except you, of course. Obviously. Anyway."

No itch needs to be scratched for this long. She turns back to her locker. Lately, whenever Fish has said anything to her, his sentences have begun to trickle into sheepish, monosyllabic utterances.

There is something unnerving about his invitation, the ease with which she could cross over into a world of smoke and illegality. She imagines a roomful of Fishes, young and quietly furious, so many eyes like slow-burning stars. She feels a thrill in her stomach, a tiny well of warmth.

ONCE A WEEK, the English instructor is replaced by the creative writing instructor, and the students release a collective sigh. They are not expected to know dates or write essays or suffer pop quizzes. No one is forced to speak, only encouraged.

Mrs. Loignon, the teacher, says that her name means "onion" in

French. She is thin and onion-pale, with permanent crinkles around a mouth that is always working on a cough drop. She keeps an infinite supply in her purse, that fat, forlorn pouch of battered pleather, always spilling pens, empty Splenda packets, and once, in front of the whole class, a packet of Marlboro Reds. Swiftly, slightly shamed, Mrs. Loignon stuffed the Reds back inside, shocking proof of some cynicism beneath her perpetual cheer.

The class, as a whole, has an anesthetized quality. Using his thumbs, a boy meticulously flips his eyelid inside out. A girl paints her pinky nail with a black Sharpie. In the chair next to Anju's, another boy is drawing a cartoon of himself, in the margin of his notebook, a cannon growing from his crotch.

Mrs. Loignon begins by reading aloud the first stanza of Andrew Marvell's "To His Coy Mistress." She performs with melodramatic gusto, the book held to her chest like a palette, her free hand wildly painting the air with her words. Her reading makes it impossible, and unappealing, to imagine any kind of carnal persuasion intended by the poet.

When she reaches the second-to-last stanza, Mrs. Loignon looks at Anju. "Go for it," she says with a smile, as if bestowing Anju with a gift.

Anju wishes this gift came with a return receipt. She hates reading aloud. Her *w*'s sound like *v*'s. Her voice, stiffened into submission, takes on the lilt of nursery rhymes.

> *Let us roll all owver strength and* all
> *Owver sweetness up into vun* ball,
> *And tear owver pleasures vith rough* strife
> *Through the i-run gates of* life . . .

After Anju finishes the last stanza, Mrs. Loignon asks what the speaker is proposing. In response, a mere shifting, a few pairs of eyes looking up.

"He's proposing to bone his coy mistress," says the cannon cartoonist.

Mrs. Loignon glares at him with predatorial stillness until he mutters an apology. She employs the silent reprimand whenever someone has broken the cardinal rule, the only rule, of creative writing class: *This is a safe space.* Anju hardly understands the rule, as being called upon to read aloud, in her opinion, creates an atmosphere of utmost threat.

Toward the end of class, Mrs. Loignon collects the student poems assigned from last week and selects a few at random to read aloud. She never reveals the name of the poet, though no one in the room has mastered the art of the poker face. The poet wears one of two masks: stunned, vacantly staring into his binder, praying for the end; or the twitchy smirk, the fidgety hand, quick to claim the page as her own.

Anju can hardly tell what is good or bad. She thinks only in terms of Pass or No Pass. Fish has told her that no one fails this class, but to write of feelings? To be given no other instruction? Facing the blank page, she is a raft at sea. She needs sails, a life jacket, an anchor, and a direction.

So far, she has been recopying the literature poems and substituting synonyms from a thesaurus ("perambulate" instead of "walk," for example; "mechanism for transport" rather than "chariot"). Her creations sound much more complicated, and therefore artistic, than the current selection from which Mrs. Loignon is reading aloud, entitled "Vegetarian's Complaint":

> *O Trout, Tilapia, all ye watery prey,*
> *No one is spared from Fish Patty Day.*
> *Battered, fried beyond compare,*
> *A Fish is not meant to be shaped like a square.*

Mrs. Loignon pauses before reading aloud the next poem. Her eyebrows rise as she scans the lines, and at the end she utters a satisfied *Mmmm.*

" 'Meditations on a Dark-Eyed Girl.' "

While Mrs. Loignon reads, Anju watches Fish out of the corner of her eye. His lips are moving just barely, perhaps along with the words though she cannot tell. His eyes are intent on the page, his pattering fingers claiming the poem as his own.

> *. . . and shadows of thinning trees*
> *like writing on the wall*
> *Tell how seasons, like people, will pass.*
>
> *But it's when I sleep that time goes still*
> *With the moon as witness at the windowsill.*
> *So whatever I have kissed in dreams*
> *I'll keep at least in part.*

The words rush a foreign warmth to her cheeks. The poem pins her to her chair. Not for all the A-pluses in the world would she turn her head, just then, to meet Fish's gaze, but she does notice the cannon cartoonist vengefully footnoting his textbook: *I wouldn't fuck Loignon with a stolen dick.*

WHEN ANJU WAS TWELVE, she came quite close to having a boyfriend.

In school, the word used for a girlfriend or boyfriend was "item." Her almost-item's name was Sri Ram. Theirs was a doomed affair, not only because Sri Ram was Hindu, but also because a girl who was rumored to be kissing a boy could just as well flush her reputation down the commode and plan for a life of parentally enforced celibacy.

They did not exchange kisses, but love notes.

His first, smuggled into her hand on the morning of the first day of school: "I like your skirt. Will you be my item?"

Because everyone wore uniforms, Anju had not been impressed by his compliment. He was a scrawny, sleepy fellow, seemingly incapable of lifting anything other than his own satchel, but the brazenness of the note charmed her. New to the class, she felt invincibly impulsive and wrote on the back of his note:

"Would you convert?"

She had no hopes that he would convert, certainly not on account of a gray skirt, but she had thought the rhyme rather clever. And if he liked her at all, it had to be for her cleverness, as she had little else in her corner.

Before class began, Anju stuck the note in her pocket, her hands placed atop her math notebook, her knees bouncing beneath the table. Linno, sitting next to her, told her to stop shaking the bench. Anju was doubly anxious, as it was her first day in Linno's math class, two years beyond her own peers. The classroom was nearly identical to her old one, the painted walls molting in patches, the buckling wooden floor, the rows of long tables and benches that made it difficult to rise from the desk in a ladylike way. But now, Anju was anxious for different reasons altogether, aware of a pair of eyes at the rear of the room, pressing into her back.

Sister Savio took roll call. *Present, Sister . . . Present, Sister . . .* Anju was focused on the present in her pocket.

"And Linno Vallara," Sister Savio said. "Next time sit in the middle of the bench. You've gotten so big you might tip the whole thing over."

Anju's knees stopped. Her heart seemed to delay between beats.

Laughter spilled from the back of the room to the front, and out of that chorus she could distinguish the timid chortle of Sri Ram.

For the rest of class, she pictured herself choking Sister Savio with her eyeglass chain. Sri Ram she would kick between the legs, as this region, to her limited knowledge, would summon the greatest amount of pain. But neither image brought peace because she felt more than rage. She was shamed by her own shame, made worse later that day when Linno told their father that she would not return to school. Anju's first day would be Linno's last.

Several days later, after recess, Anju laid a cushion of cow dung on Sister Savio's seat, leaving Sister Savio with a bull's-eye on her rear for most of the day. Unfortunately, Anju had not washed her hands with enough soap, and after sniffing each student's hands, the headmaster ordered her to stay after school. Anju received a paddling that prevented her from sitting properly for days, her rear marked far more severely than that of Sister Savio.

And like a true amateur in the art of love, Anju left Sri Ram's note in the pocket of the very skirt that had wooed him. One minute Anju was standing at the kitchen table, adding fractions, and the next minute Linno's open palm was on the corner of her book. In it: the crumpled piece of paper.

"Are you crazy?" Linno scolded her, though her eyes were ravenous for details. In the midst of laundry, she had discovered a scandal. "What is this? Who are you trying to convert?"

Anju looked at the crumple, which had once held such sweat and hope. She thought of Sri Ram, who had reportedly passed the exact same note to five different girls in the random manner of a fern casting spores into the breeze. Sri Ram had stopped talking to Anju as soon as he realized that she and Linno shared a last name. She thought of the seat next to her, where Linno used to sit, unoccupied for the past three days. Its emptiness—impossible to admit aloud—was a comfort.

But for Linno, Anju conjured a story of how Sri Ram had fallen madly in love with her, how he had wanted to convert her to Hinduism, how she had refused him, citing the First Commandment, and had traipsed away in her gray skirt, leaving him with eyes wet and tortured. And as with all her little fictions, the deeper she mined the details (her braids: swinging; his lower lip: trembling), the more the melodrama gained a truth in which she could believe.

9.

$\mathscr{A}$ S DOES EVERY SATURDAY MORNING, this one begins with a heap of warm croissants; coffee; baguettes; blueberry preserves and violet jam; wedges of Havarti, Gouda, and Brie; and a bowl of shiny, warmed olives. Mr. Solanki and Anju sit at the breakfast table, he behind his *Wall Street Journal,* she pretending to read an unfunny comic strip. Mr. Solanki chews noisily on a croissant, a smattering of flakes along his striped tie. It is as though nothing has changed from one morning to another, the previous day part of some fever dream. She hardly has the appetite for more than half a croissant, though she eats the whole out of courtesy. She might fast the whole weekend, internally grazing on a singular message:

She is loved.

Anju remembers nothing else from Fish's poem. Grammatically and practically, the actual subject who loves the object—she being the object!—is not the most important detail. That there exists someone who can love her does much to convince her that she is capable of loving that someone back.

Her insides tremble with the weight of it.

It seems that Anju is not the only one with a revelation. Mrs. Solanki usually sleeps through Saturday breakfast, but this morning she hurtles down the winding staircase in her pajamas, her robes gusting out behind her like the cape of a satin-clad superhero. She stops at the edge of the table, pauses for effect and breath. Anju has never seen her without a minimal layer of cosmetics so her chapped lips and stunted lashes add to the sense of alarm.

"Rohit," Mrs. Solanki says, "is coming for dinner."

Mr. Solanki stops chewing but does not swallow. "When?"

"Tonight. He just called."

"I thought he wasn't returning from Maine until next week."

"He is coming back early," Mrs. Solanki says. "He said he has something to tell us."

"That means he's bringing the camera. He's going to make a big show, I know it. Tell him to leave that thing at home."

"I tried."

"He should not suprise us on camera, it's not fair." Like a child refusing his vegetables, Mr. Solanki has both fists on the table. His scorn turns to vexation as he looks at his plate, as if trying to predict Rohit's announcement from the constellation of crumbs. Anju shifts in her seat, wondering if she should leave.

Mrs. Solanki, suddenly noticing her, smiles brightly. "Rohit just happens to film things in his life. Sort of like home videos." She scoops bread crumbs into her cupped palm. "It is his hobby, a very important hobby."

From the moment Mrs. Solanki begins scooping bread crumbs, the household cleaning continues without pause. An hour later, two Colombian cleaning ladies arrive, armed with mops, pails, and yellow rubber gloves. They scrub, they spray, they polish, they shimmy a feathered stick along the contours of the sculptures and vases. Mrs. Solanki divides her time between watching them and speaking on the phone, ordering a vanilla bean cheesecake to be picked up later in the day.

The more Mrs. Solanki watches the Colombian ladies, the more she fidgets until she can stand back no longer, overcome with the need to join them on hands and knees.

"But this is not *clean*," Mrs. Solanki says, reaching under the TV stand, triumphantly surfacing with a spidery wad of her own black hair. *"No clean,"* she enunciates, almost attempting a Spanish accent. The women continue to scrub at the exact same rate, back-forth, back-forth, as if chained to each other.

WITH THE APARTMENT under siege by mopping solvents, Anju is only too glad to escape.

Overnight, it seems, rows of pumpkins and butternut squash have appeared beneath the awning of the corner deli. Coolly, September is sliding into October, green leaves tipped in a yellow that portends the end of hot, lazy days.

What does this mean to Anju? That a new stylish coat is in order, especially if she is to visit Fish at his next show. Mrs. Solanki recommended a department store within walking distance, one that takes up half a block. Surely it will provide Anju with a better option than the lumpen gray thing she is currently wearing, given to her by Ammachi. "Jilu wore this when she came from Canada," Ammachi said, pulling the bloated coat from a trunk that smelled of mildew and baby powder.

Luckily for Anju, Jilu had forgotten to take it back. Turning the coat inside out, Ammachi showed Anju a number of secret inner pockets, an intricate cavern of storage systems, where one could keep various foodstuffs in case of apocalyptic disaster. "Hah!" Ammachi said triumphantly, upon unzipping a pocket and discovering an antiquated box of Sunkist raisins.

INSIDE THE DEPARTMENT STORE, Anju runs her hands over the racks of coats. She lifts one from its hanger, something long with mannish shoulders, impossibly heavy and teal blue. Wearing it is like carrying the spoils of a tiger hunt on one's back, and even the lighter coats bear a padded prosthesis on each shoulder.

"Removable!" the clerk says, reaching into the lining and surfacing with two cutlets the color of uncooked chicken. The clerk is young and heavily rouged, with man shoulders of her own. At first, she was cautious with Anju, until Anju told her that she lived nearby, at the Monarch. Immediately, the clerk warmed to her and began cracking desperate jokes, making it clear that she works on commission.

She puts Anju's cutlets on top of her own shoulders. "And if I can't use 'em here"—she puts the cutlets against her smallish chest—"I can always use 'em here."

The clerk throws her head back, laughs, like they are old friends.

Anju throws her head back, laughs, achieves a crick in her neck.

Five minutes later, Anju has retreated from the coat section, after hearing the price of the coat, which is half the price of her plane ticket from India.

She passes the makeup counters with their palettes of pinks and lavenders, past the jewel-colored bottles of perfume on shelves of glass. Well-dressed women offer spritzes from designer bottles, happily chirping the lacy names of scents like Beyond Heaven or Eau de Désir. Crossing through a patchouli and lilac fog, Anju pauses before the sunglasses rack, stopped by a familiar voice whose name she cannot place. "Anju Mol! Eh, Anju!" In the dark reflections of several lenses, several tiny Birds are moving toward her. She whirls around, her spirit lifting in spite of her guilt. In all this time, Anju has not called her. Is it possible that Bird volunteers here too?

Bird seems less excited to see Anju. Her mouth is pursed, her hands patting her head kerchief to make sure it is still in place. "Where have you been?" Bird demands in Malayalam.

"I was meaning to call," Anju lies. For a brief, ridiculous moment, she imagines telling Bird about her newfound love. "I've been so busy with school. . . ."

Bird groans at the inanity of this answer. "Every day I watch for you, but you never come. I told Mr. Tandon you were coming, but you never did. You think some immigration fairy will leave a green card under your pillow?"

Anju shakes her head.

Bird pulls a date book from her bag and flips to an open page. "How is next Monday?"

"But what is the cost?"

"No cost to meet!" Bird nearly cries her answer, so pained is she by this degree of procrastination. "I will tell him you are coming at four p.m. Come straight from school."

After jotting down the date and time of the meeting, Bird claps the book shut and waits for Anju to record the same. Anju takes down the information on the back of a perfume sample, all the while wondering how much she should owe this meeting to chance. This city can likely keep friends apart for years, such is its density, its speed. But now, in the space of two weeks, Anju and Bird are again brought face-to-face.

By the time Anju pockets the perfume sample, Bird appears to have calmed a bit. Light, dull piano music wafts around them. "You should come to my house too," Bird says abruptly. "Come and have tea. Okay?"

Anju hesitates. She is familiar with the warm, bossy aura of aunties back home, but to find it here is strange, and welcoming.

"Okay," Anju says.

"Good." From a nearby counter, Bird takes a stack of perfume samples and drops them into her purse. "This way I can wear a different perfume every month."

Her lesson, delivered unapologetically, puts Anju at ease. She asks how Bird came to find her here.

"I called the number you gave me. Said I was an old friend of yours. That Mrs. Solanki, she said you would be here."

Anju nods, slightly surprised and pleased at Bird's decision that they are already old friends.

IN THE EVENING, Mr. Solanki wears a candy pink tie and Mrs. Solanki wears a sweater of the same color, as if matching renders them a united front against whatever news Rohit will bring. Anju scratches at the brassiere that holds her shoulder cutlets in place. At the store, she told herself that she was doing a service to the coat from which she stole the cutlets, and unless the future owner of the coat possessed concave shoulders, the owner would be grateful. Anju has decided to give the cutlets a test run today, to see if they might be wearable on Monday, but can one be allergic to ill-placed cutlets? Or perhaps the irritation is due to the Calvin Klein Obsession sample that she smeared around her collarbones, one from a whole deck of cards that she stuffed into her pocket.

Her conversation with Bird continues to bother her as well. Bird was right to scold her. All this time, Anju has been selfish, ignoring her original intentions and the family whose future she meant to shape. And why? Because of homesickness—a child's excuse. And like a child, she needed to be rebuked, to have someone jog her sense of ambition.

Also, she has begun to think that there may be certain perks to the elliptical odyssey due to the many miles between home and here. The inspiration for her newfound optimism: Sheldon Fischer.

As a potential husband for Anju, Fish has two strikes against him, being both white and Jewish. No doubt Melvin would never speak to Anju again if, back in Kumarakom, she ran off with either. She knows of only a few Jews in Kerala, descended from those who migrated thousands of years ago from Palestine, fleeing persecution. Before most left for Israel, these Jews found their next-best resting place in Kerala, a land where many religious enclaves existed with little commingling, each enclave confident in its proximity to God. Diversity was fine as long as each clung to his own.

But if she were to agree to a life of here and there, if she were to accept the breadwinning role of the family, could she not demand a bit of romantic autonomy in return?

Wherever Bird came from, she is a blessing, a reminder of greater possibility. Next week, accompanied by Mrs. Solanki, Anju will keep her appointment with Mr. Tandon.

MRS. SOLANKI OPENS the front door while simultaneously using it as a shield, peering around the edge. Instead of hello, her first words are a dismayed, "Oh, Rohit."

Rohit steps into the foyer with a large video camera where his head should be, or so it seems from Anju's distance. The camera is strapped to his hand, its small screen flipped out to one side like a blunted wing. Immediately, Anju is impressed with his sparse safari style, a khaki vest with pieces of equipment jutting from the pockets, scuffed sneakers, a single duffel bag which he drops by the doorway.

Mr. Solanki smooths his tie. "Rohit, *beta,* can't we wait until after dinner for filming?"

"Dad," Rohit says, warmly ignoring his father's question. He holds the camera away from his body, its red light still solid, as he hugs his father with his free arm. He does the same for his mother, adding a noisy kiss on the cheek.

"And this must be the exchange student," Rohit says, turning his lens on Anju. She stands absolutely still, feet together, hands at her sides.

"I'm Rohit." He extends his hand, which she does not take, tensed and frozen, until he reassures her that he is not taking a still photograph. "You can move or whatever you want. Just be yourself."

AT DINNER, Anju marvels at the napkins, which have been contorted by the Colombians into the shapes of swans. They float on ponds of porcelain plates which Anju has never before seen, all of them gold-leafed and gleaming. Mrs. Solanki first fills Rohit's plate with a colorful salad, all reds and yellows with a drizzle of dressing, but he partakes rarely, spending most of his time swinging his camera from face to face as the conversation skids along. Apparently, Rohit has filmed family scenes before, such as last year's Christmas dinner and a few days in February, after his mother underwent a hysterectomy. (Mrs. Solanki seems irritated by this disclosure.) Still, no one is quite able to follow Rohit's directive to "act normal," not even Rohit, who sometimes asks his parents to repeat themselves: "I didn't catch that. One more time, please?"

"I said," Mr. Solanki sighs, "that Dr. Ummat's daughter got into medical school."

Rohit tinkers with the focus ring on his camera. Anju is fascinated by the camera and his ease with it, all the buttons and the lenses and the confidence required to fiddle with them. "So what are you saying, Dad? You're saying you wish I had gone to med school?"

"I did not say that."

"Then why'd you have to mention that Nirmal's going to med school?"

"You asked how she was doing."

"Yeah, but I asked about Nirmal the person, not Nirmal the doctor."

Mr. Solanki stabs a cherry tomato with his fork. "I do not know about Nirmal the whatever. That you can ask Dr. Ummat yourself."

Mrs. Solanki grabs Rohit's wrist. "You know who Anju has for chemistry? Mr. Haskell, remember him? He loved you."

Rohit swings his camera over, and Mrs. Solanki leans back in her seat a little, lacing her fingers over her plate with an air of false nonchalance. He pans over to Anju, who looks at the lens with no small degree of distrust. Videos do not allow for preparation. Only once has she seen herself on television, in the wedding video of a distant cousin wherein Anju glanced over her shoulder and then unsuccessfully attempted to stuff a gulab jamun the size of a Ping-Pong ball into her mouth.

"Why are you doing this shooting?" she asks.

"It's for my current film."

"Yes, Mrs. Solanki said you are making home videos?"

Mrs. Solanki stares at her greens, chewing industriously. Rohit turns his camera onto his father, then zooms in on the glass of wine that Mr. Solanki is refilling. Glancing at the camera, Mr. Solanki stops pouring and puts the bottle aside.

Rohit sits the camera next to his plate, though the red light remains on, its eerie surveillance apparently nonexistent to him, except for the moments when he looks into the viewfinder and jimmies a ring on the lens. In the form of a well-rehearsed monologue, he explains to Anju that he first caught the film bug in the late eighties, when he borrowed his father's Sony Mavica to re-create historical events like the assassination of Abraham Lincoln and the disappearance of Amelia Earhart, as told with G.I. Joe figurines. When he arrived at Princeton, he returned to filmmaking, and now he is in the thick of another project, his most ambitious to date, a personal documentary that he started on the day he decided to take an indefinite hiatus from school.

"What's it about?" Rohit asks, intercepting a question that Anju had not posed. He bends over the camera and zooms in on Anju. His concentration is that of a scientist at a microscope, his focus broken only when he looks up at her. "I don't know yet. You never know until you're in the edit room. Loosely, it's about my experiences as a second-generation brown man in a post-9/11 America.

"But since we're on the topic . . ." He picks up his camera, adjusts the focus ring, and scoots a candelabra closer to his father's plate. "This footage will be kind of underexposed, but whatever; I'll deal with it in post."

Rohit clears his throat. "Mom and Dad, I have something to tell you."

Mr. Solanki presses both hands to the table, his head slightly bowed, ready to receive the weight of this news. From beneath his well-plucked brows, he looks at his son with something between fear and stern courage.

"Guys," Rohit says. "I'm not going to be a doctor. I'm going to be a filmmaker."

Anju can hear the breath drawing in and out of Mr. Solanki's nose, shuddering the candle flame near his plate.

"That's it?" Mr. Solanki says.

Rohit says that's it.

Mr. Solanki looks at Mrs. Solanki. "I thought he was going to say that he's a gay."

"I thought so too." Glancing at the camera, Mrs. Solanki adds: "It's *gay*, Varun. Not *a* gay."

"Wait, wait." Rohit seems incapable of deciding which parent to focus on. "You thought I was gay? Why? I mean, what would make you think that?"

"Don't be angry," Mr. Solanki says.

"I'm not; I just find it a little shocking, or weird, that my own father doesn't know me."

"Your mother too. And we didn't even discuss it!" Mr. Solanki looks at Mrs. Solanki with amused wonder.

By this point, Rohit is scowling at his father, the camera listing to one side.

Mrs. Solanki squeezes her son's shoulder. "Oh Rohit, it's just that you said you had this big announcement, and you are a young single man, always talking about self-discovery and exploration and slim-fitting pants. . . ."

"Can you guys just respond to what I said? That I'm going to be a filmmaker?"

"I work in television, darling," Mrs. Solanki says. "I have been in the entertainment industry for fifteen years. If you wanted to rebel, you should've become a doctor."

"So is that what you want?"

Mr. Solanki refreshes his glass of wine and looks at Rohit, who is looking into the camera. "Gay director, straight director, direct traffic for all I care. This is not a revolution, Rohit, what you are doing. Why don't you finish this film? Or finish a degree? Finish anything. That would be a revolution."

Rohit's expression seems to gather in turmoil, his forehead wrinkling as he squints into the camera, the storm of his thoughts gathering up until he cries out, "Oh man, I fucked up the focus! It's on auto. Wait, Dad, can you say that again? That was a great line, that thing about revolution."

THE DINNER NEVER QUITE recovers its pleasant veneer, as both Mr. and Mrs. Solanki withdraw into lengthy silences and one-word answers to Rohit's questions. Darting looks around the dinner table, Anju presses the tines of her fork into a pillow of spinach ravioli. She is relieved when Rohit, with a sigh of surrender, finally turns the camera off.

There is no discussion that this family will not touch, no question unposed, no secret kept. Yet for all their honesty, all these freedoms of speech, neither Rohit nor his parents seem to know what to make of one another. They eat like strangers on a plane, eyes fastened to their plates.

Whether this is better or worse than her own family, Anju cannot tell. Among her family, the subject of Romantic Love, for example, is never addressed, like a god who could cause retinal damage if stared at directly. Best to observe R.L. indirectly, as depicted in films or television shows. Still it would be nice, Anju thinks, to confide certain thrills and anxieties in one's own sister. Even if they were on speaking terms, Anju would never tell Linno that someone had penned her a poem, nor that this same someone will be waiting by her locker tomorrow, expecting an answer.

MONDAY MORNING, Anju steps delicately from class to class. She watches herself cycle through the functions of daily life while harboring epic feelings, as expressed in centuries of poetry and painting. In love, she swabs her throat with Obsession. In love, she drinks from the water fountain. In love, she puckers her Vaselined lips at the spotty bathroom mirror where in the corner someone has written in red lipstick: THIS IS WHAT A FEMINIST LOOKS LIKE. She admires the fiery hue of the lipstick, wishes she had some of her own. Her ponytail droops and her breasts are lopsided from the cutlets, but she is loved for the sum of her imperfect parts.

By the middle of the day, she still has not seen Fish.

In math class, while proving the congruency of vertical angles, she deduces that shyness and sensitivity must be vital to poets. Men who regularly capture hearts have no need of writing down their intentions; they simply act on them. But men who pen poems do so to test the water, to work up a lather of emotion where there might not be any.

She only wishes that Fish could retire his sensitivity at will and show up at her locker with an aggressive stride, a gleam of want in his eye. Though having little to no other experience with being pursued, Anju does recall that when her father wanted a job, he wooed the employer with charm, ambition, punctuality, and a freshly pressed shirt. Sometimes none of these worked, but at least he failed heroically.

ON HER WAY TO LUNCH, Anju finds Fish in the Fine Arts Wing, staring at Linno's paintings. His arms are crossed, and when he turns to her, his expression is much calmer than expected.

He says hey.

She says hey.

He asks her what is on the cafeteria menu, a question that, Anju has learned, is the student equivalent to asking about the weather, a query posed merely to fill the time. Pork fried egg rolls. Strawberry fro yo.

She thought that she would begin the conversation by talking about his poem. She planned to explain how stunned she was by his honesty, offered undistilled to a roomful of strangers and friends, and the way his eyes, after Mrs. Loignon finished reading, hid nothing. Even in dreams, she was never so brave.

But he heads her off. An edge to his voice, he says: "Well, Saturday night sucked."

And then, to her dismay, he launches into a tirade against his mother, how she showed up at Solomon's Porch and went sniffing around for a spliff from which Fish had partaken, sure, but did not possess, and all because of this, his mother dragged him out like the goddamn SWAT team. Not only this, but the bouncer confiscated his ID. Racism at work, Fish says, or if not racism, then ageism. He is already penning a poem called "Schisms." Nodding, nodding, she feels her epic moment sliding away from her, the window of confession growing narrow, the clock run down by his aggressive babble. Not once does he glance at her propped-up bust or take a whiff of her Obsession. It is possible, she supposes, for a heroine to wrest control of her love scene, but she does not know the right words, at least none that belong in this era. All the words she knows belong to Marvell or Herrick or *Roget's Thesaurus,* all florid declarations and complex phonetics. What she wants is a quick route to intimacy, a few seismic words to close the gap between them, to make him know her completely. Her insides are coiled with the potential energy of revelation, which is why, when he sighs and glances at the paintings, when he says that by the way he likes her work, she says:

"They are not mine."

He looks at her, then squints at the card below the paintings. "Is there another Anju Melvin?"

This is not the conversation for which she planned. She surprises herself with the words she utters. "I have to tell you something."

Such intimacy in the lowered voice. Fish leans in.

"I have an older sister. When she was small, she had an accident."

Anju has never heard these words from her own mouth. They sound simple, the beginnings of a tragic fairy tale to which everyone back home has already written the end. There is fear in speaking of tragedy, as if doing so might invoke its return.

But now, speaking feels frighteningly freeing, one sentence unraveling the next as she tells him of everything until the day she stepped on the plane. How she used to feign studying while watching Linno draw. How her father made Linno the sketchbook for her seventeenth birthday, and how in a moment of desperation, years later, Anju lunged for it.

She goes on and on, while mashed potatoes and pork rolls are being consumed en masse. Every word keeps Fish in place as he listens, rapt, to the well-kept corners of her heart.

10.

LINNO WAKES TO FACE Ammachi on the adjacent pillow. Without support from her dentures, Ammachi's cheeks have sunken into hollows, and her breath comes and goes in a chainsaw snore. In Ammachi's face, Linno sees her own reflection fifty years from now, clinging to a pillow and little else.

Ammachi's eyes flutter open. She smacks her lips as if trying to remember a sweet taste.

"Mai," Linno says. "I don't think it will work."

"What work?" Ammachi mumbles, already settling back into sleep.

"With Kuku."

At the name, Ammachi blinks herself awake. "You want to what with Kuku?"

"I don't want anything with Kuku."

Ammachi raises herself on an elbow. "But why?"

Ammachi's questions follow Linno for the rest of the day. "If not Kuku, then who?" Ammachi will be satisfied only if Linno reveals that Kuku is a former convict or suffers from a brain-stunting syndrome. Neither of these excuses being true, Linno's reason—"I can't explain it"—continually leads Ammachi to ask with increasing impatience, "Explain what?"

Several days have passed since the evening of Linno and Kuku's first meeting, and not once has Linno thought fondly of meeting again. She cannot blame her refusal on his lust for the immigrant visa and neither is his blindness all that troubling, as he seems to function with little help. But during the drive home, when Melvin told her to give Kuku time, to give Kuku a chance, Linno could not muster the slightest hope. Her husband, should she accept him, led her to feel nothing at all, and this seems reason enough to say no.

How to explain this to a woman who was betrothed at thirteen?

So Linno explains nothing. She issues a final statement, Not Interested, and goes on with her work, while Ammachi grumbles off to her room, reciting a verse about humility. In the meantime, Linno gathers the mung beans she scattered over a towel last night, sprinkled with water, so that by morning they have sprouted tiny shoots like piglet tails. Melvin loves to snack on the mung beans, but have they run out? Should she buy more? It is easy losing oneself in these tiny sorts of questions, immune to larger ones.

BY WORD OF MOUTH, an unfailing form of currency in these parts, Linno is hired to paint her largest window yet, at Ninan's Sanitations Store, a purveyor of toilets and sinks.

Mr. Ninan maps the blank window with his hands, showing Linno exactly what he wants and where. He requests a soft-lipped nymph with peachy skin, slender in the waist, a sinuous black braid over her shoulder, a flirty twinkle to her eye, and below this, simply: NINAN'S.

"Maybe we should include a faucet?" Linno suggests. "Maybe the woman could gesture to the faucet?"

Ninan looks at her impatiently, tweaking the tip of his waxed mustache. He has a singular vision, and that vision is curvy, flirty, and NINAN'S.

Linno begins the painting early in the morning, the mist circling her softly while a cuckoo bird sends out its dawning call. She chalks the same face she has done time and again, the supple cheeks, the flaring lashes. The night before, she imagined that her artistic reputation would spread across the state, the country even, and by the time Anju returned, Linno's signature would hover in the corners of countless billboards, reducing the red sketchbook to a mere relic of her talents. But Ninan's demands deflate her dream, reminding her that this is a business, not art, and in business, success must be replicated rather than imagined anew. Her customers privilege predictability over creativity, and in the rendering of women, clients like Ninan believe that there is no such thing as unique beauty. A woman is either beautiful or forgettable.

Linno and Anju belong somewhere in the latter category, Anju drawing more from her mother's features, Linno taking from her father's nose. Still, they are similar enough so that when Linno looks in a mirror and blurs her vision, she can almost see her sister looking back.

But today, instead of seeing her own sister in the window's reflection, Linno sees Kuku's sister crossing the street. Linno freezes, hoping that a state of absolute stillness will throw Alice off her scent, but noting Alice's quickening pace, Linno prepares herself.

"Linno!" Alice cries out.

Linno turns and feigns shocked joy.

"I thought it was you!" Alice says. She is wearing a mauve sari, as plain as the one she wore at their first meeting, a hefty purse at her hip. If she harbors any resentment, she does not show it, and seems elated over this encounter. Alice glances up at the window. "Another job?"

"Yes, Ninan's. They sell toilets. And sinks."

The conversation lulls, allowing a window for good-byes, but Alice lingers. "I've been looking for you. I thought about coming to your house, but I didn't want your father to get the wrong impression."

Linno steels herself against the oncoming argument, that Kuku would make a good husband, that Linno would be a fool to ignore him. If Linno is so perfect for Kuku, where is he to tell her so? Linno feels her cheeks growing hot as her mouth takes the shape of a polite but firm no.

Alice is rooting through her bag until finally she withdraws Linno's napkin. She holds out the side with the fish. "You did this over tea, didn't you?"

Linno's resolve plummets. She tries to laugh and apologize, muttering about nervous habits.

"And you designed it yourself?" Alice asks.

Weakly, Linno nods.

Alice nods.

Linno wonders if she should hold out her hand to take the napkin, but something about the grave wonder with which Alice is studying the fish, biting her lower lip, makes Linno wait for her to speak.

Finally Alice looks up and asks, "Can you do it again?"

OVER LUNCH at Leela Café, Alice unfolds her tragedies, one by one, beginning with her husband, Reji. In life, he was the owner of Eastern Invites, an invitation business that specialized in wedding cards, mostly of the Hindu, Muslim, and Christian variety. Seventy years before, his grandfather had started the business, at a time when the bride's family still made personal visits to invite each guest to the impending event. Reji's grandfather took over an old-fashioned printing press left behind by the British, and cranking the handle late into the night, he pushed his small community into a new era of invitations. Over time, the invitations grew gaudier and gilded, even for those who could barely afford them. For a while, with Reji at the prow, business thrived. He and Alice bought a smaller version of the family home just ten miles away, and even a cobalt blue Maruti.

Everything was fine until two years before, when Reji began acting strangely, coming home later from work with poor excuses. He bought her an expensive turquoise bottle of perfume for no reason in particular; this from a man who bought her gifts on exactly two days per year—her birthday and their anniversary. Alice became convinced that he was having an affair. "It happens," her aunts said, shrugging cryptically, and advised her to wait it out. Like rain, it would pass.

Before Alice could investigate the possibility of other women, Reji died on the job. There are few safety hazards in the invitation business, unless one brings the safety hazards into the building, as in Reji's case— a length of rope knotted from a ceiling beam. The sweeping lady found him the next morning, his tongue fat and pink between his teeth.

From wife to widow, overnight. Alice sat at the head of his open casket as friends and relatives trudged up and down the driveway. With outward despair and longing, she looked on his body, though her thoughts were mostly congratulatory to the makeup artist, who had somehow erased the broken bluish capillaries that had spidered at Reji's temples. Drained of fluids, cotton corked up his nose, he was already a ghost.

A few days later, she heard a radio personality explain why the sui-cide rate in Kerala was so high. *"This is the paradox: in a region of such excellent educational standards, we see high unemployment, lack of social mobility, and incomplete families due to fathers or mothers working else-where. These conditions have an extremely negative effect on Malayali soci-ety, which values the concepts of honor and pride, so when this honor is made vulnerable, suicide appears to be the only option."* She flicked off the power switch with such force that the radio fell onto its back. What honor had Reji lost? And didn't they share the same honor? Was she to follow him into the flame? No thank you. This was 2001. The other day, she had climbed onto a bus to find a thick-armed woman behind the steering wheel. When Alice paused to stare at her, the driver said, "On or off?" and thrilled by her authority, Alice hurried down the aisle to a window seat.

Her inner rally died down when she learned that Eastern Invites was falling apart. Nights she spent poring over wrinkled, swollen ledgers, dragging her finger across the lines of falling numbers. Loss, loss, loss, finally punctuated by human loss. New invitation businesses had sprung up across India. Most of them were doing a great proportion of mer-chandising on the Internet, catering to the masses of migrated Indians who held fast to their fancy scrolled invitations and stone-studded envelopes, even when their children were marrying white or Chinese or Jewish or atheist. Indian invitations were in high demand. The market was going global, the globe was going digital, and Eastern Invites was going nowhere. She remembered Reji's ridiculous belief in the loyalty of customers who would continue doing business with him out of guilt, if nothing else. "What kind of guilt travels across countries?" she had argued. "They might not see you for years. Why should they be loyal, then?"

"Relax," said Reji, with the blind smile of the eternally faithful.

There were other failures as well, like the multicolor printing machine that had broken long ago, leaving the necessary parts, from Germany, never to be replaced. At the time, Reji happily lost himself in the manual labor of screen printing, which accounted for only a third of their sales. He loved the fresh chemical smell of the ink, the pressing of joyful announcements onto a piece of textured paper. But while other shops employed whole R&D departments to produce a new crop of designs each month, Reji's invitations remained the same.

Output slowed, business stalled. And there was the loan that was never repaid. And the rent that was two months past due. And the employee who had been steadily siphoning money until his recent departure. This must have been what finally tore Reji's glossy belief in loyalty. Alice pictured a boy in the back of a train, gazing out the window at the passing scenery, fanning himself with a sheaf of bills, in blissful oblivion. That image left her with a recurring dream for months after Reji's passing: Reji by the train window, fanning himself with the sheaf of bills, her beside him, sharing the moneyed breeze.

ALL THIS, even the dream, Alice relates while tearing off pieces of idli without a hint of discomfort. Linno feels smothered with someone else's secrets, an unpleasant experience, much in the same way that a stranger's body odor always smells far more repulsive than one's own. In Linno's home, and in the home of every other person she knows, families are stabilized by the preservation of secrets, the family honor maintained.

But the meal is free, the idlis plump and spongy. The waiter appears every so often with a sweaty steel jug of water or a golden bowl of sambar, spicy and sweetened with jaggery. Honor or no honor, why leave a plate unfinished?

"I sold the house and the car to pay off the debts," Alice says. "I moved back home with Kuku. All this to keep the business running, but now I want it to grow."

She has been evaluating her competition and found the flaws in their construction, the recurrence of mistakes, the poor advertising, the bland and identical websites, and worst of all, the lack of diversity in design. Ganesha this, Ganesha that. Same trunk and tusks on every card, same golds and reds and saffrons. Alice has retained half of her employees, a few salesmen to staff the shop and fifteen workers in the adjoining production house.

What she needs now is a visionary designer who won't mind working for less than a visionary's fees. She wants a breadth of designs to supply the Hindu, Muslim, Christian, Jain, Buddhist, Baha'i, mixed-marriage, secular, and fusion markets with equal appeal. The difference between her company and every other will be the personal touches, the innovative aesthetic.

And she has other ideas. Independent global vendors, like satellite salesmen, hawking their wares in the farthest wilds of Montana. Complimentary bridal packages, customized designs. Recycled paper invitations for the earthy types. Room to grow? Of course. The only way is up.

Linno watches Alice pause to draw a deep sip from her water. Where is Montana? Would she be sent there? If ever there were a time for the bathroom-excuse escape, it is now. But she thinks of the dull army of women she has yet to paint, ideal and identical and emblazoned across every window, causing her to say, with rare impulsiveness: "Where do we begin?"

THEY BEGIN with a rudimentary education.

At the production house, Alice guides Linno around three chugging machines that descend in size, introducing them with a wave of her hand. "These are the Heidelbergs. Appa, Amma, and Baby." Alice pats the largest one, a sprawling thing that steals a sheet from one side and spits another out the other, faster than Linno can blink. "Papa cost the most. Fifty lakhs, but he can print fifteen hundred pages per minute. Multicolor offset, fully automatic, and includes foil stamping as well."

Linno puts her hand to Papa, feels the raging pulse worth five million rupees.

Alice shows her the screen-printing machine, where a man is spreading black ink across a negative, and near this, a small table where two women are pasting gems to envelopes. "Kundan work," Alice calls it. Then comes the die embossing machine, the die cutting machine, the stock of mill and handmade papers, before Alice leads her out the front door of the production house and into the back door of the shop.

The shop is much smaller than the production house, and the wall shelves are nearly buckling from the weight of all the albums they support, each bulging with outmoded designs and samples from previous events. Streamers and tinsel festoon the fluorescent lights, dangling over velvet benches, where a mother and daughter are seated before a sample album. A clerk stands on the other side of the counter, slowly flipping each page and explaining the designs, to which the mother says, "We've seen that one before." The daughter dismissively nods along.

In a low voice, Alice points out the two clerks. "Prince is the one showing the album. Always wanted to be on the radio and has the voice for it too. Talks quick, scatters some English phrases here and there. None of them sound right to me, but he always persuades the customer."

At the moment, Prince is refuting the mother's claim. Animated and incredulous, he taps the invitation in the album and addresses the daughter in English: "Not possible, sista! This one is a hotcake. Very touchy, groovy card."

"Bhanu," Alice continues, nodding at the other clerk, who is staring at a computer screen. "He was fifteen when we hired him. That boy who stole from us, he offered Bhanu half the money to come along, but Bhanu said no and reported him immediately." Bhanu scratches his chest. His button-down shirt hangs limply on his narrow frame, the fabric worn thin enough to show the exact shape of his undershirt.

Alice turns to Linno. "So. Your introduction. What do you think?"

Anxiety causes Linno to go momentarily mute. How will she ever remember all this? How will she rise to Alice's expectations? She swallows, tries to compose herself. "Will I be tested?"

"Of course not," Alice says. "But you do have homework."

LINNO'S FIRST ASSIGNMENT is the Sweet Sixteen birthday party for the daughter of a plastic surgeon in Pittsburgh, Pennsylvania, an old college friend of Alice's father. The girl wrote Alice an email in advance, to express her vision for the invitation.

From: Nair, Rachna <Indogrrl@aol.com>
To: Alice <alice@eastwestinvites.com>
Subject: My Card

Dear Alice,

Hi! I'm psyched that you'll be doing my invitations. My mom said I should email you about what I'm looking for in my card.

I think the card should be both mature and fun, and should symbolize my transition from girlhood into womanhood, without being gross or lame. I think it should also be sort of fusiony, with Indian and American motifs. Maybe like 65% Indian and 35% American because that's how I'd divide myself. Nothing religious because I don't consider myself religious, just spiritual (it's complicated). I want the invitation to represent me. Like I want people to look at it and say, "That is so Rachna." Or "I wish I had an invitation like that." Or "I wish I was Rachna." LOL. J/k.

I can't wait to see what you come up with!

Thanks so much,
Rachna

After reviewing the email four times, the first thing that enters Linno's mind is a magazine article that she once read, about a team of Indian scientists investigating an aboriginal tribe in the Andaman Islands. Indians investigating Indians. According to Alice, this Rachna is Malayali, and her grandparents live in Kollam, not forty miles from Kottayam. And yet, in the space of one generation, Rachna speaks a strain of English nearly opaque to Linno, who can read *Newsweek* and *India Today* without much difficulty.

After dinner, Linno remains at the table with the printout of the email before her. She underlines the percentages. Her knees begin to tremble the way they did during math exams. She looks up at the light filtering through the dusty windowpane, and somehow it calms her, the milkiness of the light, the skein of dust, the fact that she is needed to wipe the window. She prefers this, the honest work of making the home, work that proffers sure results.

"Why are you thinking so much?" Melvin asks, lugging a plastic bucket of pump water into the kitchen. Linno rises to relieve him, but Melvin shoos her away. "I know how to heat water. You go do your homework."

She would like him to put on a shirt, in case Alice stops by, but these days, he seems too listless for shirts. Ever since her rejection of Kuku, Melvin has gone around the house in a torpor, a white towel over his shoulder. She stops herself from considering her father's mental state any further and opens to a fresh page in the drawing tablet that Alice gave her. Melvin's doubts, on top of her own, are too much to handle. She thinks instead of her painted windows as proof of higher possibility, their colors blossoming with light.

IN THE KITCHEN, Melvin stands before the hearth and listens to the quick downpour of rain on the broad banana leaves. These sudden rains have always sounded to him like the crumpling of paper, here and then gone before one manages to open one's umbrella. The wet, misty smell freshens his lungs.

Melvin strikes a match to the kindling and watches the embers glow beneath the blackened pot. The other day, he heard Ammachi asking Linno, over and over, what was wrong with Kuku. Exasperated, Linno finally answered, "I didn't feel . . . a spark." It was a line that he recalled from a woman's magazine, *Vanitha*, lying open on Linno's desk the day before. *Vanitha* is certainly not Melvin's domain, but in an effort to understand his daughter, he read the article carefully, treating it as some sort of scholarly text. The sentiments were awkwardly worded, filled with the kind of vocabulary that made singlehood sound like an elite club. "Today's woman has no need to settle against her dreams. . . . Love *you* first!" The picture showed a self-loving woman in a tank top, running through a field of red poppies, holding the ends of a red sari that billowed behind her like a windswept sail.

He watches Linno at the kitchen table, a familiar sight, her head propped against her knotted wrist, her left hand drifting a pencil over paper. Her ankles are locked, one heel twitching against the other. He sighs at the folly of youth, to think that hardships are the bricks that build a better life, to invite struggle when one could so easily wake well after dawn with eager servants preparing tea, or retire to bed after a peg of XO (not Yeksho) to sweeten one's dreams. To Melvin's mind, this is what it would mean to be Mrs. Kuku George. And if the marriage would require Linno to surrender her notion of a spark, so be it. What *Vanitha* calls "settling," Melvin calls compromise. He thought that Linno was wise enough to know as much, to recognize that the world does not abide by *Vanitha*'s definitions.

If Melvin were the father he wanted to be, he would express the ways of marriage through metaphor, using not a spark but a houseplant, explaining how love can flower when the marriage is well watered, how steady love thrives best when other factors are in place—healthy soil, good sunlight, proper fertilizer, and a well-sized pot. He imagines himself imparting reams of vague metaphorical wisdoms, the kind that are clearly based on his own experience, without having to delve too deeply into the mistakes of his past.

Linno's face, deep in contemplation, resembles her mother's. Melvin can see all her thoughts converging to a single point, like sunlight captured through a magnifying glass to kindle a piercing flame. Even if he were divulging all his secrets, she would not lift her head.

22.

AT ANJU'S SUNDAY SCHOOL, the Kapyar used to teach the Adam and Eve story in broad strokes of dark and light, serpent and heel, Tree of Knowledge and Tree of Life. The Kapyar could eulogize at length about the Garden of Eden, improvising a fanciful version filled with papaya and guava and lemon-drop trees, rivers of sweet, limitless milk, and glass bowls of Cadbury chocolates. What he never dwelled upon, however, was the moment when Adam and Eve acknowledged their nakedness and were ashamed. Even he who wrote the Book of Genesis, whom Anju pictured with a silvery beard and aeons of time on his hands, seemed embarrassed by the moment, as he spent half a sentence on it before hustling the story along.

Only now does Anju understand the shifting of feet, the averting of eyes, when you have seen too much of another. She wonders how long it took for Adam and Eve to recover from that first gust of too much truth, if they went through a period of sidling around each other when reaching for the papaya.

Such is her feeling about Fish.

HE HAS STOPPED frequenting her locker, compelled by his mother to join the golf team in order to fatten up his résumé, particularly the blank space under ATHLETICS. Every day after school, Fish hefts a giant quiver of golf clubs down the hall, rattling in the opposite direction of most students as they hurry for the double doors. He smiles less these days. He speaks up in class. He bows under the weight of all those clubs, all those swings that he will never quite master. He winces at the name of his mother's favorite golfer, the one black man she seems to love, the one that Fish will never want to be. Eventually the coach agrees to make him manager of the team, which is an equal investment of time but a lesser loss of pride.

More and more, when Anju asks him how he is doing, he simply replies, "Busy." And he is busy, undeniably so, due to what he calls his mother's "crackdown." But this is the kind of answer that glazes over another.

They still sit together at lunch most of the time, at least when he is not meeting with the several clubs that he has recently joined, such as Physics Club or Glee Club or Multicultural Club. He invites her to join the latter, but she declines, sure that he is inviting her out of pity or obligation. She also fears that they will make her wear a bindi or a salwar to school. But he has made another friend in the Multicultural Club, a ponytailed girl named Yu Zhou who keeps all her pens, pencils, and erasers in separate Ziploc bags.

It is not so terrible, Anju tells herself, sitting alone at lunch with an open notebook at her elbow. She used to feign study by moving her eyes over the words and turning the page at intervals, but she soon learned that her peers possess an extremely limited peripheral vision. She could be doing jumping jacks on the table, and lunch would go on.

UNTIL THE FOLLOWING WEEK.

All the students gather in the gymnasium for the morning assembly, where Principal Mitchell is to announce the winner of the George de Brigard Award. Microphone in hand, he stands with feet planted upon the eyes of the painted unicorn, before the rising bleachers of wilted students. The unicorn is a permanent chip on the shoulder of the school. Ten years before, the Sitwell School had partaken in a lottery with seven other schools, all of whom had declared themselves members of the high school Ivy League, to decide on mascots. Tigers, Wildcats, and Wolverines went to the more fortunate schools, while Sitwell, coming in last place, was dealt the fantastical equine. The Sitwell artist made every effort to render the unicorn with beady-eyed fury, bared jowls, a thick lingum of a horn—as much machismo as could be mustered for a magical pony.

Standing next to Principal Mitchell is a man in a seersucker suit, introduced as George de Brigard. His face is cheery and wrinkled from tanning, his clay-colored hands clapping at the mention of his own name. Taking the microphone, George de Brigard addresses the unasked question of what it takes to be an artist. Mostly he seems to be talking about himself: ". . . passion, honesty, discipline, drive, a high tolerance for bouts of regret, and the carapace with which to withstand the criticism of others that keeps coming and coming and coming. But still, my advice to you all is this: Caution to the wind. Carpe diem. Seize"—he looks from one end of the audience to the other—"the day."

Anju is sitting all the way at the end of the first bleacher, tranquilized by the sounds of George de Brigard, until he clears his throat.

"The winner," he continues, "embodies this attitude in every way. His name is . . . Andrew Melvin!"

There is some shuffling and murmuring between Principal Mitchell and George de Brigard. "It's a girl?" asks George de Brigard, accidentally, into the microphone. "Oh. *Oh*. Excuse me—*AnJEW* Melvin!"

Anju shoots up from her seat. In this moment of victory, she feels at home, spotlit and praised, culled from the rest in a way that makes all her prior isolation somehow meaningful. She hardly thinks of why her name is being called, so sweet it is to walk across the gymnasium before the many eyes that usually ignore her. She records everything to memory: the squeak of her shoe soles, the trickling applause, the number of steps she must take to travel across the glossy hardwood floor (sixteen) to receive the principal's warm handshake and a slim white envelope from George de Brigard.

Standing between the two men, she spots Fish in the audience. He watches her intently, leaning forward, holding the edge of the bleacher. Her victory deflates. She remembers what Fish said after her confession, when she asked him, "Would you have done the same as me?"

At this, he paused. "Not a lot of people would, I think. But you're the one that's standing here. You're the one who made it." His expression was not congratulatory but grave, and slightly bewildered.

Of this and events past, they have not spoken. It seems as though they never will.

12.

ℱOR THE COVER of Rachna's Sweet Sixteen invitation, Linno draws a mermaid, which seems a proper interpretation of Rachna's ratio of nationalities. Linno spends several hours drawing and erasing, erasing some more, but something about the seashell bosoms and the curvaceous flipper render the mermaid far too sexy for a sixteen-year-old. All night, she sits with her head bowed, thinking and sketching and sometimes neither, with the wall lizards as apathetic company, as still and flat as if they had been drawn there. She remembers her Sixteen, neither sweet nor bitter but bland, and the years preceding, the bandaged cocoon that came to nothing.

Bored and blocked, she riffles through Ammachi's stack of Christmas cards, which grows thicker by the year as she has yet to discard a single one. The stockings and bells are uninspiring, nor does the angel Gabriel, sent by an insurance company, act as muse. One card, sent by a cousin in Dubai, is heavier than most. Upon opening it, two planes lift from the lower half, creating a three-dimensional image of the Nativity scene. The kneeling shepherds rise up on the frontmost panel, while the wise men occupy the middle panel, and in the center is the triad of Joseph, Mary, and Jesus watched over by the white North Star. Linno studies the card for a long time, closing it and opening it, watching how the various shapes spring up and take form.

With Ammachi's sewing scissors, she cuts a page from her drawing pad, folds it in half, and makes two parallel cuts. Opening the page and pulling out the strip, she learns how to coax a small building from the crease. With more cuts, she creates several buildings of varying heights, each wall with windows. She complicates the design and constructs new ones, a process not unlike solving a jigsaw puzzle, wherein the question always remains: How can three dimensions smoothly return to two? With snips and folds and several failed attempts, she comes to replicate the Christmas card, which only fuels her curiosity as she continues to work at the kitchen table, pasting panels with grains of rice, pushing and pulling and scraping the edges, vaguely dazed as the night passes by her window and leaks into the dull blue of dawn.

LATER IN THE WEEK, Linno sets out to visit Alice's shop. She takes the bus to Good Shepherd Road, her nerves eased by the breeze that cuts through the barred windows, freshly skimmed from the paddy field's surface. Two egrets, one with prey in its beak, circle and dive around each other, meeting and parting and meeting again, painting the sky with invisible patterns.

By the time she reaches town, Good Shepherd Road is already bustling. A mini-lorry bumps along, carrying open crates of perfect white eggs, though the driver seems unperturbed by the precariousness of his burden. Bicycles whiz by with a squeaky *tring* around the fruit vendors, who build citrusy pyramids of limes and lemons on the ground, budging from their stools only at sundown.

The invitation shop is easy to overlook, wedged between a tailor shop and a hardware store. Gently, Linno pushes open the door, which tinkles at her entry.

From the back of the narrow room, Alice welcomes Linno by waving a wand of incense, attempting to slice through the sweet, mulchy smell of old paper. A slender rope of smoke dissolves toward the ceiling. Linno tries not to wonder which beam Reji chose.

After nodding hello to Prince and Bhanu, Linno follows Alice to the back room. One wall holds shelves of mill paper, each color split into a small spectrum of its own. Within the color white, there is ivory, lily, butter, and shell. Linno's gaze travels up and down the columns of tint and shade, as unable to focus as when she first entered Thresia Paint House. For Rachna's invitation, Linno decides on navy blue and rust red.

Alice seats Linno at a card table, before a set of tools arranged on a napkin, as if for a surgeon—a pencil, an eraser, scissors, glue, and various pens, a few that produce metallic ink and one tipped with a sharp, thin blade. Linno hunches over the table for twenty minutes, re-creating what she designed at home, while Alice pushes a mop between the benches. "Take your time," Alice says, but Linno needs very little, having struggled enough over the past few nights. The paper had seemed so stubborn then, impossible to shape, and the overall process of creation was as confusing as finding her way out of a maze. But now that she knows the route, it is easy to repeat.

When she is finished, Linno fans the ink on a design that is simpler than her previous plan. The card is multilayered, with the outline of a butterfly cut into the navy cover to unearth the red layer beneath, stroked with gold arabesques. Upon opening, a red butterfly springs from the gutter of the card, the paper edges whispering against each other as the wings spread wide. Beneath the butterfly are two small flaps where information and RSVP cards will be kept.

She feels a light punch at her shoulder. Alice is standing over her, beaming. "Who taught you this?" she asks, taking the card into her hands. She opens and closes it, childlike with wonder.

The very same day, Alice posts the template to Rachna's mother, along with a fixed price of $4 per card. Linno doubts that Mrs. Nair will agree to such a price, but by the end of the week Alice has good news. Not only did Rachna request 150 invitations, but 300 place cards, a whole battalion of navy and rust red butterflies.

ALICE TAKES THE BLUE PAGES to the production house, where the die cutting machine can quickly carve the butterfly mosaic into the covers and the Baby Heidelberg can fold them. In the meantime, Linno cuts the parts for the inner butterfly and shows Alice how to fit the wings together.

At first, they work in silence. Each butterfly has a personality of its own, and Linno feels a certain kinship with this early flock, which are clumsier in ways that only she can recognize. Gradually, her fingers learn to move without thought.

So far, Alice has refrained from the topic of Kuku, for which Linno is quietly grateful. Instead, Alice rambles about her favorite topic—foreigners—who have been sighted in increasing numbers throughout Kerala. Foreigners are excellent for business, she says, and their presence necessitates an interior overhaul of the office. No more tinsel and streamers, but strictly Raja Ravi Varma prints, those paintings with the plumpish, pleasant Malayali women playing veenas or holding ripebellied children to their hips. Around the clock, Ravi Shankar will whine softly from hidden speakers. The sign over the doorway will have to be fashioned anew, made to hearken after the royal mystique of Rajput kings, another task for which Linno is suited. A sign, if properly seductive, can net a whole school of foreigners.

Alice pronounces the word "foreigner" using the loving, hungry tones with which she talks of sweet kulfi. But Ammachi views them as an invasive hoard, questing with the same plundering spirit as their ancestors of centuries prior.

"They are mostly tourists," Linno argued with her. "They're not staying. They're not claiming anything."

"Oh no?" Ammachi pointed out the new billboards for Kalyan Silks, all of which featured a regal blond woman in a sari. "Hundreds of pretty girls here and this is who Kalyan chose as a model?"

There is no denying the presence of foreigners, the houseboats carrying women in airy kurta tops and jeans, tall, rangy men in Velcro sandals and elaborate backpacks, or older couples with visors and fragile crowns of silver hair, blinking away the river's glare behind insectile shades. The tourists seem either wary or ignorant of all the stares they draw, but their normal behaviors take on an odd exoticism—smoking, sneezing, strolling along. What they do not do is just as intriguing as what they do. For example: Why do they refuse to walk beneath an open umbrella on brutally sunny days?

"You know, it's rude to stare," an American woman once said to Linno. The woman must have been in her thirties, too old to be wearing her hair in those pigtails. Vulnerable blue veins branched along the insides of her wrists.

Linno wanted to come up with a sharp retort, but she was astonished that the tourist had addressed her at all, and pleased, almost gratified that the tourist had found Linno's home worthy of invasion. She saw no inconsistency in her position. Like most Keralites, she denounced the American president, American imperialism, and ate vanilla pistachio ice cream at the Ernakulam Baskin-Robbins all the same. Thirty-one flavors and the Coffee Coolatta! No ice-cream parlor, not even Vemby's, could rival it.

WHEN LINNO AND ANJU were little girls, their favorite game was called Tourists, in which they dressed up in castoffs that they had found in Ammachi's closet. Anju went about the house wearing her plastic shamrock glasses with the green lenses, her head turbanned in Ammachi's massive brassiere. A pair of pants served as Linno's cape, the ankles tied at her throat. Their names were Linda and Angel. Together they roamed from room to room, clicking pictures with imaginary cameras, shading their eyes, cooing over their found souvenirs, usually ashtrays and pencils and empty coffee tins.

From Ammachi's closet, Angel plundered a thing more valuable than any brassiere-turban. It was some sort of hat, big as a melon, ruby red with glitter, balding in patches. Angel coronated herself before her only rival could object.

At that moment, Melvin entered the room and asked if the girls had seen the iron. They were used to these tiny punctures in their Tourist fantasy and found it easy to recover their world from intruders. But this time, Melvin stayed even after Linno said that the iron was on the ironing board. Melvin was staring at Anju, who stared back from under the big red hat.

"Where did you get that?" he asked in a strange voice.

Anju put her hands on the hat. "Can I have it?"

In two strides, Melvin plucked the hat from her head. Anju looked like she might cry. "But that's mine!"

"Don't take things that do not belong to you," he said.

It was hard for Linno to picture how and why the big red hat belonged to her father. It matched none of his clothes. He had no interest in joining the Tourists. In their pant-cape and brassiere-turban, Linno and Anju pondered Melvin as if he were a perplexing native whose customs they did not understand. Melvin shifted his feet.

"Go study," he told them, which was what he told them whenever he didn't know what else to say. Big red hat in hand, he left the room.

23.

*J*N ANJU'S OPINION, Rohit suffers from an addiction to his camera. He brings it everywhere, phobic to the possibility that a witty remark might be made or a crisis might occur at the exact moment when his hands are empty. His addiction makes every banality precious and worth filming, the tying of a shoe freighted with meaning when viewed through the lens.

At first, Anju was grateful when Rohit volunteered to accompany her to Jackson Heights, where she would have her first meeting with Rajiv Tandon. She was reluctant to ask Mrs. Solanki, who seems increasingly busy with work, along with her upcoming diabetes fund-raiser. In her rush, she hardly seems to notice the comings and goings of her son, who has been staying with a nondescript entity he calls his Ex. "Probably staying with that Ex of his," Mrs. Solanki says. "He thinks I don't know, but I'm his mother. I *know*." What Mrs. Solanki does with her arsenal of maternal knowledge is unclear, but Anju can tell that the power lies in stockpiling, not usage.

When Anju meets Rohit at the subway station, her gratitude shrivels. Rohit has his camera bag slung over his shoulder, a paper cup of coffee in hand. Even before saying hello, he tells her not to worry. "There isn't a person in this country who doesn't want to jump in front of the lens. Trust me, cameras give you clout."

AS SOON AS they enter the number 7 subway car, Rohit wedges himself into the seat next to Anju's and asks her a number of questions, most of which begin with "where" and "why."

"Where are you going?" he asks.

"You know where we are going."

"I know, but for the camera. And make it a full sentence. So, where are *you* going?"

"To Jackson Heights. Sorry." She starts again. "I am going to Jackson Heights."

"Why?"

"I am going to see about how to get green card."

"Why do you want a green card?"

"No one does not want green card."

"But why do you?"

"Why would I not?"

As an interviewer, Rohit rates far lower than Mike Wallace, who, if frustrated, would not mutter "Forget it," turn off his camera, and pout into the middle distance. But Anju is happy to gaze out the window when the 7 train creaks out of the tunnel, emerging aboveground, clattering on tall tracks like a geriatric roller coaster. Queens unfolds before her in rooftops and power lines, a few distant smokestacks piping gray fluff. A cluster of brick buildings wear bright explosions of graffiti, which Rohit points out as the Graffiti Museum. A museum for works of beautiful ruin. She thinks of Linno, wonders what she would say.

Anju clutches the purse in her lap. Inside it is an envelope with $500 in cash, taken from her Art Exhibition winnings. She assumes this to be the maximum fee necessary, and the rest she will give to Linno. Linno, who has begun to haunt her days and fill her dreams, whose presence, once brought here, would right every wrong.

BENEATH THE LOFTED TRAIN TRACKS that empty into Jackson Heights, children dart across the intersection at Eighty-second Street, bold against the beeping cars. White people are a rarity here where it is gray and lively, the stores insistent for attention. Dimmed neon signs declare DENTISTA and FARMACIA, and though it is not yet evening, another sign is surrounded by blinking bulbs, like a movie marquee, peddling the main attraction of PAWN SHOP. She lingers before a barber shop that shows a pictorial menu of men beside the door, offering the shape-up, the blowout, the Caesar, the low fade, and the skin fade. Inside, a few men wait and watch as a barber applies an electric razor to a man whose newly mown head is nearly as bald as when he came into this world. Why would a man choose to speed up the balding process when baldness awaits him, a decade away? The men chat happily over the hum of the razor.

On Seventy-fourth Street, the scenery switches. No more *dentistas* and *farmacias* and menus of men, all these replaced by Surekha Designs and Butala Emporium and Rupal's Desserts, whose storefront sign offers fresh sugarcane juice. It is strange, the sense of detached belonging that overcomes her, the vague familiarity of passing through one's home to find it inhabited by another with the furniture replaced and rearranged. All around her are people who resemble her until they break into their assorted tongues, mostly Gujarati or Hindi, some Punjabi, none of which she understands. Women wear sweaters over salwars; men shuffle their socked feet in chappals. Here is Payless ShoeSource, there Patel Brothers Grocery with boxes of vegetables in a row. Beneath the deep green cucumber is scrawled: KHIRA. Beneath the bright, wet cilantro: DHANA—*2/$1.00* ☺. Strange that she should come so far from home, to Jackson Heights, to learn Hindi words she had not studied in school.

In the windows are mannequins draped with daring saris, thin as a fly's wing. Some of these hard, surly ladies are bald; others fare a little better under Beatle moptop wigs. They stand unmoved by the melodies flooding from the music store next door, the remixed drumbeats beneath the divine bellow of Nusrat Fateh Ali Khan. Anju and Rohit pass an old man hunched on a stool outside the music store mumbling, "Goprice, goprice," which Anju understands as "Good price."

She would like to absorb her surroundings slowly, anonymously, but as she walks, Rohit walks alongside, pointing his camera at her. He tells her not to pay attention to him. Everyone pays attention to him. Bystanders lean away and stare at her with the assumption that she must be famous, or at least a local TV personality. That she is neither embarrasses her. The crowds of people make an aisle through which she can pass, following her with their stares. She walks swiftly, even as Rohit stumbles to keep up, complaining that this footage won't be usable if he keeps bumping into trash cans. She walks faster.

By the time they reach Rajiv Tandon's building, Rohit is in a dark mood. They ride the elevator in silence.

AS SOON AS Anju enters the office, she hears a triumphant, "HAH!

"You've come," Bird says.

Once again, Bird's Malayalam is a balm to Anju's nerves. Anju and Rohit take a seat in the waiting room while Bird hands them Styrofoam cups of chai pumped from a large steel canister. Anju introduces Rohit as the son of her host mother. Noting Rohit's camera, Bird says, "Mr. Tandon will not like that," and returns to her desk.

They lapse into silence when Bird answers the phone. "Offices of Rajiv Tandon, this is Birdie, how may I help you?"

Birdie. The name does not quite fit, befitting of someone daintier. Also odd is the way that Bird seems far more knowledgeable in this place than in the library, phoning and filing and stapling all at once.

Anju looks around the room, her gaze passing over the gaunt African mask on the wall, the seventeenth-century map of the world, framed behind glass, and finally Rohit, who is filming her.

"Do you have enough money to get a lawyer?" he asks.

"I think so," she says.

"Maybe my mom can help you out. Or me."

"You have money? From how?"

"Different ventures."

"Why you would give it to me?"

"I look at it as another venture. Immigration is a really big deal right now."

She watches him as he watches her through the camera. To him, she must be of no more significance than a fish in a bowl. He raps on the glass only to see which way she will swim.

"No thank you," she says.

At that moment, Mr. Tandon emerges from his office. Rohit turns and extends his hand, but Mr. Tandon keeps his distance, as though his proximity to the camera might cause him an allergic reaction. He politely asks Rohit to turn it off. Holding the camera away from his eye, Rohit rattles off a number of practiced pleas and excuses. "It's for a home video, she's a close family friend, no one will see it, I just want to document her arrival."

To Anju's delight, none of this works. "We have too many people coming in here with sensitive issues," Mr. Tandon says. "So, if you would be so kind."

Mr. Tandon utters these words with a courtesy that belies the authority of his posture. He keeps his hands in the pockets of his well-pressed pants, refusing to move until his request is met.

With a weary sigh, Rohit turns off the camera, and Mr. Tandon, invigorated, extends his hand in welcome.

ANJU FEELS SAFE here in the vault of books, with Mr. Tandon's hands clasped atop her file, as if her life is now his territory. While he speaks, she tallies all the signs of his achievement—his cuff links, his gold nameplate, his tall globe that can spin and spin on its axis.

He asks Anju a few questions about her documents, whether she is registered with the Student and Exchange Visitor Information System. She answers yes with all the hope of a child wishing to please. "And you want to attain permanent status?" he asks.

"Yes."

"First let me say this is not unusual. I see cases like yours all the time. Since nine-one-one, the bureaucracy surrounding U.S. immigration has been staggering but not, in my experience, insurmountable."

Anju wishes she could write down all the vocabulary words that fall so effortlessly from this man's mouth. Rohit, slumped in the seat next to her, seems less impressed.

"What are these steps I should take?" she asks.

"First we need to make sure that we keep renewing your F-1 visa, which requires a nonimmigrant visa processing fee to the Department of State. Then we can apply for permanent status by next year."

"Is there a faster way?"

"I've known clients to achieve permanent status in half the usual time. A year or even less." He offers a small, apologetic smile. "But extra speed comes with extra fees."

"I can pay," Anju says, just as Rohit asks: "What about *your* fees?"

"Roughly?" Mr. Tandon looks up at the ceiling, calculating. "That's four hundred for the F-1 renewal processing, then five hundred for the permanent residency application, plus the expediting fees. With half my fees, taken together . . . about two thousand."

Rupees? Anju wants to ask. Rubles? Pesos? Surely not dollars. The number settles deep in her stomach, a dense and dismal sediment.

"Jeez, that's a lot of money." Rohit's tone is weirdly loud and impassioned. "Anju, what are you going to do?"

"Can I pay in pieces?" she asks.

Mr. Tandon seems to weigh her disappointment. "I'm sure we can work something out. It seems that my assistant is very invested in your future, and I trust her judgment."

Over her shoulder, Anju looks at Bird, who is speaking into the phone and jotting notes with her pen. Bird is vital to this place, at the core of its functions, and it is luck that won Anju a place in Bird's favor. Against her own doubt, Anju hears herself speaking in a steady voice:

"I can give you five hundred cash now. The rest I can send by the end of the week."

AFTER THE MEETING, Anju and Rohit part, as she is to have tea with Bird and he has a party to attend in TriBeCa. It is a relief to watch him dismantle his camera and pack the parts into a carrying case. "Great job today," he tells her by way of good-bye. It seems a strange statement, as if complimenting her performance, an accidental admission that his camera was on all along.

For a moment that takes her by surprise, she admires him.

BIRD LIVES FOUR BLOCKS from Mr. Tandon's office, in an apartment that smells faintly of Vicks VapoRub and old sweaters in a trunk. Anju sits on a plastic-covered couch, a difficult thing on which to sit gracefully without emitting an impolite noise.

Bird brings Anju a mug of chai, a box of Entenmann's chocolate-chip cookies, and two napkins impressed with McDonald's arches. "How long have you been here?" Anju asks.

"In this country? Twenty-two years, something like that."

"Do you go back?"

Bird shrugs. "There is no one to go back to anymore. Everything is changed. If I went back now, I'd just be a tourist."

Between sips of tea, Bird asks tentative questions, giving Anju little chance to ask any more of her own. Anju explains how she came on scholarship, how her family is awaiting her return.

"Your father must be proud of you," Bird says.

"I think so. I don't know."

Without looking up, Bird carefully lays two cookies on a napkin. "And your mother too."

"Oh no. She died when I was a baby."

Bird nods, seemingly unsurprised. Usually, people respond differently to this news, with sympathy or sadness, however contrived. But Bird is expressionless.

"You are here alone, then?" Bird asks. "No relatives, no nothing?"

"I have no one here."

Bird stares at Anju, then pushes the cookie box closer to her. "Not anymore."

14.

LIKE AN HOUR-OLD PIECE of gum, romance has lost all its sweetness. What Anju assumed was the smolder of gathering emotion turned out to be a dull, gray, tiring wad of nothing. With her mind mostly cleared away of pointless passions, she looks upon Fish with an acute sense of betrayal. But also a painful splinter of hope.

Against that hope, she throws herself into her studies, the only field in which she exercises some measure of control. In class, she forgoes her Ace bandage to take limitless notes, reassuring her teachers that the arthritis has temporarily lifted, though she still makes a point of conspicuously massaging her joints once in a while. Her rising grades put her at the head of the class, even above Fish, who struggles to maintain his class performance in tandem with his participation in Outdoors Club, Amnesty International, Physics Club, Glee Club, Multicultural Club, and golf. She and Fish are like two converts to different denominations, he fully devoted to his mother's dream of an Ivy League school, she devoted to her books, both unwilling to see the similarity in their pursuits. Anju wonders if her success has contributed to his avoidance of her, a thought that leads her to study doubly hard. Surpassing him is the only way to wound him, to remind him that she exists.

She also finds time to visit Mr. Tandon's office again, where she hands over all the money she has left, $900, which includes the rest of the George de Brigard award plus $400 she drew from her scholarship stipend. This leaves her with $25 in spending money for the next two months, but having no one with whom to socialize, she barely notices the loss. Bird promises that she will persuade Mr. Tandon to waive the rest of his fee. "Think of it as an investment," Bird tells her. "We will file the application this week itself."

In the meantime, Anju bends over her textbooks until her lower back aches, until her head swims with Civil War battle names and algebraic equations. She binds each fact to her memory and plows forward into future pages. Studying, too, is a kind of war, and each chapter a territory to be conquered. While so engaged, she hardly lets herself think about the doubt that needles her, that Fish might not be the person, or the poet, she thought he was.

WITH HER RISING GRADES, Anju is unsurprised to arrive at school and find a note from Miss Schimpf wedged into the slats of her locker. "Please see me in my office." At least Anju's work ethic is finally being noticed by someone, if not Fish.

She trudges down the hall, around clumps of students and boulder-like backpacks and exclusive conversations. The door to Principal Mitchell's office is open in welcome to students who do their best to ignore it, lest they be dragged into a chat. For her part, Anju looks forward to a chat now and then, even if Principal Mitchell simply asks about her homework. Anju glances in, disheartened by the empty desk chair.

She arrives at Miss Schimpf's office to find Fish already there, seated by the wall. Her reaction is one of pure elation, a smile that she cannot supress. She hardly notices, at first, that he is staring intently at his sneakers, his hands cupped together as though to trap something between them. The next person she notices is Principal Mitchell, who stands beside Miss Schimpf's desk, his arms crossed over his chest. Miss Schimpf looks up with an expression of profound sadness.

And now the significance of this meeting settles over Anju in a gentle gust. Slightly dazed, she hovers in the doorway and wonders, absently, whether she could go get her Ace bandage from her locker.

Principal Mitchell tells her to come in and have a seat. Usually he calls every student by last name, preceded by Miss or Mr., but now he calls her Anju, a foreboding intimacy. The door falls shut, gentle as a pat on the back.

"Anju, we called you in here because we have some serious things to discuss, in particular about your artwork." Principal Mitchell pauses, as if waiting for her to begin the discussion herself. "I have to ask you: Did you do those paintings yourself?"

From her throat comes a voice that she does not recognize as her own. "Paintings?"

"Yup. Did you paint them?"

"Yes, sir."

"Did you have help?" Miss Schimpf asks.

"No, miss."

"Oh, no need for 'miss' and 'sir,' " Principal Mitchell says. "We're just here to have a chat."

A chat. Again, that cozy, fireside language. There is nothing cozy about the way Fish refuses to release his hands and look at her.

Noting her glance, Principal Mitchell calls on Fish, as if they are discussing a poem or a play and little else. "Mr. Fischer? Would you like to say something?"

The noise that comes from Fish's mouth is barely a croak. He clears his throat. "She told me her sister did them."

Anju sits very still, while inside her heart falls and falls.

Principal Mitchell leans against Miss Schimpf's desk. "Anju, is this true?"

She does not answer.

When Miss Schimpf addresses Anju, her voice is dulcet, deceptively so. "Anju, what's your sister's name?"

It is cruel, the way they know things that they are pretending not to know. Anju does not answer, not out of obstinacy, but because she simply has no voice.

Miss Schimpf rises and holds up the tailor's painting, which, unbeknownst to Anju, has been spread on the desk all this time. With her finger, without touching the paper, Miss Schimpf traces a looping vine in the corner of the painting. A single gold bell hangs from her bangle, tinkling childishly. When she removes her hand, the word lifts, like a scent, from the page.

Linno.

There is a rarefied silence, of a stillness and weight that occur before an avalanche.

Anju's hand goes to her mouth, and with that singular motion she surrenders. How did she never notice? From far away, she hears Principal Mitchell beginning to talk about consequences, about the Honor Code, about violation, words that for now do little more than draw a thick, distinct line that separates her from them. Her mind reels forward through the oncoming days, when she will be asked to return the money, now in official, unknown hands. She feels herself growing light, dissolving, or perhaps it is the world that is dissolving all around her.

15.

OUTSIDE, the sounds of dawn: the *swish-gargle-spit* of Ammachi's saltwater ablutions, the *clunk* of a heavy pail set on stone. Melvin lies in bed, listening. He should be up already. He should be brushing his teeth and taming the sharp, disheveled fin of his hair, but he feels weighted to the bed, his nightmares pinning his stomach to the mattress. And again, that sense of impending wrongness, which he will not mention to his mother for fear of her antidotes.

He has this dream every so often. In it, Linno is seven years old, the age that she was when he left her behind in Kumarakom. She is wearing red ribbons at the ends of her plaited braids. He is following her down strange, labyrinthian corridors, imploring her to wait for him. Around every corner, she gathers speed, until she is running, then racing, her head a comet, her braids flaming behind her and blizzarding sparks that make him recoil with the knowledge that he is being left behind, always, by everyone. He feels childish, furious, his fatherly words turned desperate and ugly, calling her an idiot, a useless, stupid girl. Go then, if you want to go. Go and don't come back. She turns and, with the rippling nature of dreams, becomes a woman he knows, then one he doesn't, then one that may be his wife. She is crying.

Dreams are not the best place from which to draw messages, and the significance of this one, so heavy in the morning, will lighten with every passing hour. The regret that now throbs at the thought of Linno will disappear when he sees her at breakfast, picking her teeth. The day will grow harmless, and by afternoon he will forget everything. But there is only minor comfort in forgetfulness because nothing is completely forgotten, only tucked away in some other part of the brain to later betray him at synaptic speed.

AFTER ANOTHER BEDRIDDEN MINUTE, he hears the phone ring, an unlikely sound for so early in the morning. It must be Anju, a thought that brings him comfort. She has not called in twelve days, nor did she return Melvin's last call. Ammachi wanted to phone her again, but Melvin insisted that Anju was probably busy with schoolwork and the green card application. They would wait until tomorrow.

He hurries out of bed and into the sitting room, trying to smooth his hair on the way. Picking up the phone, he greets a vaguely familiar voice: "Hello? Mr. Vallara?"

After a moment's delay, he cries out, "Oh! Hallome! Miss Shiv!"

Miss Schimpf has called twice before, and each time, Melvin has regressed into his teenage self by uttering this same overly enthusiastic exclamation. Not because he finds her attractive, but because he finds her to be a person of considerable power, possessing a confident, feminine tone that fills him with well-being. Once a month, she calls with an "update," which seems like a waste of a phone card, though he feels privileged that she thinks him important enough to receive her call. Usually, she stretches each syllable so that he can understand her messages of progress—that Anju is excelling in all her classes, that Anju is making friends. This time, however, he can barely follow her rapid-fire English. He understands that something has happened, but that something remains on a lingual shelf too high for him to reach.

Linno appears in the doorway just as Melvin catches the words "remain calm." He sees his own expression, the opposite of calm, reflected in the way Linno is watching him. When she takes the phone, the last word he hears clearly is "missing."

"It's that Miss Shiv from Anju's school," Melvin whispers.

Linno wastes no time on introductions. "Hello, yes?"

Melvin stands aside, thinking that there must be a word after "missing" that he did not grasp. Anju has missed a class. Anju is missing home. "Missing" is a chameleonic word, its darker possibilities easily reversed with the right, benign context. So by the time Linno says aloud, "Anju is missing?" it is enough for Melvin to ask frantically, "What? Missing what?" while knowing the answer. It is enough to have the wind knocked out of his chest, enough to tumble him back into his nightmare, to wonder if he mistook the girl with the fiery braids. His voice barely a whisper, he calls his daughter's name.

III.

WEST WINDS

CHRISTMAS ARRIVES in a torrent of holiday cards. Teeming with them, the post office delivers the Jesus-centric cards to Christians and the more secular greetings to Hindus and Muslims, images of rosy white ice skaters and doily snowflakes, mailed in a region that possesses neither. The week before, Anthony Achen had eulogized the sweet but dead simplicity of the Christmas holiday, before the advent of store-bought trees and expensive cards. "Do you remember," he asked the congregation, while the Kapyar nodded along, already remembering, "when we would simply break a branch from a tree to bring home and decorate, and this was our tree? Do you remember when we would craft our own Christmas stars from bamboo and colored papers instead of buying them ready-made from stores? How did we arrive here in this ready-made age?"

In spite of the sermon, Ammachi demands that Melvin go to the Fancy Shoppe and buy the ready-made star that most resembles a flamboyant meteor. It is the first Christmas without Anju, but Ammachi insists, with a resolve somewhere between piety and superstition, that the ready-made star will guide her home.

Melvin returns with an extra-large star painted pink and orange, poked with holes to radiate the lightbulb within. He hangs it from the corner of the roof, just as humbler stars hover in the porches of other Christian-owned shops and homes. As children, Linno and Anju loved that first moment of illumination, as wondrous and celestial as their own private sun.

But this time, Linno and Ammachi do not stay on the porch for long, drifting off into the house toward their separate corners, their similar worries. Melvin faces the dusk alone, listening to the faint warring of firecrackers that can be heard but not seen, detonated by boys too impatient to wait until nightfall. From where Melvin stands, the trees are a chorus of protest, trembling, flailing, wringing their limbs.

Melvin, too, cannot relax, each bullet crack demanding an answer from the dark: *How did we arrive here?*

IT HAS BEEN THREE DAYS since they received the call from Miss Schimpf, who possessed little more information than what was contained in the note that Anju left:

Dear Auntie, Uncle, Miss Schimpf, et al.,

Due to a recent event, I am resigning from school. Please do not worry or come for me as I know several good and God-fearing friends who can give me suitable living facilities.

I am sorry I caused trouble. I promise I did not mean for it. Please tell my family (esp. my father) not to worry. I will see them soon. They will still worry but please explain them this note and tell them I am not in a cult or a gang. Thank you.

All the best,
Anju Melvin

Linno pictured a crumpled paper thick with smudges and misspelled words. She wanted to touch the note herself, as if clues to Anju's whereabouts would rise to her fingertips, but she assumed that the police would need it. She had always ascribed a mechanized efficiency to American police departments, believing that Anju's exact location could be found by analyzing the DNA in an errant hair she left behind. As it happened, the police had no time for Anju at all, at least not until seventy-two hours had gone by. "They get a lot of cases like these," Miss Schimpf explained. "They said that most runaways return in a few days." She added that Anju's statistics had been provided to the National Crime Information Center, an entity that sounded to Linno as large as the very country in which her sister was lost.

Mrs. Solanki also called each day, if only to reiterate her sense of helplessness. Her voice was drenched in sympathy, but there was an elegance to her teariness. "She was such a quiet, composed girl, but with the scholarship mess . . . Well, I think it was too much."

Perhaps Mrs. Solanki knew of Linno's complicity, and of her family's knowledge as well. Linno swallowed, unsure of her English. "Who is 'good and God-fearing people'? Was Anju having friends at school?"

"I don't think so. Certain students have been questioned, but she was a bit of a lonely type, you know?"

"Yes," Linno said. "I know."

Time and again, Melvin and Ammachi asked Linno to explain her sister's behavior. They seemed to think that Linno would know, believing that the mind of one sister was a mirror image unto the other. She wanted to tell them that in every person, there are private regions of the mind, infinite and troubling, that are known only to the self. Beyond the reach of sisters, friends, and fathers, these are the innermost spaces that can persuade a seventeen-year-old girl to wake up one day and walk out on her life.

Over the course of seventy-two hours, the frenzy caused by Miss Schimpf's phone call began to ferment to helplessness. Each evening, Melvin, Ammachi, and Linno took their places in the sitting room and watched the phone as if it might, in a blink, convulse to life. There were no such miracles, large or small. Miss Schimpf said she was still in contact with the police department and would call them with more news, as soon as she received it.

Because the police seemed slow in their own interrogations, Melvin, Ammachi, and Linno gently interrogated one another. They did not pose the terrifying questions, but minor ones, the kind that would not crush them in the asking.

Ammachi sat up suddenly. "Do you think she has socks?"

"Did she pack them?" Linno asked.

"I told her it gets cold there, but she is so stubborn. I had to beg her to take Jilu's coat . . ." As she scratched her knee, Ammachi's voice tapered to a surrendering "Ah."

Linno stroked Ammachi's hand. Her skin was pale and slack between the tendons like the loose skin hanging from the throat of sickly cattle. Her finger had shrunken from its wedding ring, so that the band slipped easily up to the knuckle.

Melvin tried to assure them that Anju would be back in a few days. "I know that child. She needs people around, people she knows." Melvin nodded to himself. "I know her."

TO THE NEIGHBORS, they act as though life is proceeding as always. Melvin goes to work but leaves his heart by the phone. Sometimes he can hear the phone ringing as he walks away from the house, causing him to stop and turn an ear skyward, as if straining to hear an angelic whisper.

It is Linno who answers the phone every evening, crestfallen at the sound of Miss Schimpf's voice. Though Miss Schimpf feels partially responsible for Anju's flight, Linno will not absolve her guilt so long as it keeps her involved in the cause. Miss Schimpf is their only link, however tenuous, to the uniformed policemen presiding over shadowy alleys, badges flashing like stars in the dark. But with all her phone calls and meetings with the police department, Miss Schimpf never bears good news.

"I've tried, I promise I've tried," Miss Schimpf says. Her early morning voice is a scraping sound, in dire need of moisture. "The NYPD has other things on their agenda. The list of runaways in this city is endless. Usually these cases are solved when the child comes home."

"What if she does not?" Linno asks. She shuts her eyes against the question.

"Let's just try to stay positive for the time being."

By the day after Christmas, all of Miss Schimpf's promises, once confident and gilded with optimism, have withered to weak phrasings of self-defense. "We're doing all we can . . . We're trying . . . We're hoping . . . We can only do so much." And the "we" in which Linno once took comfort—a phalanx of people committed to bringing Anju home—seems now a word to hide behind. "We" where there is only Miss Schimpf and Principal Mitchell and Sonia Solanki.

Growing impatient, Linno asks what she has been wondering for days—how exactly the school came to know of the fraud itself.

Miss Schimpf hesitates. "Her classmate. A friend."

"This classmate. What did Anju tell her?"

"It's a he. Sheldon Fischer. Anju confided in him." Miss Schimpf recounts the way in which she overheard Sheldon Fischer telling Anju's story to another student. Miss Schimpf appears to take Linno's silence as rage, adding gently: "I should tell you that he's absolutely torn up by all of this. He never meant for things to escalate as they did."

What Miss Schimpf mistook for rage is bewilderment. Anju was never particularly talented at dealing with boys. There was her minor dalliance with that waif Sri Ram, but after him, no more. Who is this boy, and how did Anju become so intimate with him? Shell Dun Fisher. Linno repeats the name twice, as if correct pronunciation might lead her to the answer.

After hanging up with Miss Schimpf, Linno tries to imagine her sister making or even admitting to such a confession. Highly unlikely, considering Anju's tendency to talk her way out of any trouble.

Except a tangle of vines.

Dread climbing her stomach, Linno recalls the corner of her painting, where she had so artfully planted her name. There were times when she thought about mentioning this to Anju, but she had no interest in speaking to her sister over the phone. Now her failure to do so seems intentional. One betrayal for another.

Absently, she worries a thread along the edge of her knotted sleeve until the thread comes loose. She pulls at the end, winding it around her finger, a tiny strangulation, though still she feels nothing.

IN TOWN, people are starting to look at Linno as though an unpleasant rash has appeared on her face, and they are mustering every ounce of self-containment to leave it unmentioned. She goes to the Chantha where Valan fishermen have spread the dawn's catch on the ground, piles of smelt, sardines, catfish, and the local favorite, *karimeen*. A thousand sequin eyes stare up at her, the metallic scales of the fish caught by morning light, the air laced with a briny smell. When she tries to bargain with one of the fishermen, he seems to assent to her price out of pity, he who makes barely enough to sustain his family for a few days, he whose collarbone protrudes as though his whole, hungry skeleton is threatening to escape his skin.

So Linno is not entirely surprised when she arrives home to find an article in a local newspaper, one of the strange side pieces that appear beside other curiosities, like the story of a woman betrothed to a tree or a boy who performed a Cesarean section on a disgraced village girl.

SCHOLARSHIP WINNER
STRIPPED OF HONORS; FLEES

New York City—A Kerala exchange student who was being sponsored by a Manhattan private school fled her host family more than three months after she arrived in the United States. The whereabouts of Anju Melvin, seventeen, are unknown.

In May of 2003, Melvin received a full scholarship from the Sitwell School in New York, which sponsored her entry from Kumarakom. Several months later, school officials found that Melvin had won the scholarship on false pretenses. When confronted with the matter, Melvin confessed, and disappeared a day later. She left behind a note explaining her intention to run away.

Since the September 11 terrorist attacks, the United States government has toughened the student visa process. Three of the September 11 hijackers had entered U.S. on a student visa.

As in the old days, Linno reads the article aloud while Ammachi and Melvin listen. The words "Melvin" and "false" and "hijackers" are stones that settle in their stomachs.

Unlike after Linno's other newspaper readings, Ammachi rebukes no one. She sits with an air of fragile stillness.

"Melvin? Just Melvin?" Melvin snaps. "They couldn't write 'Miss Melvin'?"

"Not when you've done something bad," Ammachi says. "Only when you've done something good do they call you Miss and Mister."

AT THE END OF THE WEEK, Linno phones an immigration lawyer whose number she copied from a commercial, Srikant Ramakrishnan. His silvery beard and noble bearing gave her the impression that his head and shoulders belonged inside an ornate frame. "I will not take a single paisa," he had said, "until I win your case."

Linno schedules a free thirty-minute consultation in the hopes of finding a U.S. visa that is compatible with her intentions, some sort of two-week Relative Recovery Visa. She will do anything. She will wear a homing device around her neck that beeps with every step if U.S. Homeland Security thinks it necessary. Mr. Ramakrishnan has only to point her in the right direction.

In person, Mr. Ramakrishnan seems to have aged past his televised self. His hair has surpassed its silver and begun to yellow, and his nose is as pocked and rutted as a peach pit. Linno has to repeat herself several times to explain the full story, and when she is finished, Mr. Ramakrishnan does not turn to the many tomes and texts behind him but instead scratches his nostrils, his fingers coming dangerously close to an excavation. After a sigh, he gives his prognosis with more sympathy than he might usually dole out for the free consultation.

"You can apply for the tourist visa," Mr. Ramakrishnan says. "But with your sister's situation, they would let in a flock of Iraqis before they even read your name."

On that basis, he declines to take her case, citing his overwhelming workload, a convenient loophole for avoiding the "not one paisa" promise.

WITH OR WITHOUT Mr. Ramakrishnan, Linno plans to apply with what money she has left from the Sweet Sixteen invitation cards. To this sum, Alice adds twenty-five thousand rupees.

"How will I pay you back?" Linno asks.

"It's called a bonus," Alice says. "No payback necessary."

Linno accepts the check in silence. Once in a while, Alice displays a subtle mothering quality, as when she went out to lunch and returned with a new umbrella for Bhanu because his had broken that morning. And now this check, from which Linno will not look up for fear that doing so might bring her to tears.

Alice squeezes Linno's arm. "But think of what the lawyer said. Putting your money in this is like dropping your coins into a wishing well. It may help with your own peace of mind, but it won't do any good for your sister's."

Linno turns away, briskly folds the check in half. What Alice does not understand is that peace of mind will come only when Anju is returned. Before that, any relief is simply a temporary shelter, a roof that will cave.

"I just mean that we should find another way," Alice adds gently. "The best way."

"From where? How?"

"My brother."

"Kuku?"

"I only have one," Alice says, almost apologetically. "But believe me, he has friends in high places. Ministries even."

. . .

LINNO HARDLY SLEEPS during these first two weeks. Time, with its viscous consistency, both stretches and shrinks, thins and thickens, hurtling through one week or dragging across the eternity of a minute. During the day, she works on invitations, as each new order that Alice brings is a mercy to her wandering mind. She used to glower at strangers, blaming them for the troubles they seemingly lacked, but now she harbors no envy for those celebrating a golden anniversary gala or a Mughal-themed baby shower. Instead she sees the money in each invitation, a growing sum that will somehow bring her sister back, as soon as Kuku comes up with the right strategy. Her fingers are flecked with paper cuts and smudges, but she works with a steady, fevered focus until Alice draws the window shade and sends her home.

By day, thinking feels like a kind of inefficient swimming, the way Anju used to do when she was a sunbaked little thing in knickers, kicking and kicking until she came up for a breath and noticed that she had gone just a few feet from her point of origin. At night, all Linno can do is sit at the kitchen table and try to drive the competing sounds from her mind, like the voices of Miss Schimpf and Mrs. Solanki, whose calls have grown fewer, both of them increasingly concerned with how Linno is handling everything, a question that Linno does not know how to answer. "Fine," she says. "Thank you."

Somewhere, a faucet is dripping. The pots and pans, washed and laid to dry on rags, have grown mossy with shadow. When she is lucky, darkness focuses her vision, gives contour and depth to what has transpired. Anju must have fled out of shame, but she wouldn't have left without arranging a place to go. To whom did Anju turn and can that person be trusted? Should Linno post a reward for information about Anju's whereabouts? Terrible idea. Some broken-nosed thug might kidnap her. Tape up her mouth. Put her in the boot of a car. Brainwash her. Ransom her. In another time, in another life, Linno could be penning an episode for *Sympathy*, casually playing chess with imagined lives.

GOD CREATED THE UNIVERSE in seven days, and in that same space of time, Kuku George has still not come up with a plan for Linno to pursue. Or if he has, he has failed to phone her about it. For three days in a row, she calls his cell phone, and on the fourth day, a Sunday evening, she tries his home phone and leaves two urgent messages that Kuku should call her as soon as possible.

In the meantime, Linno keeps company with the drawing tablet in her lap, trying to create an invitation for her first white client, Mrs. Judy Lambert.

Mrs. Lambert came to them by way of her tennis partner, Mrs. Nair, who had sent her Rachna's Sweet Sixteen invitation. Mrs. Lambert immediately phoned Mrs. Nair and inquired after the name of the invitation shop, what with her own fiftieth birthday bash coming up.

Judy Lambert is Alice's great white hope, the gleaming key to a pride of wealthy Episcopalian clientele who thrive on outdoing one another. She is a fashion magazine editor, opinionated, effusive, and where she treads, the pride will follow.

But while white people seem to favor simpler designs, Mrs. Lambert has especially requested some "Asian flair" to the invitation, to complement the Oriental theme of her party. "There will be Chinese lanterns," she gushed to Alice, "and origami cranes and folded fans and everywhere just red, red, red!"

Linno suggested to Alice that Mrs. Lambert might have mistaken one part of Asia for another by hiring their services. "What do I know of China? And this, what about this?" Linno held up a printout of the digital file that Mrs. Lambert had sent, allegedly the Chinese symbol for harmony. "She wants me to put this in the design. How?"

"That is your job to know and my job to sell," Alice said. "If this woman came to us by mistake, it's a blessed mistake."

But home seems the wrong place to ponder harmony of any kind, let alone that of the Chinese variety. Linno sketches without interest, intermittently glancing at the phone. Ammachi shuffles across the room and looks over Linno's shoulder. She scratches her hip. These days, she has taken to wandering about the house wearing a pink floral muumuu and a dreamy frown, her hair in a wilting knot.

"Did anyone call?" Ammachi asks.

"No."

"Where is Melvin?"

"Driving Abraham Saar." Melvin had gone despite Abraham's suggestion that he take the day off. Melvin declined, hoping that putting himself to work would put his mind to rest.

Ammachi eases into the plastic chair next to her. "What are you drawing a baby for?"

"No reason," Linno says. She crosses out her sketch of a plump, jowly head intended to be that of Mao Tse-tung.

Ammachi gazes at the curio cabinet, absorbed by the marble plaque behind the glass. "Anju was a very round baby, like a *matthangya.*" Linno already knows this story but allows Ammachi to continue. "A nine-pound gourd, that's what she was, hairy all over from sitting in the womb so long. At least that was how she looked in the picture your mother sent. I took the picture around with me, but I was too ashamed to show it to my friends. They kept asking and I kept pretending that it had gotten lost in the mail." Ammachi looks at Linno. "The picture, not the baby."

Linno nods.

"I blame your mother. She ate too much fish pickle during her pregnancy."

"That's why Anju was hairy?"

Ammachi clicks her tongue at such illogic. "That's why Anju is the way she is. Impulsive. Unsatisfied. Constipated. Always trying to push her way through the world."

Linno does not disagree. Anju is all of these things, but if fish pickle is responsible, Linno wonders what her own fetal diet was like. Perhaps plain, harmless foods like rice and yogurt, okra, a sensible gruel here and there . . .

The phone shrieks. Linno lunges for it.

On the other line, a woman's voice says: "Linno Vallara?"

"Yes?"

"Aha. Linno." The woman pauses, rallying her emotion. "Now you listen to me. I understand that you're having a tough time these days, but you had your chance with him. What business do you have breaking up a home?"

"Who is this?" Linno asks.

"There is a right way to do things, and the right way is to have the blessings of family and God, which we have. And you? You want to go sneaking behind my back, *allay*? Well, no one goes sneaking behind my back and certainly not God's back either!"

"Who is it?" Ammachi whispers loudly.

"What is this?" Linno asks. "Who are you talking about?"

"I mean my Kuku. I asked him why you called for him, *twice*, but he refuses to tell me the truth. He says this is private business."

"Whose Kuku? Who is this?"

"This is Jincy." In English, perhaps to elevate her threat level, she adds: "His *finance*. You und-a-stan? His soon-to-be *vife*."

· · ·

"I WASN'T SURE how to tell you," Alice says.

Linno and Alice are sitting across from each other at the drafting table. Alice taps her spoon on the rim of a mug—*plink, plink*—and watches the instant Bru whirl into a pasty cloud. She pushes the mug toward Linno, who ignores the offering and instead carves a spiral into a piece of paper. She listens to the hum of the printer chugging and spitting its majestic announcements.

"More sugar?" Alice asks.

Linno scrapes her blade around and around. "It's a patient man who can love a woman like that."

"Who said anything about love? They are getting married."

"When?"

"Next month. You know how it goes. Fast fast, before anyone changes their minds."

Alice watches as Linno pulls up on the center of the spiral, so that a perfect spring rises out of the table. In this, the negative space is as vital as the paper shape itself, a harmony between the tangible and intangible. She feels an idea bucking against the walls of her mind until she notices Alice staring at her with a troubled expression.

"I didn't realize you cared so much," Alice said.

"Hm? No, I was thinking about the design—"

"I wasn't going to tell you just yet, but maybe this will lift your spirits." Alice leans forward to whisper, though Prince is at the other end of the shop, taking inventory. "About your sister—Kuku seems to have found a solution."

Linno drops the spiral and sits up.

"Why didn't you say something?"

"Because he was trying to contact someone about some logistical thing . . ."

But Linno is already off her stool, zipping up her purse. "I only hope his fiancée won't be there."

LINNO'S MIND IS FLYING faster than the auto-rickshaw wallah can take them. Scooters zip past, including one straddled by a woman in a salwar, the end of her orange shawl flickering flamelike amid the smells of gasoline and dust. It is still a strange sight to see a woman driving a scooter, as just a few years back women only rode sidesaddle, perched behind their husbands, watching the road fly by. The scooter woman speeds ahead, a shrinking dab of orange in the distance. Stuck behind a bus, Linno's driver swabs the sweat off the back of his prickly neck with a kerchief that looks exhausted by its purpose.

"We'll get there," Alice says.

Linno glances at her reflection in the round sideview mirror. Who is this person—so demanding, so tense and terrified? She keeps her fingers curled around the partition bar, within a tantalizing few feet of the steering wheel.

2.

THEY ALL HAVE THEIR SOLUTIONS. Ammachi has prayer, Linno has Kuku, and Melvin has a connection.

While Linno's auto-rickshaw is beetling down Good Shepherd Road, Melvin is hurrying to meet a friend of a friend of a friend. This friend thrice removed goes by a single initial: G. Melvin wonders if he should call him Mr. G, but decides that people who go by single initials probably prefer as much brevity as possible.

G runs a secret currency exchange counter in the back of his tobacco store, where visitors can get a good exchange rate on American dollars, several rupees more than what is offered by the bank. In the late nineties, he thrived behind his clandestine counter, living off the fat of the illegal liquor market and giving a good exchange for hundred-dollar bills. But since the recent arrival of competition, he has branched out into another side business, this one more secret than the first.

What Melvin assumed was a bathroom turns out to be the heart of the side business, a small, windowless room furnished with a card table and a bare bulb that sheds an unsparing light on G's face, which is scarred not so much by brutal fights but by a skirmish with puberty. Acne has left pocks and craters of a depth that make Melvin want to look away and scrub his own cheeks clean. But he does not. He heard somewhere that two dogs at odds would continue to growl until one surrendered by looking away. Melvin will not be the latter dog.

"I'm considering you as a client," G says, "only because Berchmans could vouch for you."

With unabashed sincerity and eye contact, Melvin says thank you.

G shows Melvin two identical visas—one real and one fake—though only G can distinguish one from the other. It is clear from G's craftsmanship that he is not so much a visa counterfeiter as a connoisseur of fraud, and he handles his work with all the love of a father handling his baby girl. Not allowed to touch, Melvin squints at the sophistication in the doctoring of a signature, in the digital replication of a seal. G must have taken infinite care to produce a stamp identical to that issued by the Chennai consulate, at such a perfectly careless slant.

First they discuss fees, or rather, G gives a figure that Melvin has no choice but to accept. "This is not a sari shop," G says. "No haggling here. One lakh."

One hundred thousand rupees. A dizzying string of zeroes, but what price can Melvin put on his own daughter? What sum just to pass by her doorway and see her lima bean shape in the bed as it always was, as it was meant to be, if not for his relentless pushing?

Melvin agrees to the sum. Loans will have to be taken from places seedier than this, from persons with scars that imply worse than G's.

"Also you should know that I invest in protection. So if you tell anyone, there will be . . ." G hesitates, uncomfortable with this part of the presentation. "Consequences. You know what I mean."

Melvin doesn't, but nods unconvincingly. With an impatient sigh, G adds, "You ruin my business, I ruin you. Okay? Broken legs are only the beginning."

Melvin is not sure what to say after that. The bulb flickers as G busies himself with his visas.

"Would you be the one to . . . ruin me?" Melvin asks.

"Oh no no no," G says reassuringly, waving his doughy hands in the air, as if declining a second serving of food. "I don't have the heart for all that."

THE NEXT DAY, Melvin drives Abraham's entire family all the way to Ernakulam in order to buy kurta pyjamas at Jayalakshmi, a tall, palatial store that offers air-conditioned comfort to its visitors and sweltering chaos for the drivers trying to park around it. A man in a nondescript uniform shrills his whistle at the entering cars that slant this way and that. Beggars weave in the spaces between, specifically aiming their palms at the sunglassed patrons. A plaid-panted man passes coolly around an auto-rickshaw, but when the fingers of a beggar graze his shoulder, he recoils like an affronted turtle into the collar of his polo, crying out: "He touched me!" No one comes to his rescue.

At last Melvin drives the family back home. Abraham sits in front, his thick arm hanging out the open window, embracing his Ambassador. Mrs. Chandy and her twin sons, Shine and Sheen, are pressed against each other in the back, among plastic bags that hold far more than what they had planned to plunder. At nineteen, the boys share their father's physique, muscled and broad, but lack his ambition. Shine is always draped across a couch or dazed before the television, while Sheen prefers to loiter outside the girls' college, making eyes at the exiting students. At the moment, both boys are wearing earphones plugged into a music device about as big as a credit card. Melvin can hear the faint electronic pulsing of music that sounds American, but could be Bollywood just the same. Gone are the tablas and chendas of his youth, the songs that he could call his own, displaced by lyrics like "I love ice cream" and "Hey you sexy sexy," songs that seem neither East nor West but fall through the divide.

Before sundown, Abraham tells Melvin to pull over at a restaurant. Abraham stays in the car a moment, telling his wife and sons that he and Melvin will follow shortly.

Melvin rests his hands on the bottom of the leather-covered steering wheel, unsure of what to do with them at this juncture. He loves these old cars, their British elegance, like round-eyed gentlemen in seal grays and dove whites, loves them with the sadness of watching something slowly disappear, chased away by smaller cars, bland in their global uniformity. He ponders this so as not to appear too uncomfortable in the silence of the car, unspoken words pressing in on all sides. *How terrible about Anju.* He has been hearing this sentence quite a lot lately, and he hates the sound of it, the morbid finality, the acceptance.

"Anju reminds me of Gracie in many ways," Abraham says finally. "She has a certain vision of her life."

This, a discussion of Melvin's dead wife and Abraham's betrothed, is not what Melvin was expecting. He keeps his eyes on a scrawny yellow puppy leaning against the trunk of a diseased tree. The puppy seems possessed of a world-weariness beyond its quaint size.

"People like that do not run off without a clear plan," Abraham says. "It's not in their nature. They may take risks, but these are measured risks."

"I suppose," Melvin says. When he was small, he beckoned to a stray puppy from the other side of a street. It hesitated, then sauntered toward him just as a lorry was hurtling down the road. Melvin never told anyone of that day, not his mother or his cousins. He had never been saddled with a story that hurt too much to tell, that required a strength beyond his means to simply open his mouth and begin. And now seeing this puppy, he thinks of the one he killed, a hot and trembling pile on the road that God must have forgotten.

"I'm trying to say that she will be all right, Melvin. You will find her, and until then, she will be all right."

Though Melvin means to say thank you, the only sound he can muster is an affirmative grunt. He is reminded of the time he misspoke the name for XO. *Yeksho, Yeksho,* the mistake had clung to him all that day and for months afterward, despite the graceful way in which Abraham passed over it. If only he shared Abraham's self-possession. If only he, too, had all the right words that lined themselves up when a situation demanded it.

Up ahead, they watch the point where the road meets the sky, that thin gray line vibrating metallic in the heat. For now, they are simply two men. Not driver and employer, but perhaps, momentarily, friends.

Once inside the restaurant, however, when Mrs. Chandy invites Melvin to sit at their table, he declines and sits alone. This is partly why Melvin is considered a good driver. Quietly, he abides by the old way. He knows his place. He comforts them with the knowledge that even if the entire country is changing, the important things are not.

AFTER WORK, Melvin visits Gracie's thicket of teak trees. The trunks rise to five times his height, slender and old, shades of their fragrance borne on the breeze. The leaves cluster thickly but allow the sun to filter in pieces, casting a mosaic of light on the ground. Here in solitude, Melvin finds all the aging gravitas of a library.

He rarely visits, feeling uncomfortable around these trees. They seem to carry something ancestral and disapproving in their postures despite the fact that he never sold them, not even during the jobless times. He used to look forward to the day when he would give the land to his daughters, for their dowries, happily leaving him with nothing more than the knowledge that his final job as father was done.

He remembers when Anju, then a little girl, asked him if he regretted having had no sons. Anju's classmate Naresh had informed her that "daughters drain their Appa's finances."

He paused to think. It was important to say the right thing.

"I have excellent finances," he said. "Did I ever tell you about your mother's teak trees? Dozens of them. I could marry you off several times over."

To which Anju said, in a small voice, "Oh."

What he meant to say was this: he has never felt anything but the most engulfing love for each child, before the infant was declared boy or girl, before it was neither *he* nor *she* but *ours*, a love that turned nearly fierce at each baptism, especially at the moment when the priest took the baby and sat her vulnerable bum in a cold basin of water, chanting, oblivious to her torrential screams. From a very early age, Linno demanded to dress herself, and Melvin was quite sure that the sacrament of baptism had something to do with it.

He thrived in his flat of women, not least among them Gracie. She was smarter than he was, a fact that other husbands might have found irritating, but he enjoyed. When he read a political cartoon or editorial in the newspaper, one that he actually understood, he wanted to tell her about it, not to impress her with his learning but to hear what she might say.

And what would she say at a time like this? That these trees mean nothing, that money itself loses all value if it cannot be spent on their children.

He has thought it all out; he has staked each step of the plan. With this money, he will buy a fake visa for himself under a false, non-Islamic name. (He is still trying to come up with the name, but something plain and pronounceable. No gaping vowels and absolutely no *z*'s.) He will secure himself a two-week passage to New York, find Anju, bring her back, and they will slip right back into their lives as if nothing at all has changed. It is exactly Linno's plan, but illegal and therefore much more efficient.

As for Ammachi's plan, fat lot of good will come from praying to a saint, aloft on its pedestal, its crescent-eyed gaze fixed on a realm beyond the earthly one. Lately Melvin has begun to wonder if God is not a thing that can be seen through so clear a glass as Anthony Achen offers. He still feels the pull of his faith, but he prefers the fogginess that he read of in a Tagore poem as a boy: ". . . and the time come to take shelter in a silent obscurity." He was made to recite it from memory in front of the class, an exercise that he mostly failed except for the one line that, to this day, tolls with all the depth and truth of a church bell through his mind.

Melvin was not always so unsure. As a child, he was devout, granting particular adoration to St. Yohannan Nepumocianos, patron saint of confession, whose expression seemed somehow more benevolent than the others. But things began to change when Ammachi told him a story about her father's miraculous encounter with the saint.

Ammachi's family used to attend the northern church of St. Yohannan Nepumocianos, as opposed to the southern church of St. Yohannan Nepumocianos. Though built by entirely different denominations, both churches honored the martyred Czechoslovakian priest who, according to lore, refused to reveal to the reigning king the details of the queen's confessions. For this, the king cut off the priest's tongue and drowned him in a river. Though a little-known saint, Yohannan Nepumocianos was also the patron saint of floods, which won him the worship of two churches in Kumarakom, a land beholden to the mercy of the rainy seasons. Every year, both his churches held their annual Perunal in his honor, each festival full of competitive pomp and vigor.

One night, after a raucous Perunal at the southern church, the day before the Perunal at the northern one, Ammachi's father went stumbling home with a friend, trudging along the banks of the river. At some point, through their drunken mists, they felt the growing pound of hooves along the ground as sure as the thump of their heartbeats. And then, out of the black it appeared: a white horse galloping toward them, a robed man astride its back. As the horse passed, it struck them both so hard across the heads that the men fell unconscious. When they awoke—they found themselves on the other side of the river!

Clear to them then: that horseman was the spirit of St. Yohannan Nepumocianos, on his way from one Perunal to another. Others had seen him, too, in earlier years. And of course it made sense that he would be traveling overnight. How else could he be expected to attend both festivals?

Ammachi had meant for the story to strengthen her son's faith, but instead it filled the small Melvin with dread for every time he had to attend church and face the statue of St. Yohannan Nepumocianos. Thus far, he had operated on the belief that saints looked on from a kindly distance and did not kick mortals around on their way home from a party. To this day, he grows uncomfortable bringing his petitions to stone-cut saints and their irisless eyes. For many reasons, it seems more sensible to bargain with the living rather than the dead.

EASIER SAID THAN DONE when living with a mother like his own. Melvin is sitting on the front steps beneath a mulberry-colored sky, smoking a bidi that he found in the pocket of his shirt, the first small mercy of the week. The mosquitoes veer about but rarely bite him, bored with local blood. He listens to the thrum of winged things, the rustle of tiny lives and deaths, and wonders what it would be like to struggle as everything else in the world struggles, without sense of past or future, without regret or foreboding. But the mango trees look reproachful tonight, shimmering their leaves, in agreement with his mother's belief that they too suffer pain. He remembers how, when he found himself in trouble, Ammachi would snap a branch from the tamarind tree out back, apologizing to the tree for doing so *(I'm sorry, it hurts you, I know it hurts you)*. With that branch, she proceeded to whip her wayward son without a trace of her arboreal empathy.

"Ah," Ammachi says from the doorway. "You're home." She takes up the seat beside him, facing him squarely, and stares. "Where were you today?"

This is not unlike the time when Melvin tried to make a kite of Ammachi's shawl, an experiment that led to his very first brush with the tamarind branch. But now he is a grown man simply trying to philosophize in private, on his own front step.

"Working out some things," he says.

"Rappai saw you among the teak trees. You never go there."

An image springs to mind of his wife, clad in a sari, moving through the trees. The copper semicircle of her back, her palm thumping a trunk. This was before he took the train back to Bombay, alone, before the troubles began.

"*Enda*, Melvin," Ammachi says gently. "I know you are planning something very stupid."

"What would you have me do? Make trips to church? I'll only pray for people who have no other chance left. Not my child."

"You could make one trip. We will go tomorrow. One trip. It will help you."

Melvin shakes his head. He does not want the kind of comfort that lasts so long as he is within church walls.

"Are you selling those trees?" Ammachi asks. "Is that your plan?"

"Some, not all."

"I knew it! For what? Something illegal probably."

"Sssh!"

"My son," she says mournfully. "Trying to rescue someone in a well by jumping in after them."

"What well?" Linno asks.

Ammachi and Melvin look over their shoulders at Linno, who is standing in the doorway, breathing hard. She wipes the sweat off her nose with her sleeve.

Unable to prevail upon Melvin, Ammachi turns her frustrations on Linno. "Do you have to work so late all the time? What is this Alice making you do? Not eating, not sleeping. You're becoming just like this, like a pencil." Ammachi demonstrates the width of a pencil between thumb and forefinger.

"She's helping me," Linno says, unperturbed. Her eyes are brighter than they've been in weeks, touched by a hopeful light. "We've made a plan."

BEFORE SEEING KUKU, Linno had to remind herself that she was not the type of person to cling to her regrets. There are women who feed off the void of decisions unmade, the men they should have married, the children they meant to have, or if not a child, a chubby stone cherub. It had been several months since that first visit, and the only obvious change seemed to be the pink potted flowers flanking each step. Linno wondered if these arrived by Jincy's suggestion.

Kuku received them in his study where he was seated at his desk, prepared for them. The desk was grand, fashioned from teak, and perfectly ordered: pencils in a cup at the upper left corner, pens in a cup at the upper right, a white rotary phone, and a small porcelain Virgin Mary who stood upon a pedestal that read MOTHER, PRAY FOR US. With her arms outstretched, the Virgin faced Kuku, as if he were the deity to whom she was relaying the world's petitions. And Kuku was a happy god in his padded office chair, his hands holding the armrests, triumph all over his face.

"I think you should apply for the B-1," he said. "Temporary visitor for business visa. With this visa, Consulate doesn't have to know about Anju. They will ask business questions only." Counting on his fingers, he outlined the intentions of the business visitor—to negotiate contracts, to consult with business associates, to participate in business seminars and conventions . . .

"Negotiate and consult with whom?" Alice asked.

Kuku pulled a magazine from his desk drawer and held it to his chest like a newly earned certificate. "Desi-Club" was written in sprawling letters across the front, over an Indian girl with fat silver headphones and a jewel in her navel. "Does this say 'Desi-Club'?" he asked quickly. Alice said yes. "Okay, look on page twenty-three. Or twenty-four, I don't remember. Jincy was the one who read it to me."

As Linno seized the magazine and flipped the pages, Kuku added: "Jincy was very sorry, she wanted me to tell you, Linno. She can be a bit territorial with me."

But Linno and Alice were scanning page 23, a full-page English article with photos of models seductively bored in their bridal wear like wanton wives-to-be, and another photo of two veiled belly dancers posing hip to hip.

DUNIYA EXPO: THE ULTIMATE BRIDAL SHOW TAKES ON NEW YORK!

Remember the old days, when parents planned the entire wedding without consulting the children? Remember when young brides had to travel all the way back to India just to print their invitations and buy their wedding saris? With Duniya, Inc., those days are over! We bring South Asia to you!

Duniya Expo Bridal Show has been rocking New Jersey, D.C., and Maryland for the past Four Years and now we think it's time to take a bite out of the Big Apple. On June 1, 2003, the Duniya Expo Bridal Show will take over Long Island, featuring hundreds of wedding, food, and fashion vendors across a huge 80,000-square-foot floor. The day will be full to the brim with events, including the trade show, wedding planning seminars, spiritual workshops, demos, and world-class performances by British pop sensation Bombay Bomb Squad! So mark your calendars for this family event. We bring the deals and you make the steals!!

"We are to go to this expo?" Alice asked.

"Why not?" Kuku said. "There's a thousand-dollar fee, but it's a good investment. I know an immigration lawyer who just got a B-1 for two weavers to bring their merchandise direct to American department stores. One week, in and out."

"How do we start?" Linno asked.

"Duniya is an American-based company. You will call them. You will find out what it takes to lead a seminar at this expo. Seminar makes you sound more important. Once you pay the fees, Duniya will give you an invoice and maybe a letter to prove to the Chennai consulate that you need a business visa."

Linno tried to read the boisterous text and reply at the same time. Belly dancers, brides, Big Apple. She looked at Kuku. Quietly, she thanked him.

"It was a joint effort," said Kuku. "I couldn't have done it without my wife. Hah! Listen to me. Already calling her my wife." His chuckle thinned to a contented sigh. Linno barely heard the remark as she was busy calculating the number of weeks between January and June. For the first time that month, she felt a light filling the dark eaves of her mind, and who would have guessed that the one to throw the switch would be Kuku?

ALICE HAS BEEN WAITING to build an invitation empire, and when finally given a chance, she chooses against remodeling the shop. Her new view holds that profitable investments lie elsewhere—on the Internet.

To navigate their way into this frontier, Alice enlists the help of her nephew Georgie, a computer science student at IIT, the jewel of the family, a quiet boy who always wanted to be a cartoonist but had neither the permission of his parents nor the sense of humor to pursue it. Over the phone, Alice explains to him what she wants—a website for East-WestInvites.com, a name she chose for its global appeal. Buying the host server and building the site requires a good deal of money, but Alice possesses an almost biblical faith that the money will return to them sevenfold.

On his first free weekend, Georgie takes the train from Chennai to show Alice and Linno what he has designed. The bashful nephew that Alice remembered is now a subdued adult, fragile as a soft fruit, a young man who has spent the last two years primarily conversing with and confiding in a computer. As if arriving for an interview, he wears a shirt and tie and carries a biscuit-thin computer in its own briefcase. His fingers clatter gently against the keys, and in minutes the phrase "East West Invites" appears against pale paisley wallpaper, while beneath this the words unravel: "Welcome to East West Invites, Exclusive Invitation Boutique." In the center of the page is a crisp, sharp photo of Linno's very first card, which fades into an opened version displaying the blue and rust red butterfly.

Linno has never seen anything like this website, whose colors surpass those produced by the television. The lines are clean, the writing luxurious, the pictures dissolving from one into the next. Most girls Linno's age are Internet-savvy, having learned to type and surf in their computer classes, but since leaving school, Linno has always felt herself trapped in the pretechnological Dark Ages. It feels impossible now to catch up with the rest. Better to leave this world to Georgie, who speaks with hurried excitement about the wonders of Flash animation, continually moving his cursor and tapping on various features. A navy menu panel appears to the right, inscribed with phrases like: *Our Mission, Contact Us, Our Preferred Associates,* and *Collection.* Each phrase pulses when touched by the cursor and leads to a new page when clicked. Though most of these pages are as yet empty, Linno is astonished by the overall elegance of the design. It is like entering a wealthy, wallpapered mansion that bears little resemblance to the actualities of their shop.

"I'm paying Georgie to be our webmaster," Alice says proudly.

"See, the simplicity sets you apart from the rest," Georgie says. "Nice and clean, not too much text."

He summons up the Mission Statement, a letter signed by Alice about her commitment to quality, innovation, and style, no matter the budget: *The invitation is the gateway to a blessed event. If you want to personalize your event even more, you can work with our in-house designer, Linno Vallara, who has the vision and talent to imagine a new dimension in paper artistry.*

"You wrote this about me?" Linno asks.

"Prince and I wrote it together. We stole some of it from an American website." Alice points at the screen. "But the collection is what you need to work on. We need at least ten new designs. I'll send them to Georgie, and he will take pictures and . . . what is it?"

"Upload them," Georgie says.

"Upload them. Will you do this, Linno? Design ten more?"

But Linno does not answer, her mind already drifting to the shelves of rainbowed color, a spectra of combinations, a frontier far less foreign.

THAT EVENING, Ammachi begs Linno to watch an English film with her, one that she saw on television a month ago. She insists that Linno needs a break from her anxieties, which have etched unwelcome lines across her forehead. Linno refuses, noting how most of these outdated films have dismal titles and infantile storylines—*Home Alone 3,* for example, or *Demolition Man*—films that have been rejected by the very country that made them and funneled, like refuse, into third-world television sets. But Ammachi defends this particular movie, about "a *Madhamma* teacher who goes to a Chinese kingdom to make the Chinas speak better English." That Ammachi, who has little good to say about colonial Britannia, is giving the film a glowing review makes Linno take note.

And how lucky that she does. As it turns out, the film is neither Chinese nor British but American, filled with pagodas and gongs and bonsai trees. *The King and I* takes place in old Siam, in the court of a king played by an American actor whose painted complexion is an odd golden brown, a color too metallic for any race; his eyes are also outlined to seem aslant. Similarly, the pretty white actresses are fashioned into mincing Siamese wives who approximate an accent by speaking slowly and squeakily, whinnying behind tiny hands. And then there is the white woman teacher taking her long, confident strides within her bossy hoop skirts, her grammar as flawless as her coif, come to civilize the court. And though Linno has never seen a picture of Mrs. Lambert, she imagines her in a hoop skirt, absorbing the many marvels of this misty land.

So Linno designs a scarlet and gold-leafed card that opens up from the bottom edge. Modeled on the silhouetted set pieces of *The King and I*, a flat-roofed pagoda lifts from the back page, complete with two thin columns and two tiny steps that lead into a shallow inner chamber bearing the gold symbol for harmony. The party details are printed on the lower half of the card, in a computer font called Chopsticks.

After sending Mrs. Lambert the dummy card for approval, Linno receives a phone call a week later. "You're a genius," Mrs. Lambert says. "You've captured the essence of Asian flair. It's like you climbed inside my head! How did you do it?"

"Research," Linno says.

3.

THERE ARE THOSE in Jackson Heights, Queens, who well know the name "Action Jackson," a neighborhood group that demanded a list of "aesthetic guidelines" for storefronts in the Jackson

Heights area, as proposed by the Landmarks Preservation Commission in 1995. Store facades would be restricted to a mature palette of colors—"black, brown (not bronze), dark gray, tan, dark green and dark red." The proposal eliminated most if not all of the signs hung by Indian and Pakistani shopkeepers along Thirty-seventh Avenue, like John Muqbel's ten-by-twelve-foot candy pink awning, which disagreed with the proposal. "This is purely motivated by prejudice," Muqbel complained to *The New York Times*. "They have no right to impose this on me. I don't live in their house." But the fed-up district manager of Community Board 3 denounced the signs as "absolutely atrocious."

Along came the Apsara Salon with a sign that made every atrocity look quaint, with its crenelated edges and black-on-orange design that unintentionally evoked Halloween. If this Muqbel could get into *The New York Times*, Ghafoor reasoned, so could he. Ghafoor proudly boasted of the competitive mentality that he shared with his fellow Indians, the very reason that Indians were #1 in the *Guinness Book of World Records* in subjects as varied as "longest fingernail" and "tiniest handmade chess piece."

But the Apsara Salon arrived after the commission proved unable to control the colors that rudely bloomed along the street. And when Payless Shoes arrived with its bubbly mango-colored letters, it became clear that the street would have little recourse against crimes of design.

INSIDE THE APSARA SALON, the decor is blandly inoffensive. The rectangular main room narrows into a hallway, leading to a bathroom that wears an OUT OF ORDER sign. Favored customers know the secret—that the bathroom has always been in working order, but this is Ghafoor's way of curbing cleaning costs and the occasional sabotage of a sanitary napkin. These privileged few slip in and out of the bathroom without sullying the floor or saying a word.

But now with Anju, Ghafoor's new hire, he can remove the OUT OF ORDER sign. The new girl is from the old country, which he considers a plus, as she is ingrained to take on the most menial of tasks. She squats like only a third-worlder can, froglike for minutes on end, brushing tumbleweeds of black and hennaed hair into a dustpan. For months, the floor seemed perpetually veiled with scum, but since her arrival last week, every surface has been shiny and slippery and spotless, not a stray hair in sight.

The new girl says very little, which is understandable, seeing as how all the beauticians are either Punjabi or Gujarati and this Anju is Malayali. Ghafoor once tried to instate a Hindi-only policy to prevent sectarian conflict (and to make sure no one was talking behind his back), but implementing such a rule is like trying to cut a hole in water. The words flow around him whether he approves or not.

The only person that Anju speaks to is Bird, who brought her the week before and practically begged Ghafoor to hire them both. Luckily for them, he had recently come across the funds to do so. A rival salon called Surekha Designs had declared bankruptcy, allowing the Apsara to open its arms to Surekha's huddled, hairy masses. Still, to maintain some sense of power, Ghafoor felt the need to hold an official interview in his office, a tiny room postered over with the avatars of ruling Bollywood starlet Aishwarya Rai. Bird and Anju sat across from Ghafoor and Aishwarya the woeful bride, her marine blue contact lenses welling with unspilled tears.

"I heard about your Rajiv Tandon," Ghafoor said, setting his elbows on his desk. "Terrible, just terrible."

Bird nodded.

"Are you sure you can work at my salon after coming from a place like that? Do you remember everything about the beauty industry?"

"I do."

Ghafoor jutted his chin at the girl. "And what of this one?"

"Anju. My niece."

All this time, the girl had been staring dreamily at her shoes, and at the mention of her name, she looked up.

"I can't take a girl with no papers," Ghafoor said. "It's not like before in this country. People are watching."

Bird considered her words before speaking. "She has some problems back home. She needs the money."

"What kind of problems?" Ghafoor waved away all unuttered problems. "No, no, don't tell me. I don't want to know."

Back and forth they argued, Bird pleading and Ghafoor no-no-ing. "What about Rajini?" Bird said. "Remember her? She didn't have papers."

"I did that as a favor. But that was before. I bet you my phone is tapped so that if even I say 'Salaam aleikum,' the police make a note of it."

"Her name is not Salaam aleikum."

He cut his eyes at Anju, who sat with shoulders hunched and fingers laced. "How do you know each other?"

"I told you, she is my niece."

Ghafoor nodded. "And I am your sister."

"All these years I asked you for nothing," Bird said. "This one time. Please."

In the end, out of pity, Ghafoor agreed to take the two of them, though he and Bird haggled over Anju's wage, finally settling on $5 per hour, cash only.

"Part-time," Ghafoor said. "I will help her, so long as she is helpful."

"Thank you, sir." These were Anju's first words of the meeting.

Looking at Anju, Ghafoor hesitated. The girl was frightened, he could tell, but not in the sudden way inflicted by horror movies and tarantulas. Worry had been following her for some time, had drawn a faint line, small as a stitch, in the space between her eyebrows. If he could do nothing about the line, he could do something about the eyebrows.

"Come," he said. "Let's have someone clean up your face."

ANJU HADN'T PAID any attention to her appearance for a full week, not since the day that she confessed to Miss Schimpf and then arrived home to find Mr. and Mrs. Solanki in the living room. Mrs. Solanki's throat was wreathed in fat white beads like an oversized rosary that her fingers kept worrying. This time, there were no samosas on the elephant-ankle table.

They had been apprised of the situation, Mr. Solanki told her. "And as you know from the handbook, Sitwell has a very strict interpretation of the Honor Code. As is, they are suspending you for the next three days, at the end of which time they will make a decision as to whether you should be expelled."

Pushed or punched?

Stabbed or shot?

Thrown off a roof or thrown off a cliff?

Anju found herself nodding, her eyes lost in the carpet underfoot whose peacock blues and greens she had somehow overlooked.

"The award money," Mrs. Solanki said gently. "It would help if you could return it."

Anju swallowed hard and barely heard herself say, "I don't have it." The application had been filed the week before, the money now irretrievable.

No one spoke. There was only the clicking of beads between Mrs. Solanki's fingers. Anju could see what the Solankis assumed, that she was impoverished and distraught, that her thievery was without calculation, that poor people lacked the luxury of a moral compass. She felt small. She had brought herself low.

Suddenly, decisively, Mrs. Solanki planted her hands on her knees. "You know what? I am going to straighten this all out. They know who I am. This will all blow over, I'm sure."

Yes, Anju thought. All this would blow her right over.

DURING THE FIRST DAY of suspension, Anju condemned herself to no television, no phone, and no outdoor excursions, though with both Solankis at work, only Marta the cleaning lady was there to witness Anju's efforts at self-flagellation. Even Marta, who mostly communicated in smiles, seemed to know of Anju's guilt. Perhaps out of pity, Marta made lunch for her. Staring at the mustardy sandwich between her hands, Anju wondered if Marta would do what she had done. Having little other mental stimulation, Anju repeated this question several more times, inserting different names in place of Marta, like Mrs. Solanki, Miss Schimpf, Nehru, P. C. Mappilla, Bushes Senior and Junior. As she divvied up the sides, she was not proud of her team.

Twice the phone rang for Anju, and it was Marta who conveyed the messages to her. "Is from a woman . . . Bird?"

Anju assumed that Bird was calling about the application. "I will call back later," Anju said to Marta.

Having assumed that she could not sink any further, Anju was surprised to find that there were always new depths and sharper plunges. She learned as much on the third day of her suspension, when listening to Mrs. Solanki explain the school's decision.

Mrs. Solanki's fidgeting made her furious energy seem on the brink of coming uncorked. "It appears," she said, "that the school had a few cases last year involving cheating and plagiarism, and since then they've tightened up the rules. Of course, I find it quite odd that they didn't think to tighten up the rules every other time, for far worse crimes. Oh no. Only when we're dealing with a foreigner—"

"Sonia, please." Mr. Solanki turned to Anju. "They feel that the prize money is the main issue. Technically that money is owed to someone else, another winner."

"As if anyone else needs it."

Mr. Solanki clasped his hands between his knees. With head bowed, he looked as though he were the one being punished. He explained to Anju that they had tried to pay for the lost money themselves, but the school would not accept it. "The board feels that it's important to maintain their stance. So they have decided to expel you." Mr. Solanki visibly swallowed. His Adam's apple moved up and down. Anju wondered why it wasn't called Eve's apple. Wasn't Eve the one who lunged for it, who made the first, unforgivable mistake of wanting more than she was allowed? "They have already canceled your return ticket and are reissuing an earlier return date, at their expense, of course. And until then you can still stay with us."

Abruptly they lapsed into silence, a long stretch divided by the ticking of the antique grandfather clock.

"I mean for God's sake!" Mrs. Solanki threw up her hands, her cork burst. "That little ferret, what's her name?"

"Miss Schimpf," said Mr. Solanki.

"Schimpf!" Mrs. Solanki laughed at the very lunacy of the name itself. "She acted as though she had no idea what I was talking about! As if it is pure coincidence that an all-white institution's first expulsion in fifty years is a penniless foreign exchange student. And when I said as much, she babbled some do-gooder nonsense about her sabbatical in India, and I said, 'People like you think of foreign countries as places to plunder, natives as product.' "

Mr. Solanki, having heard several thousand versions of this speech over the course of their marriage, stared at his shoes. "And what exactly was Miss Schimpf trying to plunder with the scholarship project?"

"A feeling of inner peace. Spiritual relief. Why else do people come to India?"

"Sonia, please don't make this into one of your crusades. What is the point?"

"My point is this: they trotted her out like a poor savage. But when the savage is flawed, they throw her on the fire."

Meanwhile, Anju was looking from one to the other, imagining an intricate web of words being built in the air above her, a web that had very little to do with her.

"Maybe you should call your parents," Mr. Solanki said gently.

Anju could have laughed at this suggestion. Laughing at her terror. So this was how a person went crazy.

Instead she nodded. Her tongue had gone dead. At that moment, the hands of the grandfather clock met, causing the clock to chime "Ode to

Joy" while a blue painted bird glided out of an open door in the clock's face, its beak opening and closing, opening and closing, before gliding back into its secret chamber whose tiny doors made her want to plunge her hand inside, like a child, and strangle the sound.

LATER ANJU WOULD WONDER how she did it. How on the third day of her sentence, she shed no tears in bed. How she got up at two in the morning and quietly began to divide her things into what was needed and what was not. She kept her focus on the smaller decisions—two skirts or one pair of pants? The shampoo or the block of kiwi soap? Comb or brush? Bible or sketchbook?

Run home or run away?

She could imagine the coming months, if she went home. Ammachi would never show her face in church again. Melvin would avoid his Rajadhani Bar, perhaps preferring to drink alone. Linno would never look her sister in the eye. All of them had known of her betrayal long before Miss Schimpf's discovery, and in their silent way, they had even condoned it. Now, after running through the muck, Anju had tracked her deception all over the house, across their names as well as her own.

Run home or run away. Shame would follow both routes, but only one could possibly lead to a hopeful end.

For the first time, she began to believe her father's tales of successful immigration, people who got their green cards overnight. Someone won a lottery of sorts. Someone else found the right lawyer and in no time at all, for $2,500, Melvin said, "he took the *I-L* out of 'illegal'!" Whereas once she had scorned these stories, they now attained a hopeful sheen such as can be seen only by the young or truly desperate, and she was both.

If anyone could work such wonders, it was Rajiv Tandon. Her application was already in process, and if she were to be sent back now, the $1,000 she had spent would be all for naught. Perhaps he could speed things along. In the meantime, she would find Bird, who could show her to a temporary hostel or maybe cousins with whom she could board, for a fee. It was liberating to ruminate over the questions and options, to imagine the road ahead splitting and twisting like sinuous banyan roots rather than the dismal singular route that led home. She was free! Her world was boundless, borderless. Life had not begun until now. So what if her plan had holes? She did not pay them heed. People could become slaves to excessive thought. Instead she recalled Anthony Achen's sermon on the day she left Kumarakom, railing on about the Virgin Mary and her visitation by the angel Gabriel. *Did she doubt? No. Did she say, "Can I have a minute to think?" No. Did she say, "I am the handmaiden of the Lord. Do with me what you will?" Absolutely yes. Because when God calls, we do not think. We trust. We go. We do.*

FOR A RUNAWAY, Anju worried that she was moving a bit slowly. In fact, she was not moving at all, but hovering within the brass canopy of her brief but beautiful home, the Monarch. It was 6:30 a.m., the cold morning smudgy with mist. She watched steam ghosting out of a grate and a man in a coffee cart stacking jelly doughnuts like bricks. Nearby, two bicycles were chained to a parking sign, though the front wheel of one had been wrenched away in the night. Any minute now, the owner of the bicycle-turned-unicycle would appear and curse the city he called home.

She would miss the vanilla cake, spired and many-storied, with its sleek banisters curled like treble clefs and uniformed doormen, all kid gloves and courtesy. From this side of the glass, the man at the desk seemed less of a concierge and more like a sentry. But she had no need for these palatial entries and marbled floors, or the gym with its lofted televisions, or the indoor pool quavering with filaments of light, or the fountain and its constellations of copper coins, as if the residents of this building needed more luck than they already had.

Anju left a note on her pillow saying that she was spending the night at a friend's house and would be back by tomorrow afternoon. She wondered if the Solankis would think her ill-behaved. She wondered if they would be surprised by the mention of a friend.

On her way to the subway station, she dropped an envelope addressed to the Solankis in a blue mailbox, containing the note she had penned the previous night. Luckily, no one was around to see her hustling into the elevator in her sleeping bag of a coat, each pocket packed firmly with Fruit Roll-Ups, bags of almonds, and Mrs. Solanki's Slim-Fast bars, plus a duffel bag of her most valued possessions. She had chosen the sketchbook over the Bible, a choice that seemed blasphemous but she hoped God understood. The rest, she assumed, Mrs. Solanki would send back to Kumarakom.

As much as possible, Anju tried not to think of her family. She had struggled to write them a letter the night before, explaining her intentions, but failed to bring pen to page. Each thought of them nibbled at her courage. They would not understand the banyan tree of freedom she had imagined. Better to pretend, for the time being, that she had no family at all.

So for now, Anju focused on the matters at hand. The 7 train or the N train? Or avoid public transportation altogether, for fear of the police? The latter was not an option. Anju envisioned her face as a criminal sketch, her nose made regrettably larger than what it was, or perhaps the school would supply her class photograph: a robotic pose in which her fist was awkwardly propping up her chin.

The world seemed to spread so much farther than ever before, a cement veldt of strangers with collars up, hurrying away. Where Anju was going, no one would know her name. She would christen herself anew, seek a path around the muck. If it was possible anywhere, it was in this city, where the streets were already dense with sound—the squealing of buses and the grumble of trains underfoot, the flutter of fliers from a fortune teller's hand, the sad rattle of change in a Styrofoam cup, all the harsh, accidental music of morning.

As casually as possible, Anju descended the subway steps.

Running away. Simple as that.

IT IS ANJU'S FIFTH DAY of employment at the Apsara Salon. In the spirit of welcome, Anju's coworkers have begun to speak in English when she is present while she, in turn, has learned the cast of full-timers plus a few of their distinguishing traits.

In descending order of rank:

GHAFOOR . . . The ringleader. Looks 50, but probably 55. Formidable hairstyle. Cannot pass a mirror without glancing in it. The salon is all mirrors.

NANDI . . . née Nandini. 40. The best threader in the salon, she can weave subtle crests and arches from caterpillar brows. The word *nandi* means bull, a nickname she has earned from her heavy nasal breathing as she works on a face, the ends of the thread in her mouth, her brow furrowed in concentration.

LIPI . . . Ageless and expressionless. The best blow-dryer in the salon, she yanks the curl out of the unruliest heads of hair. She is slight but tough, a Nepali who landed on the Asian side of the genetic divide, and thus blessedly lacking in facial hair. Lipi's brother works as a sushi chef in a grocery store. "In his kimono and hat," Lipi says proudly, "no one suspects a thing. Even a Japani lady tried to talk to him."

SURYA . . . A competent waxer, able to do everything though she refuses to excel at anything in particular. She is studying to be an engineer and plans to quit in a few weeks.

POWDER . . . Surya's younger sister, age 27 (24 according to her online dating profiles), with bovine hips and unhealthily pale skin. She ascribes her pallor to her mother's complexion, though by no small coincidence, she specializes in facials and bleaching regimens.

Sometimes, when Nandi is threading a client, Anju strategically sweeps near her station, in order to study her technique. At first, Nandi's methods are swift but simple to follow—unraveling the thread, biting off the end, winding it around her fingers into some sort of web with one end still in her mouth. Her client lies back on the seat. "Hold," Nandi commands through clenched teeth, and the client's fingers pull the skin taut on each side of the eyebrow. Her regular clients always know where to hold.

But as soon as Nandi bends over her client, the process dissolves into miracle. Impossible to deconstruct how an eyebrow can be thinned by merely the crossing of threads, plucking hair by hair. The only noise is the zipping of threads and, of course, Nandi's heavy nasal breathing, periodically interrupted by her command to hold somewhere else. At the end, she mows the space between the eyebrows, scrutinizes her work, then gives the hand mirror to her client, who always responds with a satisfied nod. Nandi pats the pinkening skin with a soothing aloe gel and talcum powder, and sends the client back into the world with eyebrows that the client's husband or boyfriend will never notice. "You don't want people to notice," Nandi always says. "That is the key to good eyebrow."

But the key to threading remains beyond Anju's reach. She asks Bird, but Bird has no idea of the technique. Her eyebrows, fat and feathery, betray as much.

Lately Anju has been sweeping and wiping what is already clean, trying to seem more useful than she is. If she does not find a way to make herself useful, perhaps by becoming a threader, Ghafoor might suggest that she find a dirtier floor to sweep and wipe. She spots Bird at the cash register, counting out bills, chatting with the ladies in the waiting room with all the casual comfort of one who owns this place. Maybe Anju will not be fired, not with Bird on her side.

For Bird to care so unsparingly for a stranger, it is almost an act of sainthood. Over the past two weeks that she has lived with Bird, Anju has come to feel both guilt and gratitude for the only friend she has left in this city. Gratitude that Bird has taken her in, and guilt that Anju persuaded her to do so only by spinning another lie.

🦋

UPON RUNNING AWAY from the Monarch, Anju took the 7 train to Jackson Heights. When she emerged from the subway, the Technicolor intensity of certain signs offered at least a visual relief. She walked the route that she knew by heart, past landmarks that she recalled from her first trip, signs declaring BOLLYMUSIC WORLD and BANANA LEAF CAFÉ, past the boxes of fruits and vegetables kept behind a plastic drape to protect them from the chill. Yesterday it had seemed nearly impossible to venture out in the world with one's entire life crammed into a single bag, but at least now Anju was moving with purpose. There was promise in the air.

And yet she could not remember the exact location of Mr. Tandon's office. She stood in the lobby of the building that she had thought was his, surveying the list of lawyers that hung on the wall, each name next to a room number. Rajiv Tandon was not listed. A uniformed black man sat behind a podium, signing in each visitor with a deliberate hand, no matter how they huffed or glanced at their watches.

She hurried in and out of every building on that block and the next, dizzy with the tiny white letters she read on each wall, none of them meeting to form Mr. Tandon's name. When finally she returned to the first building, she was sweating within the plump confines of her coat.

Noticing her distress, the guard asked, "Who you looking for?"

"Rajiv Tandon," she said, and was going to give more information about Mr. Tandon's height, his coloring, his nationality, but upon hearing the name, the guard raised his eyebrows. Not in a way that boded well.

"That guy? What do you want with him?"

It occurred to her that men of good standing were not referred to as "that guy." She felt a stirring in the pit of her stomach. "I have come about business."

The guard scratched the bristle of his unshaved cheek. "Well, the only business he'll be doing is from the corner of a jail cell."

SOMEHOW SHE FOUND her way out into the cold. Her legs carried her down one block and then another, but her mind lagged behind, taking note of the unlit Christmas lights creeping vinelike around the trunks of skinny trees, the signs bearing greetings of HAPPY DIWALI and EID MUBARAK. It was a wonder that she finally noticed a pay phone.

She found the scrap of paper in her purse, worth more than the twenty-dollar bill she had stuffed next to it. Following the directions on the pay phone, she inserted a quarter, dialed the numbers, and waited. When Bird answered the phone, a sudden clot of tears rose at the back of Anju's throat, but she did not have enough quarters to cry on paid time. She said, "This is Anju."

"Anju?" There was a pause. "Where are you? Where have you been? I have been calling and calling. . . ."

Anju looked around for the nearest street sign. "Kalpana Chawla Way."

"Here? You are here?"

Anju nodded into the phone. "Yes."

"Wait inside the grocery store, by the front. I am coming."

Anju listened to the shrill purr of the dial tone and then the kindly voice of a woman telling her what to do if she would like to make a call. She felt a sharp hatred for the voice and the phone through which it came, but as much as she would have liked to slam the phone on its hook, she would not. "This is not your house," Linno once scolded her when she rested her foot on Rappai's plastic coffee table. The reprimand returned to her now. This was not her phone to slam. This country was not her house.

ON BIRD'S COFFEE TABLE was a blue glass vase that Anju remembered from her first visit. It held a bunch of dried flowers, mummified in red and orange dyes. They smelled of eucalyptus, almost pleasant, slightly medicinal. For now, this was all she could digest of the room—a flower, a hue, a smell.

Bird placed a bowl of hot white mush before her and called it Cream of Wheat. When Anju did not move, Bird pushed it closer. "You have to eat something."

In a small voice, Anju asked if Mr. Tandon had killed someone.

"Him? No!"

"Then what happened?"

Perhaps it was unwise to receive bad news on an empty stomach, but Anju was quite certain that any Cream of Wheat she ingested would come right back up in the same form.

"Please," Anju said with such frailty that Bird sighed in concession.

TWO WEEKS BEFORE, Bird had gone to work, punctual as always, to find Mr. Tandon frantically making phone calls in his office. She figured that he was working on a very stressful case, though she never guessed it was his own.

The next day and the day after, she came to an empty office and tried to field all the calls of clients who had heard rumors that Mr. Tandon had been arrested and charged with both fraud and aiding illegal aliens. Bird tried her best to assuage them, but it was impossible to assuage those who had handed over so much money, their thousands of dollars dissolving before their eyes. A Bangladeshi cleaning woman had counted out her entire life savings of $8,000 on Bird's desk, rustling each bill between two fingers with all the wistfulness of a little girl pulling petals from a flower. After news broke of Tandon's disaster, the lady shrieked over the phone at Bird, calling her Mr. Tandon's sister-fucking whore. Bird did not bite back. Where else could these people air their grievances? They were illegals, most of them. They had no voice.

That same week, the office was shut down and the New York State Bar Association disbarred Rajiv Tandon for "professional misconduct and legal incompetence" involving eight illegal immigrants in Jackson Heights. His was one of several names mentioned in a *New York Times* article uncovering the duplicities of the illegal visa business called "Dollars and Dreams: Immigrants as Prey." The article revealed that Rajiv Tandon was raised in New Brunswick, New Jersey, where he had attended a local public school, not St. Albans, as he often claimed. He had taken his law degree from Rutgers School of Law, and after clerking for a court judge in New Jersey, he moved to New York and opened his office to the pool of illegals in Jackson Heights.

The article went on to report the recent growth of such corruption: "As the number of illegal immigrants in this country has swollen to what the Department of Homeland Security conservatively estimates at nine million, so have the ranks of those who inhabit the immigration business's underbelly, posing as well-meaning advisers to those in search of a new job, a new home and a green card if not full citizenship."

After reading the article, Bird wondered where she figured on the food chain between predator and prey. All those chais she had made just to anesthetize clients before their fortunes were properly devoured. What did she know of what went on behind closed doors? But this was no excuse. She had held the hands of some of those people. She had chased Anju down and forced this predator upon her. The following days led Bird to the certainty that she could do nothing for the others, but if there was one person she had to help, it was Anju.

"I tried calling and calling you," Bird said. "I left messages. I thought you had heard somehow and didn't want to speak to me anymore."

THE "DOLLARS AND DREAMS" ARTICLE, which Bird had clipped and saved, lay in Anju's lap. She could tell that her silence was beginning to make Bird wary, but she could not stop staring at her warped reflection on the curve of the blue vase, transfixed, unwilling to return to the world of sharp angles and dead ends. But it was absolutely vital that she present herself as controlled, rational, aware of actions and consequences and their linear order. She blinked twice in the effort not to look unhinged. She took a breath.

"I have a problem."

Bird clasped her hands, her expression eager and anxious. "What can I do? Tell me, I will help you."

"Can I stay here tonight?"

"Of course." Bird glanced at the large duffel bag at Anju's feet, confused about its presence. "Do you want to call the Solankis?"

"No."

Anju would not call anyone because with a single word from a familiar voice, she would doubt herself. And doubt would not allow her to soldier on, to operate under the necessary illusion that she was alone in the world and had no other choice but to stay. If she returned home now, her family's relief would quickly fade against the disgrace that would follow. She could return only once redeemed.

For now she focused on finishing her Cream of Wheat under the skeptical eye of her new roommate. Bird would not settle for the truth alone. She, like any adult, would demand that laws be obeyed, and if not laws, then fathers. Anju's mind moved swiftly to the next lie she would tell. *Move forward, not back,* Ammachi once told her. She had been talking about how to properly sweep a floor, but still.

THOUGH BIRD IS NOT a religious woman, there are times when she feels that she is truly witness to certain small, divine mysteries. Often she thinks of that day in Tandoori Express, when she happened across the *Manorama* article that she would normally skip. What were the chances, the series of good fortunes that brought Bird face-to-face with the closest thing left of Gracie, just as Gracie had promised in one of her letters?

Bird and Anju had met. They had sipped tea in Bird's living room, so small an event to Anju, so monumental to Bird.

And now, in the same living room, Bird listened as the girl defined what precisely she meant by a "problem." Anju explained each step and misstep, from the stealing of the sketchbook to her recent expulsion. She begged Bird to let her stay until she earned back the money she had lost and maybe even worked toward obtaining a green card.

"Wait, wait," Bird interrupted. "The school expelled you, and now you've run away?"

"I did not run, I left. After the school's decision, Mrs. Solanki expected me to return to Kumarakom. What would she do with me for six months, hanging around the apartment all day? I told her, 'I'd like to stay with my auntie in Queens.' Mrs. Solanki said okay."

"And the school has no problem with you staying?"

"I am not their responsibility anymore," Anju insisted. "I'm not breaking any laws by staying. My student visa lasts until the end of June, so I have six months to apply for a visa extension and then residency."

Bird made Anju repeat herself. Was it really that simple? Impossible that the girl could tell anything but truth with such weary calm, a calm that came from having no other choice. "What would your father say about all this?"

"I called him already. I told him all about you."

Bird straightened up, her stomach sinking. "You told him my name?"

Anju hesitated before nodding. "Was I wrong to?"

"No, no. Go on."

"I told him you are a Malayali woman, a secretary and a librarian. An auntie to me here. And that you had tried to help me get a green card. I told him that you might take me in." She waited for Bird to object, but

Bird said nothing. "He was hoping that you would say yes, at least for a short time. He is afraid that if I don't finish my student visa, if I am sent home by the school, it will be a black mark on my record and I will never be allowed to return. . . ."

Bird tried to focus on what Anju was saying, but instead she pictured the Melvin she had never met. She had always imagined him handsome and bearded, muscled and demanding. And what did Bird's name mean to Melvin? No doubt he had once heard of her; Gracie mentioned as much in one of her letters. *(Melvin thinks you are a bad influence. That you are trying to take me away.)* But after all these years, it seemed that he had forgotten her name.

". . . And he has heard of many people applying for a green card and getting it," Anju continued. "So he would like me to stay with you for the time being. Till I get a better status." Anju met Bird's gaze. "He said this is what my mother would have wanted for me."

Bird looked away, fingering her sleeve. "Does he want me to call him?"

"Our long-distance connection is terrible. Better to send letters."

Nodding, Bird stared at the orange flowers, which would live infinitely in their desiccated state, dust gathering between the leaves. Her post-show wreaths and bouquets, now reduced to this. Melvin had been to one of her performances, this much she knew. But now, any conversation between them would lead back to a time that she preferred not to remember, rumors she had left behind, knowingly shrouded in dust. Did he remember the rumors? Did he connect them to the "auntie" Anju had told him about? It seemed he didn't, but he might, if Bird called. And then this beautiful chance, so fortunate for Bird and Anju both, could be lost.

"Do you want my father to call you?" Anju asked.

"No," Bird said quickly. "No need."

"So can you help me?"

This was the question that snagged on Bird's heart, an echo of the one she had uttered countless times in Tandon's office—*Can I help you?*—all the while knowing that her help would never amount to much. Now she could care for this child, Gracie's child, whom Melvin was entrusting to her.

It had taken a day to bury Gracie, but for Bird it had taken no less than a decade. Now it seemed reasonable to wonder if life did not, in fact, hinge on death, and whether the door to Gracie's life could fall open years later with an inquisitive creak.

Anju's hands gripped the sofa cushion beneath her, her shoulders hunched, waiting for the fall of Bird's judgment.

"Okay," Bird said. "Stay with me."

4.

THE DAYS SPEED BY, with no one counting them but Ammachi. The week before, Mrs. Solanki called and only Ammachi was there to answer, resulting in little more than a confused duet of syllables and half sentences. Ammachi could tell that Mrs. Solanki was slightly relieved to find Linno not at home. These weekly calls were becoming a useless routine.

A month has passed and Ammachi hardly sees Linno anymore—how late that Alice keeps her! Can she not work from home as she used to? Ammachi wonders if it has something to do with their fancy new computers, Linno's current object of infatuation. Then go marry the computer, Ammachi would like to say. It knows everything about her already—announcing her name in some strange public space where everyone from Bangalore to Brazil can see it. *The Web,* Linno calls it, a term that does not sound palatable in the slightest. "Everyone is connected this way," Linno says, making it sound as though everyone around the globe is holding hands. Why would a stranger want to hold your hand? Ammachi wonders. Probably just to yank you in his direction.

But she does not begrudge Abraham for keeping her son all day. Best that Melvin be made to work, rather than leaving him idle to concoct foolish plans. Ammachi has always felt a great admiration for Abraham, his noble bearing having bestowed him with the quiet force and equanimity of his father. She hopes that he might talk some sense into her son.

With no one to read to her, Ammachi winces at the pictures in the newspaper, but the quality is so blurry that she must turn on the television, a joyless act, as the newscaster has no time to listen to her disquisitions on current events. Melvin is not home, having abandoned whatever secret plan he has been keeping from her. In his off hours, he visits the invitation shop and helps Linno until they both take the sundown bus home.

In the meantime, Ammachi has nothing to do but go rustling through Melvin's room, halfheartedly cleaning. The mattress is buckling in the middle, despite bearing the weight of such a slight, single person. She strips it of its sheets, which smell mildly of fennel, and gathers the four corners into a bundle. Into this, she puts Melvin's dirty undershirts and goes on to sniff the armpits of those hanging in the closet. She grasps the shirt he wore yesterday and notes the bulge in the front pocket—a beaten package of his beloved bidis kept ever close to his heart. Without a second thought, she removes one from the package and goes to the back of the house for a smoke.

Throughout her seventy-seven years, Ammachi has smoked a total of three times. The first time was when she was twenty-eight years old, during a walk with her husband to see the construction of the railroad track. It was the first to be built through Kerala, then only a raised vein of earth muscling its way toward the horizon. The tracks had not yet been laid. He guided her down the berm on foot, talking about the railroad as he smoked. He had only recently taken up smoking, and she smiled privately at the way he held his bidi like a pencil.

She had heard all kinds of things about the railroad. When she was a little girl, she had heard Gandhiji over the radio, deploring the railroad's construction in the northern regions. Back then, some of the elders claimed that the British were laying the long, looping track across the country like a mechanical lasso, to drag the country back to England. Others ventured that the British were using poor Indian workers to dig up the ground, to steal the country overseas by the shovelful. Why wouldn't the sahibs do so? They tried to steal everything else. No one believed those theories anymore, but there remained a residual distrust when watching the migrant Tamil workers, glistening and dark, heaving baskets of tiny stones on their shoulders, pouring them over the slender berm. She and her husband sat on a hill overlooking the workers, watching their version of the Golden Colon take shape.

"Want?" he said, offering her the bidi.

He was only joking, but she took the bidi between two fingers and, drawing a shallow breath, sent a billow of smoke into the space between them. They had been married eleven years, and whether he loved her or not, she did not know. Nor did she know if she loved him. But she surprised him sometimes and he silently liked it, she could tell.

Now, at seventy-seven, she holds the bidi in her husband's pencil grip. She smiles faintly, but the pleasure lasts only so long. Being alone, there is no freedom in it.

AMMACHI IS APPALLED when Linno insists on missing church the following Sunday, but Linno cannot spare a single hour where work is involved. "Skipping Qurbana at a time like this?" Ammachi asks.

"Pray for me," Linno says.

The very amount of labor and time that Linno is putting into the B-1 plan confirms to her that she will get the visa. Work achieves a prayer-like consistency with every cut and fold and smear of paste, and like prayer, her work will be rewarded. It is the purest faith she has left.

OVER THE COURSE of two weeks, Linno has designed twelve new invitations for the handmade collection. She draws them in pencil, then in ink, and with Bhanu's help, she scans the designs into the computer in order to add any digital graphics or fonts. Georgie transfers the finished invitations to the website, while Prince and Alice concoct descriptions based on the terminology used in an old American catalog, words like "flourish" and "lavish" and "gaily," christening each invitation with titles like Blooming Butterfly and Zenchantment. *Made with the lovely ivory tones of our Pearl handmade paper and chiffon ribbon, the Spring Riches invitation makes a lavish and gay impression.*

A whole day is required to finish Judy Lambert's invitations, a task taken up by Melvin and Prince, who despite his usual salesmanship has all the efficiency and humor of a machine when faced with a manual task. For every five cards that pass through Prince's fingers, Melvin completes one. Melvin moves with care, pressing his fingertip to the knot of red silk ribbon, scraping away the excess threads of glue. At times like these, when the whole shop is humming with activity, Linno senses that her family's fortune will turn.

But then there are the nights. Lying in bed, Linno recalls the figures she read in the used New York City travel guide that she bought from an outdoor book table, stacked with a skyline of dismal titles and outdated *Time* and *National Geographic* magazines. That she had spotted the city name amid the surrounding titles seemed a promising omen, until she read the introduction: "New York, the fifth-largest city in the world, boasts a population of eight million inhabitants, including all the five boroughs." The sentence stopped her in the middle of the crowded side-walk, to the reproach of a bicyclist swerving around her.

At night, Linno stays up thinking. Even if she gets to New York, where will she begin? How can she know her sister's mind? It is a mad-dening circle of questions sometimes leading Linno to the conclusion that she hates her sister, though the hate does not contradict the love. Love and hate, hope and fear, all of these mingle in the same quarters of her heart.

If Anju met a friend who is helping her, that friend would be living somewhere in New York. Unless she ran off with a lover who whisked her away to another state, as far and as hazy as Montana perhaps. Linno has read stories about abducted young women, bodies turning up days later, tragedies of misguided trust. But Anju would not stray so far; she has the stomach for only so much danger. As a little girl, she once wrapped all the kitchen glasses in newspaper because she had heard of an earthquake that was predicted to hit Pakistan a week later. Anju was a practical girl, Linno thinks before quickly correcting herself. Anju *is* a practical girl. And she does not, nor will she ever, belong solely to the past.

IT IS THE FIRST SUNDAY of February, and Judy Lambert's invitations are finally finished. Alone at the office, Linno examines each card before nestling it into a white box filled with red tissue paper. On her way home, she delivers the box to Alice's house for a final review.

A servant girl shows Linno into the living room, where Kuku is seated in a plush brown chair, his face canted upward, receiving the bland murmur of the evening news. He turns the television off and apologizes for Alice, who is upstairs bathing. Linno would have been happy to leave the box of invitations on the coffee table, but Kuku invites her to have lemon water with him on what he calls the patio. Before Linno responds, Kuku says to the servant girl: "Janaki—lemon water on the patio." Janaki hurries away on her mission.

Linno follows him outside, through the veranda that wraps all the way around the house in the old, wealthy style, like a moat of white-gray marble. The tip of his cane taps with every two steps. The patio turns out to be a wider part of the veranda set up with rattan chairs and a wealth of sprawling houseplants—ferns, aloes, spider plants, baby banana trees, birds of paradise in orange pots. Janaki sets a pitcher and two glasses on a small table with intricately carved legs. Linno settles into a chair while Janaki fills each glass, then guides one into Kuku's raised hand.

"So you are finished with the Madhamma's cards," Kuku says. "May I see one?"

"How?" Linno says too soon. She bites her lower lip. "I am sorry. I mean . . ." She clears her throat, trying to think of a better phrasing for "How?"

Kuku seems unfazed. "I'm not fully blind. I can see some colors, light and dark. I can see only what is ahead of me but nothing from the corners of my eyes. I can see most colors, except red. So many important things are red," he says sadly. "I would gladly trade yellow for red."

"Oh." She gazes into her chilled glass, at the residue of lemon and sugar on the bottom. She tries to imagine his vision, the watery depths and luminous obscurities. "And you were always this way?"

Kuku nods. "When I was a baby, my eyes were rolling around in my head. My mother thought I was possessed. But my uncle was a doctor, and he found a name for my problem. Optic nerve hypoplasia." Kuku takes a casual sip. "It's a mild form, compared to most."

It is strange and slightly welcoming to speak of his disease in terms of fact and detail, rather than curse and misfortune.

He motions to her. "Show me an invitation."

Opening the box, she removes the top invitation from the stack, the best one, and fits it into his hands.

"Red," she says.

"I see," he sighs. "And what is this? A ribbon?" Linno unties the card for him and guides his fingers up the right side of the triangular roof.

"This is the pagoda," she says.

Their fingers drift down the left side of the roof. And in a maneuver that she hardly noticed, it is now his fingers guiding hers down the wall of the pagoda and across the two steps.

"Steps," he says.

She disentangles her fingers and closes the card. "We don't want to touch too much. Because of the oils, you know. From our fingers."

As she returns the invitation to the box, Kuku seems energized by the mention of oils. "Do you know what the pagoda represents? It is a place of aesthetic beauty, of spiritual shelter."

No, Linno says, she did not know that. She does know, however, the gist of what Kuku is continuing to say. It is like watching a person trip, in slow motion, and being too far away to break his tumble.

"I have always thought of you," he says, "as my pagoda."

A moment passes before she finds her voice. "I think your wife should serve that purpose."

"Well, she has the shape of a pagoda, that much I can tell." Kuku's frown is almost a pout. "I may not be able to see, but I am not stupid. All she wants is my money. All she wants is this house. And all my uncles want is to see me married so that they can believe that my parents are resting in peace. You think she likes me? Every minute she spends with me, she must be in the company of five, ten aunts."

"You are a grown man. If you don't want to marry her, then don't."

"Oh, Linno, please." He pinches the bridge of his nose, as if being harrassed by a child. "People like you and me cannot venture into the world without so much as a backup plan. I am going to marry her and that is that, unless you are somewhat interested in giving your hand to me." He hesitates with a shake of his head. "You know what I mean."

She crosses her arms over her chest, a defensive stance that she has not taken in a while, not that she forgot how different she is from everyone else, but having forgotten that everyone else notices. "Did I ever give you any reason to think that I would want to marry you?"

"Most women would jump from a bridge before they dropped a hint of interest. So prudish, people here. But you were bold enough to draw me a picture at our very first meeting. Alice described it to me."

"That wasn't for you. That was because I was bored."

Kuku begins to say something, but falters. She watches his face transform from confidence to confusion, then finally and unpleasantly, to shame. "That I did not realize."

He leans forward and places his glass of lemon water on the table. She puts hers next to his and, rising, says: "Thank you for the lemon water."

"What if you took some time to think?" he blurts. "A day or two?"

Looking up at her, Kuku appears shrunken in his chair. There is a piece of lint on his shoulder, and she wishes she could brush it away. But he would probably misunderstand the gesture just as he has misunderstood everything else, so she remains where she is and says as gently as she can, "I am sorry, Kuku, but I will never be your pagoda."

THAT SAME MONTH, Kuku and Jincy are married.

Jincy wears a puff-sleeved white sari, her throat choked with gold. Kuku wears Ray-Ban shades, a sleek gray suit, and a smile as plastic as Jincy's diamond tiara. All throughout the Mass, Linno tugs at her salwar, wary of the sweat pond at the small of her back. Ammachi wears an expression of wistful sorrow that gradually melts into a frown, her singing not unlike a hoarse lament.

Before Anju's absence, Ammachi used to thrive on social minglings, deriving some maternal power from the ever-widening circle of her acquaintance. There is tall, two-faced Sally Markose, who will hug you with one hand and cut off your braid with the other. Across the aisle from her is Oommen George, whose cancer last year whisked away his lush head of hair, ushering in a series of ladylike wigs in its wake. In front of him is Abraham Saar, straight and imposing as a pillar. His hands are clasped behind his back, causing his chest to lift, his chin raised to receive the sermon. Here is the kind of man that Linno would marry were he twenty-five years younger, a man who held the respect of a whole room with his quiet self-possession. Linno rarely spoke to him directly, harboring a deep deference for the man who had swooped into her family's life and, by giving Melvin a job, saved them from uncertainty.

Like all the fanciest receptions, this one takes place on the lawn of the Windsor Castle Hotel, beneath a sprawling lily white tent. Two great bronze bowls, filled with water and scattered with red rose petals, flank the entrance through which the newlyweds glide, like king and queen, to sit on an elevated platform. Kuku appears happy, though Linno can hardly tell what lies behind those black lenses. Since their last meeting, they have not seen each other.

After Alice serves the ceremonial tea to the new couple, Jincy's nine-year-old niece lip-synchs a Bollywood-inspired dance number, complete with pouts and blown kisses, while her mother—an older, squatter Jincy—looks on from beside the stereo with frigid intensity. The audience members solemnly watch, as if they have mistaken the evening's entertainment for a form of punishment, but Jincy joyfully claps along. After the nine-year-old strikes her final pose (hip thrown to the right, hands over heart), she bows and bows to the tepid applause, hoping for an encore that never comes.

5.

IN THE BATHTUB, Bird keeps a bucket and plastic cup whose purpose is a mystery to her roommate, though Gwen never mentions it, assuming that doing so might be a cultural impertinence. In a similar spirit, Gwen welcomes the new tenant without reservation. Bird later hears her speaking to her boyfriend over the phone. "God no, I'm not going to ask for a reduction in the rent. . . . Because she's her niece, Brian. . . . It's cultural, you know? The close familial bonds? I respect that."

Initially, it was a bond of desperation. On the first morning that Bird left for work without Anju, she detected the faint anxiety in Anju's eyes, her hand clamped over the house key. Anju clamored after her with questions: "Should I answer the door?" "What about the phone?" "But what if it's you?" It was obvious that the girl had never been home alone.

"We have an answering machine," Bird said. "If you hear me, pick up."

"Oh. Of course."

Bird was startled by the girl's nervousness, an anxiety that was also endearing. "You are welcome to call me at work," Bird told her, before leaving. "If you need anything."

"No, no. I'm fine."

Bird put her hand on the doorknob, then abruptly turned around. She wanted to say something but, reconsidering, she said good-bye and left.

Lately, Bird has begun to feel a simmering impulse to reveal to Anju the source of their connection. Sometimes she thinks that doing so might strengthen their bond, and other times the past seems heavy enough to crush whatever tenuous relation they may have formed. Telling now, it seems, would be premature. For the time being, Bird is content to simply prepare extra meals, to add another pillow to the bed, to ask Anju a question as if addressing the face she tried for so long to forget is the most natural thing in the world. As if time itself is a collapsible thing.

IN THE SEVENTIES, Bird's father was a character actor in the B-movie industry, mostly Malayalam films but a few Tamil films as well. Time after time, he played to type—a lovable, gullible, sweet buffoon—all the things that her father, in life, was not. As a child, she was confused by these two fathers, the one she preferred, lofted on a movie screen, and the other she feared and avoided.

Much later, a lover would try to convince her that her coldness stemmed from her fraught relations with her father. She was nineteen at the time and thought that they would marry, having just succumbed to the singular act that, her lover had claimed, would bind them to each other in deeply spiritual, revelatory ways. But lying in a motel bed with her supposed future husband, Bird felt nauseated by it all, the linearity of life that seemed to lead in a direction that no longer held her interest, and she was sure that she could not live with a man who occasionally gifted her with his psychiatric diagnosis. "The problem is not my father," she told him. "The problem is that I was expecting a full-length play and you barely made it through the first act."

It was surprising, that sureness, that rage—where did it come from? She had thought herself like most women, muddling prettily through her late teens, but from that moment on, she was intoxicated with the possibilities of taking a solid, solitary step into the world.

So she auditioned for her father's next film, against his wishes. "It's not a fit job for a proper woman," he said. "No one wants an actress for a wife." Bird won the part; she played the confidante of the lead actress and though she had very few lines, she delivered them in a way that must have impressed the producers, as they expanded her role as filming went on, to her father's dismay. When the film was released, it seemed from her fan mail that quite a few men wouldn't have minded an actress for a wife, but at the peak of her popularity, her father kicked her out of the house. His disapproval had more to do with competition than propriety.

Soon after, she took a room at a women's hostel in Madras and never spoke to her father again. Through a connection, she found work as a costumer's assistant on a Tamil film, and by sleeping with the director, she won her next role as a backup dancer in a mobster film that required her to wear glittery plastic pants. The director was adamant that the love scene in his film should not surpass a heated embrace, so as not to alarm the Censor Board, but where his own morals and vices were concerned, he cared nothing for ratings. Bird had thought that treading this line between sex and money would sicken her, but the nights were nothing extraordinary. The weight of a man seemed the same every time, slightly pleasant, slightly crushing; they always seemed to carry that aura of sweat and smoke and need.

By the time she was twenty-four, she was fed up with the weight. One producer, full of love and rum, slapped her clean across the face when she demanded an end to things, and then collapsed and wept into her skirt. Holding her cheek with one hand, stroking his hair with the other, she decided that this was enough.

So when Ghafoor, an old cinema acquaintance, invited her to join his drama troupe, she readily agreed. In the Apsara Arts Club there were sixteen members in total—actors, stagehands, plus technicians for music, lighting, and sound, all financed by the deep and generous pocket of Ghafoor's friend, Rani Chandrasekhar, a retired film actress who had long dreamed of being a patroness of the arts. It was Rani who selected the name Apsara Arts Club, after the bedazzling Hindu nymphs whom some said she resembled in her youth. She had withdrawn from public life years before, due to a disease that she blamed on a curse from her sister. She tried to issue a retaliatory curse, which flopped, so she resigned herself to an occasional insult. ("Always jealous, that *kushumbi*," she often sighed.) Rani Chandrasekhar, who used to command the silence of thousands, could no longer command her own hands to stop trembling, the onset of a lifelong earthquake that would gradually consume her body.

Rani offered one of her sprawling homes in Kochi to serve as a base for the troupe. Those who lived nearby commuted from their homes, but Bird stayed in one of the bedrooms. Being one of only three women in the troupe, Bird was forced to put up with the faint, fluting snores of Anita and Binal, the two other actresses whom she privately termed the Woodwinds. There was a veranda, a spacious living room, and a dining room with a long table at which they all met for meetings and meals. After two months of rehearsal, the troupe dove into the season, two hundred shows, sometimes two or three in one night. They traveled by van, slept in hotels and houses, and awoke in a new village almost every morning. It was a rare relief to return to the comforts of the Kochi house.

Bird had had her misgivings about such a lifestyle but found it fit her rootlessness. From her days in the hostel, she was used to living in close quarters with the patchwork family that came of traveling and working together, all the gentle bickering and comfort that accompanied it. The troupe was small enough for a degree of intimacy but large enough not to care when she wanted to be left alone, and no one took offense at her stretches of silence.

She discarded all her hopes of rising to Bollywood status, having grown bored of staring at the back of each starlet's head. And though she had never acted in a play before, she thrilled to the immediate energy of the audience, their rapt silence as loud as any applause. Regardless of her age, their appreciation remained taut and unconditional, so much so that Bird was able to renegotiate her contract with

Ghafoor, increasing her advance as well as her salary to one thousand rupees per show, except for the first and the seventh shows, whose profits went to the company's upkeep. Fan mail began to follow Bird again, most often from men who tried to smother her with feeling, calling her eyes the color of brandy, loading her arms with bouquets and cakes, peering over their gifts with exquisite pain and ardor. She was used to such shows of affection after a performance, but in the heat, the flowers withered quickly, and with them, her interest.

HALFWAY THROUGH THE SEASON, the Apsara Arts Club suffered a setback at the hands of Vishwas, an actor who often played comic relief in the form of an undesirable woman. Though he never complained about being cast as a woman, it seemed to inspire in him a latent belligerence when drunk. On this particular evening, he got into a brawl at a local tavern, which sent him to the hospital with a broken leg. To replace him, Ghafoor brought to rehearsal a nineteen-year-old girl named Gracie. "Boy, girl, no matter," he said. "What matters is the acting."

Gracie was a mechanical actress. She had come to rehearsals with her part memorized, but Bird could see the lines passing through her mind before she uttered them, like ill-timed subtitles. She also had a terrible habit of leaning into someone else's words, as if waiting to pounce on her own. But she was from a wealthy family, vacationing with her aunt in Kochi, and Ghafoor had promised the aunt that he would grant the girl a small part, that of a servant boy. It was a strategic move, as doing so would insure a small patronage from the aunt, but it irritated Bird to think that someday, perhaps three years hence, she would be replaced by just such a girl for whom life was as smooth and innocent as the ribbons in her hair.

Her first few lines were opposite Bird. "A strange lady is waiting at the door," Gracie said. She paused for Bird to fill the silence.

Bird stared at the girl, her confidence, her ribbons, then addressed Ghafoor, who was nodding with encouragement. "Aren't you going to correct her?"

Gracie hesitated. "Did I lose my place?"

Bird spoke before Ghafoor could interrupt. "Your line is this: 'A lady is waiting at the door. A stranger.' Not 'a strange lady.' "

"Yes, okay, thank you, Bird," said Ghafoor.

Bird ignored him. "You have to *think* when you speak. The lines come from your thoughts, not your memory. And you should be here, in this moment, not thinking two steps ahead——"

Ghafoor intervened by clapping his hands. "Okay, lesson over. Well done. Time for lunch."

THAT EVENING, the new girl claimed the only remaining bed in Rani's house, next to the Woodwinds. Upon Ghafoor's insistence, Bird found her to apologize. "Gracie Kuruvilla is the daughter of a donor," Ghafoor had said. "Not your protégée. And you, Bird, are not some guru of the dramatic arts! May I remind you that your last film was called *Boy Friendz*?"

"I'm sorry if I was rude," Bird said to Gracie, taking a seat at the foot of her bed. Gracie was sitting on the floor before her narrow suitcase, sorting through her clothes. "I get carried away when I meet such young talent."

Gracie gave her a sly, skeptical look. Her irises were as bright as new coins. "We both know I was terrible."

"You were nervous. You'll improve."

Distracted, Gracie slowed her folding of an underskirt. "I always thought that an actor steps outside of himself to play a character, but I watched you today. You were yourself and someone else, both, entirely." She made one final fold, pressing the underskirt tight as a package, and looked up. "It takes compassion to be that woman."

Over the years, Bird had earned her share of fawning remarks, but none so earnest as this. After first reading *Kalli Pavayuda Veede*, Bird could not believe in a woman like Neera, no matter how many times Ghafoor had proclaimed her to be "real." Bird had never known a woman to do what Neera had done, to renounce her own children, to leave an upstanding husband who was not an alcoholic or a gambler or a wife-beater. But that was the fresh thrill of acting, to descend inward to some common space from which she could understand a total stranger.

"Hah, what do I know," Gracie said. "All I know is I'm no good."

"You're not leaving, are you?"

"No, no. I need the adventure. Life with my aunt is too boring, and by this time next year, I will be married."

"You are engaged?"

Gracie quickly shook her head.

"Then how do you know you'll be married?" Bird asked.

"My father says eighteen, nineteen, this is a normal age for marrying."

"Hm." Bird nodded. "Then I am not so normal, am I?"

"No," Gracie said, shuffling through her clothes. "You are lucky."

With a slow smile, Gracie unearthed an album from her suitcase and held it with both hands. She stared at the cover, her face filled with light. "Now we both are lucky."

Gracie handed the album to Bird. To her, it did not look lucky but old, the corners worn, heavy with the weight of two records. On the cover was a circular symbol of two angels praying, and above this, a title that made Bird frown: *Jesus Christ Superstar.*

"Are you one of those Pentecostals?" Bird was annoyed. They had only just met and here the girl was trying to convert her.

"No," Gracie said, puzzled. "Are you?"

"My mother was Hindu. My father was godless. It's the only thing he and I have in common."

Gracie raised her eyebrows. "You believe in nothing?"

"I believe I will not like this music."

"Listen, I found it on a bookseller's table. Usually they sell religious music but maybe the cover fooled them. Just as it's fooled you." She rose, pulling Bird up by the elbow. "I saw there was a record player downstairs."

Bird began to protest that she had other things to do, though nothing specific came to mind. Promising just one song, Gracie led her along, already moving as if she knew the whole house. Bird followed her to the sitting room with its wall full of *Reader's Digest* books, the abridged versions of legendary novels whose maroon and blue spines colored an otherwise muted room.

Just as Gracie claimed, there was a record player in the corner, beneath a sprawling spider plant. Gracie put the plant aside and opened the lid. She skimmed the dust from the record player with a velvet roller the size of a lipstick tube. When she was finished, she took the first record from Bird, keeping her fingers to the edges, and slid it onto the spool.

The machine hummed. The album began to spin. Gracie dropped the needle and sat in the armchair across from Bird.

They listened to both records from beginning to end, each song building upon the next, so that even if Bird could not understand all the words, she could glean the path of the story and its players, the voices that worshipped and fought, that loved in secret and died in disgrace.

Sometimes, to Bird, the men sounded like yowling cats, but Jesus and Judas sang from a plane above the others, seething with frustration. The songs were often electronic and explosive; Bird did not enjoy them all. And yet there was one that held her as soon as the woman began to sing. Mary Magdalene was her name.

The voice poured through the speaker and swept through the room like a foreign wind, growing around Bird, gathering her up to the very heart of its lament. The woman seemed to bleed as she sang, as if singing were the last act before surrender. There were times when, in a spectacular throe, the voice rent itself with a wail and then continued on, this tearing and welding greater than the body from which it came, miraculous, invincible: *Should I bring him down? Should I scream and shout? Should I speak of love, let my feelings out . . .*

Eventually, Bird's gaze came to rest on Gracie, who had folded her legs beneath her. She was staring at the floor with her copperbright eyes, and it seemed to Bird that this was not the first time Gracie had sat with this song, almost leaning into the sounds, as if the music were a wall she could rest against. The album spun and the world spun with it, but between the two of them was a precious stillness that Bird had never felt in the presence of anyone else.

JESUS CHRIST SUPERSTAR became a household favorite, particularly Mary Magdalene's song. Worried that the record would be ruined from overuse, Gracie made another trip to the book stall and returned with *The Sound of Music,* whose angelic Julie Andrews the housemates preferred. Bird and Gracie still favored Mary Magdalene, so they saved her for rare occasions.

At dinner, Gracie always made sure to sit by Bird, though other actors did most of the talking. Chummar, with his ridiculous stories of the elephant who fell in love with his animal trainer. Raman, who claimed to have had a secret affair with Zeenat Aman that went awry because he was Hindu and she Muslim. At times Bird thought it tiring, listening to people who never seemed to leave the stage behind.

Some troupe members began to call Gracie "Bird's understudy," knowing well that if talent did not keep Gracie from a dramatic career, her father would. Such was the way with "good girls," they said, citing a goodness that had more to do with wealth than virtue. Ghafoor encouraged the friendship wholeheartedly, as if Bird's befriending of Gracie were simply part of the larger strategy to gain her father's favor.

"Keep it up!" he said. "Who knows what he'll donate by the time we reach Kottayam!"

But Bird would never drop the hints that Ghafoor wanted her to drop. She had no such designs on her friend, whom she secretly felt was far better than herself, though not because of her wealthy father or her pedigreed mother. In fact, Gracie readily admitted her dislike for her family, especially her father, who had refused to pay her college fees because the education of women was something he considered a waste. A generous dowry he would supply, but not tuition. She had wanted to study nursing, which could have taken her to Dubai or London or even New York. Like Bird, Gracie had always wanted to travel. But her father had looked down on the nursing profession and the women who daily studied and touched the ailing bodies of naked men. Sometimes Gracie said things that surprised Bird altogether, as when she added: "He has no problem studying and touching his secretary."

In spite of her parents, Gracie was confident in a way that did not apologize for itself or exact humility from others, wholly unlike any woman that Bird had ever met. She rarely wore saris, claiming that they limited her stride. She kept her toenails and fingernails a bright, raw red. She rejected the gold bangles her mother gave her in favor of a rose-embroidered ribbon or a length of lace that she pinned around her wrist. None of these details alone made Gracie beautiful; it was the easy, elegant manner in which they were carried out.

And her openness encouraged the same in Bird, who told of her early days in the industry, which to most people held a dark allure. Nothing Bird revealed from her past was shocking or repulsive to Gracie, not the motel rooms or the promotions that followed. That Bird had made her own way filled Gracie with admiration.

Sometimes they pushed their beds together to talk in the evenings. Gracie had improved her English through movies and magazines that she had collected from various booksellers, hoping one day to use the language in Europe or America. She showed Bird two copies of *Tevye the Dairyman* by Sholem Aleichem, one in English and the other in Malayalam, which they studied side by side. Gracie even memorized some of the simpler lines, whispering each word in the dark: "And sometimes God sends you a plain, ordinary passenger, the lively sort that likes to talk. And talk. And talk." And so they did through the warm, unraveling night.

Slowly Bird began to believe in the broader reaches of love. Romantic love or physical love, these were small provinces in a boundless terrain, and the love between women friends was no less than any other. There were some loves that put a period to the end of one's life, which from then on was lived primarily for the benefit of others. But Bird's was a love that thrilled her with what lay ahead, even if she could not see very far.

IN THE APARTMENT, Bird encourages Anju to hang things on the wall, so as to make the place her own as well. But Anju has nothing to hang, unless she were to take some of the sketches from Linno's sketchbook, an act that, despite her previous takings, would feel now like tearing pages from a Bible. Her favorite is an ink-pen drawing of the annual Vallankali races—two long peapod boats filled with dozens of rowers, their oars digging water beneath a sun that radiates spokes of light. Though Anju loved the boat races, her exhilaration always seemed somehow incomplete, as if she would never quite reach the nucleus of all that excitement and fervor. From the shores she watched along with thousands of onlookers, the shiny backs and curved spines of rowers, working men in their daily lives now heroes for the day, singing and plowing the water:

> *Kuttanadan punchyile, kochupenne kuyilale,*
> *(Little girl, cuckoo bird of the Kuttanadan paddyfields,)*
> *Kottu venam!*
> *(We need drums!)*
> *Kolu venam!*
> *(We need drumsticks!)*
> *Kurava venam!*
> *(We need horns!)*

There were always one or two slower boats of women in white saris, thick arms and black buns, but Anju always imagined herself the cuckoo bird of Kuttanadu, a whole boat serenading her in passing while she watched from the shore, her nose attracting a sunburn.

If then she felt close to some center of importance, now she feels a world away. Back home, she had assumed that one's very presence in New York would have a levitating effect on the spirit, but her feet drag in her heavy shoes. Perhaps this is what it means to be homesick, though she resolutely believes that such a sickness should be hidden, especially if Bird is to treat her like an adult.

Anju tries to think of her future methodically and mechanically, mapping the coming months. Bird recommends that she complete her high school degree through an online course. "No use in stopping your learning. A high school diploma will probably help when you apply for a green card. It will make you look like . . ." She tries to remember one of Rajiv Tandon's English phrasings. "An attractive applicant."

"But who will give me a diploma after I was expelled from school?" Anju asks.

Bird waves away her concerns. "Even a convicted felon can get a degree so long as he studies hard and pays the fees."

Unused to having felons for peers, Anju hesitates. "But the tuition . . ."

"That I will pay for. You never would have messed with that Tandon if not for me. It's the least I can do."

Quietly, Anju thanks her.

"It's nothing. But don't say anything to your father. He will feel the need to pay me back."

At five o'clock the next morning, Bird accompanies Anju to the Apsara Salon, where they use Ghafoor's computer before his arrival. It is a clandestine operation that requires noting the mouse's position on the mousepad before and after use. "He doesn't allow anyone to touch his precious machine," Bird says. "As if we all have hooves instead of hands."

Compared to the handheld gizmos people use on the subway, Ghafoor's computer is a fat, gray hulk, leading Anju to make the correlation that the fatter the machine, the more primitive. But as promised, Anju treats the hulk with all the care and fear of one who has never owned a computer herself. In school, she excelled in computer classes and could type faster than all her peers, but she was never good at understanding the inner logic of the computer itself. If a program threw a fit, she never knew how to pacify it and usually ended up pressing her palms to the warm monitor, frantic, like the mother of a feverish child, and finally, despairingly, shutting the whole thing down.

Bird has brought a piece of paper with the website of an online high school course that came recommended by a friend. Though intangible, the institution sounds respectable enough: James Madison High School

Online. From that day on, Anju spends the morning on Ghafoor's computer, scribbling notes that she can study later at home. No matter how early the hour, Bird sits nearby, paging through a newspaper and clipping coupons, most of which will live long past their expiration dates in her wallet.

Not once does Bird try to hurry Anju along. Bird's patience is limitless, and she mothers Anju with a care usually reserved for family, perhaps to fill some void of her own. Anju wants to know how Bird came to be so alone, but asking might be an insult. She simply assumes that Bird's story is the usual tragedy, a woman who missed marriage as one might miss a good song on the radio, by changing the station too many times in search of a better tune.

At first, Anju feels quite pleased with this analogy, as if she just made an incisive comment in class. But most of the debate and discovery goes on in her head, where there is no Miss Schimpf or Mrs. Loignon to nod as if the world revolves around her words, no circle of minor philosophers in which every answer holds the truth. There is only Correct and Incorrect and Final Score.

THROUGHOUT FEBRUARY, Anju lives mostly between two destinations—Bird's apartment and the salon. One day, while walking to work, Anju bumps into Linno, causing Linno to spill her armload of books. So struck by the impossibility of it all, Anju does not kneel to help Linno gather her books, but simply stands there, staring down at Linno, who is not Linno at all. It was the braid that deceived her. Like Linno's, this woman's braid is loosely woven.

Angered by Anju's refusal to help, the Not-Linno rises with her books and says, *"Move."*

The woman's face is petite and pretty and repulsively nothing like Linno's. Nevertheless, Anju watches her walk away and disappear into the grocery store.

In this same way, Anju happens upon Melvin from time to time, strolling along with a plastic bag swinging from his hand, or rustling through a box of oranges in front of the grocery store. She never spots Ammachi, whose look and voice are too singular to mistake. Anju learns not to approach these faux Melvins and Linnos, knows to wait and watch as their faces turn into those of strangers. Even if given the choice, she would not wish to see them in person, not yet. But still it is a painful thing what guilt and longing will do, over and over again, to the mind.

BY THE END OF THE MONTH, Anju receives a letter from the headmaster of James Madison High School Online, congratulating her for passing her high school exams "with flying colors!" She took them the week before and found the questions disturbingly easy, so easy that she wondered if she were mistaking their underlying complexity. She missed only a single question about a dangling participle, which she would have contested were there a warm-blooded teacher with whom to argue.

Bird insists on photocopying the letter and sending it to Anju's father. Obediently, Anju accepts the photocopy and later slides it into the bottom of her duffel bag.

To celebrate, Bird suggests that they go to a movie. At first, Anju protests against the expense, as every envelope of cash she receives from Ghafoor goes directly into a Folgers canister in the corner of Bird's closet. "We could rent a video," Anju says.

But Bird insists on going to the movie theater. "My treat."

At the kitchen table, Anju scans the Movies section of the newspaper when Bird says abruptly: "I used to be an actor."

Anju stares at her. "In films?"

"Mostly Tamil films."

"Which ones?"

"*Durga . . . Rajaraja Cholan . . . Idhaya Veenai.* Your father would know them. But no need to tell him," she adds with a short laugh. "They make me sound old."

Anju nods, saying nothing, which is always the case when Bird mentions the unwritten letters.

"Those movies were long before your time anyway." Bird goes to the sink and refolds a dishtowel. "Back then, as soon as a girl married, her husband would start making demands. This role, not that role. I didn't want that." A moment passes in silence before she adds, "In case you were wondering why I am alone."

"I never wondered."

"But I am not alone, *allay?*" Bird turns to Anju with a smile that makes Anju wonder what she did to deserve it. "Now read aloud the movie titles."

On Bird's recommendation, they go to a Charlie Chaplin film called *Modern Times* that is showing at the Brooklyn Academy of Music. Throughout the entire bus ride, Anju keeps her arms folded tight over her chest, her gaze averted from strangers. Since her arrival in Jackson Heights, this is her first time taking public transportation. In her attempt to seem inconspicuous, she catches her reflection in the window and finds that she looks thoroughly irritated with the world.

But when the lights darken in the theater, she forgets everything. Who is this small man in his shrunken coat and clownish shoes ambling from accident to catastrophe, none too great to defeat him? At the outset of the film, he takes a job at a factory that eventually drives him to a nervous breakdown. When Chaplin inadvertently gets dragged into the guts of a machine, his body slithering up and around the giant cogs and spools, she almost cries with so much laughter. And not far from her laughter is her pity for this man, running after a world that advances without him. Once in a while, she and Mrs. Solanki used to watch comedic movies in the home theater, but Anju never knew why and when to laugh. Sometimes she understood the jokes, but they were too dry and sharp, too sarcastic for her taste.

Bird is watching but not absorbing the film, having seen it twice before. She does not need Chaplin to make her happy. Nothing could make her happier than when she entered this theater or when she woke up this morning and the morning before with Anju by her side.

She senses that Anju is growing close to her, if not with a daughterly intimacy then with a sisterly one, as Anju has begun to call her Chachy. In that one word, which no one has called her in so long, Bird perceives the depth of her past loneliness, the hollow in her being, which has become apparent only now that Anju is here to fill it.

WHEN GRACIE WAS ALIVE, she inspired the same feelings in Bird, that need so long in hibernation, gathering its strength, its grip. Bird woke with it buzzing around her insides like a fly that would not escape a room, even after one opened all the windows and doors, as if it preferred frenzy over freedom. That feeling, that need, it frightened her. She began to wonder if she should distance herself from it.

One night, after arriving at their host's home in Kollam, Bird sat on the front steps, massaging her feet, hoping that Gracie would fall asleep before Bird went to bed. But Gracie soon found her and took a seat on the step below. She raised Bird's heel into her lap, even though Bird warned that her nightgown would get dirty. Gracie replied: "It doesn't matter, Chachy."

The steady rhythms of her fingers sought out the knots in Bird's feet, but with every knead and roll, Bird found her muscles coiling a bit tighter than before. She tried to relax by gazing at the moon; it was radiant but flawed, mottled like a bead whose paint had flaked away. She wondered if a pulse could be felt in the feet.

"I received a letter from my mother today," Gracie said. "She could not believe I'm playing a servant. She said, 'Do they know who you are?'"

Gracie pushed her thumb into a hollow in Bird's sole, causing Bird to wince and smile at the same time. "Mothers want the best for their daughters."

It was an easy thing to say, and Bird was slightly relieved to see that Gracie was not listening but staring off into the sky, her hands in gentle movement. "Maybe she wishes she were me. She could have been an actress or a singer, you know, she has a beautiful voice. I remember once, when I was small, she spread newspaper on the kitchen floor and we sat down to shell a bowl of beans. We worked, and she sang, and my father came in and pretended to read his newspaper at the table, but his eyes never moved from the same spot." Gracie's fingers went still; she held Bird's feet. "We had so few times like that."

Bird sat up and put her feet on the ground. "Thank you," she said.

Gracie hugged her knees. Bird stared at Gracie's fingernail polish, chipped into the shapes of tiny red countries with ragged borders. On Gracie, even the chipped polish was charming. Bird thought of her own mother, who was beautiful in a rational way, her features of a perfect symmetry to which everyone had been drawn. But Gracie possessed some kind of strange, specific beauty that only Bird could see, like a woman witness to an apparition.

That they had grown close in only a matter of weeks was not altogether surprising to Bird. She knew well how the cycling days and nights of troupe life could accelerate friendships and seal lifelong bonds. Gracie occupied her thoughts as soon as Bird woke and just before she drifted off to sleep. But she did not dare try and remember her dreams or imagine worlds where what she wanted was possible.

After a silence, Gracie asked what Bird would do when the season was over.

"I have a brother in California, some cousins in New York," Bird said. "I am going to ask my brother to sponsor me for a visa."

Gracie turned to face her. "You're going to California? When?"

"Most likely New York. I don't know. Soon as I can, I suppose." It was true, what Bird's cousins had said to her last time they spoke: one had to leave or be left behind. And perhaps everyone in the troupe could have used that advice. Their audiences were growing smaller as television serials attracted whole populations of viewers with the single click of a remote. At first, Bird assumed that people preferred the convenience of staying at home to watch a show, but it seemed that people also liked returning to the same hysterical characters every week, speaking of those characters as though they lived just down the street. And in any case, it would be only a matter of time before Bird herself was replaced by some young, sunny ingenue who had studied at a famed theater school, under gurus who had penned books and toured continents. No, Bird would abandon the theater before it gently, politely abandoned her.

Gracie looked perplexed by the decision, and in a small way, Bird was pleased that she had made some impact. "I always wanted to go," Gracie said. "Not to the States. To New York."

"Why only New York?"

"There are all kinds of people in New York. You can be whomever you want in that city, with no one to bother you. You can disappear." Gracie plucked at the end of her braid. "Maybe, someday, I will end up there too. People move. People find each other. We could be neighbors."

"It's a big city."

"But very organized. Everyone has a place in the phone book, A to Z. I'll find you."

And as the night went on, what began as a joke turned into a world with a logic of its own. They would live in the same apartment. They would share a garden of okra, bitter melon, and tomato, but on Bird's request, absolutely no eggplant, and nothing that was grown would belong to just one or the other, but both. When Bird said she wasn't sure if she wanted to have children—a fact she had admitted to no one until then—Gracie did not hesitate in saying, "You can call mine your own."

"So by this time next year," Bird said, "you'll be married."

Gracie did not hide her resignation. "Probably."

Bird found herself trying to effect a kind of playfulness, a girlish curiosity about marriage that had never thus inspired her. "Is there someone . . . ?"

"My father doesn't tell me these things." They were quiet for a moment, and Gracie looked up at the sky in some desperate, unblinking search for other worlds, other lives unlike her own. With her head lowered, her hands in her lap, she drew herself into a compact shape. The bone at the base of her neck protruded ever so slightly, smooth as a stone in a riverbed, so smooth it called to be touched.

Gracie said, "I wonder what kind of movies you will make over there."

And so they continued talking and pretending a world that would never exist. Years later, Bird would wonder if Gracie had ever truly believed in such a life, and if she understood what building this fantasy could do to at least one of its listeners. But Bird was not without fault. She could have ended the night long before the first streaks of pink appeared on the horizon, before they wandered down the path toward a mirage of their own making. But part of the torment was wanting the torment in all its shimmering, vexing forms.

6.

A MONTH INTO THE NEW GIRL'S EMPLOYMENT at Apsara Salon, Ghafoor must admit to himself that he made a mistake. Already there are too many beauticians, five full-timers plus four part-time girls coming in and out. He hired Anju as a favor to Bird, but he is no idiot. Bird and Anju are too kind to each other to be related. Ghafoor has considered letting the girl go, but he senses that she might be in some kind of grave trouble. Pregnant? he wonders, stealing glances at her belly. An employee wearing her disgrace in such a frontal manner simply will not do, but by the second month, when he has determined that she is without child, he tries to come up with some use for her. For years, he has been a sturdy agnostic, but he fears the karmic retribution of pushing a good girl out into the world. She may be a bad apple, but better leave that judgment to higher powers.

IT IS LATE FEBRUARY. The air has turned brittle, the wind unforgiving. Seventy-fourth Street is still asleep, the accordion doors of each store shut like so many eyelids. With rattles and clangs, up goes the door of the hardware store, then a music store, a bakery, a sari shop. Usually Bird is the one to open the salon, but Anju volunteers to arrive early on the days of her shifts, to undo the padlock and flip the switches. Glad to have an extra hour of sleep, Bird lends her the shop keys.

Inside, Anju hangs her coat on one of several empty pegs; the others have yet to trickle in. She sits on the stool and stares at the box of red flowers pressed against the window, meant to convince passersby that within these walls is a perpetual spring of tattered petals and plastic stems.

When Bird arrives, she shows Anju how to take inventory, counting bottle by bottle of product with a clipboard in her arm. "Go slow to fill up time," Bird suggests. This, finally, feels to Anju like a job of some substance, something that Ghafoor will notice. But when he walks in, he barely looks at her and instead goes directly to the back of the room, where he hangs his coat on his reserved peg. By this time, the others have already arrived. Nandi is pouring Lipi a cup of chai from her gray thermos while Powder and Surya argue over which radio station to settle on. Nandi demands the morning weather report.

Ghafoor looks around the salon, rubbing his hands together for no apparent reason. It seems that he has something to announce, though only Anju notices. She has developed the premonition of knowing when she has been singled out, when hers will be the name that is called, her hands sniffed, her hind quarters paddled. So when Ghafoor says her name, she raises her head with more dread than surprise.

"Anju? Bird? In my office, please."

"YOU WANT HER TO WAX?" Bird asks. "Are you crazy?"

Bird is standing across from Ghafoor's desk. Anju is sitting in the corner beneath the poster of Aishwarya the bad girl, who shoots a look over her shoulder, clearly aware that her rear seems nearly edible in shiny leather pants. This is exactly the sustenance, Anju decides, that must get Ghafoor through a meeting with a disgruntled employee.

"She is a child!" Bird says.

"You said she was older than a child," Ghafoor says. "If she is a child, then she should not be working here at all."

"But what if she does something wrong? What if someone tries to sue her? Everyone suing everyone in this country, you know that, and if they find out she is not licensed—"

"Powder is a certified beautician, and whatever her brain has retained from beauty school, she will teach it to Anju."

"At least let Powder do all the bikini ones."

"Powder is already busy, and Surya is leaving. I want Anju to fill Surya's shoes."

On and on they fight like a couple that has known each other too long. From Powder, Anju has learned the definition of bikini wax

("When they take off all the hair. *Down there*"). Now she weighs the pros and cons of administering the bikini wax, and while the cons are cringeworthy, they are the sorts of cons that will most likely fade with repetition. And besides, pros or cons, all will go into the Folgers canister in the end.

She has been waiting for a window in which to speak, but finding none, she interrupts with a loud question. "Do you have a lab coat, sir?"

"Why?" Ghafoor asks.

"Maybe it would make me look older. Maybe people will think I am expert in the field. Their field." Anju smiles at her own joke, then clears her throat and falls quiet.

THE WAX WARMING POT looks like an artifact of scuffed metal, centuries old, rimmed with dried, gummy sap. It sits on a hot plate that Powder has plugged into the wall, near the beige cushioned bench. While waiting for the wax to warm, Powder lists the weaponry needed to de-hair a body part and Anju takes notes: wax, wax warming pot, muslin strips, flat wooden sticks, latex gloves, postepilating soothing cream, antiseptic toner, cotton towel, paper towel, and cotton.

Powder holds up a paper diaper. "Disposable knicker. I got it at the supply store, a box of hundred."

Disposable knicker, Anju writes in her notes. She takes the knicker, folds it in half, and tucks it into her notebook.

"What are you doing?" asks Powder. "You put that on."

"Me?"

"How else will I show you? First I will do the waxing to you. Then you will do it to me."

Anju watches as Powder stirs a stick in the pot of wax. When she pulls the stick out, a long, luminous band of honey clings to the end.

"Keep your top on," Powder says. And before Anju can protest, Powder has left the room to give her some privacy.

Anju removes the paper knicker from her notebook and opens it.

And so it has come to this.

AT FIRST, lying back on the cushioned bench, Anju almost forgets her sous-navel ensemble, soothed as Powder smooths a cotton ball soaked with antiseptic toner around the area in question, keeping clear of the paper knicker. This is followed by a sprinkling of talcum. "Puts a barrier between wax and skin," Powder says.

Not barrier enough. Pain streaks across her mind like a color, a lurid splash of red across a white wall. The red flares, then fades like an echo, softening, subsiding, and just as she begins to breathe again—another *rip*. Through gritted teeth, Anju repeats the mechanics to herself: spackle the wax, smooth the strip, pull taut the skin, and yank. But it is nearly impossible to ignore the fact that she has never looked so closely at this region of her own body, let alone anyone else's.

Of course, there are more ways of waxing wrong than waxing right. Powder suffers most from this truth, trying to direct while keeping her knee hitched. "Never ever hesitate while pulling off a strip," Powder manages to say. "Do that again and I'll kill you."

When finished, Powder tells Anju to wait in the room while she convinces Surya of Anju's good work. Surya remains unconvinced but agrees to let Anju wax her anyway. "I'm doing this so that girl won't get fired," Surya says. "But I can tell just how good she is from the way you limped in here."

By the time Anju does Surya, her technique has much relaxed and improved. She keeps her mind focused on the details—the thinness of the honey, the rhythm of the rip—rather than the larger concept of her task. If she lets her mind wander, Ammachi might invade her thoughts, shaking her head and covering her eyes as if no hell could contain the depths to which Anju has fallen.

"Never write to your father about this," Bird warns. "He would never forgive me."

Anju agrees. Even if she were in contact with her father, she wouldn't know the words to describe this latest development. Perhaps she would call it a "promotion" and leave it at that.

STILL, ANJU CAN APPRECIATE those rare days of fleeting warmth, softening the snow along the sidewalks, shedding hope for a shortened winter. An old Rafi song is billowing from the open door of the music store, and passing by, she feels herself diving through a gentle wave, the tune still in her ears as she rounds the corner.

Over the past week, Anju had two clients seeking a bikini wax, and next week, upon Surya's departure, she will be promoted to the leg and arm waxes as well. The bikini clients were Powder's friends, one white and one Filipino, whom Powder had lured with a 25 percent discount. The first girl, a wispy blonde with a navel ring, knew exactly what to lift and how. She chatted through the entire process without even a wince, talking about the boyfriend into whose house she had recently moved.

"He's all like, 'I thought Jackson Heights would be more diverse, but I feel like I'm in New Delhi or something' "—*rip*—"but I said, 'Eff you, I just found a salon that'll get me a bikini wax"—*rip*—"for ten bucks and I'm not going anywhere.' " This was the type of blessed woman, Anju decided, who would shoot her babies right out, one after another, with hardly a stretch mark to show for it.

"Done," Anju said, pulling off her gloves.

"Done?" The girl looked down. "Cool."

The Filipino girl was not as lucky; she might have left claw marks in the bench had she any nails. But even with the Filipino girl, Anju felt a new certainty about her work, and no longer absorbed the pain that she inflicted. She felt instead like some sort of authority, midwifing each woman into a state of groomed well-being. Once finished, the Filipino girl even smiled at the results.

And now, with the week come to an end and the Folgers canister a bit fuller than before, Anju has permitted herself a paper cup of payasam from the bakery. Back home, she would pluck out the boiled raisins and drink the sweet, milky remains; here she intends to drain the whole cup exactly as Ammachi would have made it, cardamom, raisins, and all.

Standing outside the bakery, she takes her first sip and waits for a taste that never comes. It is a little bit like Ammachi's payasam and nothing like it at all, each spoonful adding to the disappointment. She throws it away, not wanting to ruin what she remembers. To chase an old taste is impossible, it seems, a taste perfected by memory.

IT IS MARCH. Anju flips through the calendar on Bird's wall and wonders how so many days could have collected behind her already, without her having resolved a single thing about her visa or green card.

On a legal pad, one of many Bird stole on her last day at Tandon's office, Bird writes the amount of money that Anju has earned ($625) and calculates the total of her projected earnings by April. "In time, you will have a thousand, plus a thousand from me will equal two. That will be enough to hire a lawyer, at least to start things."

"Can you talk to Ghafoor?" Anju asks. "Ask him to give me more hours? I want to start the process sooner. I only have until June."

"I tried. He said he was already booking you for arm and leg waxings." Bird sits with her head in her hand, absently breaking off the stale edges of a muffin. "What else can we do but continue as we are? I called several lawyers from the phone book and their fees were in the thousands, all of them. All we can do is wait and work." Bird looks up. "What about your father? I'm sure if you asked him—"

"I can't ask him."

"Why?"

Anju hesitates. What little money her father possesses, he would use to buy her return ticket home. And hearing his voice over the phone, she would not be able to refuse him.

"My family is too deep in debt," Anju says firmly. "We have nothing left."

"But what if there is no other way?"

"I will have to make a way."

Anju utters her words with a flat, implacable calm. Her face is frozen, all signs of life held far within. It is clear to Bird that in this instant, the girl thinks herself a woman, and Bird knows well that life can do harm to girls like that.

"Okay, okay." Bird takes a bite of her muffin and speaks between chews. "Enough melodramatics. This isn't *Days of Our Lives*. This is my day off. So let's go shopping."

ON BIRD'S SUGGESTION, they go to a department store so that Anju can at least look presentable when it comes time to meet with lawyers and officials and other hazy, important figures. In English, Bird says: "You know what *presentable* means? It means like a present, a gift. You must gift people with your appearance."

They browse racks of slacks that cling to the rear and flare at the ankle, tweed blazers that defiantly halt mid-rib. "Look at this thing." Bird holds up a semi-blazer. "If they're going to cut it in half, they should also cut the price in half, *allay*?"

Anju enjoys shopping with Bird, as it is less of a purchasing expedition and more of a Conference on the Calamities of Western Dress, a conference of two. Every garment falls into one of three categories: (1) wretchedly sluttish, and hence symbolic of the downward spiral of American civilization; or (2) a sequined knock-off of Indian styles; or (3) either of the above, but cheaply stitched by children in India with eyes the size of buttons on a winter coat. For a while, the conference involves simply fingering the collars of tops and showing the fellow attendee, "See? Made in India." Bangladesh and Pakistan also count.

They stand in a long dismal line outside the dressing rooms, their arms piled high with clothes on hangers, behind women who wear the

jaded faces of prisoners doing time. When finally they enter the dressing rooms, the conference takes a sharp turn for the worse.

It is not several rooms but one large, sad chamber with mirrors on
every wall. Before the mirrors, women are peeling off their limp
hosiery, sizing up their reflections, forcing their button flies to close over
bellies that simply refuse. To Anju, it is a horrifying sight. She is
reminded of a Holocaust film that included a scene of women in a gas
chamber. Is she the only one aware of the panorama of flesh, of graying
bra straps, of dappled thighs, of cotton and nylon stretched far too thin
by bending over to put on a sock?

"Stop staring," she hears Bird say.

She follows Bird to a patch of wall that seems relatively empty, if not
for the women to her immediate right and left and reflected all around.
Anju paces her small circle of space like a restless cat. Bird thrusts a pair
of pinstriped slacks into her hands. "This won't try itself on."

"Can I try it on over my pants?" Anju asks.

Bird is as appalled as she would be had Anju suggested trying the
pants on her head. "We are not buying something unless we know what
we are buying. And anyway what is the big deal? Powder saw you in
that paper knicker."

Anju turns her back on the woman beside her wearing lacy lingerie
and argyle socks. Tiny hairs, like magnet filings, cover her shins. "I
don't know these people."

"So what? If they see, they see. You'll never see them again."

But it is exactly this fact that worries Anju most, that their first and
only impression of her will be a half-naked one. And yet, she has no
choice. Keeping her eyes mostly fixed to her feet, she tries on piece after
piece while Bird returns each to its hanger. There is something warmly
maternal about the way that Bird evaluates each outfit with brutal criticism and care, as if Anju's appearance is more important than her own.
Bird grimaces openly at the rejects, smiles proudly at the successes,
never interested in selecting anything for herself.

While Anju changes, Bird turns to the side to allow her privacy,
thereby eliminating the privacy of another woman who is sliding a
magenta tunic onto a hanger.

"That is made in India," Bird says to the woman.

"Is it?" The woman looks at the label on the collar. "Oh no, it says
here *Malaysia*."

Bird nods knowingly. "Same thing."

ANJU RETURNS TO WORK in various combinations of her new clothing: pinstriped slacks, a blue sweater, a white blouse, and khakis. At first, the clothes seem to imbue her with their newness. She is the latest style, exclusive, and not for sale. But as the days wear on, her contentment turns temporary, a quick-flash trend gone by. All that remains is guilt, the prickly reminder of what Linno might say to all this new and useless finery.

At least Anju is improving at her job. She is now accustomed to the mild form of schadenfreude experienced by the first-time clients who enter the back room, the site of future torture. With earnest hope, they try to befriend Anju, seeking words of comfort with their eyes fastened to the medieval-looking pot of wax. Held hostage in the chair, the clients giggle nervously at the placement of the mirror, nailed to the wall opposite their splayed legs. Anju agrees that this is a terrible place for a mirror, as there are few women, no matter how shapely or waxed, who are flattered by that angle. But Anju has learned from Powder how to maintain a professional distance from the giggles and smiles, for the less she smiles, the more they respect and tip her. It is an illogical but working science.

She has also learned how to exact the least pain from a strip, and if, by accident, the client winces or scowls, Anju clucks like an old mother hen. "I see you did the shaving down there . . ." She really has no idea if someone has or has not been using a razor, but this intimate accusation usually works half the time, making the client take responsibility for what might be Anju's own shoddy work. "Terrible," Anju says. "Might as well use a vegetable peeler."

They like this persona she plays, this expert little grouch with the thick accent and occasional joke on hand. The mannerisms give her the appearance that she has been doing this for years.

Day after day, Anju waxes the thickets of arms and legs, the overgrowth in between, smoothing and prettying her clients so that they walk with chins higher than when they first entered. At day's end, she shrinks into her coat and slips into the flow of the sidewalk, hoping to disappear. Ridiculous to think that anyone from her old life would follow her here, not Fish, not Miss Schimpf, certainly not Mrs. Solanki. They seem to her like characters from a movie she watched long ago, many times over, the kind of movie wherein a strong wind rips the pages from a daily calendar so as to suggest the frantic passage of time. It seems to Anju that she has been living in Jackson Heights for much longer than three months, pulling the cord to reveal the storefront to the morning, eating dinner across from Bird every night. Have the days and hours gone fast or slow? She hardly knows, which seems a dangerous thing, this sense of time both jelling and jetting by.

And yet, there remains an underlying constant, a famished sort of feeling ever feeding on her insides, a feeling that could be quelled by calling home. But after the first call, guilt would be replaced by more guilt, longing replaced with despair. She convinces herself that in the end, her family will understand. The end will find them all renewed. So as time goes by, she grows used to the hunger, like a changeless climate, like an endless string of windy days.

7.

*A*T NIGHT, Anju always falls asleep first. Her position, which begins supine and straight, gradually rotates into a belly-flopped sprawl, while Bird withdraws to a sliver of space on the opposite side of the bed. She does not mind allowing for Anju's sprawl, and in fact, Gracie had warned of it. Making room is the first act of mother-hood, in the most literal sense, as when the body creates space within itself for someone else. Bird runs through all the possible permutations of happiness. Someday, Anju could take Gwen's room or move into the apartment next door. She could cycle back and forth between New York and Kumarakom, according to the plan she once explained to Bird, and gradually, she might come to see Bird as a true aunt, or even a kind of mother.

These are slippery thoughts, difficult to hold for very long. Anju is hardly closer to a green card than when she first arrived on Bird's doorstep, due to her utter unwillingness to ask Melvin for help. Bird wonders if she should find his address and ask him herself. That Anju continues to hold fast to her dream is admirable in one so young, but she is too young to understand that the greatest obstacle to any dream is, quite simply, time.

WHEN BIRD FIRST ARRIVED in New York, she found the days unbearable in their lengthy stillness. But being alone, she felt, was the necessary solution to the feelings she wanted to leave behind. She was unused to her band of merry, trash-talking cousins who pleasured in their disgust of American women, their vulgar attire, their mediocre meals. They perceived Bird as a kind of harmless oddity—quiet, mannered, a terrible cook, uninterested in marriage, and not as gorgeous as the rumors that preceded her. But so long as Bird kept herself available to babysit their growing warren of children, the cousins were happy to host her.

In this way, eight years went by without a word between Bird and Gracie until Bird's cousin casually dropped some news at dinner one evening. "My friend Lally—you remember Lally from church? Yohannan's father's brother's niece by marriage? *Lally.*" The cousin repeated the name as if the syllables would awaken some recognition in Bird, who finally responded with *Ah yes, Lally,* just to get on with the story. "Lally ran into your old friend Gracie in Bombay. Said she looks much thinner. Had two children and lost all her youth." The cousin shook her head with no real pity.

Gracie's name was a note that kept strumming in the hollow of Bird's ear. Enough time had passed, she decided. She had grown beyond the contours of her former life, and there was no rupture that the intervening years of silence had not mended. So from Lally, via the cousin, Bird procured Gracie's address in Bombay and sat down to write a letter.

And yet she found herself so full of words that her hand did not know which ones to transcribe. Had eight years really passed since last they spoke? To practice, she wrote a rough, disjointed assortment of things on the back of an old electric bill.

She wrote: *You want to know how tall are the buildings? So tall, a man's hat falls off just looking up at them.*

She wrote: *I heard you married and had two children. What are their names? Do they look like you?*

She wrote: *I work at the cash register in a drugstore. For lunch, my cousin sends me off with a plastic container of chapathi and chicken, but my coworkers don't like the look or smell of it. So I have started rolling up my chicken in the chapathi and folding up the ends, like a packet. The Mexicans call this* fajeetha. *I don't know what to do about the smell so I try to eat in the bathroom.*

And: *Are you happy?*

She had wanted to compose something fluid and musical, a missive deserving of quill and ink. But her letter seemed to convey one overarching thought—that in their years apart, Gracie had become an adult and Bird had regressed into childhood. Try as she might to write a more mature version of the letter, the maturity felt bland and cold, so she sent the scattered, childish version.

A month later, she received a response nearly bursting with questions but scant of answers. Had Bird seen the Kennedy son with the lustrous hair and the beautiful mouth? Did she have a garden? Did snow feel like talcum powder, and if not, what was so special about it?

My husband's name is Melvin Vallara, she wrote.

We live in Bombay. He works in a fancy hotel called the Oasis, where many sahibs stay. Linno, my older daughter, she is learning Hindi very fast. I wanted to name my younger one Anjali but Linno could pronounce only half the name. So she is Anju.

    The guts of this city spill right into the sidewalk. I am sure that New York is the cleanest city in the world. My husband's sister lives in U.S., in a place called Texas. How far is that from New York? Do you remember how I wanted to come with you?

Bird did not ask why Gracie hadn't married the man named Abraham, to whom she had been betrothed so long ago. Instead she seized upon the words that leaped from the page: "Do you remember . . ."

Yes, she remembered. She also remembered how, when she first arrived in New York, she felt as though her mind had receded into a state of waking sleep. Sometimes her cousins would clap in front of her distracted gaze and ask, "Anyone there?" while searching her eyes in jest. No, she wanted to tell them. No one was there. She was still thousands of miles away, years apart, in a dressing room in Kottayam.

Why don't you come? Bird wrote. *Melvin could apply through his sister and bring the rest of you a bit later. It wouldn't take more than a year, most likely . . .*

FOR A TIME, letters flew between them, saddled with questions and answers. Here they were again, building a fantasy that this time bore the possibility of realization. Every other week, Bird folded and sealed her growing hope and dropped it in the blue mailbox, hovering there a moment before she walked away.

Dearest Gracie,

    I moved yesterday, out of my cousins' apartment. There is only so much room where children are involved, so my new roommate is well past that age. Her name is Mrs. Spandorfer and she wears her hair in a white fluff atop her head. Mrs. Spandorfer is Jewish and tells me she remembers when this neighborhood was full of Jewish, like her, and people from Ireland and Italy. She said: We took the gays when nobody else would! She was talking about theater people in the 1920s and 1930s, who took the train from here to a place called Times Square. She said that this neighborhood will never stand still.

The good news is this—there is a space in the apartment across the hall opening up. A Gujarati man lives there with his wife, and they will be looking for a new roommate. Should I tell them to keep the space open for Melvin? They are good people, but they don't allow meat in the fridge.

Chachy, it will take some time to convince Melvin. His own sister is in U.S., but he thinks that his life is tied to his parents, who are still in Kumarakom. I let my parents go a long time ago. Sometimes I think life is easier with hateful parents. They make it easy to tell your happiness from theirs. You and I share the same mind, but Melvin still thinks like everyone else here. Slowly. Patience, patience, he says, but I feel as if I have been waiting my whole life.

Gracie, you will not believe it, but I saw Ghafoor in the window of a bakery, eating a pastry and reading the paper, as if he has lived here forever. Remember him? He said Rani Chandrasekhar died, and all the actors and technicians went looking for jobs in film—better money there. He says that he will go back home as soon as he raises enough money to put up another production. He is very sure of himself. Still I feel sorry for him. He has taken a job as the assistant manager of a grocery store. When you come, we can visit him.

Chachy, with all these adventures who will take care of the children? Anju is eating everything. Yesterday I forced her mouth open and found a cockroach on her tongue. She wants and wants. I think she takes after me.

After a month, the letters from Gracie suddenly dried up, a dearth that Bird initially blamed on the post office. Still, her hopes continued to snow one upon the next. She thought how lovely it would be to take Gracie to the Cloisters, far north on the island, and listen to that particular strain of cathedral quiet. They would walk the stone paths around the herb gardens and mispronounce the Latin names on the tiny labels.

Theirs was a sisterhood that could overcome what nearly undid them years ago, so profound, so pure was their friendship. Bird had transgressed, she understood it now. She had mistaken one feeling for another, but she would not need to apologize, not to her dearest friend who already knew her words before she spoke them. They would return to that friendship like swans returned to water with the ancient knowledge of how to swim embedded in their limbs.

So for the time being, she tried to grow accustomed to Mrs. Spandorfer's apartment. Bird's was a strange and stuffy room that Mrs. Spandorfer had preserved for untold decades under the title "Morrie and Samuel's room." The walls were blue and decorated with sailboats and potbellied bears in sailor hats. There were two narrow beds where Morrie and Samuel must have slept, but Mrs. Spandorfer refused to shift the beds from their position, flanking the portrait that hung on the wall. The boys' cheeks and chubby knees were tinted pink in the way of old pictures, one boy smiling, the other serious and self-contained. Bird did not ask Mrs. Spandorfer why her sons never visited, a filial negligence she simply assigned to the American way, but the Gujarati woman across the hall informed her that the boys, twins, had died at seven years old, in a car accident. "One died, then other followed," the woman said with admiration. "They left this world just as they came into it. Together."

A MONTH AFTER Bird sent her last letter to Gracie, there came a message that conveyed how completely Bird had misinterpreted the silence. The post office had been slow to forward the *Malayala Manorama* to Bird's new address, and when finally she sat down to thumb through the first of several old issues, she found Gracie's message in the obituary section.

KUMARAKOM: Gracie Vallara (27), wife of Melvin Vallara of Kumarakom, passed away on August 3, 1989. Mourned by her husband, her parents, Thomachen and Claramma Kuruvilla, and her daughters, Linno (7) and Anju (3).

Bird stood in the center of her bedroom with the newspaper in her hands. The nerves in her fingertips seemed to go numb. She read the obituary countless times before she fell to her knees, before the words became as distant as the beautiful roar of the sea in a conch shell.

8.

*I*N JACKSON HEIGHTS, there is no smell so pleasant as that of a sari store, for reasons that Anju cannot quantify. Packed into boxes and shipped across the sea, the saris are flung onto hangers and mannequins with the aging odor of their origins still clinging to the thread. She slides her hand across hanger after hanger of slick satins, chiffons, and silks with no interest in taking anything home. It is a minor fetish, maybe a bit odd, but she draws some faint, wordless pleasure from a faceful of custard-colored georgette when no one is looking.

She has come to value these rare hours alone, but Bird prefers to spend every last moment with Anju. It was a strange and subtle shift in Bird's behavior, the slightest need in her now that makes Anju feel alternately irritable and guilty. On Friday, Ghafoor tells Bird to stay late and straighten out the books, leading Bird to turn her plaintive gaze on Anju. "You don't have to wait for me," she says. "Unless you want to."

"I thought I would go to the sari store," Anju says. "Just to look."

"You want a sari?"

"No. Just want to see the new styles."

Bird hesitates, then consents. "Be home in an hour, okay? Don't wander too much."

Anju waves, already out the door and with every intention of wandering. She walks down the street toward the lofted 7 train as it rattles across the tracks, drowning the argument of two men gesturing wildly outside Rajan Exchange. She stands before the window of an electronics store where a television is tuned to her favorite news commentator, a marshmallowy white man with fists that occasionally pummel the desk. He begins his show looking puffy and pale, until he works himself up into a merry rage over the various wars his country is facing, including the War on Terror, the War on Obesity, the War on Illegal Immigration. She tried to watch him yesterday evening, but it was difficult to do so with Bird beside her, groaning and heckling.

ANJU CONTINUES DOWN Seventy-fourth Street on her way to the sari shop. Later she will wonder how her life might have been different had she not decided to toe a stubborn ball of ice down the sidewalk, opposite from home, had her name never been bellowed from a distance:

"HEY! MELVIN! ANJU!"

In reverse order, but it is her name all the same.

She freezes. Glancing up, she sees a bearded man starting toward her, and by the time he is within half a block, she recognizes the camera strapped to his right hand.

"IT'S ROHIT!" Like King Kong, he slaps his chest with his free hand. "ROHIT!"

Unlike most in Manhattan, people in these parts are not used to blatant disruptions of normalcy: no VCR thrown from the window of a warring couple, no street-corner evangelists, no solo protester going up and down the blocks, clanging two pots together and announcing the number of dead civilians in Iraq. No one shouting and running without reason. Heads turn, and even the two men in front of Rajan Exchange pause their argument to look at Rohit, then Anju, then Rohit again.

With no other obvious option, Anju breaks into a run.

Aside from a few triumphant badminton serves, Anju was never exactly an athlete. Running, she discovers an agility born of pure fear, of the sound of wind and soles on sidewalks, the muffled urgency of a thudding pulse. She does not think of Rohit or his intentions, only that he represents the place she once fled.

"HEY, WILL YOU RELAX? I JUST WANNA TALK!"

Unwilling to lead him to Bird's house, she has somehow run them into a residential area of narrow sidewalks and frosty lawns. This can continue for only so long before someone assumes that Rohit is a predator and calls the police. Over her shoulder, she yells: "TURN AROUND! GO HOME!"

Which comes out as a ragged gasp rather than an order.

"TURN IT OFF?" he asks. "YOU WANT ME TO TURN THE CAMERA OFF?"

She stops, her hands on her knees, heaving. Rohit stops a few yards away from her. She does not want to face him and his camera, nor is the current shot of her backside very flattering.

"Anju, listen. Can we talk?"

Still the camera is on. She would like to hurl it against the sidewalk if she weren't so sure that rising would cause her to cry.

"I don't want that camera on me," she says.

"Fine."

Once she hears the *ping,* she straightens up to face him. The camera is hanging at his side, still in his grip.

"What the hell you are doing here?" she says.

But before she can say anything more, Rohit suggests that they take their conversation to a more private place than the sidewalk. In a rare moment of agreement, they settle on McDonald's. His treat.

STANDING BEFORE THE COUNTER, Rohit begins explaining the menu items to Anju. "A hamburger is a piece of beef between two pieces of white—"

"Number five," she says. "Super-size, large soda, no pickle."

They take a booth by the wall, near a glass cabinet that guards a treasure trove of cartoon figurines from an animated movie about sea creatures. Anju had seen the commercials with Bird, who found it disturbing that computer animation could give a cartoon guppy more breadth of expression than what is possessed by most actors in the flesh.

Anju turns her attention to Rohit. His beard is new, slightly coppery in contrast to the brown of his hair, a haphazard attempt at adding maturity to his face.

"You look great," he says.

Without a word, Anju inspects her burger for pickles. Her courtesy will not be purchased for the price of a Junior Mac.

"Okay." He slouches a bit, as if to say that he is somehow surrendering a false persona and offering her the Real Rohit. "I've been looking for you for so long, it's like, now I'm not sure where to begin—"

"Why did you come here to wave a camera in my face? How did you find me?"

"All right. Easy question first: I figured that the secretary from Tandon's office was the only other friend you had. So I went all Columbo, you know, just came here on a hunch and checked with that guard in Tandon's building. I showed him your picture and he said he'd seen you around. You have no idea how long I've been combing this same strip of Seventy-fourth Street, looking for you." Rohit beams, rapping his thumbs on the tabletop, waiting to be thanked or congratulated. Anju dips a fry into a mini cup of ketchup. "As for the other question, I'm here about my film. I think you can help me. No—I think we can help each other."

"Me? I thought it was a personal film about you."

"It is a personal film. About you."

. . .

OVER THE LAST TWO MONTHS, Rohit has been hard at work in his editing suite, otherwise known as a corner of his Ex's apartment. Here, Rohit pursued the impulse that struck him as soon as he received news of Anju's disappearance—to make a seven-minute trailer that, if picked up by a production company, might evolve into a feature-length documentary film.

"My entire life I've been waiting to strike gold," he says. "That's what it's like sometimes, being a doc filmmaker. It's not necessarily the smartest or the most skilled that land on the best film. Sometimes the best film just lands on you."

The landing began on the day of Anju's disappearance, while Mrs. Solanki was sorting the mail. "I had my camera with me," he says, "because I had this feeling that something was about to go down." When Anju presses him for specifics, he admits that nothing had been going down in relation to his personal film, whose plot had long been flatlining. At a loss, Rohit had planned to conduct an on-the-spot interview with his mother concerning his childhood, hoping to stumble across some revelatory jewel of poor parenting.

"So I'm shooting her and asking her questions, which she's trying to evade by opening the mail, but I can see by the way she's using that letter opener that she'd like to slit my throat. Nothing special. I mean there are only so many close-ups you can get of a letter opener. But then there's this one letter that she unfolds and reads silently for a couple minutes before she even notices I'm still there. It's a great shot, a really slow, steady zoom. And in this deathly voice, she goes, 'Oh God. Rohit. Call your father.'

"So I just kept filming everything else, like my mom freaking out and my dad yelling. I also had those tapes of you at dinner, plus the meeting with Rajiv Tandon. I never turned off the camera." He gives a macho shrug. "I just put it on my knees. Lucky I invested in a Sennheiser mic. Picks up sound like you would not believe. I interviewed Miss Schimpf, your principal, your friend Sheldon—"

"Fish? You interviewed Fish? What did he say?"

Rohit sat back, grinning with satisfaction. "He cried."

"Cried?"

"Almost. There was definitely a pregnant pause. Anyway, I got to learn about this amazing story that all goes back to you and your sister. Linno, right? And for once, I find myself at this nexus of luck and drama and serious fucking *issues*, and I'm like, what do I do with it all? *I have to make a film.*"

"About me?"

"About immigration, both legal and illegal. About sisters, about family pressure, about the cross-cultural divide between Indians at home and Indians abroad. All through the lens of your life." Rohit is on a rampage now. When someone in a neighboring booth glances over at him, he lowers his voice to a lusty whisper, which only further attracts the neighbor's attention. "I cut a trailer of everything I got and showed it to a contact at a production company. He loves it. He thinks it's topical and riveting and he wants to fund me to make the rest if I can promise to come up with more good footage. Which is where you come in."

Rohit pauses pregnantly. Anju is overwhelmed by the choreography of this speech, each word buffed and clean and effortless.

"I know what you're thinking: *What do I get out of all this?* Well, you get the visibility of being in a full-length film and probably a string of festivals, which can't hurt your cause. And while most documentarians would consider this unethical, I'm willing to pay for a top-of-the-line immigration lawyer, so I can follow you step-by-step on your way to obtaining legal status. I won't screen the film until you've practically got a green card in your hand. I won't ask you to sign a release until the very end, and if I haven't made good on any of my promises, you refuse to sign the release and I'm screwed. See?"

At this moment, with his palms upturned on the table, Rohit resembles a lovelorn desperado, a look that he does not wear well.

"Okay, I see you're a tough sell," he says. "And that's smart. You should never agree to anything until you read the fine print."

He takes a paper from his messenger bag and triumphantly slaps it down before her. He begins to read aloud ("In consideration for my participation in the motion picture production identified above, I, the undersigned, do hereby expressly and irrevocably consent to be photographed and/or audiotaped . . .") until she asks him to stop. At the bottom of the page is a line where her signature would go.

"I can't screen a thing until I get your signature, Anju. Without you, this whole project collapses. See what I'm saying? So you can back out at any point. Though I have no idea why you would want to. I mean, this film is going to be important. The story of an illegal immigrant tunneling her way through the bureacracies of a post-9/11 America—"

"Excuse me, but I do not tunnel. I am not a worm. I walk on the sidewalk just like you."

"I know, it's just a figure of speech—"

"And I most definitely am not illegal," Anju says. "My student visa will last until June of next year."

For the first time, Rohit seems speechless. He stares at the Formica tabletop, as if trying to solve a mathematical problem in his head, and coming up empty, he leans forward to address her again. "Your student visa ran out a while ago."

"No, incorrect. My visa is valid until June, it says on my Arrival/Departure form . . ."

But something about Rohit's altered way of speaking, confused and unrehearsed, seems to prove that he is telling not only fact but truth. "You're legal only so long as you're a student. That's why it's called a student visa."

As proof, he pulls a binder of documents from his bag and flips open to a page that reads *U.S. Immigration and Customs Enforcement* in the upper corner, next to an official seal. The text is littered with terms like "alien" and "out of status." Her mind races to find ways in which Rohit might have forged the material himself, but such a ploy seems too cruel, too useless for his purposes. What she is reading is truth. She is illegal and has been so for at least two months. "For academic students (visa category F-1): Failure to maintain a full course load without prior authorization is a status violation. The student's period of authorized stay will be terminated."

SHE EXCUSES HERSELF and emerges from the McDonald's. Her breath appears and disappears like all her ideas. She fumbles her way to a bench and sits, though she can sense Rohit standing tentatively behind her, waiting for her to speak. All around her, the world is in whites and grays, the trees sweatered with snow.

But this country, she well knows, is quite full of color, too much color according to the squadron of men and women in suits, on the radio and the television. They speak of the Immigration Problem as if a pandemic is spreading through the land, a stealthy, smothering Brown Plague. "We are facing an overpopulation disaster like none this country has *seen*," said the marshmallowy news commentator. And the truth is this: Anju thought herself on the healthy, innocent end of the disaster. Not now, but someday, she would be an American citizen, and when the pestilence was closing in on New York, its swelling shadow would fall over her as it would for every other citizen. Illegals? Terrible! They cut in line. They took the spots from those who worked for it. They controlled the Mexican Mafia from a California jail cell, as evidenced by Frank "Pancho Villa" Martinez, whom the news commentator referred to as a "deadly alien." Not Anju Melvin. She was invited. But now, here she is: as illegal as a Cuban cigar and nowhere near as wanted.

At times like this, blame will do no good but is the easiest emotion to employ. Anju thinks of Bird. She was a secretary for an immigration lawyer, and she didn't know? Is it possible?

On the other hand, Bird is no lawyer. Maybe there is only so much a secretary can know. And besides, this is the woman whose Cream of Wheat and extra pillow are sparing Anju from a worse fate.

Rohit takes the seat next to her, his hands stuffed in his pockets. Hesitantly, he looks at her. "I guess it's a lot to digest," he says. "I should've thought of that before I blurted it out. I just thought you knew . . ." His voice trails off in a gauzy white breath.

He sighs. "I'll let you think things through. Do you have a computer at home?"

"No."

"Then I'll leave this with you, in case you're curious." He offers her his binder whose cover reads ANJU IMMIGRATION RESEARCH. Thick as a dictionary, the binder is full of immigration documents pertaining to her situation, all of them classified into subtopics including Student Visa Rules, Changing Status, and Interviews: What to Expect. He has written each subtopic on a neon tab, in careful print. Specific lines are highlighted according to a system that he has devised for her benefit. And under Vital Statistics, he has even listed her birthday, which passed two weeks ago, without her having told a single person.

"Information is key," Rohit says. "Where there's a will, there's a way."

And though she usually believes that such aphorisms belong on bumpers, she feels a sudden pang of gratitude. Gratitude and some small, burrowing hope. As she flips through the binder, she sees not the words but the colors, the ruler-straight lines of yellow and blue and green whose care and color-coding almost bring tears to her eyes.

NOT A DAY GOES BY without Anju in it, and Bird has come to feel as though it was always this way. She has bought eggs, milk, cake mix, and frosting, having been struck by the spontaneous impulse to bake. She enjoys this idea of herself, a domestic sort of woman with fat shopping bags in both hands, briskly walking home where a warm end to the evening awaits.

So when she arrives home to find the apartment empty, the day suddenly seems not quite right, like a painting askew. She hadn't wanted Anju to go wandering alone, but she could hardly say no to Ghafoor, who often and casually reminds her of his magnanimity where her employment is concerned. "Not many bosses would be so lenient," he says. "But I suppose I owe it all to my poor managerial skills."

At least Anju's absence enables the possibility for surprise, and with Gwen at her boyfriend's apartment, Bird can take over the kitchen. She hurries from cabinet to fridge, fetching eggs and oil and butter as the back of the box instructs, ignoring the intimidating slice of cake pictured on the front of the box. She cracks, she beats, she whisks. She ribbons the pale batter into the baking pan and checks the clock. An hour has passed since she arrived home and still no sign of Anju.

Now the day is at a slant. Where could the girl be? Did something happen to her? Bird tries to reassure herself with the memory of her younger years, how she loved to wander new towns alone and buy herself roasted peanuts in a cone of warm newspaper. It is natural for Anju to want to meander and explore. If only she would call. Has she been taken to the hospital? Melvin would never forgive Bird for such negligence. That he had trusted her at all was a miracle unto itself.

And aside from Melvin, Bird has come to need Anju, a terrifying thing at her age, to place her happiness in the hands of an unknowing stranger. But Anju needs her just as much, and their lives are twined in ways that no one would understand. Anju is everything that Bird once thought she lost.

She recalls Anju's words: *I will have to make a way.* Not a threat, but a simple conviction. Worry settles over Bird in a kind of ladylike paralysis, so that she sits perfectly upright in her chair, hands on her knees, ankles crossed, waiting for a door to open or a phone to ring. She remembers this sense of limbo and desperation, stretched out over the days of Gracie's silence, before the newspaper told Bird to stop waiting.

THERE IS A COST to thinking of Gracie so often, and the price is collected in dreams. They are seamless dreams, so nearly logical that Bird can hardly tell that she has been pulled under. Here they are, Gracie and Bird, standing in silence as sisters do, by a pond. Such bliss in this, to be near her again, watching the water ruffled by a breeze and embroidered with light. Gracie points out something beneath the surface, but as soon as Bird kneels to look, she finds that the pond has grown infinitely long and endlessly wide with Gracie a mere wisp on the opposite side. Gracie shouts and points at the pond, now a chasm, the smile swept from her face. Her voice never weakens, a warm, invincible whisper in Bird's ear.

Why didn't you come back for me? Why did you let me die alone?

BIRD WAKES to the noise of Anju's key in the lock, her neck stiff from laying her head on the table. It is dark outside. Eight thirty-four according to the clock above the stove, upon which the cake sits limp and overwhelmed by chocolate frosting. Bird presses her fingers to the underside of the table, composing herself while Anju hangs her coat. Best not to betray her relief, her irritation.

"Where have you been?" Bird asks.

"Library."

Bird waits for an apology, perhaps an admission of negligence. "You lost track of time?" she offers.

There is a pause. Bird wonders if she heard. Anju leans on the door frame and Bird can see it—something angry in the girl. Her stiff posture, her jaw. Her pockets must be hiding fists.

"Yes. Time. I lost track of time."

"Are you hungry?" Bird rises just as Anju interrupts.

"I am an illegal here. Did you know that? An illegal alien."

Bird stops halfway to the oven. "Who said?"

"The Internet said."

"How is that? Your arrival papers—"

"It was the official website of the U.S. Immigration. I am out of status." Anju bites her lower lip, and for a moment it seems that she might cry. Suddenly, fiercely, she rubs her face with her hands, through which her voice comes muffled. "*Illegal.* What would my father say?"

"Listen, many people are illegal here. . . . No one will send you away unless you do something wrong. . . . Just be a good girl and don't get sick and don't go out too much and everything will be fine. Next week I will call a lawyer about starting these things. I will call Monday itself. Promise."

"What about the money?"

"I'll give you more of my own."

"Debts on top of debts." All this time, Anju's hands have not left her face, as if trying to keep her mind intact. "I have to think of a different way. I don't want to be where I am not wanted."

The words almost tumble out of Bird: *But you are wanted, I want you here.* Stupid, frantic words like the lyrics to a desperate song. Instead she asks: "Should we tell your father?"

"No, no. It will just worry him. I'll think of something."

"Where are you going?"

"Bed."

Bird glances at the oven. "You don't want anything to eat?"

But already Anju has shut the door to the bathroom. Bird watches the door and almost goes to knock until she hears the faucet whistling water.

It had never occurred to her that Anju's visa could be revoked. How could she have known? For the first time, she envies Ghafoor his Internet.

Bird goes to the sink to do the dishes. She left a light coating of batter on the steel bowl, having been under the impression that children like to lick the leftovers. And yet perhaps she has been wrong all along, and Anju is not a child but an adult, absorbing the full weight of her mistakes and their consequences. Bird squeezes a line of dish soap onto a sponge. Water gushes into the battered bowl as she scours its sides and forces herself to consider what must be done next.

9.

ORK GIVES A SPINE to Linno's day, draws her through the malaise that descends over the evening. There is always something to be done, more now than ever before, since the website is up and running. Though Linno is given her own email address, she leaves the inboxes to Alice and Prince, who field and answer the growing number of messages. Linno feels embarrassed about using the keyboard, her hand skittering spiderlike over the letters. In the one email she returned to Rachna Nair, she sounded less like the head designer and more like the writer of a ransom note. (yOU Want extra thankyou cARD? linno.)

As Alice predicted, December and January brought a slew of clients whose invitations were to be completed by March. Women arrived with fiancés in tow, to settle upon the invitation that would embody all their conjugal hope and familial bliss; mothers came ready to bargain. Bhanu is most invaluable in dealing with tireless brides, such as the one who had him type her name in sixteen different italicized fonts just to see how they appeared on the computer screen.

But to Linno's mind, the company could use a little more impatience. True, their reputation is spreading, reaping customers from as far as Bedford, Indiana. Yes, she has designed twenty new invitations, all of them showcased and captioned on their website, but not even this can keep pace with her hopes. Sometimes, on the way home, she thinks she sees a small Anju sitting on the steps of a house, toeing circles in the dirt. The little girl looks up; she belongs to someone else. Linno moves on quickly, the pang in her chest burrowing deeper by the day.

ON THE FIRST DAY of March, a relentless rain arrives and, with it, an email from Sonia Solanki. Seeing Sonia's name in the inbox brings Linno no hope. She remembers how the woman sniffled through every phone conversation in the immediate aftermath of Anju's absence, and an email, unlike a phone call, carries news of little to no urgency. As well, the subject line "Proposal from Sonia Solanki," puts Linno in mind of the only other proposal she has ever received, more than a month ago, in Kuku's living room. For a brief, queasy moment, Linno wonders if Sonia is trying to arrange her marriage.

From: ssolanki@lbc.com
To: linno@eastwestinvites.com
Subject: Proposal from Sonia Solanki

Dear Linno,

My assistant gave me your website and email; I hope my message finds you as well as can be, despite the present situation. I want you to know that I am doing my absolute best to find Anju. I am as frustrated as you are with the handling of these matters, both by the school and by the police.

With this in mind, may I make a proposal? As you probably know, I host *Four Corners*, a daytime television show in which I, along with my three female cohosts, debate pressing issues in the public arena. Every week we present a new Hot Topic. For example, last week, we discussed abortion rights, and the week before that the lack of role models among young celebrity starlets. One Hot Topic that we have not yet touched is Immigration, both Legal and Illegal. I suggest that we present this Topic and have you on as a guest, so that you can tell your sister's story. We would be exploring questions of globalization, modernization, and the very history and future of this country. Yours would be one of several stories, but there is a very good chance that Anju might see the program (she used to watch it all the time in my home theater!) and be inspired to come forward. Or maybe someone who has seen her will see the program and inform us. We have a viewership of 3.5 million.

Of course, we would take care of the visa application, airfare, per diem, and hotel.

I write this by email so as to make things as clear as possible. I will phone you tomorrow to speak with you further, and if I get the green light from you, I will pitch it to my producer, Jeff Priddy.

I truly hope that we can work together on bringing Anju home.

Yours,
Sonia Solanki

Upon hearing the news, Alice is immediately wooed, having long been a fan of Sonia Solanki's *Mysteries of the Orient* cookbook series. "You're going to be on TV!" Alice says, radiating joy. "With Sonia Solanki!"

"I don't know. What is 'per diem'?"

Alice grows stern. "You are going to be on TV."

"How can I go on television and announce to the world my family's private business?"

They argue a bit, though Linno folds more easily than usual. Sonia Solanki could bring Linno to New York in half the time that Kuku's plan would require. Her immediate concern is twofold: how she will hide her wrist, and how she will stop herself from crying. She has seen shows of this kind and their guests, how even the most stoic middle-aged man will turn to the camera lens and, perhaps seeing his loneliness magnified in the dark reflection, will become overwhelmed by his secret sorrows and collapse into tears.

MEANWHILE, Melvin waits on the front steps. It has become his favorite place, beneath the star that Ammachi refuses to unplug and detach, as doing so would be akin to dislodging the moon. It is here that he waits for Rappai to come walking up the road as the sun goes down, to partake in their evening nightcap. Melvin has decided to limit his bar visits to once a week, occasionally relying on Rappai's bottle of bootleg arrack, so as to save money for the time when money will be needed. Linno is working hard, but if her plan falls through, Melvin has only to make a call and Plan G will be under way.

Avoiding the bar is taking its mental toll on Melvin. Its daily presence in his life provided a therapeutic calm with which he could rise above the current mess in a kind of mental, angelic ascension and tell his corporeal self, slouched at the counter, that everything would be fine. But now, on the front steps, he succumbs to the opposing pulls of pessimism and optimism. The questions tug him back and forth, questions that have no answer, so that by evening's end he is exhausted, not by physical exertion but by the futility of going nowhere.

He fears what is done to illegals over there. It is a different country than years before, trying to corral its evils. What if they catch her and question her? He is not sure who "they" might be, but he imagines sweatless men in suits and dark glasses, coolly cracking their knuckles. A girl like Anju could fumble, say the wrong thing. Melvin's cousin Kuriacko is a policeman, and once, while drunk, Kuriacko said that when questioning a suspect, there were times when he wanted to hear a confession more than he wanted to hear the truth.

Melvin gazes down the dirt path for Rappai, who is a poor conversational substitute for Berchmans. The other day, Rappai asked Melvin how Linno got to be so headstrong, a question he was tactless enough to pose only because the liquor in his veins made him so, knowing well that people do not favor the term "headstrong" when speaking of young women, usually applying it to girls who marry against their parents' wishes. Melvin asked Rappai what he meant, and Rappai held his glass up to the moon, either in awe of its powerful contents or in search of his own backwash.

"Well first, she said no to that rich blind man, and now she runs a business with the blind man's sister . . ." Rappai dispelled his own question with a grunt. "Ah, but what's the use of these questions."

"She got it from her mother," Melvin said.

Rappai fell silent, knowing better than to respond.

LINNO WAS SEVEN YEARS OLD and Anju just three when Gracie began to propose her plans for New York. Nowhere else in the States would do. Her eyes shone when she spoke of her friend who lived in an apartment outside the city proper, connected by a web of subterranean tunnels by which one could visit the brightly lit heart of the city that pulsed, unblinking, all through the night.

Around that time, Melvin's father died. Gracie phoned Melvin at work to give him the news, but he knew before taking the phone. While she told him of Appachen's stroke, a few silvery clichés crossed his mind—*It was his time . . . God wanted him*—words meant to take the place of an emotion he could not quite conjure up. All day, the news felt like nothing, and his sadness stemmed from this absence of feeling rather than the absence of his father.

Melvin gathered up his family and took the train home for the funeral, where he completed the rites of the only son. His father's face was wreathed in cloth, his nostrils plugged with cotton to suppress the draining humors of the dead. At the grave site, each relative gave Appachen one last kiss on his cold, powdered forehead, more kisses than he had ever received in life. Watching kiss after kiss, Melvin thought of the times when he and his father would go to the river, where walls of stones had been built along the banks. Appachen reached into the gaps between the stones and magically withdrew small, scrambling lobsters in his fist, dropping them into the bag that Melvin held out. "Kochu Konju," Appachen called him, Little Lobster, a name that felt almost like a kiss. But eventually, a dam was built on Vembanad Lake, blocking the salty tidal waters of the Arabian Sea, clogging the freshwater with sewage and chemicals, and the lobsters disappeared, as did the name Kochu Konju.

At last, Melvin draped the white satin handkerchief over his father's face, and as he did so, a sharp, torn cry came from his mother, a sound that he had never heard, that made his hands shake. Ammachi stood with her younger sister, Chinamma, whose husband had died several years before, a space of time long enough to heal her bruises. And there were other widows as well, with lowered lids and stone-cut faces, dressed in white chatta and mundu, the last of their kind.

Through the cloth, Melvin kissed his father's forehead before they closed the lid of his wooden coffin. For days and days after, Melvin recalled his mother's cry. It was not the sound that continued to surprise him but the fact that his parents had loved each other, a secret they had kept between them for almost forty years.

THE NEXT DAY, Gracie took Melvin to her teak trees, where she pointed out a dab of blue among the branches, a *ponman* that took flight as soon as it was sighted. It was nice, for once, to leave the children with Ammachi, to have the world as their private aviary. Gracie kept singing the same two lines from a film song, unable to remember the rest: "O blue *ponman*, my blue *ponman* . . ." He wished she knew more lines.

Melvin tentatively stepped around the trees, deep in his own thoughts. That morning, he had seen a picture of Abraham Chandy in the newspaper, as the new president-elect of the Lion's Club. It was the first time Melvin had seen the man, and even in such a small photo, he could tell how proudly Abraham Chandy filled the space. This was the man whom Gracie might have married. No woman in her right mind would have turned him down.

"Shouldn't we pay your parents a visit sometime?" he asked.

Her eyes grew wide. "Did you see my mother at the funeral? She looks like a lizard! All that weight she's losing, it makes her chin look too sharp." Melvin always found it strange the way Gracie spoke of her parents like a pair of curious acquaintances. Ever since their marriage, she had kept no real relations with her family beyond sending a belated birthday card. This was because Ammachi kept all important dates in her black address book, and when she called to remind Melvin, he in turn would remind Gracie.

Her gaze grew distant. "I wonder how much a few trees would fetch."

"What for?"

"To get us started over there."

He avoided her eyes but tried to look bewildered. He had been considering a certain decision for the past few days, and perhaps this was a window in which to broach it.

"In New York." She faced him. "Remember?"

"New York, yes . . ." He put his hands on his hips and blew out a firm sigh. "I was thinking about that. I was wondering if it wouldn't be best to stay here."

Gracie stared at him. "But we agreed, there is nothing for us in Bombay—"

"No, I mean that we could move back here. Into my mother's house."

"Here?" Hers was a tone that one might employ in reference to a leper colony. She took her hand off the tree, as if it, too, repulsed her. "Did your mother ask you to do this?"

"Of course not. But I don't want her to be alone." He gathered himself. "And what is so wrong with my mother?"

"Nothing. She is fine, much better than mine. Though she did tell the neighbors that Anju looked like a hairy *matthangya* in her baby pictures—"

"Old people have a different sense of humor."

"The point is not your mother, but mine. My mother and my father, they can't even look at me." And here, she stopped herself and began again. "You and me, we were going to start our life somewhere else. Away."

"We did go away."

"Bombay was a bad start. But if we come back . . ." She looked at the leaves, as if addressing them. "I was not meant to be here. I was not meant to live near the very people who turned me out."

"Don't be hysterical. You are their daughter."

She shook her head slowly, a gesture he hated, as it made him feel small. "People can disown their children gradually, over time, so that no one has to notice."

"Why is everything so complicated with you? Other husbands, they make a decision and the family agrees. The wife moves into her husband's home. She follows *him* around. What do we have in Bombay? What do we have in America? Just some drama woman you know whom I never even met."

"She's not some drama woman."

"Yes I know. She's *Bird*." Melvin plucked a leaf and folded it into smaller and smaller halves. As with all their recent fights, Bird's name had a maddening way of entering the conversation. This was the woman whom Gracie had called her best friend, her Chachy, someone who understood her, details that did not amount to the Bird that he remembered from the stage.

As always, Gracie came to her friend's defense. "She's doing very well there. I'm sure she gets auditions."

"And is that what you want? Auditions? Bird? Over your own family?" He felt a familiar question crawling up his throat, and though he could usually force it down during fights like these, this time, the picture of Abraham Chandy returned to him. At a loss, Melvin asked, "Why did you marry me at all?"

She looked up at the sky for patience. "Because it was time to marry. Now who is being melodramatic?"

"I don't mean why did you get married, I mean why did you marry *me*? Didn't you ever . . ." He thought he had known the answer, but recently, he had begun to doubt. "I thought this was a love marriage."

It was her turn now, to stare at him, bewildered.

"You loved me?" she asked.

"Well, yes. And I thought you could have chosen someone much better, much wealthier, like Abraham Chandy." She seemed to flinch at the mention of Abraham, but he went on. "But you didn't because you . . . because I had made some impression on you."

"When? What impression?"

"At the show. When we spoke. In the audience."

"You thought I loved you?" she asked. "Because we had a chat?"

"Why did you think I wanted to marry you?"

"For the same reason that other men did. My father, our house, our money, our name—"

"No, that was not it! Those were not the reasons at all! I loved you. And I thought I could save you from that violent father of yours—"

"Violent?"

"That bruise. On the corner of your eye. I remember it still, that color, how you tried to cover it with paint. I married you so I could save you, so you would never have bruises like that again."

His outburst left her without words.

"You didn't give me an answer," Melvin said. "Why did you marry me?"

Her face was full of a pity he had never seen across her features. This was worse than the slow head shake. He felt like a child, her secrets held in fists behind her back.

"Tell me," he said.

"My father struck me only once. The day your mother called to say that your family was interested in me. At first I refused to meet you no matter how my mother pleaded. My father listened very quietly, he didn't say a word."

"Excuse my stupidity, but I am asking why you married me. . . ." And then the answer hit him in the chest, stealing him of every sure breath. Looking at her, he wanted her to stop, but it was too late, her lips were parting with the truth he had demanded, assuming that the truth would repair every wrong.

"And then came the bruise," she said softly. "I married you because of it. If I kept saying no, I didn't know what would come next."

FOR TWO DAYS, Melvin feigned sickness so that he could stay away from as many people as possible. He wanted to speak to no one. He slept in the sitting room. His strategy worked so well that Ammachi was constantly following him around with a bowl of broken rice gruel, and when he wasn't looking, sprinkling his scalp with *rasmadthi* powder.

He could not meet Gracie's eyes. In her face was the life he had wanted, but what did his face hold for her? Stupid, misguided gallantry. He had never wondered why she had the bruise but was convinced that he would save her from receiving any more. He had recalled his aunt, whose husband obeyed no rationale as to why or when he dealt his blows.

And Gracie had never loved him. Theirs was not, after all, a love marriage. He tried not to be too sentimental about this discovery, but he felt a fool in front of the one person whose intelligence had both humbled and pleased him. No matter how long he pondered the question, he would never figure out why her parents had forced her to marry him, the fool, the son of a lorry driver, the hotel clerk with no name.

ON THE MORNING before their return to Bombay, while Gracie was running errands, he found a pale blue aerogramme on top of the dresser, sealed and addressed to Bird. Without another thought, he held it up to the lamp to try and decipher the writing, but three layers of translucent Malayalam made an impenetrable wall. He thought how easy it would be to steam the thing open over the stove. Immoral, yes, but who was this Bird to weasel her way into their life, to widen the cracks that already existed in their marriage?

What were they conspiring?

And here he stopped. He left the letter alone. For him, truth was not freedom. Truth bound you up in shame.

Later in the day, while Melvin folded his shirts for packing, Gracie attempted a cheery babble in his direction. ". . . and did you know the price of an egg has gone up by fifty paisa? But I know how your mother likes *mota* curry, so I bought a half dozen." She paused, noticing the aerogramme on the dresser. "My letter. I forgot to send it."

He glanced at the letter and went back to folding. She was staring at him.

"Did you read it?" she asked.

"It is not addressed to me, so no."

She sat on the edge of the bed, next to his shirts.

"Have you packed?" he asked. "We should take an early train tomorrow."

"I could tell you what I wrote." She picked a stray hair from one of the shirts. He continued folding to demonstrate his new philosophy: coming clean only made you dirty. He had no interest in it. "I said that we won't be coming to U.S. anytime soon."

He folded a bit faster, hoping to finish before a fight began.

"I said that Kumarakom is not as small as I thought, and I have friends here and there. And I'll never find a *ponman* in New York." Gracie leaned in and searched his face. "I said I choose this life."

At last, he sat on the edge of the bed, a stack of shirts between them.

"Have you packed?" he asked in a tired voice.

"No," she said.

"Are you going to?"

"No."

The next day, as Gracie suggested, he boarded the train to Bombay alone. He would work two more weeks to earn his last paycheck, pay the remainder of the monthly rent, and then pack up everything valuable for home. In total, they owned very little, enough for a man to handle by himself.

On the platform, they stood: Melvin, Linno, and Anju in Gracie's arms. Linno wore a red headband that kept sliding down her forehead, and Anju's eyes were in constant wonder of her surroundings. These were his children, from whom he had never parted. He kissed their cheeks. He found that it hurt to step away from them.

"Eat before it gets cold," Gracie said, jutting her chin at the tiffin in his hand. Inside were a few idli and a sambar that Ammachi made almost unbearably spicy, a final combat against Melvin's sickness that would, instead, afflict him with diarrhea a few hours after eating.

People began to board the train. Melvin did not know how to say the words so near to his heart, so unfamiliar to his tongue. Instead he said everything else, each sentence wrapped in the warmth of her silences.

"Don't forget to lock the door."

Good-bye.

"That lower lock too."

I'm sorry I stopped talking to you.

"Of course the dog is there, so you don't have to be afraid."

I will miss you.

"I will call when I get there."

Soon it will be better.

"Go on, then," Gracie said with a smile. "At this rate, you'll be sitting in the luggage rack."

Once aboard, he could not get a good view of the window, squished as he was next to a man of considerable girth. He did not have to see Gracie to know her face, her posture, one arm holding Anju, the other hand in Linno's. Perhaps within that upright frame, behind her bright, wifely optimism, all her hopes had frayed to regrets. He would never ask or know. It was the last time he would see her.

10.

A WEEK AFTER the first email from Sonia Solanki, Linno learns that Mrs. Solanki did not receive the "green light" for her proposal.

Mrs. Solanki calls Linno at the office. "That idiot Priddy thinks I should stick to the special interest bits, all things related to cooking, even though obviously I can only conduct so many segments on seitan vindaloo!"

"This means we will not apply for visa?" Linno asks.

"I'm so sorry. You see, Jeff's main concern is this: If we don't have Anju, then where is the story? Without a reunion, there's no ending and the audience would feel . . . unfulfilled. Unsatisfied."

Unsatisfaction and unfulfillment—but this is exactly Linno's problem, just as it has always been. Were she satisfied and fulfilled, she would be someone else. But perhaps this is Mr. Priddy's point: audiences want to hear from Someone Else, a person whose story can be smoothly digested from beginning to end.

"Linno? Are you still there?"

"Yes."

"Listen, do you think Anju reads *Me & You* magazine?"

"Sorry? What is it?"

"It's a magazine with more readers than my show has viewers. They usually publish fluffy things about famous people, who is carrying what purse and so on. But I play tennis with the features editor, and she's been looking for more special interest stories, pieces about ordinary people who are sort of . . . extraordinary in their own way. Anyway,

I have been trying to think creatively about this, and I think I can pull some strings."

UNTIL RECENT TIMES, the most famous member of the Vallara family—though ancestral—was P. C. Mappilla, whose portrait still features prominently in the sitting room. Since then, heroes have grown few, and Linno knows even less of family heroines. If anyone, Linno thought that Anju might earn a spot on the wall next to Mappilla someday.

So when Mrs. Solanki says that *Me & You* magazine wants to feature Linno as a special interest story, her first thought is that Mrs. Solanki has her confused with Anju. Mrs. Solanki explains how the piece will feature two other people as well—one of them missing a foot and the other missing an arm. The piece will be called "Miracle Workers."

Linno's response: "They couldn't find anyone missing a head?" She and Alice are pasting yellow rhinestones to floral envelopes. "I'm going to tell Mrs. Solanki to find another miracle."

"Why didn't you tell her on the phone, an hour ago?"

"She kept talking and talking, that woman! She said, 'This will be great for your business, get your name out, publicize your website . . .' "

"Maybe somehow reach Anju."

Linno sighed. "She mentioned that."

"Well, then?" Alice gently blows on her studded envelope. "Am I using too much glue?"

"Yes. What is wrong with those Duniya people? Why do you think they aren't returning my calls?"

"Because they probably get too many calls. Mrs. Solanki is right. This magazine might get their attention, and it will help with the visa application. Didn't she say your picture is going to be bigger than all the others, maybe take up the whole first page? You can't say no."

"But I can refuse to answer personal questions."

Alice throws up her hands, nearly toppling her plastic bag of rhinestones. "The magazine is called *Me & You*. If they wanted to know about the invitation business, it would be called *Invitation Business*. They want to know about you, and what's wrong with that when you've done so well?" Alice picks up another envelope to embellish. "You always think someone is pointing a finger at you. But this is not about your accident. It is about what you did after your accident."

Listlessly, Linno sifts a handful of stones through her fingers. She wonders if they will expect her to wear short sleeves. To be proud of her deformity. That kind of thing happens in America all the time it seems, that defiant hubris, that fist-in-the-air mentality. Or stump-in-the-air, as the case may be.

THE PHOTOGRAPHER, Jade, is a sweaty white woman with a man's haircut. She wears no jewelry other than the camera hanging around her neck and an ever-present smile, enthralled by the newness of her surroundings. "The colors in this country are fabulous," Jade says. "I've taken three rolls of film just on my way to your shop! You people are really unafraid of bright red."

"An auspicious color," Alice says.

Jade nods solemnly. "Love it."

While Jade sets up her lights, Alice insists that Linno use the lipstick that Alice brought with her, a shade of red auspicious enough for a prostitute. Linno blots most of it onto a handkerchief. Meanwhile, by the window, Jade has arranged such an elegant shrine of custom-made cards that Linno feels like some sort of imperfect offering. She has never seen her cards this way, open all at once—her first butterflies, the pagoda, the Manhattan skyline, the triptych of elephant heads, the triple-tiered birthday cake, a bouquet, a leaping star, a peacock and a sunrise and a lotus all in bloom. Linno sits on a stool in the center of her pantheon, wrists crossed in her lap.

"Just try to get comfy," Jade says. When this does not ease Linno's stiffness, she adds, "Think pleasant thoughts."

Linno thinks of the time she taught Anju how to swim by a stone footbridge that spanned a stream. She remembers small silver flecks of *poonjan* fish and the little boy on the bridge above them, obliviously peeing into the water while Anju clung to Linno, hands fastened about her neck, squealing. Anju's watery weightlessness, her primal need stripped of pride, these made Linno feel strong and loved in ways she would never admit aloud. "Don't let go!" Anju begged, fearful on several counts. "Don't let me go!" And though Linno laughed to reassure her sister, she answered without a trace of teasing to her voice: "No, never."

THE NEXT FEW WEEKS are uneventful. Linno dedicates the entire time to a royal blue wedding invitation that opens into a peacock's tail, scalloped around the edge and studded with faux emeralds. The bride's father, a hedge fund billionaire, requested an invitation that would acknowledge Indian Independence Day, as it was also the date of his daughter's wedding, without using the color orange, which the billionaire's daughter considered "overdone and simply over." It is Linno's most involved job, requiring two weeks for completion. During her lunch breaks, she phones Duniya about sponsoring her visa, but no one responds to her messages.

After finishing the last invitation, she goes to dinner at Alice and Kuku's house, which has become Kuku and Jincy's house, as the decor now implies. Portraits of Jincy's family grace the bookshelves, the walls, and the top of the new television, a gift from Kuku to Jincy, which he learned of upon its delivery. "So far from my family," Jincy says over dessert. "I need a little entertainment."

Kuku notes that her family lives ten minutes away.

"But still it is a sorrowful moment when the girl leaves her family and joins her husband's." Jincy glances at Linno, and finding no empathy there, reaches over and clasps Alice's hand. "Chachy, you know what I'm talking about."

Linno recalls the ceremony performed before Jincy's wedding wherein she received her mother's blessings, a symbolic gesture of departing her family. In Jincy's case, all pathos was drowned by the soggy chorus of sobs, a cued symphony of aunts and sisters, while Jincy and her mother clung to each other. Interlocked like this, the two reminded Linno of a crumpled butterfly unable to rid itself of its cocoon. As Jincy went down the steps amid a decrescendo of noise, her mother wiped her eyes and looked around. "Anyone for tea?"

Linno rose to leave. "I should go. It's late."

"So soon?" asks Alice.

"Let me and my driver drop you off," Kuku says.

This, Linno was not expecting. Throughout dinner, Kuku hardly directed a word at her, which Linno thought was only appropriate, considering the way their last private discussion ended. But Jincy brightens at the suggestion. "All right, then. Let me pack up some dessert for you to take home. Promise to return my Tupperwares? They were wedding gifts. Not just any old plastic containers."

Linno promises.

"People borrow and borrow the Tupperwares," Jincy says, shaking her head. "It's hard to be generous with no more Tupperwares."

. . .

DUSK HAS SETTLED by the time they climb into the car. Kuku takes the front seat while Linno sits behind the driver, giving her an angle on Kuku's jaw. He unwraps a peppermint from plastic and pops it in his mouth, and for most of the ride, the only sound is the rumbling engine and the candy clacking against his teeth.

When they near her home, Linno suggests that they let her out, so she can walk the narrowing road alone. The driver slows to a stop. Suavely, Kuku hands him a rolled bill and suggests that he go buy himself a pack of cigarettes. The stall across the street is closed, but the driver seems to know this is coming and gets out of the car with no questions asked.

Linno puts her hand on the door handle. "Good-bye, then."

"Wait." Kuku raises a hand. "I won't waste your time. I came along for one reason—to ask you a question."

"If this involves a pagoda, I don't want to be asked."

He clicks his tongue as if it is foolish to reference such distant history. "I want to talk about my sister. Alice."

Kuku shifts in his seat so that he is nearly facing Linno while she, at a loss, waits for him to continue. He sighs, allowing for a moment of dignified silence, which is broken by the mating croak of a toad.

"I'm sure you know that Alice and I have had a hard life. Loneliness can make you do strange things, can make you imagine feelings where there were none before." Almost wistful, Kuku tilts his head. "I know. I was lonely once. Alice looked after me in those times, and now it is my duty to look after her, as well as the reputation of our father's name. So I have to ask you. What is the nature of your friendship with my sister?"

"The nature?"

"You know what I mean," he says. "Don't make me say it."

"But I have no idea what you mean."

Kuku presses his lips together and then finally blurts: "Are you in love with her?"

Linno stares at him until he repeats himself.

"I know what you said. Are you mad?"

"When you refused me that first time, Linno, I accepted it. When you and Alice decided to spend night and day together, I said fine. But I have been hearing things. Not just from anyone, but from a respectable source."

Linno fights between two urges—the desire to push her way out of this car and the need to know more. "From who? From who have you been hearing things?"

"From Abraham Saar."

It is as though he has reached into her head and rattled her brain as he would a snow globe, and try as she might to construct a thought, she cannot. Abraham Saar, who absorbs the Sunday sermon with his eyes closed. Abraham Saar, who took them to Kovalam Beach long ago, who spread a large blue sheet over soft sand and staked the corners with stones.

"Abraham Saar was a great friend of my father," Kuku continues, "and he invited Jincy and me to his house for dinner. Afterward, he and I were having drinks on the porch and I let it slip that you refused my hand in marriage, which he could hardly believe. But then he told me I should be careful. He said, 'She might take after her mother.' He had had several drinks by then. I asked what he meant. And he told me." Here, Kuku pauses, knowing to step carefully when speaking of mothers, however scandalous the story. "He told me how he was meant to marry your mother. How he found out about the relations she was having with another woman. Some kind of traveling actress in a local drama troupe. He said, 'Gracie was a headstrong girl, but I would have married her if not for that.' "

Linno's tongue moves slowly through a syrup of half thoughts. "Abraham Saar?"

Kuku nods. Only then does he seem to recognize that she has known nothing of this affair.

"Of course, I will never tell anyone of this," he says. "Not even Alice, if the answer is no. But Jincy also felt I should have this conversation with you. After all, she is very concerned about the family name, now that it's hers as well." He softens his voice. "Jincy has read that these inclinations might be genetic. Which is why we wanted to make sure that you . . . that your feelings for my sister are of a proper kind."

She hears a noise in the bushes, a rustle of birds in the dark. The toad resumes its lonely, interrogatory croak.

"Linno?"

"One minute," she says. Tupperware in hand, she gets out of the car and wedges the Tupperware just behind the rear wheel. When she re-enters the car, she takes the front seat.

"Shashi?" Kuku asks. She presses down on the brake and puts the car in reverse, as she has seen her father do many times before. "Are you wearing perfume?"

"This is not Shashi."

"Linno? Are you crazy? Are you licensed?"

Though Linno has never driven a car on open roads, she doesn't plan to go very far. Letting up on the brake, she reverses about a foot, until she hears a faint and satisfying pop. She then puts the car in park once again.

"Stop the car!" Kuku yells, his hands gripping the door handle.

"We are stopped."

"Then get out of it!"

Linno obeys. She gets out of the car. On her knees, she fishes out the bag of crushed Tupperware and rasmalai, and circles the car to Kuku's side just as Shashi is hurrying back across the street. She tosses the bag into Kuku's lap. "Jincy is too generous with her Tupperwares," she says.

"Linno? Linno!" Kuku leans out the open window. Walking away, she can still hear him barking into the night. "You listen to me, Linno! I am trying to be discreet but I had to ask! Just because something is genetic does not make it right!"

A RUMOR WILL METASTASIZE if one lets it. Linno decides that the quickest way to remedy this one is to never mention it again, not to Alice, who may have heard by way of Kuku, and especially not to Melvin and Ammachi. It pains her to think that Abraham Saar is privy to knowledge that her own father does not possess. Now the mere thought of Abraham Saar fills her with discomfort, and she feels ashamed, made naked by what he knows.

Alice comes to work the next day and the next without any change in her behavior, so Linno assumes that Kuku was satisfied with his investigation, if not with the mangled Tupperware. Linno will ignore what was said, and in doing so, the mother she knew will remain intact. Dead people should be treated as sculptures, dusted on occasion but never shifted too drastically, and life has made Linno particularly skilled at this, at turning her back on what should be left alone. As a child, it was Anju who tried to make Linno look at the feathery smudge of a tire-flattened bird or the pat of cow dung in the shape, she insisted, of Sri Lanka. Unless tricked, Linno never looked.

But she cannot help but consider the kind of woman who would love another in that way. She once saw a pair of white tourists in town, a girl holding hands with a boy who, upon closer inspection, had breasts! Not flaccid man-breasts but those born exclusively of estrogen! The "boy" had mastered boyishness in the shuffle of her walk, the careless haircut with cowlick, the khakis shapeless and rumpled. It is too far a jump between these features and Linno's mother, who frowned upon ladies with short haircuts. When their neighbor in Bombay cut her hair into a bob, Gracie took to calling her Mrs. Mushroom. "All cap, no face," she said.

Occasionally, the phrase comes streaking through Linno's mind, raucous and taunting, throwing up its skirts at her while she goes about the most banal of tasks. Brushing her teeth—*an affair with another woman!*—or calling Duniya, Inc.—*an affair with another woman!* What is most disturbing is not the thought of her mother masquerading with cowlick and khakis, but the chance that she might have harbored a love that had nothing to do with Linno and Anju and Melvin, a love that scaled uncertain heights, that ran upstream, along its own dangerous course, a love that Linno will never understand. However much she might want to, she cannot defend a mother she barely knew.

When such thoughts creep up on her, Linno closes her eyes and grits her teeth, thinks: *I. Will. Not. Look.*

LINNO ARRIVES at the shop to find the *Me & You* article laminated and posted in the front window. She stands before it, trying to reconcile the face before her with the one she had assumed was hers all along. In the picture, sunlight falls softly across her left side, and her eyes seem larger than usual, captivating and flecked with light. For the first time ever, when looking at her own picture, her gaze does not go directly to her knotted wrist.

Linno notices that Alice clipped only the part of the article that praised her invitations, leaving out Linno's answer to the question of whether or not she planned to visit the States.

"I am wanting to," Linno said. "My sister, she is there. She is liking it so much that she did not call me in too long. I very much wish to see her."

According to the date on the article, the picture ran last week. Linno wonders what Anju thinks of it, whether Linno's voice and face might jolt her into action or cause her to withdraw further from them. Or maybe this picture will lead nowhere at all.

"So?" Alice says, emerging from the shop. She is beaming. "Pretty good, isn't it?"

"We shouldn't hang it here."

"Why not?"

"It will send the wrong idea. That I am vain. Or dead."

"You should be vain!" Alice says. "If I had a picture like this, I'd turn it into a full-size poster."

Linno follows Alice into the shop, inhales the comfort of percolating coffee. Bhanu is on the phone with a customer, and Prince is seated before the computer, driving the mouse in circles.

"Doesn't Linno look good in the picture, Prince? Bhanu?"

Bhanu nods emphatically while listing the different shades of white. Prince, who cannot be bothered with anything outside the screen, offers efficient English: "Very gorgeous."

Linno pours herself a mug of coffee. "I suppose I don't know what makes a woman beautiful. I don't look at women that way."

"What way?" Alice asks.

"In a way that notices a woman's beauty."

Blowing on her coffee, Alice winks. Linno wishes she hadn't. "Lucky for you, maybe someone at Duniya does look at women that way."

It takes a moment for Linno to make sense of Alice's statement. Duniya. Linno nearly spills her coffee as Alice sits her before the computer and clicks on the message awaiting her.

From: neha@duniya.com
To: linno@eastwestinvites.com
Subject: Re: I WOULD LIKE TO BE SPONSORED FOR VISA

Dear Ms. Vallara,

Greetings. I am the president of Duniya, Inc. We greatly apologize for our delayed response, but we receive hundreds (!!!) of emails with similar subject lines, as you can imagine. Yesterday, luckily, our intern brought your email to our attention, as well as an AMAZING and moving piece about you in *Me & You* magazine. Not only this, but we have visited your website and find it to be one of the finest displays that we've seen. We literally cooed over your creations! Your work and your life story are truly truly INSPIRING, and we would be thrilled to have you lead a seminar on wedding invitation trends during our June Exposition.

We can speak more via phone, once you know the details of what kind of booth and seminar you would like to put together. I am sure we can provide you with whatever support materials you need for your visa application, after you send us a check for $1000 made out to Duniya, Inc.

I look forward to speaking with you.

All the best,

Neha Misra
President
Duniya, Inc.

Bhanu looks over at the commotion with a puzzled face, never breaking his on-phone presentation voice ("Yes ma'am, most people prefer gold leafing on the eggshell . . ."), all the while wondering why Alice and Linno are jumping up and down like little girls.

IV.

TRUE NORTH

l.

VITAL TO ANJU'S INVOLVEMENT in the film is an imperfect equation that she has formulated over the course of Rohit's rambling pleas:

Anju + documentary film = immigration lawyer = green card = Anju's rise from illegality and failuredom

He has promised these things, in so many words, over pastries and buttery, creamer-tainted coffee. Most of his credibility comes not from his own appearance, especially not with that coppery smear of a beard, but lies instead with his silent partner—the camera.

It is sleek yet hefty, a James Bond among cameras with the stylish plume of its microphone and its dark, seductive lens. Without the camera, Rohit is just a boy with idle hands in the pockets of his Dolce jeans, for whom the world holds neither consequence nor challenge.

On one occasion, Rohit reluctantly eases the camera into Anju's hands, hovering about as though she is an ogre handling an infant. She slips her fingers under the strap, as she has seen him do for the past two weeks, and weighs its expensive, humming power in her palm. She puts her eye to the viewfinder, expecting spectral visions, slightly dismayed by the black and white of it all. At the end of a branch, she sees a lone leaf twirling against the wind. The control is exhilarating, the power to record the last moment of this leaf, to potentially capture the seething essence of nature. Gently, she nudges the zoom button, as she has noticed Rohit doing whenever he thinks she is saying something of import, usually about her family. This happened the other day, when he asked her to call Linno on his phone card, while he filmed.

At first, shifting her feet before the pay phone, she resisted. Rohit peeked from behind his camera when she hung up the phone, her quarter and dime jangling into the coin return niche. "What's the problem?" he asked. "Don't you think they want to hear from you?"

She had no doubt they wanted to hear from her. But after that first blissful greeting, the inevitable questions would come tumbling: What has she done? Why has she done it? How will they survive this disgrace? If she calls, they will arrange to bring her home, and she will be as much a child as when she left. Each day she does not speak to her family serves to harden her resolve. "I will not call until I have good news," she said. "Until you get me the immigration lawyer."

"I told you, I'm in touch with an attorney. With a couple, in fact." But as usual, Rohit gave no specifics on the subject, preferring instead to swaddle her in vague encouragement. "I know times seem tough right now, but the thing is, you have to start from zero for the audience to care about your problems. So in the end, when everything works out, the audience will totally love you and be on your side. It's called *the dramatic arc*, see what I'm saying? Now." He put his eye to the camera. "Go ahead."

It was comforting to think that Rohit had made himself the dramatic architect of her life, that he felt so zealously optimistic about the future. But as she put her fingertips to the depressions of the silver keys, she could not dial. She did not speak, but by Rohit's silence, she could sense that he was slowly pushing the zoom button, closing in on her.

At the time, she did not understand why he so loved the combination of silence and slow zoom, but now, as she pushes closer to the leaf and its frantic dance, she understands the heightening of emotion when coming closer and closer in the attempt to comprehend, to find significance, to see something of one's self in the leaf.

ON THEIR SUNDAY OFF, Anju and Bird go for a walk in Central Park, which, when they arrive, seems as bad an idea as Anju initially suspected. Ever since her first meeting with Rohit, she has harbored the disquieting feeling that gazes are trained upon her wherever she goes, pairs of dark, alarming eyes beneath wide-brimmed fedoras. It does not help that the fedora seems to be in style, as she has seen two different preteens wearing them on the 3 train. No doubt some detective movie has fed this theory, but she has the illicit sense of being Wanted, and not in the tragic way of children's faces on milk cartons. The INS has her under surveillance, watching her from parked sedans, teasing her with this limited semblance of freedom. She wonders if there is something foreign about her gait.

But Central Park, she must admit, is fantastically groomed and beautiful. All around are the trillings and cawings of wildlife, though rarely seeing any insects and birds gives the feeling of walking through some sort of nature-themed park, the noises emitted by carefully hidden radios. They walk into a place called Sheep Meadow. Bird sits and Anju lies on her stomach, watching the white people play their games of catch and kites, backed by a deep green border of trees and, beyond this, a bevy of handsome buildings against a fading sky. From Anju's vantage point, the meadow is so broad, so subtle in its changes of velvety green that the land seems to curve with the earth. There is a beauty here of which she will never be part, but this is the pleasant melancholy of witnessing anything beautiful, the wish to enter and become it.

"Relax," Bird says, offering her an open bag of salted almonds. "No one is looking at you." No one except for a disturbingly fearless squirrel. It stares with hostile eyes even after Bird shoos it away, as if biding its time.

"So what did you do yesterday?" Bird asks. "On your day off?"

Anju delays, picking almond skin from between her teeth. She has been trying to keep Rohit a secret from Bird, at least for the time being, as she is sure that Bird will disapprove of the film idea. Bird hates movie people, finds them untrustworthy, making the blind assumption that Anju trusts Bird enough to believe in her judgment. But ever since Anju discovered her illegal status, she finds herself sharing more silence than secrets with Bird, perceiving that autonomy and adulthood require a measure of distance. Still, the silence feels wrong.

"I tried to call my family yesterday," Anju says.

Bird stops chewing. "You reached them?"

"No one was home."

For a time, they watch the disks flung through the air, the flight of a rainbow-colored kite on a string, an animated tableau of comets and planets against a field of blue.

"You never told me about your mother," Bird says. "How did she die?"

"My mother?"

Bird nods.

"She drowned in the sea." Speaking of her mother's death, after all these silent years, feels more strange than sad. "I don't remember my mother. My older sister does, but she never speaks of these things. My sister was there when she died."

Bird squints at her as if from a distance, absently plucking a few blades of grass. "Did your sister ever tell you about that day?"

Anju had tried to coax the subject from her sister on one or two occasions, long ago, and she had watched Linno's expression cloud over, stowing her memories in some sealed mental space. A familiar image returns to Anju's mind, formed in part from Ammachi's description and her own imagination: a rigid little Linno, the way she was found that day, with dirty feet and eyes that would not blink. "All we know is that she drowned herself."

Here, Bird stops plucking. "What do you mean, drowned herself?"

"It was a suicide."

"How do you know that?"

"Everyone knows."

"And a thousand years ago, everyone knew the world was flat." Bird brushes the crumbs from her skirt, somewhat forcefully. "Everyone knows only what they are told. Easy that way."

In the gauzy blue of dusk, the signs and windows of the buildings have suddenly, without notice, turned luminous at once. A neon sign reading ESSEX HOUSE glows red. Anju wonders how long she should wait before changing the subject.

"And she loved you and Linno," Bird says softly.

"Maybe she did, maybe she did not."

"But I'm sure she did—"

"Not enough. Not enough to stay."

Careful with Anju's anger, Bird remains quiet.

"How did you know my sister's name is Linno?" Anju asks.

Bird looks up. "You said so."

"I did?"

"Many, many times. Linno this, Linno that . . ."

But always Anju has tried to do just the opposite, attempting to keep her family at arm's length from everyone else.

"Of course, I don't know how your mother felt, do I? Who knows another person's mind? I'm sorry. Just it is hard to believe . . ." Bird removes a handkerchief from her pocket and blows her nose, which clearly does not need blowing. And then, in a belated attempt at providing comfort: "Very sad, your mother's story. Very, very sad."

INTERVIEW. One of Rohit's more intimidating terms. When he says that he wants to interview her, she thinks of a bare, white room, her hands fidgeting under a spindly table, the camera in the corner like a cop. She thinks of a confession.

According to Rohit's instructions, she goes to his Ex's apartment for the interview, wearing a blue shirt rather than her best blouse and skirt, whose floral pattern Rohit has deemed "too busy." His Ex resides in Little Italy, between streets whose titles sound like jams, Mott and Mulberry, near a butcher shop that seems ill at ease among its svelte young passersby. Signs announce its presence in the windows: THIS BUTCHER SHOP WAS IN MARTIN SCORSESE'S 1ST FEATURE FILM, *WHO'S THAT KNOCKING AT MY DOOR?* AND IS THE LAST REMAINING "OLD TIME" FAMILY BUTCHER SHOP IN LITTLE ITALY. BEST VEAL, MEATS, AND POULTRY, CHOICE BEEF. Anju enters a neighboring brick building and climbs four flights of misshapen stairs, seemingly molded by generations of heavy-footed people. By the time she arrives at the door, she finds that the Ex has left.

"Where is your Ex?" Anju asks. "She is living here, no?"

"Yeah, yeah, she just wanted to give us some privacy," Rohit says. He nervously scribbles something in his black Moleskine notebook, the same kind, he once told her, that Hemingway carried. She did not think it appropriate to ask who Hemingway was. "This interview is going to be pretty personal, and it's important that you're totally comfortable."

Anju surveys the large studio apartment, a bed coyly hidden behind a great span of bookshelves where the books have been arranged according to the color of their spines, a spectrum of literature. It is the only orderly thing about this habitat. A cereal bowl sits on the coffee table, a green flake petrified to the bottom. A small, unplugged television faces a wall, as if being punished for its ineptitude, and on top of this, a tall burgundy boot with a lethal heel.

Rohit has uncluttered an island of space for the interview. Anju sits at a round table by the window, whose shade Rohit keeps opening and closing, deeply bothered by the view of the fire escape. He puts an ash-tray full of pennies on the tabletop, then takes away the ashtray and replaces it with a fat vanilla candle. Stepping back, he stares at the candle meaningfully, chin in hand.

"All right." He stands by his camera, which he has set up on a tripod. "I think we're ready. Don't look directly into the camera, okay? Just meet my eyes, like we're having a conversation."

Throughout the shoot, his eyes dart up and down between his camera and her gaze, and she senses that his mind is thusly divided, his interest in her words only partial. He nods emphatically, even when she has said nothing of import. He seems to hope that his nodding will inspire her to offer up some precocious gem of wisdom, some well-phrased message that deserves to be hugged by quotation marks in his Moleskine book. Part of her worries about the state of her hair, which she forgot to check before taping began, but maybe mussed-up hair is appropriate for the Starting-from-Zero look.

Q: What did you hope to accomplish by coming to the States?
A: My family is not a poor poor family, but we were having bad luck, and I thought I will change our luck by coming to U.S. I was having high marks in school and my teachers were saying I will do great things, so I was believing this too. And then when you believe something should happen, you will make it happen, whichever way. Even if the way is maybe little bit crooked, still it is going in up direction. Like that fire escape.

Q: Well, fire escapes go up or down. But okay, so speaking of downward spirals, are you referring to your sister and the scholarship?
A: Yes.

Q: Are you sorry about that?
A: Of course I am sorry. I went from number one in my class to pulling hairs in a beauty salon.

Q: Can you say "I am sorry for faking my scholarship application"? It'll just make more sense in the editing.
A: I am sorry for faking the scholarship application.

Q: If you could go back, would you *not* do what you did?
A: Now you are trying to make me be little.

Q. What?

A. You are being belittling to me.

Q: I'm sorry, I take it back, then. Why don't you tell me about your sister?

A: Linno. My sister's name is Linno. She is older to me by four years. She had an accident when she was small from playing with this *mala padakkam*, how do you say . . . fireworks. The doctor took away her hand. Cut it off, I mean.

Q: That must have been a traumatic experience.

A: What is the meaning?

Q: Traumatic, like when you're traumatized by something. It haunts you. It messes with your head, makes you upset or angry or sad.

A: I don't know. We do not talk on these things. After the accident, Linno always was cutting her sleeve to tie her wrist, so that no one will see it. One time—I was younger then—I cut the sleeve of my best Christmas dress and tied mine also. I remember Linno saw me walk around like this and she was very traumatize with me. She ran into the bedroom. My grandmother thought I was making fun at Linno—I was not—but she beat me for that and for cutting my dress. My grandmother, she shorted the sleeves. Still it did not look right.

Q: Hmmm . . . (nodding)

A: There is no more to that story.

By the end, the interview has whetted Rohit's appetite. He badgers Anju to let him film Bird as well. "We need some interaction with your roommate. With Bird, I mean. Don't you think she's a key figure in your story?"

"Key to what?"

"No, I mean that she's important. She's the one who took you down that road with Tandon in the first place. And now she's become your benefactor, in a way."

"She does not like movie people," Anju warns.

"Trust me, I've heard it all. I'm in documentary. We're the least loved of the bunch."

Rohit pushes EJECT on the camera. With a tiny growl of gears, a panel on the camera's side juts open and offers up the tape. Rohit writes on a sticky label—ANJU FILM INTERVIEW I—which he presses to the tape with pride.

"My mom would love to get her hands on this footage," he says. "To be honest, I kind of got the idea for this film from her."

"Mrs. Solanki?"

"She was trying to get this episode together for her crapass show *Four Corners*. She even called your sister about it, I think."

Anju's breath catches in her throat. "Linno, she called Linno? What did Linno say?"

"I don't know. The idea tanked, I think."

"Oh." Disappointed, Anju wriggles her fingers into Bird's water-proof gloves, which are as large as oven mitts. "I did not know your mother is making documentary film also."

Rohit throws off a dismissive laugh, almost a snort. "If what she does is documentary, then I'm Errol-fucking-Morris. She does talk show segments, you know? They're, like, short and packaged and slick, like MTV. There's no real depth, no complexity to what she does."

Anju nods. Whenever he speaks of his film aesthetic, she feels comforted by his confidence, his panache, cut to *this* and fade to *that*. She also feels a vague pity for him. Piece by piece, he nestles the camera parts into the cushioned niches of the bag while she watches him in silence, thinking how safe and sad it is to put the bulk of one's love in an inanimate thing.

FOR THE SAKE OF THE FILM, Anju allows Rohit to come over to the apartment and speak to Bird when she arrives home from work. Anju forbids him from turning on the camera until Bird agrees to being filmed, a rule that Anju will not allow him to bend, out of loyalty to Bird.

Anju perches nervously on the couch while Rohit moves the blue vase from the coffee table to a side table and turns on all the lamps he possibly can. He is appalled by the darkness, baffled by the fact that Anju and Bird could survive here in this cave they call home. His own is as ruthlessly bright as a hotel, but since arriving here, Anju has come to prefer the forgiveness of shadows. She thinks of her bedroom back home and its single window as familiar to her as a member of the family.

How well she knows its view, its moods, as when the light comes hard and glinting through the bars or lugubriously blue, and shadows travel across the room, marking the passage of hours.

The front door opens. Anju sits up straight, though what she was planning to say—*I've been meaning to tell you . . . I believe this is the best way to . . .*—flies out of her head along with her courage.

In steps Gwen, flushed from the cold. She pulls off her lime green galoshes before noticing Rohit and the video camera on the coffee table. "Oh hey. What's going on?"

"I'm Rohit." He raises his hand in a swift hello as he goes for his camera.

"We said no camera," Anju says sharply.

"No, no, it's cool," Gwen says. The tip of her nose is charmingly ruddy. "Is this for a project or something?"

"I make documentaries. Actually, I'm making one about Anju here."

"Oh yeah?" Gwen pulls the elastic from her ponytail and fluffs her hair. "Very cool. Did you do something special, Anju? Something I don't know about?"

"She's done a lot." Pointing the camera at Gwen, Rohit presses the RECORD button.

Usually, when Gwen enters a room, Anju withdraws to her own so as to minimize conversation. She is fairly sure that Gwen thinks that she knows very little English, a comforting assumption that allows Anju to continue on her silent orbit within the apartment, without the collision of a conversation. But she does think it strange that the shampoos and creams of virtual strangers should occupy such intimate positions in the bathroom. Anju uses Bird's efficient and unlabeled bottle of shampoo plus conditioner. Gwen's shampoo is called Pure Blonde, a golden bottle whose fliptop is always open, like a taunting tongue. Once, on impulse, Anju used the Pure Blonde on an inner lock of her hair, but it did nothing to "release the golden tone and caramel essence of each strand."

Gwen is saying something about Truffaut's auteur theory and the *caméra-stylo*, to which Rohit is murmuring, *mhm, mhm*. Holding the camera to his eye, he asks, "So do you know Anju's story?"

"Does who know Anju's story?" Bird asks from the doorway, both arms saddled with grocery bags. She steps past Gwen and into the living room, but Rohit keeps the camera rolling. "Who are you? Why are you filming in my house?"

"This is Rohit," Gwen says brightly. "He's making a documentary about Anju."

Bird stares at Anju, brow furrowed, the bags still in her hands, which are ashy from the cold. Anju elbows Rohit, and he lowers the camera.

"Since when?" Bird asks in Malayalam. "We didn't discuss this."

Silence follows, during which time Rohit turns off his camera and puts it on the couch. He picks up the blue vase with both hands, as if it has suddenly gained in value, and sets it in its original place on the coffee table.

Gwen backs into her room, her brightness diminishing with each step. "I'm gonna hop in the shower."

IT COMES AS NO SURPRISE to Anju that Bird is uninterested in befriending Rohit. Neither is Anju all that offended, on Rohit's behalf, that the only "interaction" he witnessed was Bird pointing at the door and asking him to leave. In fact, he seemed prepared to leave yet confident that he would return, adding: "I'll let you both talk this out."

Now Anju watches Bird preparing dinner, wondering how to talk things out when all of Bird's words form incredulous questions. "You want to let this boy follow you around with a camera?" Bird breaks a fistful of yellow twigs over a pot of boiling water. "You are an illegal. How much attention do you want?"

"He says that attention is good, when directed the right way. Attention can help."

Bird goes back and forth between the fridge and the stove, muttering, "Salt, salt." She pulls a clear jar of salt from a high cupboard. "So you trust him."

"Yes." And she does. Trying to mimic his magnetic sense of urgency, she translates his words into Malayalam. "Because my best interest is in his best interest. He wants the same ending that I do—citizenship in the States. He promised to get me the best lawyer because his parents know many powerful people."

"What about your father? Maybe we should get his opinion."

"But in the meantime, I will keep filming with Rohit. If my father says no, I will stop."

Bird opens the jar and spoons a heap of salt over the twigs, which have softened and curled into a wreath of noodles. "Why do you need this Rohit? I told you I would help you."

Anju chooses her words carefully. Over the past two weeks, Bird has grown strangely sensitive, hurt when Anju did not want to watch *The Price Is Right* with her, irritated when she learned that Anju's clothes were still in her duffel bag rather than folded in the dresser.

"I want to move forward," Anju says. "All this time I feel I've been walking in one place."

"You think I am holding you back?"

Anju says nothing.

Bird busies herself in hurt silence while Anju slowly closes the lid on the salt jar. She spots an ant burrowing a tunnel through the white sand, not far from its colleague working an inch below. Her mind falls through the past months, to Linno and Tang in sweaty steel cups.

"This is sugar!" Anju says, holding up the jar.

Bird sips from the wooden spoon. "Oh shit hell dammit!"

Anju stares at Bird, stunned by her unlikely string of curse words.

Bird snaps off the stove, nearly taking the dial with her. In one motion, she pours the noodles into a colander, steam drifting off the hot, sweet mess.

AT NIGHT, Bird lies on her sliver of bed, listening to the fuzzy drone of Anju's snore. Bird hadn't noticed, but earlier in the evening it had rained, leaving the windows gemmed with droplets that redden each time a car's headlights go streaming past. Bird had imagined this day turning out much differently, with spaghetti marinara that she would make from a recipe out of *Good Housekeeping* magazine, quickly perused but not purchased under the disapproving eye of a magazine vendor.

And to come home to this—to a camera in her face. To hear that Anju has been cooking up some disastrous Make-Me-Famous recipe, fed to her by a boy claiming to be a filmmaker. Could they possibly be in love? No, Anju is more discerning. Bird remembers him from his visit to Tandon's office. There was something untrustworthy about him, about the way he barreled into a place with his camera, the way he seemed to be examining you through a lens even when he wasn't. Why doesn't Anju listen to her elders, or in this case, her elder? And why did she take so long to unpack her bags, waiting until Bird simply hung up her clothes for her?

It is almost as though Anju feels no real attachment to Bird.

The thought of this is a weight upon Bird's chest. Feeling queasy, she rolls onto her side, facing Anju, whose lashes are fluttering between dreams. Merely looking at the girl makes Bird wish for so much more

than what she has, makes her think, *This is the closest I have come to home.*
A thin wind escapes from Anju's mouth, which in sleep belongs to her
mother and during the day belongs to someone else. Anju looks nothing
like the baby in the photograph that Gracie sent so long ago, of chubby
Linno seated on an upturned crate, Anju in her arms like a surprised
sack of flour. Maybe Bird could tell Anju that she and Gracie were
acquaintances. Friends of friends. She could paint over the past in a
clean dull white, but the loss of that landscape, carefully preserved all
these years, would erase her as well.

HAD BIRD RECOGNIZED her last day with Gracie when it came,
she would have devised something better to do than sit in the dressing
room. It was the opening night of their Kottayam performance, which
had taken place outdoors, on the Thirunakkara Maidan, with the statue
of Gandhi looking on from the north and two pale minarets in view
from the east. All had gone well, it seemed. Gracie had tempered her
lines, and rain had not swept away the show at intermission, as it had in
Thiruvananthapuram. But while the others had gone off to celebrate,
Bird preferred to take her time as she sat before the mirror and removed
her makeup. Gracie perched on the ledge of the dressing room table and
spoke of a man in the audience who had liked her ruby red hat. "Strange
fellow. Something sweet about him, but definitely not his nose. His
sneeze could topple a small child."

"You went into the audience?" Bird said. "You can't do that."

"Why not? My part was finished, and I wanted to see you up there."

"Because there should be some space between us and them, some
mystery. People can only believe from a distance."

With a damp towel, Bird stroked the makeup from her cheeks, the
coats of pink and peach, until her face was marbled with flesh tones. On
the counter were the compacts from which the colors came, slender
brushes resting neatly beside them, and a steel bowl of water.

Gracie sighed. "It doesn't matter anyway, whether his nose is big or
not. He is not the one I'm marrying."

Bird's hand stopped mid-stroke. "Your family made a match?"

"Six months from now I will be a married woman."

Slowly, Bird dipped her rag into the steel bowl. She steadied her
voice. "I thought it was a year."

"My father found me someone sooner." His name was Abraham, she
said. A dignified name, such that belonged to the sort of man who would

raise an army of sons. "My father says it is dangerous for a girl to be alone for too long. She might start to like it. And my mother says, 'Always pluck a bud before it fully flowers.' "

Bird looked at the girl before her, nineteen years old, eager and angry, bright but unsure. The ceiling light skimmed the outline of Gracie's hair; seated beneath her, Bird felt herself within some fleeting shade. "I've always thought," Bird said, simply to fill the silence, "that a flower is best on its second or third day of blooming."

Gracie nodded; Bird could not read her thoughts. Turning to the mirror, Gracie dipped the end of a clean rag into the bowl and drew the rag across her eyelid. The kohl was smudged but still there.

"Not like that." Bird unscrewed the lid from a jar of Vaseline and dabbed some onto a clean rag. She stood up and steadied Gracie's chin with one hand while wiping her eyelid with the other. The kohl came away in thick streaks of bruisy black until finally her eyelid was slick and shiny, her lashes like thorns. Gracie kept both eyes closed as Bird stroked the rag across the other eye, now more slowly, gently, taking the time to contemplate the features that she might not see in another six months, down to the finest detail, to the pink tendril of a vein on across an eyelid. This was the face that Abraham's hands would hold and study for years as age carved its way around the scant freckles, the mouth. Bird removed the rag, but she did not remove her hand from Gracie's chin. The muscles in Gracie's throat shifted up and down. With her eyes still closed, she reached for Bird. She laid her head on Bird's shoulder, and Bird, too, closed her eyes.

In that moment, the world was in perfect balance, undisturbed. Bird's sense of smell blossomed briefly so that she could pick apart the layered air—the dull sweat, the sultry perfumes, the sprays and Vaselines, Gracie's breath. Bird felt the shape of her friend curled into her chest.

Bird opened her eyes to the sloping curvature of Gracie's neck, where she could distinguish the finest layer of down. Her own nose was not more than two inches from that shallow. Bird lowered her head and rested her lips, briefly, in that spot. The earth did not shudder. In fact, it was the world beyond these walls that had suddenly dissolved, along with the man Gracie would marry and the sons she would mother, the houses she would have, and time itself. There was only that fine, soft shallow which Bird met once again, for the last time, feeling Gracie's breath flowing calmly through her throat.

There was a noise at the door. Gracie sat up. Sharply, she called out: "Who is it?"

Someone had seen. This much Bird knew. She could not have imagined, then, that the someone was Abraham, with flowers in hand, that he had lingered and watched until, startled by his own sound, he hurried away with his heart full of turmoil and wonder. And what had he seen? An embrace, a kiss, which led him to form a story of seduction and sin, so that when he went to Gracie's father the next day, he painted a picture much closer to what he believed than what he had seen.

But now, in the dressing room, Bird could not help but lie, if only to reach for a moment lost. "It was nothing," she said.

At last Gracie looked back at Bird and smiled the kind of smile that was tossed off at a glance, brisk and clean. The kind of smile that tidied things up, that took a step back. Gracie slid off the counter and moved to the door.

"We should join the others," she said.

For years, Bird would remember Gracie disappearing through the door, and she would imagine any number of ways that Gracie could have turned, could have come back inside and stayed for longer with her head on Bird's shoulder, forever ignorant of the world pressing in on them, hovering from the doorway, watching.

2.

GHAFOOR IS THRILLED at the prospect of having the Apsara Salon featured in a full-length documentary about ethnic beauty salons, but he demands a day's notice for the shoot so that he can "prepare." Rohit warned Anju not to confess the true topic of the film while he, in turn, promised not to disclose the name of the salon.

To Ghafoor, Anju tries to explain what Rohit once told her about the editing process, how all the many hours of shooting must be condensed into a ninety-minute *dramatic arc*, one that will not necessarily include the Apsara Salon. Ghafoor laughs away her warnings. "Well then, Miss George Lucas, we will have to do our level best."

Over the phone, Ghafoor and Rohit settle on a Wednesday shoot, but after Ghafoor hangs up, Bird complains of a burgeoning ache in her stomach. "My appendix," she tells him.

"Are you going to the hospital?" he asks.

She manages to wince and shake her head at the same time. "Could be appendix. Could be something else. I'll wait it out at home."

And while normally Ghafoor interrogates all sick leaves, today he says, "Okay, see you Friday." He has known Bird long enough to know that she is faking it, that she hates cameras as much as she hates the bearded ladies who come in expecting a face lift from a simple threading session. But he cannot be bothered with Bird's negative energy, nor does he want an invalid shuffling up and down the aisles, hands on her belly; if he wanted that, he would've invited his mother. No, the Apsara Salon must exude cool and comfort, and the employees must be neat, well-chappaled professionals, as close to pretty as possible.

At the cash register, Ghafoor thumbs through his shoe box of cassette tapes, trying to decide whether old Bollywood music or carnatic music will be appropriate to set the mood. Powder suggests her own bhangra-reggaeton remix tape courtesy of DJ Kaur, which he vetoes by ignoring her.

"Rohit will ask you to turn the music off," Anju says, recalling one instance when he roamed Bird's apartment with his headphones on, searching for the vague sonar hum that was ruining the shoot. When finally he concluded that it was the neighbor's music, he knocked on the suspect's door, to Anju's horror, and asked Mrs. Ortiz to turn off her radio for the next thirty minutes. The solely Spanish-speaking Mrs. Ortiz nodded, closed her door, and turned up the radio.

"Rohit is his name?" Nandi asks, combing the finished eyebrows of her client, who is gripping the arms of her chair as if it might launch her out. "You know this man?"

"He is not a man," Anju says quickly. "He is student only."

"How did you meet him?" Lipi asks.

"At a social function." For the past six months of her employment, she has kept her personal life as shrouded as possible, which usually means listening to other people's stories and contributing very little of her own. "In the park. A church function in the park."

The other stylists seem doubtful.

"Enough dillying and dallying," Ghafoor says. He tells Powder to buy some flowers tomorrow morning, before work. "Cheap and colorful. Now who is going to dye my mustache?"

Just then a mother and her teenage daughter walk through the door, faces that Anju does not recognize. The mother looks around, unsure, while the girl gnaws on her fingernails. "May I help you?" Anju asks.

"I would like brow and lip threading. And she," the mother glances back at her daughter, lowering her voice, "wants the bikini wax for some reason, godknowswhat. She says swimming, but I tell you, children are crazy these days—"

"*Mom,*" the girl says. "It *is* for swimming. I *swim*. God."

Anju seats the mother with Lipi and guides the girl toward the back. She has had several girls like this, those who claim the same official alibi—swimming—and who demand the kind of waxing that Anju has unofficially termed the Eve.

"Really?" Lipi asks, after the girl and her mother leave. "At her age?"

Anju shrugs, expertly pulling off her gloves. "Not even a fig leaf."

ANJU CANNOT BLAME Ghafoor for ecstatically assuming that the salon will appear in the film. She herself had a difficult time understanding that the past two months of shooting, from February to March, would mostly be discarded on what Rohit calls "the cutting room floor." It never occurred to her what it meant to condense so much time in such a way, until Rohit showed her a scene that he had edited on his computer, from the first time they met for dinner at the Solankis' home.

What Anju remembered as lasting two hours had been chopped down to six minutes. The discussion was not just shortened but shaped beyond recognition, airbrushed and paled to a bleak semblance of its previous self. In the scene when Rohit announced to his parents that he was going to be a filmmaker, the subsequent shot showed Mr. Solanki refilling his glass of wine and giving his wife a look that, after any other shot, could have conveyed his curiosity or indigestion, but its placement after Rohit's announcement sent the story in a different direction than Anju remembered. And as well, there were many close-up shots of Mr. Solanki pouring red wine into his glass, more than Anju remembered having occurred in so short a space of time. Gone was the discussion about Rohit's supposed gayness, and Mrs. Solanki correcting Mr. Solanki's grammatical usage of "gay." Instead, the scene clumsily jumped to Anju asking Rohit questions about his film, and Rohit answering that he didn't know what exactly the film would be about, a much more reticent answer than the one Anju recalled. Cut to: Mr. Solanki refreshing his glass yet again, before adding, "Why don't you finish a film? Now that would be a revolution."

This Mr. Solanki was not Mr. Solanki. This Solanki was mean and abrupt and alcoholic, shooting stiff looks at a soft-spoken wife who, likewise, was wholly unlike the version Anju knew. They had been edited into neater, simpler paper-doll versions of parents, dressed in outfits of frustration by the son who wielded the narrative scissors. And the problem lay in this—that time, once pruned and reordered, could tell a different story entirely than the one that Anju remembered. Was the scene Anju remembered even the one that had occurred? Did it matter? The only story that mattered was the one told by the very person who was doing the pruning and shuffling, and for the first time, Anju began to wonder what outfit he was designing for her.

WHEN ROHIT ARRIVES the next day, the salon is waiting for him. Mismatched bouquets of long-stemmed carnations and peacock feathers sit in vases at every stylist's station, and the movie star posters that used to panel the walls have been replaced by Rajasthani tapestries of garba raas dancers and one long panorama of a Mughal emperor on a royal hunt, loaned by the trinket store down the street. For the first and only time, Ghafoor demands that everyone leave their shoes at the door, not for the preservation of the motherland's customs, but for the preservation of the Oriental rugs that overlap all the way to the back of the salon, and are also on loan. If an employee should spill on the rug, Ghafoor calmly threatens to extract a sum from her paycheck. He has also directed everyone to wear salwars of "the red and marigold color palette," and Anju, having none, borrows one from Lipi. "Spill on this," Lipi says, "and I extract it from your paycheck." Anju cannot tell if Lipi is joking or serious, so limited is her palette of facial expression.

When Rohit begins to shoot, it seems fairly obvious that the film is not, as Anju claimed, about beauty salons. Rohit follows Anju up and down the floor, even when she is doing nothing more than taking a box of Kleenex from one end of the store to the other. He lurks behind a vase of flowers and feathers to film her while she answers the phone. He zooms in on the notebook where she writes "CANCEL" next to her two p.m. appointment. This was her only appointment for the day, so she spends the rest of it thumbing through the notebook, trying to look diligent, which is even more difficult than actually being diligent.

Meanwhile, Ghafoor is roaming from station to station in a khadi kurta pyjama as opposed to his usual brown slacks, arms crossed, feigning expertise. He looks in on Nandi's work, nods approvingly. He meanders over to Powder's station, where she is blow-drying straight a client's unwieldy shrub of curls, and points at the curly half of the client's head. "You missed this section," he murmurs and walks on, oblivious as Powder cuts her eyes at him. Sensing drama, Rohit goes over to film Ghafoor and the others.

Anju watches Rohit sidling about, zooming in on a face, drawing back to include Ghafoor's directions. Today, she feels a kind of camaraderie with the camera and almost takes pleasure in the importance that it gives her. She wishes she could rise to the occasion by doing something of use, weaving brows like Nandi, the thread between her teeth. Already Rohit has documented her descent from student to illegal, but now she wants as much attention given to her ascent, from hard worker to citizen.

In the early afternoon, Anju receives a walk-in client, a white girl with long orange hair. White girls are rare but not foreign to the salon. This girl seems to thrive on her rarity, wearing a belted shirt that stops a few inches below her rear, tall burgundy boots, and nothing resembling pants.

"I'd like a bikini wax," she says to Anju.

Rohit moves close to them, but the pantless girl does not turn her head. Anju writes down her name—Jaclyn—and says, "Come with me."

Still filming, Rohit steps aside, then follows Anju and Jaclyn to the back room. Anju stops short of the door. "What you think you are doing?" she asks Rohit.

"I'm filming you work," Rohit says. "Otherwise it'll just look like you sit around all day."

Though this is exactly what Anju does, she prefers not to emphasize that fact. "This you cannot film."

"Oh no, it's cool by me," Jaclyn says. "Ro and I go way back."

"You know each other?" Anju asks while Rohit brings the camera down and nods impatiently. She glances at the burgundy boots. "You are his Ex?" she asks Jaclyn.

"Um," Jaclyn says, as if trying to decide from a menu. "Yes and no."

"I asked her to come," Rohit says. "As a favor."

"And I'm about due for a wax anyway." Jaclyn punches him in the shoulder. "He's paying for it, though."

Anju looks from the camera to Jaclyn to Ro.

"I know what you're thinking," Rohit says. "But all documentary is a form of manipulated reality. As long as you conform as much as possible to some skeleton of the truth, it's fine."

Anju notes how Rohit expands his vocabulary whenever he is trying to convince her of something. The only argument she can depend on is this: "I don't like some man in the room when I am trying to wax."

"Look, I'll keep my distance. I'll even lock it down on the tripod, no handheld. It'll be totally tasteful and artistic, not like a porno at all."

The sudden presence of the word "porno" in the conversation makes Anju ill at ease.

Jaclyn steps in with a carefree laugh. "Oh, if you're worried about me, I honestly don't care. I mean, Ro has seen, like, all of my student films. If that's not naked, I don't know what is."

AT THE END OF THE DAY, after Rohit, the stylists, and a freshly waxed Jaclyn have left, Anju helps Ghafoor put the place back in order. She refills the water in the vases, though the carnations have already begun to sulk. She unpins the tapestries while Ghafoor rolls up the rugs and slumps them against one another in the corner. He whistles an off-key rendition of "How Do You Solve a Problem Like Maria?" from *The Sound of Music*, happy with his performance earlier in the day. "Do you think he liked us?" Ghafoor asks.

"I think so," she says.

"We looked professional, isn't it?"

Tired of these questions, Anju points at a framed poster on the wall. "Where do you want me to put this?"

"I think it was professional to have everyone's salwars matching-matching. Like the Air India flight attendants." Ghafoor sprays Windex onto a paper towel, which he squeaks up and down the glass of the frame in question, the *Doll's House* show card Birdie had forbidden long ago. When finished, he stares absently at the words: *Apsara Arts Club presents . . . Kalli Pavayuda Veede.* He taps the first and largest in the receding list of cast members, *Birdie Kamalabhai.* "Good thing this woman didn't come. If she saw this show card, she would take it down herself."

"I never saw it before."

"That is because of your auntie. She makes me keep it in storage." He polishes the plastic frame. "Does she ever speak of those days?"

"Not really."

Ghafoor looks offended. "Did she tell you that I was a director?"

When Anju says no, Ghafoor grows indignant, gesturing heatedly with his Windex bottle. "Well, maybe she thinks she fell from the pedestal, but I am proud I was ever up there."

Still irritated, Ghafoor shifts over to wipe the next frame while Anju gazes at the *Doll's House* show card. He remembers the first time he hung it on the wall, which led to Bird's cheeks turning a rare shade of pink. She would allow any wall hanging but that one, for reasons she would not explain but that he attributed to the nonsensical dramas of the female species. "But it is the nicest decoration I have," Ghafoor argued. And more than that, these show cards represent the best and purest part of himself, the version of himself that he always aspired to be and now can only look back upon with melancholy fondness, though the world around him has changed absolutely and no one remembers the man he was. If there were some subtler way of reminding the world, he would. Often he wonders: How many like him are out there, behind cash registers and brooms, with the best part of their lives behind them? How do they bear the weight?

He is mummifying the Mughal portrait in bubble wrap when he realizes that Anju has been asking him a question in the smallest voice he has ever heard from her.

"Who is this?" she asks again, her finger on the glass of the show card.

He goes over to her and squints at the smallest name on the cast list, next to Anju's fingertip.

"Gracie Kuruvilla," he reads, the name meaning nothing to him.

"Do you know her?"

Ghafoor wipes her fingerprint from the glass. This girl has no idea how many actors came in and out of the troupe, not to mention lighting technicians, sound technicians, music technicians, and God knows who else. He was the *director,* he is about to remind her, sometimes hated but always needed as is the way with people in power, when, with a start, he remembers. "Ah, Gracie Kuruvilla! Of course I remember. Tragic girl. Her part was very small, but her parents were important people—"

"Where was she from? Gracie, I mean." It seems to take some effort for Anju to say the name.

"From some small place in Kerala. Near Kumarakom or . . ."

"Chengalam?"

"Ah yes, she was from Chengalam. Did you know her?"

"What else?" Anju insists. "What else about her?"

"Oh, I hardly know. Her parents pulled her out of the troupe all of a sudden, never even made a donation. You should ask Bird; she and Bird were great friends back then."

"Bird? My Bird?"

"Yes, but people grow out of these old attachments. Gracie married some local boy. Bird came here."

Anju neither moves nor nods but seems to anticipate every word with unblinking eyes. Her gaze slowly returns to the show card. For years, Ghafoor considered himself an expert in direction, yielding subtleties of emotion from even the dullest actors, but he has never learned how to coach people through the narrows and depths of their actual problems, their true vulnerabilities. There, he does not pry; one's own troubles are enough.

"Come, come." Ghafoor plucks the *Doll's House* frame from the wall. "At this speed, we will get home by midnight."

AT HOME, Bird emerges from the bathroom, her hair wrapped in a terry-cloth beehive. She is rubbing lotion between her fingers, from one of Gwen's bottles; the fragrance seems to be blossoming all over the apartment from this single, surreptitious usage. Hearing noises in the kitchen and assuming that these belong to Gwen, Bird almost heads straight into her bedroom before she notices Anju easing into a chair at the table.

"It's late," Bird says. "Where were you?"

"Helping Ghafoor clean," Anju murmurs. Her eyes are fixed to the saltshaker in the center of the table. "We were talking."

Bird gives a short, false laugh. "And what did Ghafoor say that was so interesting?"

"We talked about my mother. You and my mother."

Bird nods automatically, her mouth going dry. She walks to the sink for a glass of water but absently opens the silverware drawer instead.

"He hung up the posters from your plays," Anju says. "There was one with my mother in it."

A glass, a glass for water.

"He said you were close."

Bird turns the faucet on and watches water rising in a mug that was here when she moved in, same as the rose-rimmed dishes and the plastic tablecloth and the perpetually empty chairs. She tries to collect Anju's words, to make sense of what has transpired. Ghafoor's show card, his stupid pride and joy. The one time she was not there.

"Did you know my mother?" Anju asks. "Gracie Vallara? Or I suppose she was Gracie Kuruvilla at that time."

Mug in hand, Bird takes a seat across from Anju. So this is the moment that Bird has been waiting for, the pivotal point at which she can lay her secrets open and close the gap between herself and Anju, between herself and Gracie, between this world and the one before. In a single evening, she can tell her version of the story, open the grand velvet curtain on the truth according to Bird.

But Bird looks at the girl across from her whose face is clouded with suspicion and confusion, and suddenly all words are lost to her. They fly from her like wintering crows, and in their wake, the old questions return: What can she possibly say to honor the past? What words can do justice to the truth without chasing Anju away? Gracie chose her life long ago, and here, across from Bird, is the fruit of that choice. Here is a girl with her mother's calves and puttering snore, who inexplicably dislikes Pop-Tarts, who lunges after what she wants even when wounded. What would Gracie have wanted her to know?

As Bird forms her next words, she feels a crumbling within her, the tiny, extinguished death of a dream. It requires all her strength to conceal the loss, to say calmly:

"Sort of. The name is familiar."

"Only sort of?"

Bird scratches her throat, then sits up suddenly. "Oh! Did she have thick eyebrows? Shaped like"—she draws an eyebrow in the air—"commas almost? And she was very thin?"

"Yes. In her pictures, she looked thin."

"Hah!" Bird claps her hands. "Of course I remember! You are her daughter?"

"You did know her, then?"

"Yes, yes, I knew her, I knew everyone in the troupe. That's how it is when you travel in such a way, eating meals together, brushing teeth together. She seemed like a very sweet young woman, and smart." Bird nods with wonder. "My, my. Her daughter. Sitting here. How small is this world!"

"Oh. Ghafoor was wrong, then. He thought you knew her well."

They fall silent. With her hands in her lap, Anju looks despondent, and Bird, for her part, wishes they shared a kind of mother-daughter language, of nourishing hugs and held hands. For such a small world, the space from person to person can span a whole sea.

"It is strange, isn't it? That you met her . . . and then you met me . . ." Anju's voice trails off. "My father never told me she acted in plays. But my father never told me many things."

"I knew her before she married your father."

Anju nods. "Ghafoor said she had only a small part."

"Sometimes small parts are the ones to remember."

EVERY TIME Anju picks up any phone, she speaks for as brief a period as possible, imagining that a network of operators can track her location and send it to the INS. She prefers pay phones to Bird's landline, though most pay phones have been uprooted in favor of cell phones. In Kerala, too, she has seen cell phones in the hands of men and women, bleating strange tunes from their pockets and purses. Even serious-looking businessmen seem to take pleasure in selecting their tune; once, on a bus, she heard a cell phone chuckle maniacally before its owner, a middle-aged man, picked it up without shame. But what pleasure it must be to take someone's voice with you, what weight it must lift from the word "good-bye."

Rohit's phone is a miniature computer, able to accomplish the tasks of a whole entertainment center—surf the Internet, check the weather, watch clips from the *Godfather* trilogy (which he does often). She would not be surprised if he told her that his pocket-machine could compose music as well. And yet for all its tiny functions, the phone often fails in its primary task: to connect Anju to Rohit himself. He could be avoiding her calls, as she has become rather obsessive about the immigration lawyer. But it is April now, and how could there be no progress?

"I'm telling you," Rohit sighs over the phone, "there is progress."

"Please explain the progress." Anju grips the cordless phone and turns away from the salon window, ready for a verbal tussle if this is what is needed. It is 6:45 a.m., well before anyone else will arrive.

"Anju, it's, like, *dawn* over here. I know you're in Queens, but aren't we in the same time zone?"

She shushes him, wary of the operators knowing her coordinates. "No, not the same. Difference is that your life is very comfy and nice, and my life is going no place."

Immediately Rohit goes into deferential mode, a mechanical response she knows well. "I understand, you're right. No, you're absolutely right. It's just, it's early, I've got a hangover . . ."

"You said you would meet a lawyer last week, but did you?"

"Actually I did. A few days ago. His name is Charles Brown, and he's with one of the top firms in Manhattan dealing with immigration law."

Anju's free hand grips the curly cord of the phone. "Already you met?"

"And we're having a follow-up call today."

"Why you did not invite me to this meeting?"

"I didn't want to get your hopes up because I'm not sure about him yet. I'll know by today. But in the meantime, maybe the guy has a website. Why don't you look him up?"

Anju fumbles for paper and pen. "What is the web address?"

"I don't know. Just type his name into a search engine." He describes the steps, where she should go and how. "It's like, if you type in 'Rohit Solanki,' my entry at the Rolling Oak Film Festival comes up. And also the Louisville Watertower Film Festival, I think . . ."

"So I type in what?"

"Rohit Solanki. Oh sorry, I mean Charles Brown. *C-H-A-R-L-E-S*—"

"Brown, yes. Okay, thank you, call you later." Anju hurriedly hangs up, both due to her operator surveillance theory and so she can fiddle on Ghafoor's computer before the others arrive. Fumbling with several of Bird's keys, she finally unlocks the office door. She reminds herself to return the mouse to its position in the lower left corner of the mousepad.

Following Rohit's directions, she types the names into a blank strip of space: *Charles Brown*. The Internet lags. She jostles the mouse, trying to shake the sand in the hourglass icon.

A sentence appears on the computer screen: *Did you mean <u>Charlie Brown</u>?*

Below this, a carpet of text unscrolls from top to bottom, most entries referring to a bald cartoon boy. A "Charles Brown" appears beneath these entries, a musician whose albums include "Snuff Dippin' Mama," "The Best of Charles Brown," and "Charles Brown Sings Christmas Songs." Clicking on each page, Anju finds that the grand, godly sprawl of Charlie Brown has mostly trampled the existence of all smaller Browns. She gives up.

But the lack of a website has not altered her mood. At long last— a lawyer, one with strategies and plans! Perhaps attached to a firm triad of names! Anju imagines a silvery-templed type with a noble jaw and pictures of grandchildren on his desk, which he will reach across to shake her hand.

The cursor blinks in the search engine space, after the *n* in "Brown." Such a luxury it is to be able to paddle carefreely along the Internet. She begins to type her name. *A-N-J* . . . but then stops upon imagining what might surface. Perhaps that *Malayala Manorama* article about her scholarship. She prefers not to know what else, if anything.

Who can she search for? The first name that comes to mind, always and now, is Linno. Knowing that she will find nothing, Anju types Linno's name in the search engine anyway. Linno is an uncommon name. Anju expects the search engine to politely ask her: *Did you mean Linda?*

When she presses ENTER, several entries appear. The first three belong to a site called East West Invites. Anju presumes this must be a mistake, after reading the snippet of information below the first entry: ". . . with the spectacular creations of head designer Linno Vallara whose invitations were featured in *Me & You* magazine . . ."

An alternate Linno Vallara. Probably born here, an NRI, a non-resident Indian, or, as Powder likes to say, a "Not Really Indian." Or perhaps a Bombay socialite like the Solankis, one with connections and wealth to hoist her to these entrepreneurial heights. But something about the phrase "beautiful creations" makes Anju linger over this entry. And as if this Linno can tell her something about her Linno, Anju clicks the mouse.

The computer brings her to a picture of a woman who, as Anju suspected, is not Linno at all. She is older, with a bun and a stiff schoolmarm smile. Above her are the words "Meet Us." Next to her is a small block of print that begins, "Alice Varghese, president of East West Invites, is a leading visionary in the invitation industry . . ."

Anju scrolls down to the picture below that of Alice Varghese. Unlike the latter photo, this photo was taken by a window, by someone who understands the subtle pleasures of natural light. The colors are rich, the phosphorescent sunlight sifting through the window, illuminating the side of the woman's face. The woman is surrounded by a flock of open, intricate invitations, as if she herself is a goddess sprung from the heart of a small shrine.

By some strange, mental mitosis, Anju feels herself dividing into the part of her that is looking and the part of her that is falling, a vertiginous sensation that increases the longer she looks at this Linno, who, unlike every other Linno Anju thought she saw in the streets, is the only one that does not look away. Here are her shoulders that used to hunch over a sketch, now held back with a degree of modesty. Here are her moon-pale fingernails; here is her knotted sleeve laid plainly on her lap.

Anju forces herself to stop looking at the picture so that she can read further. Slowly, she gleans that Linno has become the head designer for an invitation company called East West Invites. That she has been featured in major magazines. That people come to her, specially, for invitations like the ones featured in these other photographs, a resplendent bouquet, a blossoming peacock, whole cities built of folds and holes, and many more such miracles made by her hand.

Again, there comes that flying, falling feeling. Disbelief replaced by a restless churning in her stomach. The questions pelt her from every direction, ones with answers that she cannot even begin to guess, so spellbound by this photo of her sister who is not frozen in time, as Anju assumed she would be. If home belongs to those who are there to watch it change, then what of sisters who change even faster? All Anju can do is put her elbows on the desk and her head between her hands, staring until Linno's face begins to shift and blur. Anju wipes her eyes. She has never wanted for something or someone so despairingly. These are the feelings she has kept so long at bay, but the tide of them now pulls her under, gutting her of every tear she has not yet wept.

BIRD IS THE FIRST TO ARRIVE, just as Anju is buttoning up her coat. "I brought you a pastry," Bird says to Anju's back. The pastry looks like a limp mattress laid on a napkin along with a tiny plastic pillow of icing. "I didn't squeeze the icing yet."

Anju turns around, her coat buttoned up, aware that her skin is sallow, her eyes swollen and red. No matter how many times she rinsed herself at the bathroom sink, the face that stared back in the mirror was tear-streaked and impossibly tired. "I feel sick. I think I'll go home."

"Do you have a temperature?" Bird puts her hand to Anju's forehead but Anju moves away. "Why don't I come with you?"

"No. I just need sleep."

"But should I walk you home at least?"

She must summon up some effort to say it, but Anju has no reserves of courtesy left. "I would like to be alone."

Bird pauses, slightly wounded, then folds the pastry into the napkin. "Okay. If you like."

Anju moves past her into the pure blue day, the kind that arrives like a reward after last night's rains. She pulls her coat closed and continues down the sidewalk.

AT BIRD'S APARTMENT, Anju sits in front of the television watching a Kairali news report on the Indian Parliamentary elections. She pictures Ammachi nodding along to the current talking head, a political expert who pounds a fist into his open palm, revving his rhetorical engines. ". . . and this social unrest we *cannot* ignore. *Unemployment* among the poor. *Malls* built on top of slums. The current BJP government cannot respond to the seven hundred million poor who have been *abandoned* by the high-tech boom." The next clip shows a BJP rally crowding the street in front of a Tamil temple selling incense sticks that bear the BJP slogan, *India Shining!* Another clip shows a clay-tinted elephant on its elbows and knees, a voting machine awkwardly mounted on its back.

Anju was hoping to watch some sort of home or human makeover show, something dull enough to prevent her from thinking and lying in bed, curled as she was for an hour, unable to sleep. She could hardly focus on the television. Her mind was shrouded by a thick fog, so that all she heard and felt was the sad, plodding thump of her heart. At some point, her heartbeat stopped. And then she realized that the sound came from the padded footsteps of the person upstairs.

She turns off the television when the phone rings, presuming the call to come from Bird, but it is Rohit, fresh from his meeting with Mr. Brown.

"Now look who's avoiding who," he says playfully. "They said you took a sick day? Good for you."

"What did the lawyer say?"

"A lot of things. Are you sitting down? I have something to tell you. Something that really came as a surprise to me, so I hope you don't think I misled you. I mean, this is the first time I'm learning this too, but just remember, it's all good news. . . ."

AT THEIR FIRST MEETING, Rohit was discouraged to find that Mr. Brown was a rather unintimidating presence, shrunken within his oversized tweed suit, afflicted by a lisp not unlike the whistle of a kettle. While Rohit poured out Anju's history, Mr. Brown did not interrupt but simply removed his glasses and wiped the lenses with a pocket handkerchief. After putting the glasses back on his nose, he asked: "But how do you know she's illegal?"

"It said so on a website," Rohit said. Mr. Brown raised his eyebrows. "An official website. The Department of Homeland Security website. It was in the rules. It said that if you default on your school attendance then you're immediately illegal."

"I see," Mr. Brown said, in a tone that meant Rohit had not seen enough.

Mr. Brown went on to describe the American immigration system as "a broken-legged beast." Outdated, unwieldy, unable to enforce its own rules. "It could be that this girl's school reported her to the police, but they never reported her to the INS. Schools fail to do that sometimes. In which case, she'd be legal until the departure date on her Arrival/Departure form."

"What would happen then?"

"Well, if she wants to continue her education, she could enroll at a college of some sort. I had one client who enrolled at the York School of Medical and Dental Assistants. She extended her visa for two years. When she finished, she got a job offer, which got the ball rolling on her permanent residency application. It all comes down to time, luck, and money."

The meeting ended with Mr. Brown offering to look up Anju's status himself as he rarely, but discreetly, did for other clients. Several days later, Mr. Brown called Rohit with the same information that Rohit is passing to Anju now:

"So as it turns out, the school never reported you. You're not illegal."

It takes her a moment to decipher the content of his words.

"Anju? You there? You're *legal* is what I'm saying."

ROHIT HAS BEEN TALKING for so long that Anju's ear has grown hot from the receiver; still she does not move. "Illegal," "legal" . . . the two words float around her head while Rohit continues his stream of giddy talk. She waits for some kind of thrill or relief to surge through her body.

"Now what?" she manages to ask.

"Now we find a college, some kind of two-year program. Maybe that medical-dental school? We'll have to do some research about financial packages and stuff. I mean overall, it's probably like a seven-year process. These days it could take up to nine. But Mr. Brown is optimistic—"

"Nine years?" Anju unfolds her legs and sits up. "It will take nine years?"

"Well, I don't know. It might. I mean, that's probably more like an upper limit, so it could take a lot less."

"How much less?"

Sensing the stiffness in her voice, Rohit hesitates. "It's hard to say. But Mr. Brown said . . . I mean it would definitely take, like, seven to nine years for everything to fall into place."

Today, it seems, Anju will never stop falling. The ground will never rise to meet her feet. "I thought you said . . ." Her voice loses strength. Rohit has always been contagiously optimistic, but he never once explained a time line. "I thought, because my visa took only short time—"

"We're talking green card here, Anju. *Citizenship.* I know seven to nine sounds like a long time . . ."

Seven to nine sounds like a jail sentence.

". . . but think how gratified you'll be when you bring your family to the States to become naturalized citizens. This is the immigrant story, you know? I mean, my parents were the same way. They got here with just two suitcases to their name, but they worked their asses off, and now they're living the American dream—"

"Your father has a villa and a street both wearing his name."

Rohit pauses. "Who told you that?"

"He did."

"Okay. True. But my point is that this is what people do to get what they want. Trust me, these years are just going to fly by. You'll make the money you need to make, and Mr. Brown will get you the green card, and I'll be here to film it all along the way. When I'm not back at Princeton anyway."

"You are going back to college?"

"Yeah, my mom won't let me defer forever. But this film is my main thing. Maybe even my thesis. I'll just go back and forth on the weekends or whatever, for however long it'll take. And who knows what'll happen in that time? Maybe I can even go to India and interview your family. How wild would that be? This story is so rich, and it'll only get richer with time. All the best docs take, like, *years* to make, and I'm willing to put in the effort—"

"I want to go home."

And though Anju is sure he has heard her clearly, Rohit asks: "What's that?"

"I want to go home. To Kumarakom. To my family."

She listens to the rigid silence on his end.

"Go home?" For the first time, Anju hears a thin, hairline fracture in the usual cool of his voice. "Right now? What kind of ending is that?"

"I don't want this film anymore."

Shock renders Rohit speechless, but only briefly. "You don't care about all the time that you and I have already put into this thing? This is my life, Anju. This is the first time that something I've worked on has had any significance for me."

"And what if nothing works out?"

"Well then, we'll film that too. I—" He expels a slow, deathbed sigh. "Why don't you meet Mr. Brown with me? We'll hash things out, we'll even film it. Hey, we can make your indecision part of the film itself, you know, to show how complicated these decisions really are—"

"The decision is not complicated. I want to buy a ticket home."

"Well, then buy it yourself."

He utters this sentence so coldly and quickly that she almost skims over its meaning. "You will not help me?" she asks.

"I am trying to help you, Anju, but I'm also trying to make a good film. Like I said, I think that both these things—the film's best interest and your best interest—converge really nicely for everybody. Right? Listen." He switches to his Real Rohit voice with all the ease of Superman sliding on his Clark Kent spectacles; the change is just as unconvincing. "I know it's scary out there. I shouldn't get upset with you. Let's just take a day off from each other before we say things we don't mean, and I'll call you in the morning. Okay?"

She grips a handful of her own hair, tightly, but makes a calm, affirmative noise through sealed lips.

"I'm on your side, Anju. You know that, right?"

"Thank you. Yes. I know."

ANJU HAS $875 in her Folgers canister. The bills, uncurled and classified by their meager denominations, surround her in a semicircle, a configuration that seems appropriate for a sum that amounts to only half of what she needs. A flight to Delhi would cost about $1,000, but the flight to Kochi and the bus to Kottayam would cost $400 more.

Around noon, Bird calls to check in. "You are sure you don't want me at home?"

"Home." The word itself has crawled under Anju's skin, so that she cannot hear it without wincing inside, like hearing a wrong note in a familiar tune.

"No," Anju says. "I am fine. I think I might go for a walk. To see a friend."

"You mean that boy with the camera?"

Anju hesitates. "I will not be home till later."

"Fine. If you have to."

Anju hangs up and reviews her options, which takes almost no time, as she seems rather optionless at the moment. She does know that the answer lies no more with Bird than it lies with Rohit. She will not leave this country with debts. Slipping the bills into an envelope, she zips her savings into her coat.

She hopes that the Solankis are not out of town.

IT IS EIGHT P.M. when Anju boards the number 7 train, the vein that takes her to the coiled heart of Manhattan. There, she switches to a downtown train that rushes her to Chelsea. A group of boys in wind-breakers and popped collars board the train along with her, passing a plastic bottle of clear liquid between them. As their night begins, another day ends for the puffy-ankled woman sitting in the corner, clutching her purse and dozing along the many stops until her destination.

Anju exits the train but takes a seat on the subway bench, where each sitter is allowed only the cubby of space between two slabs of wood. A homeless man lies slumped over two seats, defiantly malodorous. Unable to think properly in his company, Anju wanders to the tracks.

I have failed. It is necessary for her to repeat the sentiment several times, as many times as is required for her body to unflinchingly bear the sting. From the moment she returns to the Solankis' home, her failure will be present in every disapproving pair of eyes, and she should not shy away from it. She should accept it, like the blow of a severed branch, like another mouthful of Bird's Cream of Wheat.

On the tracks, a charcoal rat rustles with enthusiasm in a fallen pretzel bag. Anju once saw a Malayalam movie wherein the heroine, a young girl caught up in a forbidden love affair, flung herself before the bright eye of a roaring train. The suicide, the screaming, the plaintive violins, all this equaled a box office success. She imagines doing the same, hurling herself into the path of the number 1 train, which would give Rohit a spectacular ending, not a dry eye in the audience. Her last words over the phone, his attempt to save her, and then cut to: her body in an open coffin. Rohit interviewing Bird. Bird interviewing Rohit. Some closing thoughts, some tears, maybe some text about the high suicide rate in Kerala, and fade to black.

She realizes that her hands are in fists. This is all a kind of thievery, the business of steering someone's life. Happy or sad or unforeseen, her ending is hers.

ANJU EMERGES FROM the wrong subway stop but decides to walk the rest of the way. She used to like the dark glitter of the neighborhood at night, the clatter of important heels on cement, the slick black windows of bars manned by dour bouncers, watching taxis prowl past. While climbing into a cab, a girl has her finger in one ear and her cell phone against the other, yelling: "We're going to Orchard and Stanton! . . . ORCHARD AND STANTON!"

Anju walks in a direction that someone told her was west, and someone else, with equal conviction, called east. She continues. Forward, not back, every block same as the last until finally she reaches the Monarch, a pale and spired Goliath among the surrounding brick and stone. She stares up at the spires with a clarity of mission that will send her, slingshot, over her doubts. But even biblical heroes must have suffered their butterflies.

IT IS HALF PAST NINE when Anju strides through the glass doors of the Monarch as if she never left. All is the same, as enchanting as it always was—the cloudy marble, the fountains, the red carpet so soft it seems to melt underfoot. She hardly remembers the version of herself that passed beneath the expansive brass arms of the chandelier on that dizzying day in December.

The doorman must be new, a young man who seems apologetic for mistakes he has yet to make. She gives him her name, hoping that the Solankis are there when he dials them.

"Anju Melvin," he says into the phone. He looks up at her, his eyebrows raised, and mouths, *Right?* She nods. "Anju Melvin. Yes, yes I'm sure . . . Mhm . . . Yes."

THE ELEVATOR RISES. In the corner is the tiny television screen tuned to the news. A weatherman warns of an approaching cold front from the east: "Bundle up out there, if you're not already!" The ground presses into the soles of her feet.

As the doors slide open, Anju sees Mrs. Solanki waiting in the door frame, her arms hanging by her sides. She is wearing her pale pink pajamas.

"Hello," Anju says.

"You're here."

Mrs. Solanki wears a strange expression, hovering somewhere between bewilderment and anger. Only now does Anju fully understand what she has done to this woman, and more of these realizations are yet to come. But before Anju can apologize, Mrs. Solanki catches her in a hug. Not the flimsy embrace of acquaintances, but simple and strong and fortifying.

3.

*I*T IS MAY OF A YEAR that still feels new to Melvin. The sky shares his sense of promise in its cloudless blue, the same shade as the oceans in an atlas. Today is Sunday, and tomorrow Melvin will accompany Linno by train to the Chennai consulate. The consulate people have had a month to review her B-1 visa application, and now, after a personal interview, they will decide if she should be crowned with a visa. Melvin made this trip before, with Anju, and has decided to wear his second-best shirt, as he did the previous time, for luck.

When they first received notice of the interview, Melvin phoned Abraham to take four days off from work. He felt anxious calling, then irritated that calling a man two years his junior would make him feel anxious.

"You'll be gone all week?" Abraham asked.

"Yes, I'm going to Chennai." Abraham waited for Melvin to continue. "The Consulate Building. I have business there."

"Is everything all right? I only ask because this is short notice. We have a wedding in Ernakulam that week. . . ."

"Linno has a visa interview." There was a certain pleasure to be had in hearing himself say these words.

"Linno?" Abraham asked. "Your Linno?"

"My Linno."

"That's wonderful news!" Melvin was taken aback by the earnest excitement of this response. "So she is going to America too?"

"I hope so," Melvin said. "It's not for certain."

"What a blessing, your daughters." Abraham grew serious. "And what of the younger one? Have you heard from her?"

"No, but I think we will. Very soon."

"Of course. She's probably getting her green card as we speak. Ambitious, your children. Wish they could talk some sense into mine."

Melvin gave a tense laugh, but Abraham's tone seemed genuine. Here was a man who had every reason to dislike Melvin, who had saved Melvin from a long drought of unemployment. It was a strange thing now, to feel pity for Abraham and impatience for his sons, who listened to their father no more than they listened to the old songs. Melvin wished that he could do something for Abraham, and though he was in no position to do so now, he allowed himself to imagine that maybe someday he would be.

THE MAYHEM OF the upcoming election—rallies, speeches, slogans, signs—has barely slowed Linno's pace. Days and nights she and Alice have worked to put together the seminars for the Duniya Expo, designing new invitations and business cards, making phone calls, and exchanging emails with potential partners who can hawk their wares in Chicago, Philadelphia, Miami, and other hotbeds of the South Asian populace. For Linno, most of these activities are for the benefit of the Chennai consulate, to prove her business credibility.

Where Anju is concerned, Linno will answer only what is asked, but nothing more. With Georgie's help, she has researched dozens of immigration websites that make the process sound swift enough that she may escape specific scrutiny. Usually, the questions concern business alone without delving into personal matters. She has also been researching several tourist books on New York, preparing a method to comb the city, block by block, in order to find Anju. Her brain is a map of boroughs, with multicolor rivers of subways. She will visit police stations and post signs for Anju's whereabouts. She will speak to every person with whom Anju shared a single conversation, a list that includes Anju's host family, her teachers, Shell Dun Fisher, and with all the meticulous logic of a detective, Linno will bring Anju back.

Linno will not disclose to the Chennai consulate that for the past three days, she has fallen asleep at the kitchen table with her head in her arms, thus accounting for the shadows that rim her eyes. What keeps her awake is not her work but that inevitable moment of paralysis when she will step off the plane and all the maps and routes will flee her mind. The city that she thought she understood will rise before her, beclouding the tourist books that sought to reduce it to a digestible size. For the time being, a map allows her to pretend at some sort of control over a roiling city, allows her to forget, tentatively, this world of unknowns in which she is so very small, so powerless.

.   .   .

LINNO AND MELVIN take a two-hour train ride from Kottayam to Ernakulam, where they buy tickets for the express train that will take them to Chennai. The platform in Ernakulam smells of sweat and smoke; it is swarming with passengers and wiry coolies whose heads are turbanned in towels so as to balance luggage that surpasses them in weight.

As soon as Linno and Melvin join the currents of boarders, two coolies appear and offer to tote their bags onto the train, a job that requires only one coolie since Melvin can carry his own. One of the coolies hoists Linno's suitcase onto his head while the other hustles alongside his partner, against Melvin's wishes. "It's okay, it's okay," the noncarrying coolie says. "We're cousins."

Halfway down the platform, the coolie puts the suitcase down and extends a hand toward Melvin.

"Fifty rupees," he says.

"But you haven't even taken the bags on the train yet!" Melvin says.

"Fifty now," the coolie says, "and twenty-five more to finish the job. Plus what about my cousin here?" The cousin nods energetically, silent as a mime.

"Your cousin did nothing."

"Hah, he put the suitcase on my head!"

Not wanting to be late, Linno bargains them down to twenty rupees more. For all their negotiations, the coolies are deft and graceful as they veer around without bumping heads or stepping on feet. Linno and Melvin follow the coolie cousins into the train car, where they slide both suitcases onto the overhead rack and, grudgingly pocketing their payment, hurry off the train to aid other needy passengers.

Across from Linno and Melvin is a dignified old man with a tall umbrella over his knees, his wife next to him holding a plastic bottle of water. They are college teachers in Chennai, they say, and have just enjoyed a few days' vacation in their hometown of Ernakulam. "And you?" the man asks.

"We are going to the consulate for her visa interview," Melvin says.

"So young to have a visa!" the woman says. Linno smiles, now even more anxious at what might be another possible objection made by her interview officer. She is twenty-one years old, too young to be interested in anything less than moving permanently to the States. She fingers the knot of her sleeve and looks out the window.

Melvin listens to the teacher, who, as it turns out, is also the founder of what he calls a "public health organization." One beautiful summer's day, the teacher was walking to work when out of nowhere, like a revelation, excrement landed on his head. "*You*-man shit," he declared. For days, the teacher had walked this same route to work, beneath the bridge of a lofted railway, never knowing that he should be wary of such unannounced shrapnel. For the teacher, the experience was repulsive, yet formative. He started a website (www.railshit.com) and an online petition to pressure the railway industry into rethinking their in-car potty system, which turned out to be no more than a glorified hole in the floors of the cars. "The more I talked to people," the teacher explains, gesturing with the steel tip of his umbrella, "the more I realized that I am not the only victim. Do you know how much total waste falls from our trains every day?" The man snatches his wife's water bottle as a visual aid and gives it a shake. "Three hundred thousand liters of waste per day. *Per day!* How can India be shining if shit is raining from our sky?"

Melvin agrees to visit the website.

"I still don't like that website name," the teacher's wife says. She shoots her husband a look. "Maybe First World has better plumbing, but we don't need their dirty talk. It's not polite."

The husband raises an open palm in the way of a patient saint preaching to his flock. "Usually I am a courteous person. But the day I resort to pleasantries in this matter will be the day I wear someone's crap as a hat."

EVENTUALLY, thankfully, the teacher and his wife fall quiet. Linno thrills to the first lurch, the shudder of metal all around her until the world is streaming by in blues and browns and greens, flares of clouds cut by the flight of birds. Passing through a paddy field, Linno sees a flash of red and, squinting, makes out a lone red Communist flag stuck at the intersection of two berms. Farther down: a few women with backs bent at acute angles, their hands pulling through the wet harvest as their mothers and grandmothers have done for years.

Melvin and Linno decide to take turns sleeping so that one of them can watch the suitcases. He is the first to climb up onto the berth while she stares out the window beneath, thinking ahead to the next forty-eight hours, which may be among the slowest of her life. Rappai's mother warned her about the whimsy of the Chennai consulate, as told to her by a cousin who arrived for a scheduled interview, only to be turned away because the American ambassador was paying a visit that day. When the cousin requested to speak to a manager, the official raised a finger and, with ominous drama, said in English: "Give me any more trouble and you will never set a chappal in the U.S. of A."

NEVER HAS LINNO spent so much time in lines as she does at the Chennai consulate. At least in line, she has a vague sense of order. Her father, on the other hand, was left standing outside the gate, as only applicants were allowed to enter. And though she would have liked an ally, she has now grown familiar with the back of the person in front of her, who seems oblivious to her fixation on the nape of his neck. His hair ends in a neat, straight line above his collar, though a few strays compromise the integrity of his hairline. Sometimes he blots his neck with a handkerchief, despite the air-conditioning.

Thankfully, they are now inside the building, in the prescreening line. Outside, Linno and Melvin waited along with fifty or sixty others, some of whom seemed to have no appointment at all. A man was strolling up and down the line, muttering in Hindi, beyond the lazy ear of the security guard: "You'll never get an interview at this rate. My agency can book a slot within three days, no problem. You can even book several dates in case you get rejected today." He had a lumpen cauliflower of a nose and eyes that never lingered on one focus for long, always darting to the street. These features made him a dubious ally, but still he continued down the block, casually sowing pessimism. "Three thousand rupees for an appointment within two days. See me at the photocopy shop next door."

Most preferred the sweat that came from standing in the heat to the sweat that came from taking a risk. Sighing, wilting, they turned their faces forward. But there were those toward the end who looked at the consulate building, then at the cauliflower man, at the building, at the man. With a shrug, the second to last in line hurried down the street while everyone stared after him, unsure whether to feel envy or pity.

WHILE IN THE PRESCREENING LINE, Linno overhears the man in front of her telling his neighbor that this is his second time at the consulate. He works for Dell, Inc., in Hyderabad, and is applying for the H-1B visa to take him to the States as a skilled professional. Last time he failed, but this time he will succeed since he took the trouble of visiting the Visa God of Hyderabad.

According to the man, the Visa God was Lord Balaji, an incarnation of Lord Vishnu. Happiness, prosperity, and fertility were Lord Balaji's previous causes, which attracted only a few visitors a week to the Chilkur Balaji Temple. Several years ago, the temple priest decided that Lord Balaji deserved more attention, so the priest decided to broaden the god's interests by dubbing Him the Visa God.

In droves, they came. A hundred thousand worshippers per week. The religious and nonreligious. The young and the old. According to the priest's directions, they walked eleven laps around the temple, and when closing hour came, the worshippers jogged. In Hyderabad, in the midst of the newly sprouted offices of Dell and Microsoft and General Electric, even the deities had to keep pace with the local need.

"This irrational country," said the other man, shaking his head. "More fodder for foreign people to make fun."

The man shook his head and argued in a low, fervent voice. "No, we are not the irrational ones. This process is irrational. U.S. receives thousands of visa applications in a single hour. They give out visas like miracles. You may get it, I may not. With so many applicants, how can they use logic? There is no logic. Totally random. And where there is randomness, there is room for religion."

Unfortunately, it seems, the man will have to create even more room for Lord Balaji. He is dismissed from the prescreening line because his identification photos are not of an appropriate size. Linno feels a pang for the person whose movements she mimicked in the security line, where the guards patted them down and thumbed through their folders for electronic devices. The officer directs him to the nearby market where a new photo can be taken. When the man turns, Linno glimpses his face, sallow and sedate, like a zoo animal tired of shrieking against the bars of his cage.

BY THE TIME Linno reaches the personal interview line, it is three hours past her scheduled appointment. One after another, the hopefuls go to one window to give their fingerprints, then to another window to meet their decisions, good and bad. It seems that there are many rejections, which usually require more time as those applicants try to make sense of their fate. One of the more desperate rejects crouches so as to speak into the small microphone in front of the glass partition, rendering him a wretched hunchback. But everyone is courteous with the official administering the news so as not to upset him, low though he might be on the totem pole. Those who fail today will likely try again, and who can afford an enemy behind the glass?

Rumors have been traveling down the line, most of them worrisome. It is said that the interview officers obey their own individual strands of logic, some just, some cruel, some mathematical, like the one who accepts only every fifth applicant that stands before him. One of the officers is a China, and of course everyone knows what Chinas think of Indians. But maybe he is a Japan? A Japan would be better. Japans hate Chinas, don't they? So by extension, a Japan might like an Indian.

At last, for better or worse, Linno finds herself face-to-face with the China/Japan. "Hello," he says with an American accent.

"Good morning." It is long past morning, but she is reluctant to stray from her rehearsed greeting.

He is young, but to Linno's mind, all Asians look five years younger than they are. She once met a newlywed Chinese woman in the waiting room of a beauty salon, where her Malayali mother-in-law had brought her. Unabashed, the Chinese woman stuttered a few garbled sentences of Malayalam to Linno, which could have meant either *It is difficult for me* or *I want to sing.* To which the mother-in-law gave a silvery laugh of pride. As soon as the Chinese woman disappeared into the back, the smile on her mother-in-law's face fell away. To Linno, she said: "I sent my son to Hong Kong for studies. You see what he brought back? *Kando?*"

Linno hopes that her interviewer looks more favorably upon her than the mother-in-law upon her Chinese daughter. He takes her folder and thumbs through her papers. "Why do you want to go to the United States?" he asks.

She answers with automated ease. "I wish to represent my company, East West Invites, at a wedding convention sponsored by American company called Duniya, Incorporated. Duniya has history of bringing foreign businesspeople for their convention." As she continues to answer questions about her employment, all these words mean little more to her now than *I am sophisticated, I am worthy, I am sophisticated, I am worthy.* She attempts the posture of a politician's wife, shoulders held back, dignified yet modest. She recalls one of the suggestions on an immigration website that Prince found for her: "Dress up nicely and keep smiling! Give a good impression of the Indian people!"

"How long have you been working for this company?" he asks.

"Six months."

"That's not very long. What if you find a better job in the United States?"

"I will be staying here itself. I am head designer of East West Invites."

Across the counter, she passes a letter of financial support from Alice and a letter from Duniya, Inc. Along with these, two salary slips and a bank statement recently inflated by a loan from Jilu Auntie. The interviewer breezes through the papers and turns to his computer. He types for a moment, then stares at the screen, his chin in his hand.

"Do you have any family in the States?" he asks finally.

Her throat tightens. "Yes."

"Who?"

"My younger sister, Anju. She is there on student visa."

He is nodding slowly, still looking at the screen. She feels a small hatred for the computer and its potential to tattle on her circumstances. What does it know? Is the screen telling him all the things that she has not?

Taking a breath and maintaining her smile, she plunges into her closing argument. "As you can see from the evidence, I show a desire to abandon U.S. I have strong family ties, work responsibility, and permanent residence in my home country . . ." Her voice fades as she tries to remember what comes next, but the interviewer steps in.

"I'm sorry, but we cannot make a decision at this time. This application is pending investigation."

His decree is as a pin to a balloon. She stares at him for a moment before realizing that her smile is no longer necessary.

"You'll have to keep checking in for the status of your application," the officer continues. He is apologetic, to a degree.

"What they are investigating?" she asks.

He shakes his head. "I can't really say."

His face is an impenetrable mask reserved for the hundreds of Indians that press their questions against the glass each day, searching for any place to hang a hope on that mercilessly smooth pane.

Does he know about Anju? Does he think Linno will not abandon the States? She wants to shout, bang against the glass. Except for her, no one wants to abandon the States! Look at the man in the next booth, dancing his way out of the room with "yes" all over his face. Look at the couple clutching their file folders, both retired, both miraculously walking out of here with a ten-year visitor visa so as to end their days in their son's

Florida condo. Who among them does not want to nest in the U.S.? What game is this of smoke and mirrors? She is the only one with an exit strategy in mind, the only one who does not want to stay.

Her eyes go to the clock behind him, and it seems, for a moment, that she can hear every tick of the second hand. "If they reject me, how long until I can again apply?"

"As soon as you want." The official peers around her to see how many others are in the waiting room. "But you'll have to make another appointment."

4.

CONSOLATION DOES NOT COME EASILY to Melvin. He never knew how to touch his wife on those days when he came home from work to find her biting her fingernails or lost in her tea. When she fell into such moods, he employed an isolationist strategy of keeping to his own quarters, which was difficult in a two-room flat peopled by three females of varying sizes and tempers. He sensed that he was to blame. Wasn't he always? Even when her complaint was lodged against a neighbor (someone stealing her underskirt from the laundry line, for example), Melvin sensed his complicity. In America, there were no laundry lines! There were water machines and underskirts galore! Oh, he knew his wife, he did, enough to carry on the whole fight in his head, taking the liberty to add a reconciliatory love scene at the end, though not a word had passed between them.

And now, by instinct, he avoids Linno as well. They arrived home that morning, rumpled and ill-rested from another overnight train, and she immediately went to her room, refusing breakfast. Ammachi hovered at the edge of the bed, Linno's cup of chai going cool in her hands.

Melvin roams the perimeter of the house, puffing on the last bidi in his pack. In Chennai, he had waited by the gate rather happily, having felt no gastric hint of ill fortune to come. He bought a roasted ear of corn, rubbed with lime and spices, and nibbled on this while eyeing the other applicants with pity. He peeled a mango and shared it with an old man who was anxiously waiting for his wife to emerge with a visitor's visa which would allow her to visit their pregnant daughter in Chicago.

The old man was so nervous he could eat only a few bites, no matter how much Melvin encouraged him. When the man's wife emerged weepy and empty-handed, Melvin was ashamed of his own small pang of hope, that a "no" for this wife meant a "yes" for Linno. Guiltily, he gave the old man his only other mango before the couple made their way home.

But as soon as Linno emerged from the consulate building and found Melvin at the gate, he felt something crumple in his chest. His stomach had betrayed him. *Pending investigation* . . . "About Anju?" Linno asked him. "Did someone tell them? No one even knew we had applied."

Were Melvin in a lucid state of mind, he would acknowledge that there might be several ways that a visa officer would be informed. He might conjecture that the investigation could have nothing to do with Anju at all, but rather a glitch in a system so overworked that at times its decisions rank among acts of God. But at the moment, he has only blind, fatherly vengeance on his side, and as soon as he hazards a guess, his body fills with a furious eureka, as close to a holy experience as he has had in years. For the first time, he knows where he is going, what he will say and how loud. Isn't this the P. C. Mappilla in his blood, the ore of resolution? It was the absence of God that made Mappilla's faith so unbreakable, the vacuum that enabled preachers to bellow on God's behalf about what was godly and what was not. Melvin's faith is just as firm in this way, thriving on Anju's absence.

Melvin quashes his bidi underfoot and walks down the road.

Halfway down, he stops to look back at his house. He has heard of illegal immigrants living in America for years, gathering piles of money and returning home to sons who have surpassed them in height. Will Anju be one of those? Remaining until she is someone else? Will she know this house or, like a spirit, will she simply pass over it, presuming that it belongs to strangers? This is still her house, even more so now that she is not in it, and so long as Anju is gone, it will be a haunted, unfinished thing. Not a place of rest but a place of unrest, her hair in the combs, her shoes in the doorway, her echo in every room.

ON THE STEPS of Abraham's veranda, Melvin waits for the servant to fetch his employer. Melvin studies the small wasp's nest growing beneath the eave of the roof like a solid gray goiter, a wasp floating languidly around it. At a safe distance from this are two white wicker chairs and a table between them. So many places to rest in this house, to linger and idle and scheme undisturbed. Melvin will not sit down, as he has never done so for the entire time that he has called himself Abraham's driver. Usually he leans against the car, waiting, but this time he has arrived on foot.

Abraham emerges, wiping his hands on his munda. "Ah, Melvin! I was not expecting you."

Melvin points at the roof. "You have a wasp's nest up there."

"Oh yes, about that. Do you think you could help me with it today? Mercy wants me to call an exterminator, as if I'm made of porcelain. . . ."

As Abraham complains about the price of exterminators, Melvin remembers his original mission. Before he can interrupt, Abraham says, "My God, I almost forgot. How did it go in Chennai?"

"Badly."

Abraham sighs. "It's the Mexicans. Taking up all the spots in that country. So what did the officials say?"

At this, a pivotal point in Melvin's life, he feels himself steered by a new philosophy. Thus far he has believed that a boy becomes a man over the course of years and lessons and mistakes, a stone worn smooth by an ocean. But now it seems he was quite wrong. A man is made in a series of moments, an evolution in bursts, and maybe this is his final turn. These thoughts come to him not in sentences but as a tidal throbbing in his gut, a *now, now, now.*

Melvin crosses his arms over his chest. "You know what they said. You told them yourself."

"Told what?" Abraham tilts his head, a movement whose subtlety sends a fissure through Melvin's resolution; perhaps he is wrong. Too late now for doubts such as these. The first words have been fired and the rest come in bullets.

"You called. You told them about my Anju."

Abraham hesitates, then brays a laugh of disbelief.

"They never would've known," Melvin says.

"Who fed you this nonsense?"

"Before I left, I told no one about this meeting, no one except you. How else would they find out?"

Abraham gathers himself up, fits his hands on his hips. "I don't like this tone, Melvin. It is not the tone an employee takes with his employer."

"I am not only your employee. I'm Gracie's husband—"

"Melvin—"

Pure madness, this train of words without brakes. "And for this, you never forgave me. For this, you wanted to get back at me."

"Who are you to tell me about forgiveness?" Abraham jabs a finger at his own chest. "I have been very forgiving! How easy do you think it was for me to hear your name with hers? She was mine, she was to be my *wife*." On "wife," he hits the back of a wicker seat, as though Gracie would be sitting right here were it not for Melvin. "And then you bumble into the picture as if you of all people could belong to a family like that."

"She told me you did not want her. You gave her up."

"So I did. But just because a man does not want his dinner doesn't mean he wants the servant to step in and have it."

Servant. They have crossed into terrain where neither meant to go, and now the word sits between them as it always will, implacable and pulsing with life.

"My wife hired you out of pity and politeness," Abraham says formally. "Were it up to me, we would never have met."

"I am not your servant. You are not my master."

"I don't need you to remind me of what I am. You are the one needing reminders, so here is one. There are only two good reasons a man should have more than his share of the world—by being born into that share or by earning it. You did neither and ended up with more than you deserved."

With his heel, Abraham kicks up the edge of his munda so as to tie it around his waist. "If not for me, Melvin, you'd still be stuck at that bar, asking Berchmans for a peg of Yeksho."

The Ambassador key has grown warm in Melvin's breast pocket. He thinks of hurling it at Abraham's forehead so as to scar him, to brand a permanent reminder onto his skull. But these are fantasies. He and Abraham are too old to survive old feuds, too young to be free of the past.

Instead, Melvin drops the key into the wicker seat where Abraham's Gracie would have sat.

Abraham refuses to glance at the key. And though Melvin is already down the steps, Abraham shouts after him with all the volume and vigor of a real-life Mammootty: "I'll take care of the wasps myself!"

AND SO, in an effort to reinstate his manhood, Melvin has entered an early retirement. He always imagined that he would be older when he retired, dentured and content, surrounded with grandchildren to guide him by the hand through the waning years. Instead he finds himself bewildered by his recent explosion, and having nowhere better to go, he ends up at the Rajadhani Bar.

The bar swelters with the alluvial heat and musk of its male patrons, the ceiling fan slowly whisking the air to no great effect. At this hour most men are at work, so only one customer sits at the counter, chatting with Berchmans. Melvin takes a stool farther down and orders a peg of brandy, neat, something to send a gentle kick to his brain. Outside, a jeep passes with a bullhorn perched on its roof, through which a voice bellows: *The twenty-first century will be the Indian century! The country's future is in your hands!*

Melvin takes his drink and grimaces, the liquid razing a path down his throat. He calls out to Berchmans. "This stuff gives you a headache before you even swallow." Melvin drops the glass onto the counter. "Don't you serve anything other than battery fluid?"

Berchmans saunters over, studying Melvin's anger from a distance. "Not for what you're paying, I don't."

"So if I were rich, you would give me the good brandy?"

"Of course."

"If I were someone like Abraham Chandy? Is that it?"

"Melvin, what is this? How could you be Abraham Chandy?"

"I'm not saying I'm him! I am saying I deserve better, I deserve the same—"

Melvin stops himself; his voice has begun to tremble. Berchmans is staring, as is the other customer, his brow furrowed behind a bottle. Melvin cannot lift his eyes from the counter. Carefully, quietly, he adds, "I deserve a nice thing. Once in a while."

He presses his hands to his eyes, which have grown suddenly full. Now, finally, he acknowledges his failures, the loss of his job, his wife, his daughter, and all the ways in which he is to blame. Now, when he feels smaller than he ever felt before, now he is a man.

After a moment, he hears the unscrewing of a cap, the clink of glass against glass, the pouring of liquid. He feels a hand brush his shoulder. When he opens his eyes, his glass is brimming with gold.

Melvin thanks him.

Berchmans nods and moves away to clean some glasses. Berchmans is good in this way; he senses who wants to speak further and who does not. Even if Melvin wanted to talk, he would have no idea where to begin or how to utter the word "servant" as Abraham did, a word that had flown in long ago, unnoticed, and made its nest. Melvin knows he was never a servant, but to be perceived as such beyond his knowing is even more shameful to him than being one.

When Melvin was a child, his family could afford to employ a part-time servant, an old man so committed to social custom that he refused to answer to his first name, Kelan, and would respond only to the full name that included his Untouchable caste: Kelan Pulayan. Back then, Ammachi told Melvin of the way life used to be, when Paravans and Pulayans would even walk backward in the streets if an upper-caste person were coming their way, according to rules that ran old and deep as rivers. But when Kelan Pulayan's son, Kochu Kelan, came of age, he rebelled and converted to Islam. Kochu Kelan showed up one day in the backyard, growing the beginnings of a beard and wearing the white cap of his new religion.

"The temple doesn't want us," Kochu Kelan said. "Only before Allah can we show our face."

"Then go." Kelan Pulayan's decision was quiet, as he had never once raised his voice while in Ammachi's employ. "But don't ever show your face to me."

From the doorway, Melvin watched Kochu Kelan tromping back the way he came, his hand steadying his topi. Kelan Pulayan's back was to Melvin, still and straight as a tombstone as he watched his son. And then he returned to chopping wood in calm, even strokes.

Though years have passed since Melvin first met Gracie, what pains him most from that time was his ignorance, his neglecting to understand that he lived in the same world as Kelan Pulayan. The customs that decided where Kelan Pulayan would worship and to what name he would answer, these were the rules that put Melvin beneath Gracie and Abraham above them all. This is the web that time has built, of which they are all a part. This is what Abraham will not let Melvin forget a second time.

5.

ON THE THIRD DAY of Anju's stay with Mrs. Solanki, Rohit phones with a voice full of brash adolescence. Anju is sitting at the kitchen counter across from Mrs. Solanki. When Anju hears his voice over the speakerphone, she stops swiveling on her stool and holds the counter with both hands. "I called the woman that Anju was staying with, Mom. She said you guys have had Anju for days."

The phrasing sounds plucked from a hostage-and-ransom movie, causing Anju to shrink into her chair. But Mrs. Solanki looks non-plussed. "Ah, Rohit, I was wondering when you would call, *beta*. I would've told you if you had called but you never call. Let this be a lesson—"

"Is Anju there with you? Let me talk to her."

"She told us about the film you are trying to make."

"Not *trying*, Mom. I *am* making it. I'm sorry I didn't tell you, but I didn't want you getting involved."

"After all my crying and searching. All you did was film me without saying a word." With a huff, Mrs. Solanki puts a closed fist on her hip though her eyes possess the playfulness of a person at advantage. "Sometimes, Rohit, I think you can be very insensitive."

"Look, are you going to let me talk to her or do I have to come over there?"

Mrs. Solanki raises her eyebrows at Anju, who shakes her head.

"She is in the shower. But let's have dinner at La Tache this evening. Can you come? I will make reservations."

"But they probably won't let me film at La Tache."

"Exactly, *beta*."

This phone call goes much more smoothly than the one Anju made on her first night back with the Solankis. Bird answered with fear in her greeting, a fear that soon turned furious. "Where are you? How could you run off like this?"

But when Anju, with measured words, explained that she was not coming back to the apartment, that Mrs. Solanki had agreed to send her to Kumarakom, Bird grew quiet. She did not pose a question or inter-rupt with a word.

"Please don't tell Rohit," Anju said carefully. "If he calls for me."

"Come back. You should come back. We should talk about this, Anju Mol. Have you talked to your father recently?"

"My father knows nothing about all this." Anju took a breath. "I never told my family about you. I have not spoken to them since December. When I ran away from the Solankis."

To this, Bird responded with stark silence.

"I never told anyone about you," Anju said. "Not the Solankis, not the school. I lied to you. I thought it was the only way to convince you to let me stay."

When finally Bird spoke, her voice was dry as if from disuse. "But you said your father was sending you letters. . . ."

"He wasn't. And I never wrote."

For a time, there was only the sound of Bird's breathing.

"I'm sorry," Anju whispered.

"I don't understand. This is not the way you say good-bye. As if I am no one to you."

"Chachy, are you crying?"

"No," Bird snapped. "I'm laughing."

Then: *click* of the phone hanging up. A good-bye as abrupt and wounding as Anju's own.

LA TACHE IS THE TYPE of restaurant that makes Anju want to serve the waiters herself, so elegant and calm they are, like soon-to-be starlets fully aware of their upcoming discovery. From memory, they recite the specials like sonnets and bring them on trays balanced on single hands, orbiting around one another without touching, part of a grander firmament of gold and crushed velvet and wood the color of semisweet chocolate.

The waiter slides out a chair; Mrs. Solanki slides into it. She orders a Bombay Sapphire martini and then says to Anju, "I'll need it to get through this evening."

In mutters, the Solankis try to negotiate who should break the news to Rohit, but before anything is resolved, Rohit strides through the revolving doors. Mr. Solanki says quickly, "You talk, you talk."

Perhaps as an unsubtle show of defiance, Rohit wears a red T-shirt riddled with purposefully torn holes as opposed to the slacks and suits of everyone around him. When he reaches the table, he gives his parents a sullen nod. "Anju," he says tautly, and sits down. Under the table, Anju rubs her clammy hands on her knees.

A basket arrives, carrying a cloth-covered bundle roughly the size of an infant. They spread their napkins on their laps while a waiter peels back the cloth to reveal a pile of rolls. Anju wishes, for a moment, that the waiter might prolong his stay by repeating his sonnet of entrées.

"So." Rohit looks at his mother, then his father, and lastly Anju. "Someone want to tell me what's going on?"

Before anyone can reply, Rohit shakes his head as if to reject a silly thought. "Listen, Anju, it's not like I care if you want to have a reunion with my parents. In fact, I think that's great, especially for the film. I'm all about reunions. They're poignant, they're cyclical, they're redemptive. But what's the use if you're going to do something like that behind my back? How am I supposed to incorporate it into the story? With a title card that says: *Anju decides to reunite with her host family?* No, we'll have to stage it again, but it's going to look stagy, that's all I'm saying. And I know what I said about manipulating reality, but staginess is obvious."

Anju stares at the basket, her cheeks growing as warm as the swaddled rolls. "I am not doing your movie anymore," she says.

It seems as though her words are slowly lowering onto his shoulders, causing them to sag. "I thought we talked about this."

"We did, but I did more thinking and I think I am right."

"So what, you went to my parents so they could buy you a ticket back?" Rohit raises a finger at the waiter and orders a vodka and Red Bull, a cocktail that makes Mr. Solanki wince. "Is that it? Because if so, this film is really going to tank. What's the point? Money bails you out. The end. Who's going to care?"

"Rohit, if I may." Mrs. Solanki takes a sip from her martini to create an authoritarian beat of silence. "What it all comes down to is Anju's decision. She told us everything that happened over these past few months, how she was living in Queens, how you found her and started making this film. It's an extraordinary story."

"Yeah. I know. I *discovered* it."

"But now Anju is taking the reins. With my help." Mrs. Solanki presses her fingertips to the base of the martini glass, as if to keep it in place. "As you know, I've been trying to get this episode off the ground for months now, and Jeff is finally on board—"

"Episode of what?" Rohit asks warily.

"An episode of *Four Corners* dedicated to immigration. It's a very hot topic right now. And Anju's will be one of the featured stories." Mrs. Solanki squeezes Anju's shoulder. "She came to us with the idea actually."

Slowly, Rohit's face slackens. The irritability slides off his face, leaving his features blank as a dish.

"Now we know you probably think that this is unfair," his father says gently. "But you have to think of it from Anju's perspective."

"My show will give her more visibility," Mrs. Solanki says. "Think of how her story will spread. I'm sure there will be agents interested in representing her for life rights."

"Life rights?" Rohit says.

"You don't know what life rights are?" Mrs. Solanki seems to take pleasure in educating her son. "It's when a production company purchases the story of someone's life in order to make it into a movie. Probably a TV movie in this case, but it could go for quite a sum, a bildungsroman like this, about *immigration* no less. Anyway, we'll go to India, shoot the reunion, and air the episode next month. Excellent timing!"

"And my documentary? What about my documentary?"

"Well, you said yourself it would take years for that to happen, and it's so rare to get a wide audience for documentary. Even a theatrical release would be like winning the lottery. I mean, darling, you must think of what is in Anju's best interest." Mrs. Solanki fishes an olive from her martini and sets it on the corner of Rohit's saucer. "There. You like olives."

All this time, Rohit has not moved. His expression reminds Anju of a time in Jackson Heights when she watched a child's newly scooped ice cream go tragically *splat* onto the gum-splotched sidewalk, the utter disillusionment with the world before a deluge of tears. "You mean *your* best interest," he says.

"And mine," Anju says. "Your mother's people are paying me also."

"Three thousand dollars," Mrs. Solanki says, "plus the return fare home and per diem."

Anju turns to Rohit. "I thought you said that the subject is not receiving payment?"

Rohit slams his hands down on the table. "They aren't! Not in documentary! It's unethical. But this is reality TV crap, all packaged and prettied up, no ethics at all, and if that's what you want, then fine, go and get it."

"Rohit," Mr. Solanki says. "Your voice."

Mrs. Solanki slices open a roll and spreads a sliver of butter on each half. "I know you've never wanted my help, but this could lead to better opportunities for you too, better than this film would anyway. So what I want to ask you, Rohit, is this: Would you like to be an associate producer for this episode?"

"Yeah, right. So I can bring you coffee?" Rohit studies the olive for a moment. "Make me first camera."

Mrs. Solanki rolls her eyes. "Rohit, I've seen your films."

"First camera."

"Second camera. And you release your documentary footage to us."

Rohit chews on the inside of his cheek.

"I am letting you shoot second camera," Mrs. Solanki says, "and you haven't even seen the inside of a classroom in a year."

"Fine. Whatever." He disembowels a roll and plows the soft stuffing through a pool of olive oil. Rohit looks at Anju. "So it was all for the money, huh? No devotion to the art of the thing."

Anju stares at the remains of his roll. Of course, the money was only part, though a large part. She could tell him of the night in the subway with her pungent neighbor, how she decided that working with Rohit disturbed her, the way he nudged her into doing this and that, the way he tried, time and again, to force her life into a palatable time line and shape. The Anju in his film would be a cracked reflection or, at best, a broken shard of herself. And maybe Mrs. Solanki would distort her life just the same, but so would the local newspaper, and so would the local rumors. At least, by then, Anju would be home.

6.

BIRD SITS ON the plastic-covered couch, watching an episode of *Four Corners*. She has closed the blinds. She has set her heels on the coffee table. It is 11:05 on Tuesday morning, and for the second time in her employ at the Apsara Salon, she has taken the day off. Two weeks have passed since Anju left her side, and though Bird never elaborated the details to Ghafoor, he has been careful with her, more lenient than before.

On television, the four cohosts huddle around their cozy table, each of them holding their mugs, the Young Creationist hiding behind her glossy hair, the Still-Sexy Elder crossing her legs. Sonia Solanki has just announced that she will be taking tomorrow off, in order to tape a segment in India that will air in two weeks, about a fascinating young woman named Anju Melvin and her travails upon emigrating from India to the United States. The conversation slides into the topic of immigration, then illegal immigration. "Call me crazy," says the Young Creationist, "but I think people who enter illegally are breaking the law, and people who break the law should be sent back. Period." The Creationist receives a few claps and a rallying "Yeah!" egging her on. "We've got to address this problem at the root."

"Well, you're grasping at leaves," Sonia Solanki says, gesturing with a pen, rendering her the most erudite of the group. "Our country is heavily dependent on illegal labor from the millions of undocumented workers who are already here. They are more necessary to our economy than you think."

One person in the audience claps.

Bird is hardly paying attention to the conversation as it unfolds, focused instead on Sonia Solanki. Her long, unaging neck and her lacquered fingernails. Her crisp, clean words and her posture, that of a dancer. Bird shouldn't be jealous but she is, not simply because Sonia whisked Anju away, but because here is a woman entering the latter half of her years with grace, who is watched by thousands every day, listened to and talked about. Quite simply, she matters.

Does Bird? Will Anju look back on this strange streak of time and recall her with any warmth? Bird clings to the memory of Anju in the kitchen, asking the question, *Did you know my mother?* It was so easy to forget, sometimes, how vulnerable Anju was, how still a child full of doubt and wanting, and how the loss of Gracie had stained her as well, though she was too young to remember anything but absence.

DURING THE COMMERCIAL BREAK, Bird goes to the nightstand by her bed and from the drawer pulls out an empty chocolate tin. From this, she retrieves the last of Gracie's letters. The paper is blue and cottony soft, the creases delicate from disregard, having been opened and read on so many occasions. There was a time when Bird knew the look of every word, could string each line in her mind's eye like pearls on a strand.

April 6, 1988

My dear Chachy,

It has been a long silence, but this will be a short letter. I am writing to tell you that I won't be seeing you for some time, maybe never, unless you come to see me in Kumarakom. We have decided to live with Melvin's mother. His father has passed away.

Just yesterday I saw a man climbing a betel nut tree—have you ever seen it? They are tall and thin, these trees. They look so fragile compared to the others. But a man climbs all the way to the top to cut the betel nut, and when he is finished, he does not climb down to climb up the next one. He throws his weight back and forth, still holding on to the treetop, so that the tree bends forward and backward, farther and farther, until he can grab the neighboring treetop and jump onto that one. The betel nut tree is thin, but you can't break it, it's so strong. You know my meaning? It will not break because it bends. The same with me.

I know you will say that I lost my sense of adventure. You would be right. But I have my girls now, they are my life. And we have our smaller adventures. Linno is as high as my waist—we measured. She is sleeping on the edge of the bed while I write you this letter. Anju tends to roll on top of her, even though there is more than enough room for both. For such a little one, she spreads like a starfish in her sleep. They are your girls too. I would've made you godmother if you were here for their baptisms, but you can be something else to them, something better. You should know these things for when you meet them, because you will someday.

Please forgive me. And don't take too long to respond.

Your loving friend and sister,
Gracie

The television show has resumed, and it comes to Bird from the other room like the faint noise of an ocean. She remains on the bed with the page in both her hands, grateful to her younger self for preserving it. She presses the letter to her face, then her chest, and stays like this for a very long time, long after the show ends, watching the sunlight cross her lap.

The phone begins to ring, but she lets the answering machine pick up.

Ghafoor's voice: "Bird, are you there? I don't want to bother, but I am looking at the appointment book and it seems that you double-booked Mrs. Majmudar and Mrs. Mazumdar. Mrs. Majmudar is the one with a wedding to go to, but Mrs. Mazumdar will jump on my head if I push on her too much. I think you should call and explain, lady to lady. Bird, come now, I know you are there. Hello? Pick up, Bird. Are you there?"

And hearing her life calling to her, she puts her past back in the chocolate tin and takes up the phone.

"Yes," she says. "I am here."

7.

THE JFK AIRPORT has not undergone any major changes since Anju's last visit. Near the ticket counter, a father and son squat before their suitcases, a small one and a bulging one, trying to shift the contents so as to magically reduce the overweight status of the latter. Surrounded by soaps, loofahs, T-shirts, and boxes of Old Spice aftershave, the man and his son look mystified by the arithmetic of it all. The son mutters at the father in a tongue that Anju does not recognize, but whose tone roughly amounts to: "I told you not to tell anyone we were going back! Half of this is for people we don't even know!" Which is a refrain Anju heard in Hindi during her first foray into an Air India terminal, where the ticket takers seemed proudly empowered by their authority to turn whole duffels and pullmans away.

In her own suitcases, Anju has stuffed a number of gifts for her family, mostly clothes, but also more selective purchases. Among them: a Jesus nightlight for Ammachi and a tiny hula dancer doll that Melvin can affix to the dashboard of Abraham Saar's car. Its hips jimmy at the slightest tremble so the doll will hula enthusiastically on Kumarakom roads. The most impressive gift is a used book for Linno titled *The History of Art*. Each page is slick, with a pleasant chemical smell, the space taken up by a famous painting and a brief block of text. The yellow sun and crescent moon unscrolling from coils of gray cloud in *The Battle of Alexander at Issus*. The white turban of an Arab and the black top hat of an Englishman, framed by the arch of a giraffe's bending neck in *The Nubian Giraffe*. "With the development of communication links," the caption reads, "traders of the early nineteenth century were able to travel farther and farther afield and return with increasingly exotic gifts."

She wishes she could call home, to see what other exotic and unexotic gifts her family might want, but Mrs. Solanki told her not to. "We want that element of surprise," she said. Anju recalled Jilu Auntie's gifts from years prior, of Tang and cake mix, so Mrs. Solanki bought ten boxes of yellow, marble, and chocolate cake mix, five canisters of Tang, and two jars of Ovaltine.

Wearing saucer-sized sunglasses that attract more attention than they are meant to repel, Mrs. Solanki pulls a mud-brown suitcase senselessly covered in gold initials that are not her own. Rohit and the rest of the camera crew keep their lives in their backpacks, having to carry their own equipment as well. The first camera operator's name is Petra. She wears a black tank top and cargo pants; her arms are sleeved in green tattoos. At first, her mere presence seemed to inspire a sense of competition in Rohit, which gave way to intimidation, then absolute deference. At the airport, Anju overhears her directing Rohit to "stay out of her way" and to "look for the other angle." He seems to fail both directives quite often, leading Petra to give him one of her many grim lessons.

"Don't jump the line!" she yells at him. He keeps his head bowed. "Do you know what I mean by that? Didn't you learn it in school?"

"I didn't finish out the year," he says, for the first time, without pride.

Anju feels sorry for him, especially after all that transpired, though it quickly becomes clear that Rohit not only benefits from Petra's teachings but that he is also beginning to adore Petra of the green tattoos. He seems to delight in the way she muscles him around, the way she snaps her fingers at him, how she depends on him for extra batteries which he obediently keeps charged, one per pocket, and feeds to her like an animal trainer in full thrall of his shark.

"Go shoot some b-roll," Petra tells him. "But be discreet. And no more slow zooms, okay? I wasn't impressed by those."

Rohit walks away, rubbing his cheek and smiling sheepishly, as if Petra has just nuzzled him.

Mrs. Solanki and Anju sit on a bench while Petra talks to the sound guy, Billy, a lanky, friendly man with headphones perpetually collaring his neck. He carries the boom microphone like a hockey stick, down by his side, and tells anecdotes about his children whenever possible. "I named my daughter Daytona," he told Anju. "After the beach where she was conceived." The last member of the crew is Roy, the producer. His age is ambiguous due to the white blondness of his hair, and his shirt is open two buttons too far, revealing a turquoise stone on a hemp necklace. Caffeinated and rigid and fidgety, Roy is the one to explain to Mrs. Solanki what will be shot and how. He spreads his discomfort, like flu, to whomever he speaks.

For the most part, Anju keeps her distance. While waiting to board the plane, she sips on a beverage that she had thought would be coffee, but looks instead like a tall cousin of the sundae, all weightless cream laced with chocolate powder. When Mrs. Solanki sits next to her, Anju asks: "You are sure we should not call my family to inform them? What if no one is home?"

"If no one is home, then we'll wait," Mrs. Solanki says between sips of espresso.

Anju brings a spoonful of sweet froth to her mouth, then drops the froth back into the cup. "My stomach is tossing and turning."

"Mine too." Mrs. Solanki's eyes are bright and espressoed. "This is going to be tremendous."

BUSINESS CLASS, Anju learns, is all about space—the space to stretch and sprawl, armrests aplenty, to receive champagne in a glass, to wash one's face with a warm wet towel handled by silver tongs, to stare out the window or into a book as the economy passengers file past.

Never has Anju been more ill at ease.

Early in the journey, Mrs. Solanki goes to the bathroom while Petra positions herself near Anju. "So," Petra says, angling the camera at Anju, "will you miss it here?"

Nodding seems like the right answer, but instead Anju says: "I am not sure."

Petra waits. It is a comfort, Anju thinks, her patience, the way she lets a person's thoughts take shape.

"There is one woman. I was calling her like a big sister or auntie, because she was family to me almost. She was helping me very much." Anju looks at her hands. "I will miss her."

These stilted sentences do little justice to Bird, whom Anju worked up the nerve to visit four days before. She arrived to find Bird in her flannel robe, civil but leaden, smelling of Gwen's tea rose lotion. An abandoned cheese slice sat on the arm of the couch, both still in their plastic sheaths. Bird and Anju stepped awkwardly around each other, as if a camera were in the room, forcing them to monitor their words and movements. Anju packed her clothes into Mrs. Solanki's rolling suitcase, and intermittently, Bird brought a few extra pairs of shoes into the room, egg-white sandals and gray flats that Anju thought dowdy and Bird called "sensible."

"Thank you," Anju said.

But Bird did not move, simply stood in the doorway, staring at the sandals in her hands as if they had asked her a question.

"Your mother . . . ," she said finally.

It seemed to require a great effort to expel the rest of the sentence, which Anju predicted to be the opening lines of a gentle, genuine moment, something like *Your mother would be proud of you.*

Bird met her eyes. "Your mother and I were friends."

Anju waited for something else until she realized that this was all Bird wanted to share. "Okay," Anju said.

Bird nodded and straightened up, somehow restored by her own words. "Keep an eye on the shoes, especially at church." She went to the suitcase, where she fit the sandals next to the flats.

On her way out, Anju glanced at the blue vase, the dried flowers, the plastic-covered couch. And though she had seen the couch so many times before, she had never noticed how forlorn it appeared. It seemed as though Bird would never remove the plastic covering, as if she would continue to preserve the fabric beneath for a cherished guest, one that would never arrive.

AN HOUR LATER, the entire crew (including Rohit, who has seated himself next to Petra) is snoozing away, having taken the sedatives they brought with them. These are people who swallow pills like candy. Mrs. Solanki offers Anju some of her Ambien, but Anju refuses, afraid of the side effects. She has heard of people who sleepwalk on such pills and others whose pulses stutter to a stop, though her own will not allow her to rest anyway. There are times when her mind conjures up images of Linno and Ammachi and Melvin, and no sleeping pill or sedative could keep her heart from leaping to greet them.

8.

*A*LONG WITH THE SMUDGY SUNRISE, there comes the feeling that today Linno must go to church.

She tries to defeat the feeling by going to work, where by ten a.m. she is useless, answering phones in automated tones and ruining three invitations in a row simply by cutting where she should have folded. Easy mistakes, but none that she would usually make.

Alice looks at her with tender worry, a look not unfamiliar to Linno in these last few days, since she returned from Chennai. Each day seems a repetition of the last, the same "on-hold" music when calling the consulate number, the same sense of limbo provided by the official who informs her that the application is still "pending investigation." Yesterday Alice suggested hiring a lawyer to speed things along, but today she sends Linno home early. "Get some sleep," Alice says. "We'll see about the lawyer tomorrow."

Linno takes the bus home, but traffic is slow today due to a frenzy all along the river, people gathering around the banks. The passengers squint at the water, where fish can be seen moving and bobbing just beneath the surface. "*Karimeen pongi!*" says a passenger. "They've risen!"

"Are they dead?" someone asks.

"If they were dead, they'd be on their sides . . ."

"But *karimeen* always stay deep down in the water."

"Why are they moving so slowly?"

"Pesticides. What else? It'll be in the newspapers tomorrow."

Linno exits at the next stop, unable to stand the slow haul of traffic. With every bus that arrives, a herd of people push their way out, wading into the water for Kumarakom's most famous fish. Some of the men remove their mundus to use as nets, splashing around in tiny shorts. Usually, only nets and rods can trap the swift-swimming *karimeen*, but now they wander into bare hands, bodies that barely possess the energy to resist, numbed by whatever fresh chemical has stunned them. Years ago, Linno witnessed a whole plague of fish floating along the river after an overdose of pesticides from the paddy fields, eyes staring up at the sky. But this picture is stranger, grotesque, nauseating: the sight of so many men, yelling, scrambling like fish themselves around a dangerous bait.

LINNO MAKES HER WAY across the nearby bridge where lorries tremble past, billowing veils of fumes behind them. The humid heat feels skintight, but she keeps walking, waiting to be struck by the sight of the church she has visited for most of her life.

For years, Linno has been attending Mass without a proper confession, and in this quiet fashion, she has received the host into a mouth still full of an untold sin, pretending a piety that she cannot claim. Today she will sit opposite Anthony Achen and form the words in a cleansing rush, and he will assign her a recitation of prayers, and in some slow, divine way, everything will be absolved and the world she knew will return to her. Maybe this is the missing part of her visa application—the stamp of the divine.

This morning she dragged herself onto her feet, dizzy, knees flaccid as the blood rushed to her extremities, to the very tips of her fingers. She awoke with the knowledge that life comes in circles of cause and effect, of fault and consequence, that her own accident and her mother's accident are connected in some indissoluble pattern, that her mother's death was the first in a series of mounting failures, a tumble of dominos to which Linno gave the first push, and in punishment, five years later, she lost her hand. How easily she pretended to forget all this, what with her designs and her cards, her face in a magazine. But now, as then, she is being punished for a crime for which she never atoned, and she will continue to be punished until she does. She has clung to action rather than prayer, presuming that there is no use in turning her gaze inward rather than outward. Inside is a world of regret so vast and deep that to linger there feels as impossible as skipping around the ledge of a well. But no more impossible than giving up her sister, and that she will not do, not until she has visited every lawyer and consulate, every priest, guru, imam, and astrologer, anyone who might bring hope.

AFTER AN HOUR of wandering, Linno feels very far from her home and her mission. She walks past an empty bus stop, its bars leprous with peeling paint, past a mulberry tree soaking the air with its sweet ferment. A wall borders the road, postered with political faces, sickled stars, slogans of *India Shining*. Now that elections are over and votes are being tallied, new posters will cover these, perhaps a fair, moon-faced actress from the latest Tamil movie. As a child, Linno used to watch the poster man carefully plaster each quarter of the mural until he stood back, the entire wall filled with a beautiful, unspoiled face. Then he would pull up a corner and rip a long scar through the cheek, which he would press back down, an ingenious solution to the pilfering of local boys who might want to mural their walls at home. They could not do so without destroying her; nothing came without cost.

Linno continues past the posters. Crammed with schoolchildren, an auto-rickshaw waddles past her, in the opposite direction of a man driving his butter-colored cow with a stick. The cow is as malnourished as its owner, its ribs raised like the bones in an old pair of hands. She feels as doleful as the cow, and slow, filled with its haylike smell and its sadness. Is this what it means, then, to be depressed? To watch the steady unraveling of her life and have no impulse to take up the thread? To be more absorbed by a stain on the mirror than by her own reflection? She shakes herself free of these thoughts, thinks only of her meeting with Anthony Achen.

And now, in the distance, she can see the triad of steeples awaiting her, each with its pale, petaled cross. It is not far, the church at the top of the hill. A lorry noisily hobbles past, kicking up dust from its bumper where someone has painted in yellow letters DISTANCE CREATES LOVE. She imagines herself running after the lorry and hopping onto the bumper and riding and riding until an immeasurable distance grows between her and Anthony Achen, who will soon be sitting across from her, his knuckles whitening with every word until he banishes her from his presence. The ground begins to move beneath her, the road ripples and buckles like water. There is nowhere to look that is not moving. She takes hold of the wall which seems to go on and on, a ribbon without end, a question without answer, an apology without pardon. She closes her eyes and presses her forehead to the back of her hand. In her ears is the trill of a bicycle bell, the thick whispers of windblown leaves and then, simply, her breath.

IF LINNO KNEW that the only person at church today would be the Kapyar, she might have changed her mind about confession. In fact the Kapyar spends more time in the church than anyone else by his account. Not that anyone would ask or care that the House of God does not clean Itself. The Kapyar is the one to rinse the lip prints from the chalice and wipe the carved wood stations of the cross that hang along the walls. He pauses before the picture of Jesus with Veronica and raises his fingertip to the gaunt profile of Christ, feels the knifelike line of His cheekbone not unlike his own.

The Kapyar would have liked to be a priest, but his father had refused the calling, responding instead to a call from a sizable dowry. Being employed by the church, the Kapyar thinks, is the next best thing. And he fulfills his duties with utter gravity, fully aware of the children who call him the Crab. Once, he twisted the ear of one boy particularly hard, a multiple offender who had bullishly snorted loud enough to provoke a hesitation from Anthony Achen. After Mass, the Kapyar heard the boy say to his cohorts: "That Kapyar, that son of a *veshya*."

The words embedded themselves in the Kapyar's chest, caused his mind to stagger back into a moment of childhood, when he came into the house to find his mother fastening the last hook of her sari blouse as the landlord put a roll of rupees on the table. At the time, he thought: *But she should be paying him.*

One boy's curse is another man's truth. The Kapyar used to tell himself that he was not (he thought) the son of a whore, but now that the words have been thrown down before him, the Kapyar is reminded of that slender, crippling *maybe*. No, he is not that: he is the Kapyar who tugs the Sunday bells; who collects the weekly moneys, watching to make sure that the same hand that deposits fifty paise into the basket does not withdraw a rupee; who travels four miles on foot from a small hut by the side of the road, built atop the matchbox shack where he and his mother and father once lived in a careful semblance of oblivion.

AFTER THE KAPYAR lowers the bolts on the two front doors, he can sit on the stone steps outside and open his thermos of tea in peace. A peace that dissolves when he sees a young woman in the distance, making her way up the road to church. He puts the cap back on his tea and rises, shielding his eyes against the sun. It is Melvin Vallara's daughter, the elder girl who messed with firecrackers, who, by the Kapyar's mental records, recently abandoned church altogether. But now there is something strange about her, something wounded in her eye and dazed in her gait. The closer she comes, the wearier she looks, and by the time she reaches the Kapyar, she looks as though she might collapse, as if the only thing holding her up are the words she is trying to expel between gasps.

"Anthony Achen?" She swallows in a way that seems painful. "Where is he?"

"Anthony Achen isn't here," the Kapyar says.

"But . . ." She looks around. "But I came for confession. When will he be back?"

"Not today. He doesn't live here."

She stares up at the steeple, her arms hanging by her side. A slight wind could knock her over.

By this time, it seems that this Vallara is benignly crazy. But do crazy women carry handbags? She is parchment pale, on the verge of fainting, so the Kapyar braces her elbows and guides her into a sitting position on the steps. "Have you eaten?" he asks.

"Not today."

The Kapyar unscrews his thermos and pours a cup for her. "I only drank from this side—" the Kapyar begins to say, but she seems not to care as she drinks.

She holds the cup in her lap and stares at the dregs for a time. It seems to the Kapyar that the young woman is regaining some color, that she seems almost able to rise and return home. He is about to encourage her to do so when the woman turns to him.

"I still need to confess," she says.

"To whom? I am the only one here."

"Then you."

He argues against this, but she will not listen. "Don't you understand? I am the Kapyar, not priest. Not even deacon."

It goes on like this, "please" and "no," until it is clear that the woman has no intention of leaving. With a face like that, desperate and imploring, she might even follow the Kapyar home, and he is not the sort of man who would appreciate that. Nor would his wife.

"Please," she says.

Days come in unforeseen shapes. The Kapyar thinks of his childhood, a string of pretty days until the one with the landlord and a blouse hook undone. It was not the worst of his memories but the beginning of knowledge that he did not want. And yet he never hated his mother for it. He treated her gently, aware that she deserved much more than what little this life had given her. So it is the thought of his mother as much as the plea of this woman that leads the Kapyar to nod in assent.

"Parraya," he says. "Tell me."

IT BEGINS WITH GRACIE, holding out a pair of white knickers, into which Linno steps while gripping her mother's shoulder. One foot, then two.

Linno is seven and old enough to dress herself, she believes, but her mother is anxious about the choice of outfit. Linno's navy sailor dress with white piping matches Anju's smaller, superior version, a matchingness that renders the smaller girl cute and the bigger girl juvenile. But Gracie could dress them in twin rice sacks for all Linno cares. Her entire being cries out for their destination: *To the beach! To the beach!*

Kovalam Beach. Linno's father has told stories of sand so fine it can be sifted through a piece of silk, water as bright as the aqueous eyes of a porcelain doll. No real place can adhere to such standards, but with her father back in Bombay, Linno will forgive him his fairy tales. Her mother says he will return by the end of the month and then they will go to Kovalam Beach as a family. Until then, Linno loves the beach before she sees it because he loves it too.

"BE NICE TO ABRAHAM SAAR and Mercy Auntie," her mother says, while waiting for the van that will deliver them to the beach. She is wearing a rose-colored sari of a slippery material that will not suffer from the saltwater. In her arms is Anju, sucking on her white piping, showing off her muffiny diaper. "This trip was his idea. He is paying for the van as well. So make sure to thank him."

But a grown, bearded man like Abraham Saar roams above the world of puerile pleases and thank-yous. The other day, he and his wife visited Ammachi and Gracie to invite them for a day trip to Kovalam Beach. Gracie was as stiff as the chair in which she sat, but Mercy Auntie seemed warm and at ease, explaining how her father and Gracie's father had been classmates long ago. "Just come," she said. "Another couple is joining us. It will be a nice welcome home, don't you think?" At first Gracie began to protest, but Ammachi encouraged her to take the children, and Linno nearly sprang out of her seat when her mother said, "All right."

But now, the imminence of Linno's thank-you slightly tarnishes the day to come.

When the van arrives, they squeeze into the farthest back seat. In the first row is the other couple, a dour man and his wife whose bun hangs like an overripe fruit on the verge of falling, pinned with a garland of jasmine. Behind the couple are Mercy Auntie and her broom-thin boys, who seem to believe that Linno and Anju are where girls should be—out of sight. She wants to ask if Shine feels pain when Sheen falls down, and vice versa, but Shine and Sheen glance at Linno with their round, froggy eyes and at once commit themselves to never look upon her again.

As the van rumbles to a start, Gracie nudges Linno in the arm. Gracie raises her eyebrows at the front seat, where Abraham Saar is seated next to the driver. When Linno looks away, her mother taps her elbow. "Say thank you," she whispers.

From the back, Abraham Saar's head looks large and hairy and indestructible. To squeak out a thank-you, to cause not only his head to turn but also those of his driver and his wife, Shine and Sheen, the dour man and the jasmine wife, seems suddenly a gargantuan task to ask of a seven-year-old.

Her mother pinches her arm. Linno jerks away.

"I thought you were a good girl," her mother whispers, rocking Anju to sleep.

"NO," Linno says. She is quiet, not good. These are not the same things.

Shine/Sheen glances at her, then whispers into his replica's ear behind a cupped palm. Linno sticks her tongue out at the both of them. *"Eddi."* Her mother's voice is knife-sharp. "Do it again and I'll drag you back home by that tongue."

"Everything okay?" Abraham Saar bellows over his shoulder. "Comfortable?"

"Yes, very much!" Linno's mother says. "My daughter, she wants to say thank you, but she feels embarrassed. She's shy."

Linno stares at her knees, heat crawling up her throat. Every child knows that this exact sentence—*She's shy*—inspires a litany of shaming responses related to *Oh* and *Aw* and *Why so shy?* On cue, Mercy Auntie emits an artificial *awww,* as if Linno belongs in a muffiny diaper of her own.

And here, her mother says the kind of thing that can destroy a postcard-perfect day. "Just like her father."

Abraham Saar gives an awkward laugh.

Linno stares at her window, where a moth's wing is stuck to the out-side of the glass. Into the hollow of Melvin's absence, Linno's mother has tossed a careless joke. She has laughed at him, at Linno, at herself and her life. Last week, Linno saw how her father had grown so sickly and sad around her mother, who only recently relented over the issue of moving to America. Linno hates the idea of America. She hates that country for casting such a spell over her mother, who for so long could imagine no other life than one lived there. She remembers waking in the middle of the night, searching for her mother's shape on the charpoy. Gracie's voice cut clear through the dark. "Go to sleep, Linno Mol. I am here, aren't I?" And though it was a question not meant to be answered, still it seemed open to more than one possibility.

9.

*I*N THE VAN, Anju takes a window seat in the back, next to Mrs. Solanki, while Petra swivels around in her row to continue film-ing. The sound man wedges his fuzzy microphone by Anju's knees, while Rohit checks the batteries. Roy sits up front, gripping the window frame to steel himself against the oncoming buses, which seem to swerve around them at the last possible minute. "They really come out of nowhere, don't they?" he remarks.

The driver smiles with his paan-stained teeth and youthfully whips the steering wheel around a charging auto-rickshaw. "This is old road," the driver says. "No lanes, like in National Highway."

The National Highway. The Golden Colon. Ammachi's voice drifts back to Anju like a sweet, stale smell.

"How do you feel?" Mrs. Solanki asks, the same question she has been asking all along the way. If Anju possessed the proper words, she would say that the whole thing is strangely ordinary. The sunbright paddies and their healing greens, the buses panting plumes of smoke, the berms, the bridges, the Kalyan Silks billboard, the thickets of yellow bamboo, the coconuts and mangroves and the pile of burning trash, the rise and fall of her stomach mapping the hills and hollows of the road, the sweat and the dung, the rippling heat, the convulsed reflection of the sun in a puddle, and the ginger-colored road.

But it is exhilarating, too, to feel so ordinary in these surroundings. It is a sign of coming home.

For the sake of Petra's camera, Anju resorts to her high school vocabulary list. "I am nauseated?" She looks to Mrs. Solanki for approval of this word.

Mrs. Solanki looks deeply interested, yet perplexed by the answer. "Nauseated? Do you want to stop?"

"Not bad nauseated. Good nauseated," Anju specifies. Complex words for complex emotions. "I am inebriated with joy."

10.

By the time they arrive at Kovalam Beach, Linno's mouth is a fixed line and her lips hurt from the effort. She has privately decreed that a smile will not cross her face for the rest of the day, at least not for her mother. She imagines her smilelessness plaguing everyone in the van, a pox of guilt spreading over them until they beg her to cure them with kindness and smiles. To which, after taking a seat in the front, she does.

Her father was right, of course, about Kovalam Beach. She sifts the white dust of sand through her fingers; she tastes the brackish air. The tide slowly sticks out its tongue at the coast, then politely recedes, leaving opalescent shards of shells in its wake.

Abraham Saar spreads a large blue sheet over the sand and stakes the corners with stones. The boys run off to build a fort of sand, but seeing that they are too close to the shoreline, their mother walks over to advise them to move a few feet back. She bends over them, her braid swinging in the wind. With a stick, Linno draws her name in the sand, but Anju keeps waddling through her handiwork and finally demands the stick.

Linno moves some distance away to write her name in peace. When she looks back, she picks out her mother from the small throng of adults. Gracie is leaning onto her palm, tilting her face to the sky, while Abraham Saar lies on his side and plays with Anju. Her mother's eyes are closed, her face relaxing with every breath. It is strange to see this combination of three, a tableau of an alternate family. Stranger still is when Abraham Saar looks up at Linno's mother without saying a word, mired in thought. Gracie does not notice him. Linno keeps waiting for him to look away but he does not.

Just then, Gracie opens her eyes and sees Linno staring. They blink at each other, as if from across a great distance. Turning, Linno's mother asks something of Abraham Saar, who shades his eyes and nods quickly. She rises, brushing off her knees, and approaches Linno.

Her mother stands tall and shadowy, silhouetted by the sun behind her. "Shall we go play a game?" she asks.

Quick as that, her mother offers reconciliation, but Linno does not want it yet. The impact of her anger should be more lasting than this. Despondently, she asks what they would play.

"Hide-and-seek," her mother suggests.

"Where?"

Gracie looks past Linno, at the sickled coast of the beach. "I know a place. I used to go there with my cousins."

Linno follows her mother down the shore. Of course she wants to play with her mother, fully aware of the precious rarity of such an event, adults agreeing to the rules of play, rules beyond their own making. But Linno deems it equally important to cling to her pouty indignation, at least for the time being, if that is what it took to get her mother's attention in the first place.

22.

CHILDREN, on their way home from school, scuttle along the sides of roads in chatty clusters, backpacks bobbing against their narrow shoulder blades. Anju recognizes the uniform of St. Anne's Catholic, navy jumpers and light blue blouses like the ones she used to wear, worn by little girls with familiar faces. Every face, though belonging to a stranger, is familiar.

Mrs. Solanki leans forward and taps Roy on the shoulder. "Shall we discuss how we will shoot the reunion? I'd like to make a plan so I'm prepared. Minimal surprises, you know."

Anju listens as Roy and Petra roughly outline the proceedings, who should stand where and say what. When they are within walking distance of the house, Roy says, the crew will travel on foot so as to better capture the actual moment of embrace between Anju and her sister. That moment is "key" to the reunion itself. Petra tells Rohit to cover Anju's left side, staying wide and out of the way. "Just look for the open angle," Petra says. "See where I am. Don't crowd my shot."

Rohit says okay several times, clearly worried that he will never be able to satisfy Petra, let alone on this day, on this shoot, an event no less pivotal than a rite of manhood.

Mrs. Solanki turns to Anju. "As for you, Anju, just remember: bigger is better. You know what I mean? Don't be embarrassed in front of the cameras. Feel free to cry if you want to."

Anju nods and shifts her gaze out the window at the passing green. *Bigger is better:* she has heard this phrase before, in a sandwich place where the XL cup of soda had been replaced by an XXL tub. She wishes once again that she had called Linno ahead of time, at least to warn her of the camera carnival around the corner. Might Linno be frightened? Furious? It seems unfair to creep up on her with a lens or two, capturing her before she has assented. Anju said as much to Mrs. Solanki, days before, to which she replied, "Do you think Rohit ever asked me before he started shooting? With family, these sorts of courtesies can be ignored a bit."

But "courtesy" is too small a word in Anju's mind. To take a person's photograph without her permission or awareness seems akin to stealing. And hasn't she stolen enough?

12.

THE SUN is slowly tucking itself into a lavender cloud as Gracie leads Linno to a solitary spot on the beach. It is a long walk away, over a small bluff, but well worth it, Linno decides, as the piles of slate gray rocks provide ample room for hiding. The water whips the rocks in great flares of foamy white. Storks perch on the higher peaks, and everywhere is the pleasant reek of fish.

Gracie names four rocks to delineate the boundaries, making it impossibly easy for the seeker to find her prey. "The ocean is out of bounds," she says.

"But why?"

"No."

"Amma, I can hold my breath for a full minute. I was practicing."

Her mother is unyielding on the issue of dry land. "Want to count first?"

Linno accepts with limited interest. In a drab tone, she counts from one to twenty, her hands pressed to a rock, her eyes pressed against her hands. She can hear her mother rustling off to her left. When Linno is finished counting, she turns around only to spy her mother's toe peeking out from behind a rock not three feet away. She stares at the toe, irritated, her intelligence insulted. Here is her mother, trying to make up for betraying her in the van, but unwilling to play to the game's fullest potential. Presuming, as always, that Linno is younger than she really is.

When it is Gracie's turn to count, Linno prowls about with feline silence and wedges herself into the crevasse beneath a giant boulder. She must keep her body flat and her head turned to the side in order to fit. The stone smells damp and mineral, possibly the home of various wriggly things, but in true hide-and-seek, hiders make such sacrifices.

At first, Gracie searches in silence and then begins to tease Linno aloud. "Whoever wants ice cream after the game, raise your hand! Just me? I guess I'll eat ice cream all by myself."

After roaming around for a few more minutes, Gracie calls out: "You know you have to stay in the boundaries, don't you?"

Silence.

"Okay, Linno Mol, I give up. Come out. You win."

Three times Linno sees her mother's chappals passing back and forth across the narrow sliver of her vision, and each time, her mother's feet pick up speed. "*Eddi!* Come out, I said!" An irritated quiet. Then, the fading slaps of footsteps.

Beneath the rock, Linno discovers how a game of hide-and-seek can make her mother love her better: a person is more important in her absence than in her presence. The longer Linno keeps herself hidden, the more frantic her mother will become, realizing finally that this is her family, whom she loves so greatly that there will be no more taunting or fighting, no more thoughts of running away to the States.

Linno meanders down other lanes of thought, of chocolate ice cream, of stupid boys and their exclusive forts, before she remembers her mother. Only then does Linno realize how her mother's voice has vanished, though she cannot remember when exactly it did so. She wiggles out from under the rock, startled by the gusts of wind that tug at the hem of her skirt, the needles of straight, gray rain.

LINNO CIRCLES, trying to spot the rose of her mother's sari. There is no one in the distance. She climbs over rocks and scrapes her knee on her way to the water. A spot of blood stains the white piping of her skirt. Her mother will be furious, not only about this but about Linno's ruthless, stupid dedication to hide-and-seek. The wind squeals in her ears.

When Linno reaches the shoreline, she removes her chappals. The sand is wet and supple beneath her feet, squelching between her toes, but she keeps her chappals looped in her fingers. Ruining her dress as well as losing her chappals would double the beating she is sure to receive. But a beating would be better than this. There is nothing unexpected about a beating; the fear of the branch is a familiar one.

Over and over she cries out *Amma*, then *Ma*, then nothing.

FAR IN THE DISTANCE: a pink petal on the water. Linno squints, barely breathing. A splotch of pink and black. Faintly, Linno can hear her mother shrieking her name.

Linno screams for her mother.

The pink petal turns. It has a face. The face is Linno's own. Terrified, wet and windswept, her braid a drenched rope around her throat. Her mother has walked right into the water, submerged up to her chest, her arms spread to keep herself balanced among the rowdy tides.

Relief and joy spread through Linno's body. She goes splashing into the water, but her mother waves her arms in the air, as if telling Linno to stop. Linno stops. The water laps at her ankles as she watches her mother stumble, thrown off balance by her waving.

It happens in an instant. Her mother slides under the waves.

LINNO STANDS WATCHING for a very long time. She waits for her mother to bob up again, gasping, waving. But the water, having no memory, moves on.

It is almost as if her mother is playing a trick, about to strike out of the water like a dolphin, glistening and laughing. Was that even her mother at all? Or one of those buoys warning swimmers to keep to their limits?

The air turns colder, and Linno's body seems to go numb. Her mind as well. Was it her mother? Was it a vision? Was it just a pink petal? If any of these things, it could not be her mother, it could not be that they would dredge her up from the waters tomorrow morning, with blue lips and blue fingernails. It could not be that they would find Linno in a few hours and ask her questions to which she would respond by staring into thin air, mute. For now she hurries back to the rocks and scoots into her old hiding place. She presses her cheek to the sand. She has only to wait.

THE WOMAN SEEMS FINISHED with her story. She stares off into the distance as if her mind has replaced the open road with the ocean of her telling.

The Kapyar realizes that it is his time to speak. What would Anthony Achen say? Is there a prayer to absolve such things? Surely the Kapyar is not the one to administer it.

"I am sorry," he says.

The woman seems not to hear or care.

"But I cannot forgive you. I am only the Kapyar."

"I know," she says finally. "I thought it would feel better to tell it."

"Does it?"

She shakes her head.

The Kapyar nods, convinced. He has never seen someone leave the confessional with a smile.

They sink into silence. He can imagine explaining this to his wife, how a young woman stumbled to church and spilled her story into his

lap. Strange, his wife would say, though it would be strange only in ret-
rospect. For now, it is all rather quiet and ordinary, two people on a step,
a thermos of tea between them.

"So what happened then?" the Kapyar asks.

The woman looks at him. "I told you. They found my mother.
Dead."

"And then what?"

"The funeral."

"And then?"

"What do you mean? That's the end."

Now it is the Kapyar's turn to gaze at the road. At moments like these,
he feels his age. He says to her, "Nothing is the end."

WHEN THE WOMAN finishes the tea, the Kapyar helps her to rise.
She is shaky on her feet but seems better than before. "Thank you," she
says.

The Kapyar makes a noise to mean, *It's okay.*

Probably they will not cross paths again, or if they do, maybe the
woman will not remember him. Or pretend not to remember. This is
life, tides moving the sand into unpredictable whorls and chance config-
urations, the gentle collisions of strangers. For a long time, he watches
her go down the road, to make sure she is safe, because he is the Kapyar
and this is his job.

13.

THE VAN PASSES a bridge that runs over a slender section of
the river, where a woman has waded knee-deep into the water to
lash her laundry against a rock. Another woman, perhaps her daughter,
wads up a soapy garment and kneads it like a ball of dough. Usually
Anju loves this sound, the crush and crunch of milky bubbles against
stone, but she feels the sudden urge to vomit.

"We're close, aren't we?" Mrs. Solanki asks her.

"I feel nausea," Anju says.

"I know, dear." Mrs. Solanki smiles, remembering Anju's previous
use of the word.

The driver pedals the brake as he navigates a curvy, rutted road. The passengers jostle about, holding on to their seats and their equipment. Every bump in the road is a belated lurch in Anju's stomach; she can feel her lunch beginning to stir. It would be ironic and frankly humiliating if, out of all the foreigners in this vehicle, it would be she whose constitution could not handle the masala dosa they ate two hours ago, from a roadside tea shop.

Anju turns her face to the window. The curving wall is painted with advertisements. Here, a glassy-eyed woman in bridal jewelry, her hand against her face, beside the words ALAPPAT JEWELLERY. She recognizes that sign, her mental halfway mark between home and church. Beneath the Alappat sign, there used to be a Bata chappal advertisement, and beneath that, an old Mohanlal movie poster. She takes pride in the fact that she knows the sedimentary history of this wall. Soon after the Alappat ad, they pass a woman in a brown salwar kameez walking in the opposite direction.

Later, Anju will remember this moment above all others, how unremarkable it is, how delicate and small, this wrinkle in her day.

Immediately her body is filled with a frantic electricity as she whips around in her seat, almost cracking her neck. It is too late. The woman slips out of view as they are coming out of the turn. Anju's hand fumbles for the door lock. Mrs. Solanki is asking her a question. Anju can feel a seething in her chest, her voice clawing its way from the depths. They have not gone far from the curve before she cries out to stop the car, stop the car.

"What is it dear?" Mrs. Solanki asks. "Are you going to be sick?"

Anju manages to nod as she stumbles out of the van.

"Rohit, go with her," Mrs. Solanki says.

"Um, clearly she'd prefer another female to hold back her hair," says Rohit.

Through the open windows, Anju can hear them arguing over who should go until Roy suggests that they both give her some privacy. She hurries up the road from which they came, her chappals flapping loudly. Anju can feel the anxieties shedding from her body like a snake writhing out of its old, translucent skins. Is this what it is like to travel in time—part of you pulled forward as if by a little girl's hand, part of you floating above, watching from where the world is timeless?

As she rounds the bend, the woman in brown is there, farther away now but still trudging with her head down. Even from this distance, Anju can distinguish the clumsy braid.

Anju looks back over her shoulder. No cameras have followed. There is no one on this stretch of road but Linno and herself.

Finding her voice, Anju calls her sister's name.

14.

*A*ND NOW LINNO IS STOPPED by the sound of a voice in her ear, as far and as close as a memory. She listens to the sizzle of insects in the leaves but, afraid to linger, she continues on. Already she spent every last ounce of strength to pull herself from the steps of the church, where the Kapyar must have thought her crazy. Hearing voices, maybe she is. The possibility makes her move faster, as though she might outrun her own mind. There was a time when she thought she heard her mother's voice calling to her as if for dinner or a bath, and every time Linno strained to hear, she felt her heart straining as well, like a balloon stretched too thin, until she forced herself to stop remembering, forced herself to forget until.

Until.

Her name again. And breathing, heavy and not her own. She stops, sure that if she turns she will find that she is as alone as she ever was.

She turns around.

"Linno," Anju says.

The distance between them is only as wide as a well. And in Linno, a familiar dizziness returns, from trying to net a butterflying hope. In a blink, this all could disappear.

"Anju?" Linno whispers. It is not possible. She blinks, and Anju is still standing before her. Anju's eyes are bright and wet in a face much leaner than when she left. She takes a step forward.

"Oh." Linno's sound is no more than a sigh. "Oh," she says, and they reach for each other.

Acknowledgments

I'd like to thank Nicole Aragi, whose energy and kindness inspire me always, and Jordan Pavlin, my wise and endlessly generous editor. Thank you to Leslie Levine and everyone at Knopf, and to Jim Hanks and Lily Oei for smoothing the process.

My gratitude to my teachers: those at the Columbia Graduate Writing Division, especially Nathan Englander, Jamie Manrique, and Alan Ziegler. Thank you, Anne Glosky. And to Frank X Walker and Kelly Ellis, who gave the first nudge.

Thank you to those who patiently walked me through their various worlds of expertise: Chandradasan, director of Lokadharmi Theatre Company; Prabuddha Kothari from Regal Cards; and Arlene Lyons, wizard of immigration law. I also drew from several articles in *The New York Times,* particularly "Dollars and Dreams: Immigrants as Prey" by Gary Rivlin and "Neighborhood Report: Jackson Heights; Landmarks Proposal Intensifies Debate Over Store Facades" by Jane H. Lii.

I owe much to those who have read this book in earlier forms: Jenny Assef, Karen Thompson, Sheela Maru, and Vivek Maru, from whom nothing escapes. And to Ragdale, for the space and time to begin.

To my extended families on both sides of the world, especially my ammachis, Rachel Kurian and Mariakutty Lukose, who have been generous with hymns and love. To Neena, for earlybird calls and sisterly guidance; Raj, caring brother and grill maestro; and the ever loyal Christine, who has read every single word.

And finally, to my mother and father, for wondrous stories and wisdom and figs. All my love and thanks for making each day a blessing.

A Note About the Author

Tania James was raised in Louisville, Kentucky, and is a graduate of Harvard and Columbia. She has published her work in *One Story* and *The New York Times*. She lives in New York City.

A Note on the Type

This book was set in Fournier, a typeface named for Pierre Simon Fournier *fils* (1712–1768), a celebrated French type designer. He was also the author of the important *Manuel typographique* (1764–1766), in which he attempted to work out a system standardizing type measurement in points, a system that is still in use internationally.

Composed by
Creative Graphics, Allentown, Pennsylvania

Printed and Bound by
Berryville Graphics, Berryville, Virginia

Designed by
Iris Weinstein